THE BELIAL PLAN
A BELIAL SERIES NOVEL

R.D. BRADY

SCOTTISH SEOUL PUBLISHING, LLC

BOOKS BY R.D. BRADY

Hominid

The Belial Series (in order)
    The Belial Stone
    The Belial Library
    The Belial Ring
    Recruit: A Belial Series Novella
    The Belial Children
    The Belial Origins
    The Belial Search
    The Belial Guard
    The Belial Warrior
    The Belial Plan
    The Belial Witches
    The Belial War
    The Belial Fall
    The Belial Sacrifice

The A.L.I.V.E. Series
    B.E.G.I.N.

A.L.I.V.E.
D.E.A.D.
R.I.S.E.
S.A.V.E.

The Steve Kane Series
Runs Deep
Runs Deeper

The Unwelcome Series
Protect
Seek
Proxy

The Nola James Series
Surrender the Fear
Escape the Fear

Published as Riley D. Brady
The Key of Apollo
The Curse of Hecate

Be sure to sign up for R.D.'s mailing list to be the first to hear when she has a new release!

PROLOGUE

MADRID, SPAIN

1502

Marguerite stared at the women who surrounded her, her friends, her sisters. There were twenty-two of them. Most had Marguerite's dark hair and eyes, taking on the looks of their adopted homeland with skin bronzed golden after generations spent in the sun. Their hair had darkened as they wed and had children over the generations in which they'd made this land their home.

But some maintained the red and blonde hair from their people of long ago. In age they ranged as well, from twelve to sixty-three.

Marguerite fell in the middle of this group at thirty-six. She had been their leader, their spokesperson for five years, during all the tumult. The Inquisition had forced many groups into the shadows, too afraid to speak out. Many had disbanded. That was never an option for Marguerite and her sisters. Their duty was too great.

Besides, this world, it was hard. It was meant to be. Suffering in this life meant greater understanding of why we were here, why we exist. But even she paused at the glimpses of the future her visions had shown her. *Give me the strength to face it.*

These women were more than just followers of the Great Mother. They were the protectors of her final legacy. Even through the death of her husband and children, Marguerite could see the need to protect the Great Mother's legacy, and protect it at all costs. At the same time, the Mother's greatest lesson was so simple, so perfect: love. Embrace it, share it, teach it. That was all anyone need do. That was all that mattered.

She glanced to where the other fifteen normally stood. Their numbers were reduced in body but not in spirit. *May the Mother speed you on your journey, sisters.*

Her own family had gone on, but she would see them again. They had been in each other's lives for eons. And one day, she would join them again. Part of her longed for that day, but a larger part of her knew her job in this lifetime was not finished yet. And she would not shrink from what needed to be done.

No matter how painful it will become.

She turned her gaze to the women looking up to her in expectation. "Our sisters have gone ahead with our most sacred relic. They do so to protect the legacy of the Great Mother. Even now, forces move to strike her from this world's memory. But we will not let them forget. She is seen in the kindness toward a stranger, in the compassion for an enemy, in the openness to new cultures and new ways. We are her last soldiers. We pledge our lives and our bodies to her mission. And we pledge to find her in this world and be her example for all to see."

Marguerite reached for the ceremonial wine and raised it high. "May the Great Mother and her message of peace and love spread like wildfire across the world."

"Make it so."

"May those with hearts of anger and darkness see the light."

"Make it so."

"May the day dawn when we let go of the material needs of this world and embrace the needs of the soul above all else."

"Make it so."

"May the—"

The door at the back of the room swung open with a bang. All the women rose to their feet with a cry as six men filled the space. All were armed and wore chests of metal, the red cross signaling them as members of the Inquisition.

Marguerite sprinted to the back of the room. "Run, sisters!"

The men spread out into the room, but the sisters were well prepared for this moment. The strongest rushed forward with Marguerite, giving the young and the old a chance to escape. The women did not wait for the men to attack. They were a swirl of movement as they launched themselves at the weak points of their targets: groins, knees, and eyes. The first six men were taken down quickly, not expecting the skill of the women—but Marguerite could see additional forces coming.

"Escape, sisters!" Marguerite yelled.

As one they sprinted for the exit.

One of the men managed to get to his feet; he grabbed Enique, only fourteen. With a ferocious cry, Marguerite kicked out his knee, then slammed her open palm into his face. As he lessened his grip on the girl, Marguerite yanked her from his clutches and pushed her toward the back. The terrified girl sprinted away.

Marguerite managed only a step before a fist collided with her jaw. She crashed to the floor, her jaw ringing with pain, and she could feel a tooth loosened in the back of her mouth. She heard a stone door slam shut, blocking the women's exit. Her heart cried out with fear at the slam of the lock, but she'd known this moment was coming. She had insisted upon it. *Goodbye, sisters.*

A man yanked her up by the hair. She winced but clamped her lips shut to keep from making a sound.

The man twisted her hair, forcing Marguerite to turn to him. He glared down at her. A scar ran down the left side of his face, cutting through his eye, leaving it white. "Do you know who I am?"

Marguerite spat blood in his face. He backhanded her, and she nearly passed out as her jaw screamed in pain. He shook her roughly. Tears sprang to her eyes.

"Where is it?" he demanded.

"Safe from the likes of you."

"You think the women who fled through that tunnel have escaped? We will run them down. We will catch each and every one. And if you don't tell me where it is, one of them will."

"None of us will betray the Great Mother."

He inspected her closely, then spoke softly, causing the hair on the back of her neck to rise. "No, I don't suppose you will. But tell me, will you sit back and watch your sisters as my men have their way with them? Will you stay loyal to your Great Mother then?"

Marguerite's stomach rolled at the thought. "They can not tell you what they do not know. What you seek is long gone from here, and none of us know where it has gone."

"So you say. But you would never reveal its location, not without some motivation." He thrust her toward one of his men. "Make her talk. However you need to."

A second man grabbed her roughly by the arm. The brute that held her smiled, revealing three missing teeth. "Aren't you pretty? But you won't be when I'm done with you."

A man stepped into the room. Unlike the others, his skin was smooth and unmarked. But Marguerite knew he was not untested in battle. This man, she knew him well, not with her own eyes, but through the Great Mother. She started to shake and noticed a tremor run through the giant of a man holding her. *Oh Great Mother, help me.*

The man cast a calculating look around the room before heading toward Marguerite. All the other men dropped to one knee. Marguerite was shoved roughly to the floor as the man holding her did the same.

The man stopped in front of her, but the brute that held her kept her face crushed to the dirt floor. "Where is it?" the man asked, his voice soft, but the command there nonetheless.

The man who had first grabbed her spoke, his eyes still on the floor. "She says it is not here. But we will get her to talk."

The man walked toward her, and Marguerite felt liquid run down her legs. "Stand," he commanded.

The brute who held her yanked her to her feet, her shoulder jolting painfully. Marguerite tried to stand tall, but her knocking knees would not cooperate.

"Look at me."

Taking a breath, Marguerite looked up into the devil's handsome face. His blue eyes peered into her brown ones.

"You are scared. You should be." He nodded to the brute. "Take her to my tent. I will question her."

Terror crawled through Marguerite, but she refused to let these men see it. Instead, she pictured the women who had escaped. *Run, sisters. Run.* Then she pictured her husband, son, and daughter. She looked into the man's face and smiled.

"What are you smiling at?"

"I will see my husband and children soon."

He leaned close, his breath on Marguerite's cheek. "No. You won't."

She looked up into his face, knowing the pain he would put her through, but also knowing that at the end she would finally find peace. *Yes, I will.*

CHAPTER 1

BALTIMORE, MARYLAND

Three months ago, the crisis center dedicated to finding Delaney McPhearson had moved from Henry's office on the third floor of the Chandler Headquarters main house to the second floor. In the almost six months that they'd been looking, everything here—all of the leads, hints, and information on Laney's movement—had been carefully reviewed, investigated, and crossed off. Nothing had panned out.

While Henry and Jake had agreed the search would continue, they could no longer make it the sole focus of everyone's lives. Henry went back to running the Chandler Group, and most of the analysts had been pulled off to focus on other tasks. Jake, though, was still fully involved in the search. It was his primary mission. Not that that focus had helped; Laney was nowhere to be found. And as much as all of them hated to admit it, there were other responsibilities they needed to attend to.

Now Jake walked along the line of three whiteboards attached to the long back wall. Everything on here was related to the search for Laney: pictures from surveillance cameras of women who might be Laney, sightings from across the globe, the report from the incident out in Colorado. Every spare space was covered with information—and not one single piece told them where Laney was.

The more Jake looked for her, the more he realized why she'd left. And he realized it wasn't just Laney who needed to adapt to her role. They all needed to. Laney—she was the general, which meant the rest of them needed to follow her lead. And for Jake, that had been incredibly difficult. He had years of military experience that Laney did not have. He had more experience in conflict. And he had his male ego; he could admit now that he had difficulty with letting a woman, especially one he cared about, run into danger.

So wherever she was, he knew she had made the call to leave because no one else would be willing to do it. That's what leaders did. They made the tough calls.

And even though rationally he knew all of this—and even though rationally he accepted it—he was still driven to find her. Even if that was not what she wanted.

He stopped at the picture of Drake. It was a publicity shot from the man's agent. Drake glared at the camera in what the agent had informed Jake was his smolder look.

Jake still couldn't believe this Las Vegas entertainer had managed to grab Laney from the house in Colorado and disappear with her. Drake had last been seen carrying an unconscious Laney into a plane.

Jake had his people running down Drake's history, but it was as elusive as his current whereabouts. Drake had been in Vegas for close to twenty years, although from his photo he looked to only be in his thirties. But before that, there was no trace of the man. He walked into Vegas fully formed with a show and capital and not a clue as to where he had been before that. Of course Jake now knew the man was an archangel. But he was supposed to be on sabbatical. So whose side was he on? From what Jake had read of the man, Drake had allegiance to only one person: himself. So what the hell was he doing in the middle of all of this?

The door opened behind him, and Henry Chandler ducked his head under the doorway to step inside. Angela Hartlett, his assistant, followed. Angela was in her late twenties with dark black hair and brown eyes. She'd been a recent hire, to handle some of the work overflow. She was professional, efficient, and focused.

She was talking to Henry as they entered. "So I will speak with the office in Milan and contact the Japanese group to see if they can move up the deadline on the Scoba project. Anything else?"

"That should do it for now. Get some lunch and I'll be back upstairs in an hour or two," Henry said.

Angela made a note on her tablet. "Okay. Great. See you then. Hey, Jake."

Jake nodded. "Angela."

She smiled and bounced out of the room, closing the door behind her.

Jake raised an eyebrow at Henry. "I take it we're still pretending we don't know she's FBI?"

"Yup."

Henry sank into a chair at the end of the conference table. Since Laney had gone on the run, the surveillance on Jake, Henry, Patrick, and most of the Chandler Group had ramped up. They all had people tailing them. Their phone calls were recorded. Their online activity documented. The United States government was leaving no stone unturned in their attempt to track down Laney.

And they weren't the only ones. Two Israeli operatives had broken into Jen's home in an attempted abduction last month. Jake smiled, picturing the scene when he and Henry had arrived. Jen had been filing her nails in her living room while the two agents lay unconscious and hogtied on the floor next to her. They'd contacted the FBI after that, and the State Department had assured Henry they'd had no idea the Israelis were working on US soil. Jen had agreed to not press charges, but only to avoid an international incident. They had enough attention on them as it was; she knew they didn't need any more. But boy, had she been pissed.

Jake nodded toward the door. "Anything from her cell?"

"She's been checking in with her handler, but she can only report on my business dealings. Her ASAC is getting a little annoyed."

"Do they have anything?"

"Not that I can tell. I don't suppose there's anything new here?"

Jake took a seat across from Henry. "A few more sightings. One in Bolivia, one in the Netherlands, and one in downtown Sacramento. And none of them Laney."

"Jake, I know you want to find her, but I think you need to accept that we're not going to."

Jake narrowed his eyes. "What are you saying?"

"Not what you're thinking. I don't think she's dead. I just think Drake—he's been around for a while. And until he decides to let her go, or until she figures out how to get away from him, we're not going to find her."

"I just don't get why he'd stick his neck out. I mean, from all reports he's a playboy who only cares about his next hit of adulation."

Henry shook his head. "There has to be more to him than that. You know what he is."

An archangel—one of the highest ranks of angels. He was instilled with the duty to protect the tree of wisdom for at least for part of his time on earth. But when he wasn't on duty, living it up seemed to be his only goal.

They had met one other archangel: Ralph, Victoria's guardian. Ralph would have laid down his life for Victoria and was loyal to the end.

Jake's gaze flicked to Drake's picture. *So what about you, Drake? Are you loyal to someone too?*

"Jake, you need to step back from this. It's consuming you."

Jake sighed. He knew Henry was right. But he couldn't help but feel responsible. He should have known she would try to run. That she would try to keep the rest of them from getting caught in the net that had slowly encircled her. But he hadn't.

Jake ran a hand over his face. "You're right. I know."

"Let's start small. How about we go grab some lunch? Yoni's on the estate. We can grab him too."

Jake smiled, picturing his friend. "Actually that sounds great."

Henry stood. "Good. Meet you downstairs?"

"I'm right behind you."

Henry headed out of the room, and Jake let his smile drop as he turned his chair to take in the board again. His eyes roamed over all the clues that had taken them nowhere. And then he looked at the picture of Laney in the middle of it all. He loved her. He always would.

But somewhere along the way, that love had shifted. He would still lay down his life for her. And he knew without a doubt that she would do the same for him. But he didn't want her to do that—not for any of them. All he wanted was for her to let them help her.

He sighed. *Where are you, Laney?*

CHAPTER 2

The woods within the Chandler Preserve bloomed with life as Noriko walked quietly down a well-worn path. She marveled at how different the woods were here compared to the plant life she had grown up with on Malama Island in Hawaii. There it had been all palm trees and exotic flowers. Here, there were oaks and flowers that lasted only a season or two before fall caused them to crumble away and winter buried them under white.

Baltimore was as different as could possibly be from her upbringing, and she loved it. The cold took a little getting used to, but the crispness in the air, that was incredible. And there was another huge perk about living in Maryland.

Noriko went still, squinting at a bush in front of her, before a rustle behind her caused her to whirl around. A Javan leopard, yellow with black spots, charged toward her with a roar. Noriko braced herself as the cat barreled into her.

She slammed onto her back with a grunt. The cat stared into her eyes with its unusual green eyes, its paws on her shoulders.

Noriko stared back. The cat let out a ferocious growl, then leaned down and licked Noriko's cheeks. She laughed, turning her head to try and avoid some of the cat's affection. "Ugh, Tiger, you are *not* a humble winner."

Tiger stepped off her, and Noriko put a hand on his back, using him to help pull herself up. As soon as she was standing, Tiger leaned into her, rubbing his head on her thigh. With a laugh, she leaned down and scratched his side. "Yes, I still love you."

A girl a year younger than Noriko, with curly dark hair and bright blue eyes, stepped into view, a pure white panther with blue eyes at her side. "He won again, huh?" Lou Thomas asked.

Noriko grinned. "He always does."

Lou and Noriko had met when Laney had brought Noriko back from Malama Island. The two had become fast friends. When Laney had gone missing, Henry had asked Noriko if she would mind staying for a little while to help the cats get settled. She'd expected it to be only a few months, but it had now been close to eight months since she'd last been home to Malama.

And she couldn't head home quite yet. "Did you find her?" Noriko asked.

Lou nodded. "Yeah. Come on."

Most of the cats were doing all right. They revered Laney. But it was actually Lou, Rolly, and Danny they viewed as members of their pack. The three of them had been made members because they had helped save the cats from the lab that had created them. These were not regular Javan leopards. No, at the behest of a particularly sadistic Fallen, the DNA of Javan leopards had been mixed with the DNA of a Fallen. The result was a whole new species, one that was larger than leopards, with most standing four feet at the shoulders—although the vets thought Tiger might actually grow a little larger than that. But more critical than their immense size was their intelligence. They were almost on par with a normal human being.

In Laney's absence, Noriko had taken over their care. Although Henry took care of providing for their basic needs— food and shelter—Noriko was in charge of their emotional needs.

Like Laney, Noriko could understand and communicate with the cats. Except Noriko's abilities didn't stem from a ring, but rather a unique genetic heritage.

Noriko was a member of Honu Keiki, the descendants of the people of Mu. And the descendants had brought more than ancient stories with them through the generations; they had brought abilities. These abilities had been diluted over time, but a little less than half of the members of Honu Keiki still had some form of psychic ability. Noriko was unique in that she had two abilities: the ability of prophesy, and the ability to communicate with animals.

As she and Lou walked through the preserve that Henry had created for the cats, Noriko sent out feelers trying to gauge the feelings of the cats nearby.

"How are they doing?" Lou asked.

"All right. Although the walls make them unhappy." Because of all the attention on Laney and all those connected to her, walls had been erected around the estate to keep the world's prying eyes from seeing the cats. But the long arm of the media had still managed to get shots. A few helicopters had flown over, and they'd even used satellite feeds. But while most commented on the cats' size, they didn't know what else made the cats so unusual.

"Yeah, well, they're not the only ones. We all have walls around us these days," Lou said.

Noriko held out a hand. "Hold up."

Lou stopped. "What?"

Noriko nodded down the path. "Wait for it."

Two black Javan leopards sprinted into view. They stopped short and looked at the young women for a moment, grins on their faces, before sprinting away. But that small pause was long enough to see the small dachshund with a patch over one eye sitting in a saddle on one of the cats' backs.

Rolly Escabi and Zach Grayston blurred into view a second later.

Noriko grinned. "Princess looks happy."

Rolly smiled. "Yup. Thanks for suggesting it."

"Which way did they go?" Zach asked.

Lou pointed down the path. "That way."

The boys took off again.

Lou looked at Noriko. "Princess really was okay?"

"Oh yeah," Noriko said.

The dachshund had been rescued from the same lab as the leopards. Unlike the cats, nothing extra had been given to the poor little dog, only taken. Rolly had been unable to leave her behind when he and Lou had investigated the place.

Noriko smiled, thinking of how happy Princess seemed. "Ever since she lost her leg and eye, she's felt so slow. So unhappy. Seeing the cats and their speed, she was jealous. So yeah, riding on Kingston's back, Princess is very happy."

"Well, that's one patient handled. This way to the other one."

Lou led Noriko off the path, through the brush, and up a small incline. Snow stayed at her side.

Noriko knew where they were heading. There was a ledge on the other side of the hill that provided a pretty good view of the enclosure. As they approached, she could hear Danny Wartowski, age seventeen, one of the head analysts of the Chandler Group and all-around nice guy.

"So I figured out if you use gold as a shield," Danny was saying, "it would protect the transmitter long enough for me to duplicate the signal."

"Well I'm pretty sure *that* topic of conversation would put me into a depression," Lou muttered.

But Noriko didn't say anything as they came around the hill. Danny looked up, his relief clear. "Hey there."

"Hey," Noriko said, her gaze quickly shifting from Danny to the cat next to him. "Hey, Cleo."

Cleo lifted her head, then dropped it back down with a sigh. Danny and Lou exchanged a worried glance.

"I've got this," Noriko said. "Why don't you guys give us a little time?"

"Sure, sure." Danny got to his feet. He nodded to the insulated bag on the ground. "I brought some bacon, but she wouldn't take any."

"I'll see what I can do," Noriko said.

"Okay, we'll, uh, meet you guys back at the house." Lou tugged on Danny's sleeve, and he followed her back through the trees. Snow walked over and licked Cleo's cheek before following them.

Tiger walked over and curled up next to Cleo, laying his head gently on her back.

Noriko walked over and sat on Cleo's other side. She ran a hand along the cat's side. *Hi, Cleo. How are you doing today?*

Cleo just sighed again in response.

I know you miss Laney. But you know she loves you. She would never leave you unless she had to. There are people after her. She was trying to keep everyone safe. And you would know if something happened to her, right?

Yes.

So she's still all right? Noriko asked the question hesitatingly, hoping the answer remained the same.

Still sleeping.

Still sleeping. Cleo had had that response for the last five or six months. Noriko had tried to understand what she meant, but the communication was not perfect. And Cleo seemed frustrated when Noriko pointed out that she didn't understand. So Noriko just accepted the words.

Well that's good. If she's sleeping, she's not hurt.

Cleo opened one eye to look at Noriko. And somehow, using only one eye, she managed to convey annoyance. But Noriko was happy for the response. Anything was better than apathy.

Importance and arrogance crept into Noriko's mind. *I've protected her.*

I know. But just like you've protected Laney in the past, she's trying to protect you now. This time, you can't protect her. You just have to trust her.

And just like that, the arrogance and importance disappeared. *It hurts.*

Noriko's heart clenched. She leaned her head into Cleo's, gently rubbing behind her ears. *I know, Cleo. I know.*

CHAPTER 3

"Patrick, the Holy See is losing their patience," Father Sean Kirkpatrick pleaded. "You must denounce her."

Patrick paced along his kitchen island. *They're not the only ones losing their patience.* He'd been on the phone for forty minutes with Sean. The phone calls had been occurring every week, each time with the same topic: the church was requesting he denounce Laney. "I have told you my answer, Sean. I will not denounce Laney. If that is the requirement for reinstating me, then I will never be reinstated."

Even though he meant the words, they still sent a chill through him. The church had ordered him to denounce the actions of Laney four months ago. Patrick had refused. They had forced him to take a "sabbatical," but to be reinstated, they demanded he put out a statement to the press denouncing Laney's actions and calling on her to turn herself in.

As far as Patrick was concerned, it was would be a cold day in hell before that happened. But the idea of never being a priest again—it terrified him. Being a priest wasn't a job. It was who he was. But this price? No, they were asking too much.

Sean sighed deeply. Patrick and Sean had gone to the seminary together. They had kept up a close friendship even as they had gone different routes in the church. Sean had gone to work behind the scenes, eventually making his way to the Vatican. Patrick had never wanted that. He had wanted to work with people and to further the archaeological understanding of the church. But despite their different career tracks, Patrick considered Sean a friend. One he'd had for over thirty years.

"I worried when you adopted her that it would become complicated," Sean said.

"But you supported me. I always appreciated that."

"I knew how much you loved your sister."

The mention of Fiona brought a fresh bloom of grief to Patrick's chest. She had been his best friend since they were children. Her death, even though twenty years ago, still felt unreal.

"When she died, I saw how hard it hit you. And when you learned of the situation Laney was in..." Sean paused. "I knew you were serious when you said you would leave the priesthood. And I knew that would be a loss for all of us."

Sean's words brought back not only the pain of Patrick's sister's loss, but the guilt of not protecting Laney. And with Laney's current absence, that was guilt he felt anew. "I cannot do what they are asking. She has done nothing wrong." Patrick let out a bitter laugh. "In fact, she has done everything in her power to protect those who cannot protect themselves. I will not turn my back on her."

"But Patrick, the church is in a bind as well. Delaney has been publicly declared an enemy of the state. She is wanted by multiple countries."

"And she is *innocent*. I remember someone else who was branded a criminal by those in power. Tell me, do you think the church would have ordered us to turn our back on Him as well?"

"You cannot equate your niece's situation with that of Jesus."

"Why not? After all, Jesus is in all of us, isn't He?"

"Patrick, this line of defense, it will not go over well."

"I do not care! She is my daughter. I will never turn my back on her, especially not in response to public opinion. I know who she is. I know where her heart lies. The church is on the wrong side in this. *You* are on the wrong side in this."

Sean was quiet for a moment. "I wish I could see this situation as you do. But I cannot. The public reports on your niece, they are compelling. She is guilty, Patrick."

"No, Sean. She is not."

The stalemate hung heavy across the phone. Finally Sean spoke. "I will speak with them again. I will tell them you need more time."

"I will not change—"

"Patrick, let me do this for you. I know what you are saying. I know you will not change your mind. But perhaps something will happen to change theirs. Do not throw away this chance. It may be your last."

Patrick stilled. "They're thinking of defrocking me?"

"It has been mentioned. But we are not there yet. Let me buy you some more time."

Patrick wanted to tell Sean to shove his offer. But that was his anger talking. He closed his eyes. "Thank you, Sean."

"I'll speak with you next week, all right?"

Patrick sank into a chair. "Yes. Next week."

"Take care, Patrick."

"You too."

Patrick placed the phone on the kitchen island and looked around the kitchen. It felt so empty. He couldn't remember the last time anyone had been over here. Not that Patrick had been avoiding people, but Laney had been the center. She had glued them together. Without her, it felt like there was nothing holding them together. The words to Yeats's "The Second Coming" ran through his mind: *Things fall apart; the centre cannot hold.* She had been the center.

Samyaza stood unsullied by public opinion while Laney had

been forced into hiding. And no one save those closest to Laney seemed willing to stick their neck out for her, even those who believed she was innocent.

Over the last six months, Henry, Jake, and Patrick had met with official after official to plead Laney's case. They found people who did not believe Laney was guilty, including many who'd had the misfortune of crossing Elisabeta—yet they would not publicly offer Laney their support. The cowardice both angered and disappointed him.

And right now it felt like the church wasn't any better. The church had left him voluntarily not out of conviction, but because they didn't like that the smear campaign against Laney had also cast a spotlight on them. They were looking to mitigate that effect, but Patrick wouldn't help them. He couldn't. And he knew they were growing restless with him. And soon, he would have no say in what they decided. A lifetime of service, and he would be cast aside to assuage the fickle wants of public opinion.

He glanced at the clock, and with a start he realized the phone call had taken up more time than he had thought. He'd need to hurry if he was going to make it there in time. He grabbed his backpack and hurried to the door. Because while there might not be anything he could do at this moment to help Laney, he could still fulfill her last request of him.

He paused at the door, debating whether or not to get changed out of his civilian clothes and into his clerical clothing of all black. But he shook his head, opening the front door instead. He had a sinking feeling that he would be spending a lot more time in the future with more colorful clothing.

CHAPTER 4

BEVERLY HILLS, CALIFORNIA

The swans circled lazily through the pond on Elisabeta Roccorio's fifty-acre Beverly Hills estate. She watched as one ducked its head underwater for a snack. She loved the beautiful creatures. So graceful, so serene.

It had been six months since Delaney McPhearson had been sidelined. But that had only been the first part of the plan—isolating her from those who would defend her. That part had worked spectacularly. The second part of the plan, however, was proving more difficult than anticipated.

Elisabeta had planned on giving Laney a month to seep into the background, to allow the need to find her to grow. And then, when the desire for Laney's blood had reached a fevered pitch, Elisabeta would offer her up on a silver platter.

Dead, of course.

But that moment had come and gone. And despite Elisabeta's efforts, Laney had avoided all of her people, and had removed any digital footprint of her movements as well. It was as if she had simply disappeared.

But Elisabeta had not let this slight delay in her plans keep her from moving forward. No—Delaney out of sight was just as helpful to the bigger plan she had in play. Elisabeta had spent these last six months researching her targets. The pure number of targets had been immense at first, but slowly she had whittled them down. Now she had one group that she believed was the most promising, and a second and third target on deck, in case the first group did not turn out as planned.

But she had a feeling those secondary targets would be unnecessary. She felt it in her bones—she would find what she needed in the first group. And finally, this endless cycle would cease.

The movements of the targets and their guardians had been meticulously worked out. She knew which ones would fight and which would be too overwhelmed to do anything. And now finally, *finally*, she was ready to move.

But confident as she was, Elisabeta never placed all her eggs in one basket. There was one other possibility that could give her what she wanted. She frowned. For that possibility to pan out, the ring bearer must live. And that was not something Elisabeta was willing to tolerate.

She finished her walk, rounding the far end of the pond, and headed for the garage. A tall muscular man with dark hair and eyes, a tribute to his Spanish heritage, stood waiting for her next to a running Maybach. A tingle ran over her skin as she approached. He nodded at her, then opened the car door. Elisabeta slipped in without a word.

Hakeem got into the driver's seat. They were heading to a charity event for homeless kids or pets or something. Elisabeta couldn't remember. And didn't really care.

Actually, that wasn't true. She cared that it was taking her away from her work. But she had to maintain her appearance.

She glanced over at her aide, Hilda. Plain, with prematurely gray hair that was always pulled into a tight bun, the woman was ruffled by nothing. "Go," Elisabeta said.

"It appears the US government is still deciding what to do with the residents of the SIA facility. A decision is expected later today."

"What's the holdup?"

"The optics. They crucified Matt Clark in the press for running a fiefdom. They can't exactly do the same."

Elisabeta grunted. She had no use for politicians. Ostensibly, they were put in position to help and serve the people. But she had yet to meet one who helped anyone other than himself or herself. "And McPhearson?"

"Still no sightings. She is completely off the grid."

"How is that possible? I mean, she was grabbed by a Vegas entertainer, for God's sake. The man doesn't have any training, does he?"

"Nothing has popped up so far." Hilda hesitated.

Elisabeta narrowed her eyes. "What?"

"I hired a new investigative agency, and they came up with something—but it doesn't make any sense."

When Delaney had gone missing, Elisabeta had ordered her tracked down. The last image seen of the woman was her being loaded into a plane unconscious by a Vegas entertainer named Drake. Her team had pored over the entertainer's life, looking for something that would indicate where he had gone. Drake had been in residence in Vegas for nearly two decades. His physical appearance had changed little in that time, but very few Vegas entertainers aged naturally due to makeup, top-notch dermatologists, and plastic surgeons, so pinning down the age of any of them by sight alone was impossible.

According to the report she received, Drake was best known for sold-out shows, a lavish lifestyle, and a bevy of one-night stands. Not exactly the type who would be able to easily slip into the shadows.

And yet that was exactly what he had done. More perplexing, there was no record of the man prior to his Vegas stint. She had

had three different teams investigate him. They had all come up empty. Drake simply did not exist prior to moving to Las Vegas.

But Elisabeta had known it was only a matter of time before her people uncovered his history. No matter how well people covered their tracks, they always left traces of themselves—high school yearbooks, old neighbors. People could always be found. It was just a matter of getting the right people to search.

"What have they come up with?" she asked.

Hilda handed Elisabeta a printout from the file in her hand. It was a picture from feudal Japan—one of the only shots taken of a samurai warrior tribe.

Elisabeta frowned as she scanned the shot. Two dozen men in ornate armor stood stone-faced, staring at the camera. "What does—" Then she caught sight of the person Hilda wanted her to see.

The man did look like Drake. He had the same sharp cheekbones, the same arrogant expression. Elisabeta's gaze flicked to the writing in the top right-hand corner: *Spring, 1854.* She frowned.

"There's this one as well." Hilda handed her another photo. This one was from early Las Vegas, 1946. It was the same man, looking the same age. He wore a fedora and stood at the bar next to Bugsy Siegel at the Flamingo Hotel. The caption said his name was Hank.

Hilda nodded toward the photos. "I—I don't understand how it's possible. The team did a facial recognition search on the web looking for any hits. The program crawled through images across the globe with no hits—and then it spit these out. The program said it was him. But it has to be a relative or something, right?"

"Yes, that must be it," Elisabeta said. She felt lightheaded, knowing there was one other possibility to explain the similarity. One that made it much more likely that McPhearson would be able to stay hidden.

Shit. She's found an archangel.

She did not remember this particular one, but then again, she did not remember all the details of her past incarnations.

A vision filled her mind: a bloody battlefield, a warrior slicing through men with a roar.

Then the image was gone. But Elisabeta knew what it meant—she had run into this man before. She narrowed her eyes. *But why are you involving yourself now?* It bothered her not knowing.

She handed the pictures back to Hilda. "Have them dig into the background of these pictures. I want to know everything you can find about these men."

"Yes, ma'am."

"Where are we with Project Genesis?"

"The subjects have been selected. The teams are just waiting for your go-ahead."

"Send them."

She smiled, settling back against the leather seat as Hilda made the call. The archangel didn't matter. He'd hidden McPhearson away, and there had been no sign of her—which meant there was no one to stop her.

And once Project Genesis was completed, no one would *ever* be able to stop her.

CHAPTER 5

ADDISON, WEST VIRGINIA

The hall of the SIA facility in West Virginia had added a few more unfamiliar faces since Patrick's last visit. Of course, there always seemed to be new faces lately, since the FBI had overtaken the day-to-day activities. He and SIA agent Mustafa Massari walked together down the hall. They passed yet another unfamiliar guard in black tactical gear, but Patrick didn't say anything. He knew there were ears everywhere.

The SIA facility, or actually the former SIA facility, had been established to contain Fallen and nephilim who could not be held in regular prisons. With their abilities, regular prisons had no chance of keeping them contained.

As the existence of the Fallen and nephilim had been a secret when the prison was created, the prison itself had long been a well-kept secret within a very small circle in the US government. But after Laney's unmasking, the world of the Fallen and nephilim had been thrust into the spotlight, and so too had the prison. There were cries of dismay across the country at the lack of constitutional protections for the inmates incarcerated there. And

Patrick understood those concerns. Truth be told, he agreed with them. But at the same time, he knew why the facility had had to be kept secret. And from what he knew personally of some of the inmates, this was exactly where they belonged.

Patrick and Mustafa walked past yet another guard that Patrick did not recognize as they stepped into the elevator. As the doors closed, Patrick turned to Mustafa. "Have they let the former guards go? I don't recognize these men."

Mustafa shook his head. "No. But all SIA agents have been moved to the office. None of them are allowed near the cells."

"Why?"

"They aren't trusted."

Patrick shook his head. He'd seen this before. The drawing of lines between former allies. Us versus them. It had happened during the Civil Rights Movement and again after 9/11. And it never ended well.

The door opened, and they stepped out, turning right before Mustafa buzzed them through a security door.

"Any word yet?" Patrick asked as the door closed shut behind them with a thud.

"No," Mustafa said. "But the ruling should come down today."

The prison had remained largely the same since the federal government had taken over, but the decision of what to do with the inmates housed there was a current topic of discussion over at the Department of Justice. The first group that had arrived had opened one cell and had lost half their team before Mustafa and his men had been able to take the inmate down. That inmate had been one of Amar Patel's men. Amar Patel was a particularly reprehensible Fallen. He had been gathering Fallen, sometimes just teenagers, together for Samyaza.

That incident had slowed the government's approach. And it had let them know that the world was so much more than they realized. Patrick hoped it had also opened a few eyes to the dangers of the Fallen, so that perhaps they would look at Laney a little differently.

"A group of politicians flew in yesterday to see Cain," Mustafa said.

Patrick raised an eyebrow. "How'd that go?"

Mustafa grinned. "Fine. Until Cain took off his sunglasses."

Cain, the biblical Cain, was another guest of the facility. The Bible stated that Cain would bear the mark and all would know not to kill him—but it never described what that mark was. Turns out, it was pitch black eyes without a drop of white. It would halt anyone in their steps.

In addition, anyone who tried to harm Cain would receive sevenfold that injury in return. Patrick had seen the devastation of that curse first-hand.

"This is where I leave you. But I'll be back in two hours to see how it's going," Mustafa said.

Patrick glanced at the FBI agent at the end of the hall. "You're still not allowed near the cells either?"

"No. I don't know what they think we'd do. Let them out? No one would be that stupid."

Patrick wasn't so sure that was true when it came to politicians. "Let's hope you're right."

CHAPTER 6

ADDISON, WEST VIRGINIA

Three hours later, Patrick was still in Cain's cell. He wanted to stay with Cain until the decision about the inmates came down. He had a feeling Cain might need the support.

The chess table was set up in its usual spot. Patrick sat across the board from the immortal. He moved his pawn and looked up.

His adversary quickly moved his queen, a small smile on his face. Patrick knew he was no challenge for the man. But Cain didn't finish a game too quickly; instead he drew it out. Patrick knew these matches, and Patrick's visits, were a break in Cain's monotony, a taste of normality. And the immortal seemed to enjoy his company.

And to Patrick's surprise, he felt the same way. When Laney had asked him in her letter to visit with the world's first murderer, he hadn't known what to think. But lover of history that he was, he had thought it would at least be an opportunity to perhaps learn of times long past. He had never expected that he would enjoy the conversations as much as he did. Laney had told him that Cain was not what he seemed—that there was a peace to him now. Patrick had thought he had just fooled her.

I should have trusted her, he thought, studying the board again.

"How is Cleo doing?" Cain asked.

Patrick looked up. The sight of Cain's black eyes no longer jarred him. "Not good. She misses Laney. It's taking a toll on her."

"I think it's taken a toll on all of you."

"You're not wrong."

"So I take it there's nothing new?"

Patrick shook his head. "No. Every Fallen we've run down has been cleared."

"So you're still thinking Drake is linked with Samyaza? That he grabbed her for Elisabeta?"

Patrick shrugged, but he felt himself tense up. He hated not knowing where Laney was. "We're trying all angles. I mean, there's no reason for Drake to involve himself in this. From what we know, his focus seems to be on enjoying himself above anything else. I can't see how this fits that pattern."

Cain watched Patrick for a long moment before he shrugged. "I suppose."

Patrick frowned. "You have a different idea?"

"Hm," Cain said, studying the board.

"Hm? What does that mean?" Patrick narrowed his eyes. "Do you know why Drake would involve himself?"

Cain sighed. "I should not have said anything."

"Well, you did. So keep talking."

Cain studied him for a moment before speaking. "Drake—this is not his first time on earth. He has been here before. He has known Laney before."

Patrick was stunned. "He has? When? Where?"

"When she was Helen."

Patrick's mouth fell open and he tried to imagine who Drake could have been. He didn't know much about the flamboyant archangel except that he seemed to enjoy life, if not its responsibilities. But was he just watching, or was there some greater purpose to his existence on earth?

"He's been around since the Bronze Age?"

Cain shook his head. "No. As you know, he is on a type of sabbatical. He's one of the Guardians of the tree. But no, when he knew Helen—Laney—he was not an archangel. He was human."

"Human? Is that possible?"

"Drake was a special case."

"So he was mortal? Did he know what he was?"

Cain shook his head. "No. He had the abilities of the Fallen, but he had no idea he was more than even that. He was born, he lived, he died—like every other human."

Patrick felt his jaw falling open and slammed it shut. Drake was an archangel. From his canon, he knew archangels were the elite of the angels—the strongest, the most powerful. Ralph had been an archangel—loyal, compassionate, powerful, and Victoria's right-hand man. But Drake was the exact opposite.

"Were they close?" he asked.

"Very," Cain said softly.

Patrick's jaw dropped again. "He wasn't Menelaus, was he?"

"No."

Relief swept through Patrick. At least there wasn't an old romantic relationship to worry about. "Who was he?"

"Achilles."

Patrick shook his head, thinking of *The Iliad*. "Helen and Achilles didn't know one another."

Cain gave Patrick a smile. "As you know, the reports of history are written by the victors and rarely tell the full story—or even the true story. Achilles and Helen knew each other. And I can say, without equivocation, that if Drake is the one who has taken Laney, he will make sure absolutely no harm comes to her."

Patrick stared at Cain for a long moment before shaking his head. "Somehow, that does *not* make me feel better."

CHAPTER 7

BALTIMORE, MARYLAND

Lunch with Henry and Yoni had been good. They'd gone to a brewery near the estate, and Yoni had sweet-talked the waitress into giving them a free round. That man would never change. Now Henry and Jake were in Henry's office waiting on the Japanese delegation. Jake had agreed to run security reviews of a plant they were building in Ohio.

Jake stretched out his legs. He needed a run. After this business was completed, he'd run a few miles and then hit the bag for a while. Henry was right. They needed to get back to life. As much as he hated to admit it, Laney coming back was not in his control.

Across the room, Henry's desk phone rang. Absentmindedly, Henry picked it up, his eyes still on the file on his desk. "Yes?"

Henry sat up, his face still. "What? No, they— But—" Henry stared at the phone before placing it back on the receiver.

Jake got to his feet. "Henry?"

"Hold on a second." Henry dialed the phone and paced, but no one answered on the other end of the line. Henry punched the disconnect button before striding toward the door. "We need to go. *Now.*"

Jake hurried along next to him, practically running to keep up with Henry's long strides. "What is it? Is it Laney?"

Henry shook his head, not slowing down. "No, no. It's the SIA facility. The government has decided to take all the prisoners to their own facility."

Jake shouldn't have been surprised, and yet he was. When the world found out about the SIA facility, there had been a public uproar; it was cast as an extra-government entity subverting a fair and just legal system. And now, apparently, they weren't concerned about that anymore.

"What? What about civil rights? Trials? Due process? All that flag-waving they've been doing?"

"Apparently they think the Fallen are too dangerous to let the public know they exist. A force arrived at the facility ten minutes ago. They've already started to transfer the patients."

"What? Do they even know what they're doing?"

"I don't know. I tried to reach Mustafa. He's not answering."

Jake felt a pit open in his stomach. "Patrick's there. He was visiting Cain."

"There's more. The inmates are no longer under the control of the FBI." Henry pushed through the door leading outside.

"Who's in charge now?"

"The ETF."

Jake's jaw dropped open. *Oh shit.*

CHAPTER 8

ADDISON, WEST VIRGINIA

Patrick stretched, feeling a twinge in his lower back. The game had been good. He'd lost of course, but the conversation had made it more than enjoyable. They had discussed the Peloponnesian War—the ancient Greek war that began in 420 BC between the Athenians and Spartans. The war had shifted power so much that the vital city-state of Athens had been reduced to rubble and Sparta had become the leading city. *Helen's legacy,* Patrick thought.

Patrick shot Cain a quick look before he started putting the chess pieces back in the box. *To have seen so much history.* Patrick was not ashamed to admit to a twinge of jealousy at all that Cain had witnessed. But perhaps the cost, always separating yourself from others, was not worth it.

Cain took the chairs and pushed them against the wall, then took the box from Patrick and placed it on a shelf above his bed. Patrick pushed the table back against the wall. This was their cleanup routine. They didn't discuss who would clean up what, they just each played their role, like a well-known dance.

The game put away, Patrick looked around Cain's cell. Over the last few months, the restrictions on Cain had been eased so it was a more comfortable room. A bright blue comforter was on the bed, and a Monet print, *Madame Monet and Child*, was on one wall. Not for the first time, Patrick wondered at the choice. The print depicted the wife of Claude Monet sewing in a garden with a small child playing at her feet. Patrick thought perhaps it was more revealing than Cain intended—a longing for the sense of family and love that the picture conveyed.

Books lined the shelves above Cain's bed. Two comfortable club chairs had even been moved in and put in front of the TV. Patrick knew that in part, that luxury was due to him. He and Cain had spent hours sitting in those chairs speaking about days long gone.

Patrick glanced toward the door where the FBI agents stood. He knew that he should get going, but honestly, there was nothing waiting for him back at the estate. He could go to the school; he loved the kids. But he was on his own there for the most part. He was the kids' parental figure, not their friend. Here, he had companionship. And until he became friends with Cain, he'd never realized how much he'd missed it.

"Say, you wouldn't have been in Scotland before the rule of Bruce, were you?" he asked.

"You mean did I know William Wallace?"

Patrick nodded.

"I spent some time with him. He was a fascinating man."

Patrick grinned. "Any interest in watching *Braveheart*, and you can tell me where they went wrong?"

"Dinner from the Secret Garden?" Cain asked. The Secret Garden was a Korean barbecue place nearby.

"Absolutely."

"Well, I think my schedule's clear."

Footsteps hurrying toward Cain's cell caused both of them to turn. The FBI agent who stood outside the cell was joined by six other agents—except all of the new agents had a different patch on their black uniforms. Patrick squinted, trying to make it out. *The ETF? Who on earth are they?*

One man stepped forward. There was cruelty in the narrowing of his eyes as he leered at Patrick and Cain in the cell.

The FBI agent nodded at the newcomer. "Agent Seward."

"You're dismissed," Seward said, never taking his gaze from Patrick and Cain. There was no hint of kindness in the man, and he only strengthened Patrick's doubts in any government who would give this type of man any authority.

Patrick frowned. "What's going on?"

"I think you should go, Patrick," Cain said quietly.

Seward stepped up to the glass wall of the cell. "Patrick Delaney, you are ordered to exit the cell immediately."

"It's *Father* Patrick. And what is the meaning of this?"

Seward narrowed his already small eyes. "Exit the cell immediately, or you will be charged with obstruction."

"Obstruction?" Patrick asked.

"Last warning. If you do not remove yourself, we will remove you."

Patrick turned his bewildered gaze to Cain.

Cain nodded back at him, although Patrick could sense his confusion. "It's all right, Patrick. Go on. They probably just want to interview me again."

Patrick curled his hands into fists, knowing Cain was wrong. Something was off here. He noted the shackles one of the agents in the back held. And from the way the agents were tensing, he also knew that whatever was about to happen was wrong.

"I'll tell Henry and Jake," he said. "We'll find out what's going on."

"Thank you, Patrick. For everything." Cain extended his hand.

Patrick shook it without hesitation. "I'll see you soon."

Cain just smiled in response.

"Now, Father Patrick," Seward barked.

With one last glance at Cain, Patrick made his way to the door.

An agent pointed at Cain and yelled. "Stand against the far wall."

Another agent stepped up to the door and glared at Patrick. "Move."

Patrick knew surprise was splashed across his face. He had been in and out of this prison a few times a week for months, and no one had ever spoken to him like this. His anger began to simmer. There was no reason for him to be spoken to this way.

Cain put up hands and walked backward to the far wall. The door in front of Patrick slid open, and he was grabbed roughly and pulled from the cell.

"What are you doing?" Patrick yelled as Seward threw him to the floor.

"Patrick!" Cain yelled, stepping forward.

"Fire," Seward ordered.

Two agents stepped into the doorway and shot darts into Cain. Both men dropped to the ground. Cain stumbled; whatever drugs were in those darts were taking effect quickly. The downed agents were pulled out of the way as four others moved into the cell and surrounded Cain.

Patrick started to get to his feet, but a knee in his back forced him back down. "Stay down," Seward growled.

"What is wrong with you people? This isn't necessary."

The agent didn't answer him.

Inside the cell, Cain dropped to his knees before pitching forward. The agents moved in warily before turning him over and placing cuffs on his legs and wrists.

Patrick watched in horror as they put a bag over Cain's head, then rolled in a dolly and laid it flat. Cain was lifted onto the dolly and strapped to it.

"Where are you taking him?" Patrick demanded.

The knee in his back pushed down harder, and Patrick winced. "You don't get to ask questions. Seen your *niece* lately, Father?"

Seward grabbed one of Patrick's wrists and yanked it behind him. Pain shot up Patrick's arm and through his shoulder. His other arm was grabbed just as roughly, and zip ties were wrapped around his wrists.

"*I'm* being arrested?"

Patrick was hauled to his feet as the four guards walked past with Cain.

Seward leaned down toward Patrick and glared. Spittle flew onto Patrick's face as the man spoke. "If it were up to me, you'd be tossed in a cell with the rest of these animals. So don't tempt me." He turned Patrick around and shoved him forward.

Patrick stumbled and crashed into the wall. He used his shoulder to straighten up, anger burning through him—anger at the treatment of him, at the treatment of Cain, and at the attitude of the guards.

Seward grabbed him by the shoulder and shoved him toward another agent. "Put him with the others."

The agent took Patrick by the arm. Patrick started to look back.

"Don't," the agent holding him warned.

Patrick swallowed and let himself be pulled forward. *What on earth is going on?*

CHAPTER 9

Jake flew the Chandler helicopter himself to West Virginia. As they approached the facility, he turned to Henry. "Do we have permission to land? Or is someone going to take a shot at us?"

"Hold on." Henry pulled out his phone and made a call while Jake glanced at the silver-haired man in the back seat. Brett Hanover, the head of the Chandler Group's legal department, sat there, his eyes wide.

"You all right, Brett?"

Brett swallowed. "Um, yes. This is only my second time in a helicopter, and the last time, it was a little slower."

"Oh? What was the first time?" Jake asked.

"Um, honeymoon in Maui."

"Must have been nice."

Brett grabbed on to the straps holding him to the seat in the back. "Honestly? I didn't really enjoy it. Turns out I don't like riding in helicopters."

"Well, we'll be down in just another few minutes."

Brett nodded but didn't seem comforted by the time assessment.

Henry disconnected his call, and Jake raised an eyebrow. "Well?"

"With a great deal of unhappiness, we have been granted access to land."

"Great."

Jake all but nosedived the chopper toward the ground. Brett gave out a little yelp, but Jake didn't slow the approach.

The agents who had been looking into Laney had been growing more and more frustrated at their lack of progress. In fact, the whole US government was beginning to look foolish at their inability to find her. Jake was pretty sure that was why the ETF had been placed in charge of the facility. As the ETF worked under the auspices of Homeland Security, and by extension the PATRIOT Act, they had been given a great deal of leeway with rules and oversight. Putting them in charge was like letting a fox guard the chicken coop. With the pressure mounting to show something, a group with a long leash and little oversight didn't seem like the best choice.

Jake knew that the pressure to do something would be pushing down to all aspects of the government associated with this debacle. Which meant anyone caught in the crosshairs would not be treated well.

And Patrick… he was tough, but the idea of him being pushed around by agents didn't sit well with Jake. Patrick had taken on the role of father, or kindly uncle, to all of them. If Jake couldn't protect Laney, he was damn well going to make sure Patrick was okay.

CHAPTER 10

The sky was gray as Patrick was pushed through the front doors of the facility, his wrists still restrained behind his back. The first agent had passed him off to someone else, but not before Patrick overheard them talking. They weren't just moving Cain. They were moving all the inmates.

The elevator dinged behind him, and Patrick glanced over his shoulder as four ETF guards stepped off and surveyed the lobby. One guard pushed the dolly holding Cain. They wheeled him outside, and Patrick watched as Cain was taken to a waiting armored truck.

"Where are you taking him?"

"None of *your* business." The agent grabbed Patrick roughly by the arm and pushed him to a small area surrounded by temporary fencing. A group of about forty people was inside—all staff from the facility, all with zip ties around their wrists.

Mustafa pushed through the crowd, his eyes large. "Patrick."

The agent pushed Patrick against the fence and glared at the group inside. "Back up."

His mouth tight, Mustafa backed away, keeping his eyes on the agent. The guard by the gate unlocked it, and Patrick was shoved inside. The gate shut behind him.

Mustafa rushed to his side. "Are you all right?"

"Fine, fine. But they took Cain."

Mustafa nodded. "They're taking all the prisoners."

"Where?"

"No idea. But they started with Cain, after they escorted all of us here. Now they're going for the rest."

Patrick glanced at the tall towering man in the back: Hanz, Cain's former guard. Patrick lowered his voice. "Do they know some of the guards are, uh, different?"

Mustafa shook his head. "No. Matt never put it in any of their files."

"Good. Where *is* Matt?"

"He's in DC, meeting with the DOJ. I'm guessing getting him to DC was part of the plan to make sure this went off without a hitch."

Hanz moved closer to them, nudging his chin in the direction of the east lawn. "Someone's coming."

Patrick tensed. Hanz was a Fallen, which meant he could only be sensing a Fallen or nephilim heading their way. *Oh, please, be the good guys.*

And then a familiar face appeared from around the side of the building, followed by two more familiar faces. Henry, Jake, and Brett.

Henry scanned the area, then nudged Jake, pointing him toward the fenced-in area. The three men hurried over.

Henry reached the area first. "Are you all right?"

An agent stormed up to them. "What are you doing? Get away from there."

Henry glared down at the man. "Are these men under arrest?"

"I haven't decided yet," the agent sneered. "And unless you want to suffer the same fate—"

Brett stepped forward. "Actually, due to the fact that you have both cuffed them and locked them in a secured area, you have legally arrested them." He turned to Mustafa and Patrick. "Have you been read your rights?"

Patrick shook his head.

"No," Mustafa said.

"I see." Brett turned back to the agent. "So you are unlawfully holding these men."

"According to the PATRIOT Act, I can."

"Really? You're saying you believe these men were involved in terrorist activities?"

"Damn straight. This one"—the agent gestured to Patrick —"has a friendship with one."

"And what evidence do you have besides friendship?"

"He's also related to Delaney McPhearson. That should be enough."

Patrick glared. "My niece has done nothing wrong."

"Yeah, sure." The agent walked off, Brett hurrying after him.

"Don't worry, Patrick," Henry said. "We'll get you out—all of you. Are you all right?"

Patrick nodded. "They took Cain and are gathering the rest right now."

Two choppers appeared in the sky, coming at the facility from different directions. Mustafa frowned. "Who's that?"

"Are they with you?" Patrick asked.

Jake shook his head. "No."

No one spoke as the choppers flew closer. Soon, the names of two different news stations could be seen on them.

"Great," Jake growled.

Patrick shared his sentiment. After the treatment of Laney, neither of them was particularly fond of the news media.

The doors to the facility opened, and federal agents marched out. An outer layer of agents held weapons at the ready while an inner layer escorted several individuals attached to stretchers, a drip attached to each of their arms.

"At least they were smart enough to drug them for transport," Jake said.

Henry nodded.

It took an hour for the Fallen to be removed from the building and loaded into waiting vans. Finally the stream of stretchers and agents dried up. Patrick and the rest of the SIA staff remained in the fenced-in area throughout, and Jake and Henry stood with them. Brett argued with someone on the phone for almost the entire hour.

"That's not right," Mustafa said quietly, watching the doors to the facility close behind the last stretcher.

"What's not right?" Patrick asked.

"They're missing one."

"Are you sure? Maybe you miscounted," Henry said.

Mustafa shook his head. "I didn't."

"Who's missing?" Jake asked.

Mustafa opened his mouth—then his gaze flicked to the doors, his relief obvious. "Wait. Someone else is coming."

Two agents stepped out, a woman held between them. But unlike the others, she was not bound or drugged. Tears trailed down her face, and she looked around fearfully.

"Son of a bitch," Jake said.

The former ruler of Honu Keiki—Xia, but known to the world as "the priestess"—looked small and fragile between the two large agents. Her dark hair hung down to her waist, and her eyes looked smaller, older, without the makeup she normally wore. She held on to the agents, playing up the damsel in distress.

"Those idiots," Henry hissed.

"Why isn't she restrained?" Mustafa asked.

One of the agents leaned down and whispered to her, seemingly needing to encourage her to move. She looked up at him and nodded, taking a deep breath. Then she started to walk with trembling legs.

The agents accompanied her slowly, and the priestess continually looked around. To anyone else, she probably looked like she was terrified of her surroundings. But Patrick had the feeling she was scanning for threats.

Then the priestess's gaze fell on Jake and Henry. Her lip curled in distaste. Before anyone could yell a warning, she grabbed the heads of the two agents that held her and slammed them together with a heart-stopping crack.

"Oh my God," Patrick said.

Hanz and three other Fallen guards stepped in front of Patrick and Mustafa. "Get back," Hanz ordered, as Henry and Jake took off toward the priestess at a run.

The FBI agents didn't respond as quickly, seemingly shocked by the transformation of the priestess from helpless victim to violent predator. And that was their undoing. The priestess leapt on one agent and twisted his neck before he could even pull his weapon. She was on another as he pulled his weapon, turned him so that he was her shield, and bulldozed him into the three agents across from her.

Jake dove for the agent that had been killed, wrenching his shotgun from around his arm. He unloaded it at the priestess, catching her in the ribs. She whirled around. But Henry caught her from the other side with another borrowed weapon.

Patrick held his breath as they advanced on the woman. The remaining ETF agents seemed to gather themselves and joined in, all weapons trained on the priestess.

All weapons except two. Those were aimed at Henry and Jake. "Drop it! Drop your weapons!"

With a muttered curse, Jake dropped his weapon to the ground. Henry did the same.

"On the ground! Face down on the ground!" the agents ordered.

Jake and Henry did as they were told.

But Patrick kept his gaze on the priestess. None of the other agents had fired, and Patrick knew she would already be healing. "What are you waiting for?" he whispered.

"They don't understand what she is," Mustafa replied, his gaze also glued to the drama in front of them.

The priestess reached up with blinding speed and grabbed the barrel of the gun closest to her, wrenching it from the man's grasp.

"Open fire!" someone yelled—and then all that could be heard was the cacophony of gunfire. The priestess jerked back again and again as blood appeared across her torso. Finally, she collapsed to the ground. "Get restraints on her now!" the agent in charge yelled, his voice shaky.

"She's not dead," Jake yelled. "She'll heal. You need to drug her —now."

The agent gave an abrupt nod, showing he'd heard. "Medic!" he yelled.

A small man rushed over, his skin unnaturally pale and his hands shaking as he quickly plunged a needle into the priestess's skin.

Patrick let out a breath, knowing that at least the immediate danger was over.

Overhead, the news choppers circled. Mustafa nudged his chin toward them. "They got all of that."

Patrick nodded. "Yeah. Now let's see what they make of it."

CHAPTER 11

BOSTON, MASSACHUSETTS

Three of Mary Jane McAdams's four redheaded kids bolted from the car as soon as she had it in park.

"Get back here and take something!" Mary Jane yelled through the open car window before they were out of shouting distance.

Her two teenage sons grumbled to a stop, and her daughter had the decency to look a little sheepish. Joe and Shaun, ages seventeen and sixteen, made their way to the back of the car. Shaun opened the back as Mary Jane walked around.

"What do you want us to take?" Shaun asked.

Mary Jane stared at the sky, searching for patience. The back of the car was filled with two coolers, three chairs, an umbrella, a stroller, and a bag full of soccer gear, and all of it needed to be taken—which after a decade of soccer games on weekends, all three of her children knew well.

She peered in at the gear. "Gee, I don't know. What do you think?"

Shaun grinned, peering at her from the corner of his blue eyes. "Nothing?"

She ruffled his hair. "Ha ha. Now start grabbing stuff, Muscles."

Joe, a year older and almost six inches taller than Shaun, reached in. He'd shot up over the summer, and Mary Jane knew Shaun was hoping he'd catch up. "Muscles?" Joe said. "Are we doing that Opposite Day thing again?"

With a grumble, Shaun shoved him. Joe shoved him back.

Mary Jane stepped between the two of them. "Okay, okay. Before this devolves into a boxing match and I have to wipe the floor with both of you, *in* front of all your friends, just grab as much as you can and head over to the bleachers."

"Yes, Mom," Joe said.

As he grabbed a chair, swung it across his shoulders, and picked up one of the coolers, Mary Jane realized how strong he had actually become. A few summers ago he was dragging the cooler along the ground. Now he looked like he could take both coolers at once.

Not to be outdone, Shaun grabbed the same amount, although he moved a little more slowly toward the bleachers. And with a pang, Mary Jane realized it wouldn't be long before both boys were heading away to college.

Her daughter Molly grabbed the stroller and unfolded it. "I'll get Susie."

Mary Jane cast a glance to the youngest member of the McAdams clan, miraculously sleeping through the craziness of her siblings. "Thanks, honey."

Molly smiled and pushed the stroller around the side of the car. And Mary Jane realized that Molly, at age thirteen, was growing up quickly too.

Mary Jane pulled out the soccer bag and the last chair.

"She's still sleeping. You still want me to take her out?" Molly asked.

"No, that's okay. Take the bag, would you? Go warm up."

Molly leaned in and ran a hand over her little sister's face before grabbing the bag from her mom. After a quick glance around, Molly leaned up and kissed her mom on the cheek. "Love you, Mom."

And Mary Jane wanted to hold on to that moment, because she knew it wouldn't be long before her daughter would be embarrassed to even be seen in public with her. "Love you too, honey. Now go give 'em hell."

Molly gave her a smile, slung the bag over her shoulder, and jogged over to where her team was practicing.

Mary Jane closed the hatchback and walked around to the passenger door. Two-year-old Susie, known within the McAdams's larger family as "the surprise," lay with her head tilted to the side. She had the McAdams red hair and light blue eyes rimmed in a darker blue.

She opened her eyes and blinked sleepily.

"Hey there, sweetheart."

A smile spread across Susie's face, and Mary Jane's heart melted a little bit. When she'd found out she was pregnant again at forty, she hadn't exactly been excited. She had been looking forward to her and Billy actually getting to spend some time together and reclaiming a little of her life. Then Billy had died in a car accident, four months before Susie was born, and Mary Jane's plan for her life had lurched right off the tracks. She'd struggled to pull herself and the kids together. Her extended family all lent a hand, but there was no denying that a giant hole had formed at the family's center.

And then Susie was born. She was a lifeline for all of them, a reminder of why life was good.

Now the grief was still there—it would always be there—but all Mary Jane could think about when she looked into this little face was that Susie, and the rest of her children, meant that Billy was still here. And all she felt was love.

She also realized that her family hadn't been complete until Susie came along.

Mary Jane extracted Susie from her car seat. After a quick snuggle, she put her in her stroller, along with Mr. Binxsy the monkey and her sippy cup.

After locking the car, she slipped the keys in her pocket and headed for Molly's field. Molly's game was scheduled to start in about fifteen minutes. Other families were already set up.

Mary Jane watched Molly practice on the field with her team and felt a burst of pride; the girl was a natural. Molly was quieter than her brothers, but on the soccer field she was ferocious. Mary Jane grinned as Molly dribbled around one of her teammates and took a shot. The ball sailed into the top right-hand corner of the goal. *That's my girl.*

Molly grinned and turned to jog back toward the sideline as the coach called them over. Then Molly's head whipped back toward her mother, her eyes large. "Mom!"

Mary Jane frowned. "What's—"

A blow landed across the back of Mary Jane's head, and her whole world went black.

⁓

"Wake up, Mom. Please wake up."

Mary Jane's head throbbed as Molly's words made their way through. She felt cold. Why was her bed cold? Slowly, she became aware of more sounds around her, then a cool wind. Did Billy leave the window open? *No, Billy's gone.*

She opened her eyes and blinked in confusion at the sky above her. What? She turned to Molly, who sat clasping her hands, tears in her eyes. "What happened?"

"Oh, Mom." Molly fell on her, hugging her, her shoulders shaking.

"Hey, hey, it's okay. I'm all right. Just—God, my head hurts."

"Mom!" Shaun and Joe sprinted up to her. Molly sat back, and Mary Jane sat up slowly, the world swimming for a minute before it righted itself. A crowd had collected around her.

"Take it easy, Mary Jane. We've called an ambulance and the police," said Helen Aciccio, one of the moms from the team.

As if on cue, Mary Jane heard a police siren drawing closer. "The police? What happened?"

"Someone hit you on the back of the head," Joe said, looking close to tears as well.

"What? Who?"

"We don't know," Shaun said.

"Oh my God. Susie? Is she okay?"

Shaun exchanged a glance with Joe, and Molly burst into tears.

Mary Jane's chest squeezed tight as she looked around. "Where's Susie?"

Shaun knelt down. This boy, who just a few minutes ago she had thought looked so grown up, now looked like a scared child. "She's gone, Mom. Somebody took her. We gave chase when Molly yelled, but we couldn't catch them. Honestly, we didn't even see them. It was a blur."

Mary Jane struggled to her feet, looking wildly around. "What do you mean she's gone?"

"Mom." Shaun took her arms and looked into her eyes. "Somebody hit you and took her. We've looked. Half the people on the field are still looking. But we can't find her. She's gone."

Mary Jane stared at him. "No. That can't be—" She looked around at the faces of the people surrounding her. She looked down at Molly, who was still on the ground sobbing, and at Joe, who was knelt next to her, his arm around her shoulders, wiping at his own eyes.

Mary Jane stumbled, her knees refusing to work. Shaun grabbed her before she could drop. Her gaze fastened on Susie's stroller, which lay tipped over. Susie's sippy cup had rolled a few feet away, and Mr. Binxsy lay face down on the grass.

Mary Jane's whole life once again lurched off the tracks. *She's gone. She's gone. Susie's gone.*

CHAPTER 12

BALTIMORE, MARYLAND

The lock stuck, and Patrick struggled to turn the key. Exhaustion washed over him along with a feeling of powerlessness. *Please.* Finally it released, and he all but stumbled into his cottage.

The ETF had held them for eight hours. Jake and Henry had been charged with obstruction. They were still being held. *Because apparently saving the lives of ETF agents is a crime now,* Patrick thought bitterly.

He looked at the stairs. The idea of climbing them to reach his bedroom seemed a Herculean task at the moment. Instead, he headed to the kitchen to brew himself a cup of tea. He went through the motions, his mind running through all that had happened today. Cain was gone—the rest of the inmates as well. He'd been detained. Henry and Jake were locked up. It was too much.

He took his mug of tea and some slices of cheese to the living room. Placing the drink and food on the side table, he sat on the couch and pulled a blanket over his lap. He grabbed the remote and turned on the TV, hoping there was something on that would allow him to forget the misery of today, even if just for a little while.

He skimmed the channels; nothing caught his interest. A few of the news channels were talking about the SIA facility, but Patrick quickly moved on, not wanting to hear their opinions. But then his hand stilled. A picture in a box next to the anchor's face made his heart lurch. *Laney.*

The brunette anchor sat facing the camera, her demeanor serious. "There has been a stunning development in the Delaney McPhearson case. As you no doubt remember, Delaney McPhearson caused an uproar six months ago when video surfaced of her saving a busload of children on the Francis Scott Key Bridge. McPhearson, who works for the Chandler Group, saved the children with what can only be called psychic abilities.

"But the public love affair with McPhearson was short-lived, as other videos surfaced showing what was dubbed a callous disregard for human life. McPhearson, once hailed as a hero, was quickly vilified. Soon it was alleged that McPhearson had staged the incident on the bridge and had been the mastermind behind the attack on the Temple Mount in Israel. Video even surfaced of McPhearson brutally ending the life of the cult leader known as the priestess. Through her legal representatives, McPhearson denied all wrongdoing but refused to answer any additional questions.

"But soon rumors started to swirl that there was a larger mystery at play. That McPhearson was not the only individual out there with special abilities. People stepped forward to argue that McPhearson was a hero and to recount stories of how she had saved them.

"But there were still those tapes. The recording of the death of the priestess was particularly damaging, as Delaney McPhearson snapping the woman's neck was clear for all to see. The case was cut and dried.

"Or is it? Video has now surfaced that once again forces us to look at the case of Delaney McPhearson. By now, everyone has seen the video from the government facility in West Virginia. The woman on the tape has been identified as the priestess—the woman Delaney McPhearson allegedly killed. And yet the priestess, who has been portrayed as an innocent victim, is seen in the tape killing federal agents with incredible speed and strength. If I did not know the camera operator personally, I might even think it was faked. But it's not. There is more to the priestess than we have been told. In the video, the priestess is shot multiple times, but a short time later, she leaps up, apparently healed, and manages to kill yet another agent before she's taken down in a hail of bullets. Even then, she is not dead. She is cuffed and drugged before being taken away.

"Even before this incredible footage, over a dozen individuals were removed from the same facility, drugged and bound. Which begs the question: Do they have the same abilities as the priestess? And what exactly is the United States government doing with them?"

The anchor turned to a different camera angle. "But I find myself asking a different question. What is Delaney McPhearson's role in all of this? Is she the evildoer the governments of the world have made her out to be? Or is she as she first appeared, a hero trying to save as many people as she can?

"With some digging, I've learned that McPhearson has made some powerful enemies. And powerful enemies can warp and influence the public's perception. So who is Delaney McPhearson, really? We know now she did not kill the priestess. We know that her actions at the capital months ago saved hundreds, if not thousands, of lives. The same can be said for her actions at the Temple Mount. According to those who label her a murderer, she did all of that for the attention.

"But if that's the case, where is she now? The woman has a PhD. She had to know the publicity could easily turn against her.

So why direct it at herself? When we look back at her life, there's nothing to indicate a person who seeks the spotlight. Quite the opposite, in fact. So—was there a rush to judgment in this case? Was the need to find an enemy so great, that we chose the first one offered up?

"I for one believe there is much more to this story than we have been led to believe. And I for one look forward to hearing Delaney McPhearson's side of the story."

Patrick shut off the TV, his mouth hanging open. Rationally, he knew it was only one news report. There had been hundreds that vilified Delaney.

But now there's one that doesn't. And as much as he tried to quell it, he couldn't help but embrace the small burst of hope that flared inside him.

CHAPTER 13

BALTIMORE, MARYLAND

Noriko was getting worried. Cleo's bouts of depression came and went, but for the last few months, they'd been happening more often. The last one had lasted days.

Noriko had rarely left the preserve. She had been wracking her brain to figure out a way to help her. She'd scoured the internet, but psychoanalyzing a genetically altered leopard was not one of her skill sets. Yet even she knew that Cleo needed something to focus on, to distract her from worrying about Laney.

With the restrictions Henry had put in place, the cats rarely left the grounds. Even Cleo's trips to the school had been curtailed. To make up for that, Noriko, Rolly, Lou, Danny, and Zach had been visiting here as much as possible. Henry had even constructed a house on the grounds that would allow people to stay overnight—and for the last three months, at least one human had stayed every night to reassure all the cats, but mainly Cleo. Noriko had all but moved into the enclosure.

When she wasn't here, she was either at the school or the

estate. But here was where she felt the most at home, where she felt like she could do the most good. Besides, with her sheltered upbringing, the lack of electronics and modernity at the preserve actually made her feel more at home.

Today, Noriko had been sitting with Cleo for an hour, just keeping her company. Tiger stayed with them as well. Tiger had grown closer to Cleo than any of the other cats, although all the cats were concerned about Cleo's fragile state. They all spent time keeping her company. It was pretty amazing. Like the humans in Cleo's life, they, too, seemed to have worked out a schedule to make sure Cleo was rarely alone.

Noriko met Tiger's gaze over Cleo's back.

Better.

Yes. I think she's a little better too. Noriko's stomach growled.

Food? Tiger's eyes lit up.

Noriko laughed, and even Cleo seemed to perk up. "Yes. I think it's time to eat. Cleo?"

Cleo stretched and stood. Tiger nudged her affectionately as Noriko also got to her feet.

"Okay. Let's go see what's on the—"

Tiger's head snapped toward her a second before he raced to her side.

Noriko reached out a hand as the edges of her vision went dark. *Oh no.* Her legs trembled, and she felt Tiger slip under one arm, Cleo under the other, catching her as she started to fall. Cleo let out a roar.

The vision began before she'd even touched the ground.

A child cried somewhere in the distance. Noriko turned around and around trying to find the source, but all she could see were gray clouds. And then one cry was joined by dozens more. Noriko put her hands over her ears as the cries joined together, drowning out everything. It became painful. Only focus on one, she warned herself.

Then all went silent. Slowly Noriko lowered her hands, and she heard the one cry.

"Where are you?" Noriko called out as she walked forward, following the sound.

She pushed past the clouds, which somehow had substance to them. The child cried louder. Noriko had a sense of the child somewhere ahead of her, but she also sensed there were more children around her.

She pushed through the clouds and into a clearing. There, sitting in the middle of the space, was a gray stroller, its back to her. Noriko walked slowly toward it. As she came around the side, two little feet in pink sneakers kicked into view. Noriko knelt down in front of the child. Blue eyes filled with tears stared back at her from a pale face framed by red curls. The child's breaths came out in hiccupped cries.

Noriko took the girl's hand. *I'm here. I'm here.*

The girl's cries stopped, and she held tightly to Noriko's hand. *Find me.* The words drifted through Noriko's mind, and the hair at the back of her neck stood straight up. *Find all of us.*

CHAPTER 14

BALTIMORE, MARYLAND

The image of the little girl stayed in the forefront of Noriko's mind as her surroundings came back to her. The first thing she became aware of was the hand brushing the hair away from her face. She opened her eyes to see Lou above her; Noriko's head was in her lap.

Lou smiled, some of the worry dropping from her face. "There you are."

"Hey," Noriko said softly, still a little lightheaded.

"You okay?" Danny asked from next to Lou.

"Where'd you come from?"

"We were coming to take you out to lunch." Lou nodded across from her. Noriko turned her head to see Rolly, Zach, and Danny watching her, concern across their faces.

Rolly took her hand. "We heard Cleo roar, and even without your abilities we knew something was wrong. Tiger raced out from the trees and led us to you."

Noriko nodded. Her head was beginning to clear, and the pounding receded.

Tiger walked up and put his face right in front of Noriko's, staring into her eyes.

"I'm okay," she assured him.

He stared into her eyes for another moment before nodding and stepping back. He disappeared into the trees.

"Well, if he think's you're okay, then I guess you are," Rolly said.

She started to sit up, and Zach was immediately there, supporting her back while Rolly pulled her upright. Noriko looked at the concern on the faces surrounding her. In the short time she'd been here, these four had become her group, her tribe. No, not four. She looked beyond the humans in front of her to the large black cat who sat silently watching her. *Five.*

Cleo stepped forward, and Rolly scooted to one side. Cleo leaned her head into Noriko's. *Find the child.*

I will.

With a nod, Cleo stepped back, then disappeared into the trees in the same direction as Tiger.

Noriko reeled again at this connection she had with Cleo. Somehow Cleo saw her visions. None of the other cats did, although they could all sense when she was about to have one. Danny thought it might be because Cleo was older than the other cats, and that one day the other cats would have the ability to see the visions as well. Noriko didn't know whether that was true, but she liked the fact that someone else could see what she saw. Being able to share the burden, even if it was with a giant leopard, was a comfort.

"What did you see?" Lou asked.

Noriko was once again humbled by the easy acceptance her gifts had received among this group. One of the reasons Honu Keiki kept to themselves was because they had been taught since time immortal that their abilities would make them targets in the larger world—that they needed to keep themselves separated to allow themselves to not be corrupted and disbelieved. But Noriko had yet to experience any of that. She had found a group of people who never questioned what she could do. Perhaps it was because three of them had abilities of their own—strength, speed, and enhanced healing. And Danny... well, as a genius, he had his own type of ability that kept him separated from others. And somehow, together, their differing abilities were what made them all normal.

Noriko nodded. "It was a vision."

"What was it this time?" Zach asked.

She'd only had a few visions over the last few months. None of them had been violent or with the overwhelming urgency of this one. "It was about a child." She shook her head. "No, children. They were crying. One, a little girl, said I had to find them."

Lou frowned. "How old?"

"Two, maybe three at the oldest."

"Could you describe her?" Danny asked.

"I can draw her. She was very pale, with red hair and really blue eyes."

Danny's mouth dropped open. His surprised gaze flew to Lou.

Noriko looked between the two of them. "What?"

"It's not possible, right?" Danny asked.

"I—I don't know. I mean—" Lou shrugged, words obviously failing her.

"What are you two talking about?" Zach asked.

"Victoria," Danny said. "If she was reborn right after she died, she'd be about two right now."

"But she wouldn't look the same, right?" Rolly asked.

"That's the thing—she does look the same. Every lifetime, she looks exactly the same," Danny said.

"So you think it's Victoria who called to me?" Noriko shook her head. "But that can't be. It wasn't just one child. One spoke to me, but there were dozens of voices. And she asked me to find *them*, not just her."

"Either way, we should figure out what's going on. I'll get

started." Danny stood up and strode away. Lou looked at the others, then quickly followed him.

Noriko looked at Rolly and Zach. "Is he okay?"

Zach shook his head. "Victoria—she was his grandmother, and he really liked her. He misses her. And now with Laney gone, his world's in turmoil right now."

"But, I mean, there's no guarantee it's her," Noriko said.

Rolly looked to where Danny had disappeared. "Once you've spent a little more time with the Chandler Group, you'll realize there's no such thing as a coincidence. So my money's on Victoria having something to do with this."

CHAPTER 15

The exterior lights were all on, giving the main house of the Chandler Estate an almost festive atmosphere. Built in the late nineteenth century, the house had been modeled after Jefferson's Monticello, although built on a much larger scale. A rounded roof supported by four tall columns dominated the front entry. Two large wings expanded out from either side.

Patrick could almost see the ancient carriages pulling up to the front door and letting out their guests. He and Laney had spent one evening in front of the building with a picnic basket, just talking about what it must have been like throughout time. The memory made him smile, but it also made his heart ache.

His burst of hope from last night's broadcast had dissipated throughout the day as no other journalist or program picked up the thread. They reported on the SIA facility and the search for Laney, and some even speculated that she might have helped the priestess. Of course, those same anchors had labeled her a murderess months earlier, after the tape of the confrontation between Laney and the priestess had come to light. The anchors seemed oblivious to their own hypocrisy.

Patrick knew he was not handling any of this well. As time went on, he was growing more and more stressed. He and Cleo seemed to have that in common. Oh, he was pushing through his days, saying the right things. But inside, he was slowly dying.

Cain had helped, actually. He'd been one of the few distractions. And one who never seemed to tire of talking about Laney. And now Patrick got to worry about what was happening to him as well. He held no illusions about how they were going to treat the immortal. He would be a lab rat subjected to every test the US government could conceive of. The same US government that had tried to kill Laney.

Patrick didn't like how dark his thoughts became when he thought of his government's role in Delaney's plight. Patrick was a patriot. He had been a Marine in Vietnam, and like they said, there was no such thing as a former Marine. But his allegiance was not blind. The government was taking steps that didn't conform to Patrick's picture of this country. The US did not torture, it did not declare its citizens guilty without trial—and yet, that's what they had done to Cain and Laney.

Patrick knew there were good Americans in government. He knew there were people who believed in what America was. But the people running the show right now, they were not those people. They were looking for political expediency, and apparently constitutional protections meant little to them.

Patrick could not get behind that.

He walked slowly up the marble steps. The door opened as he approached, and Angela Hartlett, Henry's assistant, stepped out. "Father Patrick, how nice to see you."

Patrick gave her a nod. "Ms. Hartlett, it's nice to see you as well."

She held open the door for him. "They're in the dining room. Dinner smells great."

She looked at him expectantly, and Patrick bit back a sigh, knowing she was angling for an invitation. But seeing as how they were going to be discussing their next steps, and Angela was FBI, he didn't think inviting her along was in any of their interests. And the duplicitous nature of her job just made him more tired. How had it come to this—that the US government had inserted spies to check on the Chandler Group? After everything they had done, this was how they were being treated.

Patrick gave her a small smile. "I'm looking forward to it. Have a good night." He slipped past her, not missing the look of annoyance that crossed her face.

He shook his head as he made his way down the hall. *God never gives you more than you can handle.* The phrase wafted through his mind. Earlier today he'd read Job, to remind himself that it could be worse. But he was getting a little angry at the Almighty. Laney had been through enough. They had all been through enough. A little break would not be out of order at this point.

And that was the other problem: his faith was wavering. It was hard to believe in an almighty and loving God when everything around him seemed to be targeting the good guys.

Patrick knew priests often had points where they questioned their faith and the choice they'd made to dedicate their life to the church. But Patrick had never questioned before, not in the decades he'd been with the church. But all of this... it was almost too much.

Patrick could hear voices in the dining room. He paused just outside to pull himself together. Everyone in that room had enough on their plates. They didn't need to be worrying about him on top of everything else. So he pushed down all his fears, all his concerns, like he had been doing for months. Taking a breath, he schooled his features and stepped inside.

"Evening, everybody."

CHAPTER 16

The Chandler staff had once again outdone themselves with dinner. A beef Wellington with five side dishes, salad, and handmade bread dominated the center of the dining room table. It looked and smelled amazing.

And yet, Henry knew very little of it would be consumed. No one had much of an appetite after the last thirty-six hours. He and Jake had been released late last night, although he knew the ETF was not happy about that. But Brett had explained exactly how much he would crucify the US government in the media if Henry and Jake were charged after saving ETF agents' lives.

Jen sat to Henry's right, Jake to his left. Matt and Mustafa sat next to Jen. All the critical people that were left in this little ragtag army. And all of them looked defeated. They were just waiting on Patrick.

As if summoned by Henry's thoughts, Patrick appeared in the doorway. Henry's first impression when he saw Patrick was one of worry. This was all taking such a toll on the priest. He looked so tired, so beaten down.

Henry stood. "Patrick. Good to see you."

Patrick smiled, taking a seat. "Smells good." He lifted the silver dome covering the plate in front of him. Mustafa and Matt exchanged greetings, and the three exchanged small talk for a few minutes.

Henry retook his seat, exchanging a glance with Jen. He could almost hear her voice in his head. *He'll be all right. Let's just give him a focus.* "Okay, if it's all right with everybody, I thought we could speak while eating. A lot seems to be happening."

Everyone nodded.

"Now, Matt, Mustafa, I'm hoping you've learned something about where they've taken the Fallen from the SIA facility."

Matt blew out a breath. "Not yet. But I have my people working on it. I think the most likely place is a black site in the country. I have people combing through records, but by their very nature, it won't be easy to find."

"Is there any other source you can tap?" Henry asked.

Matt hesitated. "There's one. You'll be the first to know it if bears any fruit."

"What about this Seward from the ETF? Have you learned anything about him?"

Mustafa grimaced. "Nothing good. Moses Seward was a cop in Chicago for ten years before shifting over to Homeland Security. His police record had a number of excessive force complaints which never went anywhere."

"Well that's not good," Jen muttered.

"No. And his Homeland record isn't much better. It shows he was reprimanded a few times, although no details are in his file."

Jen raised an eyebrow. "He was reprimanded by Homeland? The group's that's okay with rendition and waterboarding?"

Matt grimaced. "I know. Right now he's second in charge of the External Threats Task Force."

Patrick frowned. "External Threats? Wasn't that created after 9/11?"

Mustafa nodded. "Before 9/11 it would have been considered

extralegal and would never have been allowed. But they've used the PATRIOT Act to extend their enforcement capabilities."

Henry knew that the FBI were not the only ones who had seen an opportunity in the PATRIOT Act. The PATRIOT Act, designed to give law enforcement additional tools to protect Americans from terrorist activities, was actually rarely employed in terrorist investigations. In fact, the provisions of the PATRIOT Act were now used primarily in the war on drugs, not terrorism at all. A 2011 report detailed how terrorism was the focus in less than one percent of all requests. In particular, the sneak and peek searches —searches where the subjects were not informed that a search had been conducted—were extensively employed.

"So what exactly does the External Threat Task Force do?" Patrick asked.

"That's the problem," Matt said. "Their objectives are extremely vague. Officially, they're charged with investigating any threats that infringe upon the well-being of the American people, as well as safeguarding national security."

"That could mean anything," Jen said.

"Yeah. And so far, that's what it looks like. They've been involved in the drug war, militia groups, white nationalists, trafficking, even white-collar offenses."

Henry frowned. "The PATRIOT Act removed many of the safeguards in place for normal citizens if they were implicated in terrorist activities. I'm guessing this task force is using all the same tools?"

"Yes," Mustafa said. "Secret courts, secret warrants, secret searches, arrests without probable cause, indefinite holdings, and no notification of family about those holdings—the task force has used all of them. We know of at least thirty people who have disappeared and are believed to have been rounded up by the ETF."

"What about enhanced interrogations?" Patrick asked.

Matt nodded. "They have taken advantage of every other facet of the PATRIOT Act. It's hard to believe they wouldn't take advantage of that as well."

"How the hell is this legal?" Jake asked.

Matt shrugged. "It's a post-9/11 world. After the attack, people wanted to feel safe. Congress and the Senate rushed the PATRIOT Act through to say they had done something. They didn't think through the long-term effects. They didn't think about how it could be applied beyond terrorism."

"And the definition of terrorism within the act itself all but guaranteed the act would be used for other activities," Henry said. According to the act, a person was considered a terrorist if they posed a danger to human life and if their actions were intended to influence or coerce a civilian population or government, or cause mass destruction, assassination, or kidnapping. But that was extremely vague.

Critics argued that rather than being an exceptional tool for fighting terrorism, the PATRIOT Act had now become a common tool for everyday law enforcement.

"Certain segments of the government were counting on that. Waiting for that," Matt said.

Henry knew Matt was right. Some segments of the government had never been happy with the restraints that had been placed upon them when it came to ensuring justice in the United States. Criminals were criminals and deserved to be treated as such—that was the rallying cry of the group. The problem was, in the United States defendants were innocent until proven guilty—a long, imperfect process.

But the PATRIOT Act stripped all that away, allowing the United States to lock people up without charges and keep them locked up for years. And that approach opened up its own can of worms. Thanks to the act, 779 individuals were in Guantanamo Bay, 674 of them were never charged, and of those charged, only eight were found guilty. And of those eight, three convictions were overturned and an additional three were partially invalidated. A total of 709 had been transferred, and nine had died. Only one was transferred to the US to be tried. And sixty remained. Sixty percent of detainees were found to have never been associated in any way with Al Qaeda or the Taliban.

But the problem was actually larger than that. While it was true that the vast majority of individuals locked up in Guantanamo Bay did not have terrorist leanings prior to their incarceration, research indicated that many *did* have those inclinations afterward. Research indicated that inmates incarcerated for terrorism charges were more likely to become radicalized as a result of their incarceration even if they were not supportive of terrorism. So the mass incarcerations, far from reducing the terrorist threat, actually increased it.

Henry had to wonder if incarceration would have the same effect on the Fallen population. Not that the individuals who had been incarcerated at the SIA facility had been innocent. But was it really that big a stretch to think there might be calls for locking the Fallen up, any Fallen, when their existence became known? Right now, that would be half the people at this table. And the other half could be locked up for conspiring.

"What about on Capitol Hill? Any talk there?" Patrick asked.

"Oh, lots of talk," Matt said. "The people in the loop are adamant that the existence of the Fallen remains hidden. Others outside the loop are beginning to ask questions. There have been too many public incidents. Our existence is going to come out. We need to prepare for that."

Silence descended on the room.

Jen finally broke it. "Any idea *how* exactly we should do that?"

"I have the PR department already working on that," Henry said.

Jake raised on eyebrow. "The PR department? Seriously?"

"Henry's right," Matt said. "Look, everything these days is about spin. They need to be ready to explain the Fallen. Point out all of the good they've done. And they need to be ready to make that argument as soon as this all hits the fan."

"You think it's going to come to that?" Jen asked.

"I think it's amazing it hasn't happened already," Matt said.

"What about Cain? You know they're torturing him," Patrick said.

"No," Jake said. "Out of all of them, he's probably the only one that's not being touched."

"But that doesn't mean we're going to leave him there," Henry said. "As soon as we have some intel, we'll figure out a way to get to him."

"Where's Samyaza in all this? She's been awfully quiet since her interview," Jake said.

"According to the team we have on her, she's focused on business. There's hasn't been a hint of any plans," Mustafa said.

Jake frowned. "There's no way she's sitting quietly. She has to be up to something. She went to an awful lot of trouble to expose Laney."

Matt sighed. "True. But right now we have no idea what that is."

CHAPTER 17

Danny tossed and turned. He flipped his pillow over, looking for a cool spot. Then he lay on his back, staring at the sky. Noriko's vision had shaken him, and he couldn't get the image of a young Victoria, helpless and crying, out of his mind.

It's not her. It's not. He'd convinced himself of that hours ago, throwing himself into a programming project with a rapidly approaching deadline. But at one point he'd pulled up the data on all the births the week after Victoria had died. He'd created the file months ago with the crazy idea that maybe somehow he would be able to find her.

Even he had to admit it was like looking for a needle in an immense haystack. She could have been reborn at any point after her death, making the potential pool that much larger.

"It's not Victoria," he said out loud.

His black shepherd mix, Moxy, lifted her head from the dog bed next to Danny's bed. Normally she slept on the bed with Danny, but she'd gotten fed up with all his squirming an hour ago and had hopped down to the floor.

"I'm okay, girl," he said. And she lay her head back down. But he wasn't okay. *It's not Victoria*, he reminded himself as the sketch Noriko drew flitted through his mind. The girl from the vision, whoever she was, was not Victoria. But he couldn't shake the feeling that Victoria was somehow involved.

Go to sleep. There's nothing you can do now.

But his mind refused to shut off. Victoria... She had understood him, had accepted him immediately. He'd never felt that before, not even from Henry. He and Henry had danced around becoming a family for almost a full year. But as soon as Victoria had met him, she had declared him family, biology be damned.

And he couldn't get the feeling out of his mind that she needed him now. Danny had gone back and forth on whether to tell Henry. Laney's disappearance had really taken a toll on him, and he'd only in the last two months been able to crawl out from under the weight of that worry. And Noriko had reminded Danny that she didn't always learn what her visions referred to. Sometimes they weren't literal, but symbolic. But Danny had known in his heart that he had to say something when he learned for certain that this wasn't an abstract vision. Because he'd put a name to the face: Susie McAdams from Ashburnham, Massachusetts.

So he'd spoken with Henry, Jen, and Jake after their dinner meeting. It had been hard to watch the fear cut across Henry's face, and Danny had prayed he wasn't unnecessarily worrying him.

Henry had told him that he'd look into it. Jen and Jake would go to Massachusetts to speak with the McAdams family early tomorrow. They told Danny to leave it to them. Still, Danny could not get the idea out of his head.

Finally he threw off his covers. Moxy stretched next to him and got her feet. "Come on, girl."

He opened the door of the bedroom and looked around. He was in the student wing of the Chandler School. Unlike most of the kids, he had his own room. Seeing as how he'd finished high school when he was eight, it seemed kind of ridiculous to treat him like a regular student. But he liked being near his friends when he stayed at the school.

He walked quietly down the hall, and was unsurprised when the door at the end of the hall opened and Lou stepped out. "What are you doing?"

"I couldn't sleep."

"You're bothered by Noriko's vision."

"Yeah. You?"

Closing the door behind her, she fell in step with him, giving Moxy's head a quick rub. "Same. So what's the plan?"

"I just thought I'd run a couple of searches and see what I can find."

"Well, I guess I'll go with you," Lou said.

Ten minutes later, they were in Danny's office at the school. Danny booted up the computers and started writing a search algorithm. Lost in his work, he was shocked when he saw that an hour had gone by. He turned to Lou. "Hey, you don't have to—"

Lou was asleep on the couch, Moxy curled up next to her, a blanket over the two of them.

Danny smiled and turned back to the computer. He finished up the algorithm and set it up to run. He executed it, then pushed back from the desk, feeling exhausted all of a sudden. He headed for the couch across from Lou. Grabbing the blanket from the back, he curled up. *I'll just close my eyes for a few minutes.*

∼

"THEY'RE IN HERE," Rolly yelled.

Danny sat straight up on the couch. "What—huh?"

Rolly chuckled. "Morning, Danny."

Danny wiped his eyes and the side of his mouth. "Hey. What's going on?"

"Zach and I stopped by your room this morning and you

weren't there. And then we couldn't find Lou." Rolly wiggled his eyebrows. "So what have you two been up to?"

Danny felt his cheeks flame red. "What? No. I mean—"

"Ignore him, Danny," Lou said from the other couch as Moxy hopped off and trotted over to Danny. "He's just teasing."

"Right. I knew that," Danny mumbled, petting Moxy.

Zach stepped into the room. "Oh, there you guys are. What are you up to?"

Rolly opened his mouth with a smirk, and Lou blurred across the room to clap a hand over it. "Danny had an idea about Noriko's vision, and he wanted to try out some searches."

Rolly frowned. "I thought you already identified the girl from the vision."

Danny rubbed his eyes. "We did, and Jen and Jake should be arriving at her family's home any minute now. But Noriko said she heard lots of cries, which got me thinking…"

"Find anything?" Zach asked.

"I don't know." Danny headed to the desk. The other three followed while Moxy curled back up on the couch. Danny scanned the search results. The searches had finished running an hour ago; he must have slept through the beep. He frowned. *This doesn't make any sense.*

"What is it?" Lou said, looking at the data and shaking her head. "I don't know why I think looking at the screen will answer that question for me. Please translate."

"For those of us who do not speak numeric," Rolly muttered.

"It's—well, I set up a search last night. Noriko said there was more than one child in her vision. So I set the parameters for a female child born within the last three years with red hair and blue eyes. Then I set it global."

"Okay. And?"

"Well, red hair and blue eyes is actually the least common hair and eye color combination in the world."

"Wait, seriously?" Zach asked.

Danny nodded. "For someone to have both, each parent has to carry the recessive genes for both, which only one percent of the world population does."

"So how many kids with that combination are born in one day?"

"Only 1753."

"Only? That seems like a lot."

"Not when you consider that 353,000 children are born each day. And then slightly more than half of those are female."

"Okay," Lou drew out the word. "So how does this help?"

"Well, I cross-referenced those births with missing child reports."

"And?"

"And something really weird popped up." Danny went silent.

"Feel free to share with the rest of the class," Rolly said.

"Right. Sorry. Well, a pretty significant number of those children have gone missing."

"That's horrible. But I mean, don't children go missing all the time?"

"Yes and no. 797,500 children were reported missing in a one-year period."

"Again, that seems like a lot," Rolly said.

"It is, but not all of those are what we usually mean by 'missing children.' 203,900 were abducted by family members, and 58,200 were abducted by non-relatives who knew the child. Only 115 were classified as being taken by a stranger."

"What about the rest?"

"That's where it gets difficult: runaways. Children who intentionally left home. Sometimes they return, but the stats aren't updated. Sometimes they don't return." Danny gestured to the screen. "And obviously kids this young are not running away. But according to this, there's more. There was a spike in missing children who were all born within twenty-four hours of each other, all with red hair and blue eyes."

"The *same* twenty-four-hour period?" Zach asked.

"When was that?" Lou asked quietly.

Danny stared at the screen before answering, hoping that maybe he had missed something. But he knew that the fear that had cropped up in the back of his mind as soon as Noriko had explained her vision had been all too accurate.

"The twenty-four hours after Victoria died."

CHAPTER 18

The charity event had been a bore, as Elisabeta had expected, although she did find an on-the-rise actor who had managed to keep her entertained for the last four nights. She leaned over and ran a finger down Atlas Younger's toned back. Despite the ridiculous name, he had been fun.

Atlas rolled over. "Hey." Twenty-two years old, the star of a cable TV show, and desperately looking to break into movies. His body was toned to perfection. Perhaps it was even a little too large, but that's what steroids would do to you. His brown eyes looked up at her, a smile barely moving the skin on his chiseled face—the beauty of youth.

"So, last night was fun. You do all right." He looked her up and down. "Bet you enjoyed yourself."

And then the stupidity. If only he would stay silent, he would be the perfect bedroom partner. "You were adequate."

He laughed. "Adequate. Sure. So I was thinking, maybe today you could introduce me to that director you were speaking with at the charity thing the other night."

Elisabeta smiled and patted his cheek. "Get out." She pulled away and started to stand.

Atlas grabbed her arm. "Hey. You can't treat me that way."

She looked down at the hand wrapped around her wrist. She reached down and yanked his pinky backward.

He let out a scream and scrambled back. "You bitch! You broke my finger."

"Bitch? You called me a bitch?" Elisabeta stormed around the bed.

Atlas's eyes went wide.

She yanked him up by the hair. "I don't like that word." She pulled him from the bed, dragging him along the floor.

"Let go, let go."

She pulled him out onto the balcony, and before he could breathe, she picked him up by the neck. "Let go? Sure thing." She launched him over the railing. He screamed as his body fell the two stories down. He crashed into the concrete surrounding the pool with a crunch of bones.

Two pool attendants looked up, then hurriedly averted their gazes. One of her security guards blurred into view.

She waved to Atlas's body. "Take care of that."

"Yes, ma'am."

Elisabeta headed back into her room. Honestly, how women tolerated the behavior of the men in this world was beyond her.

An hour later, she had showered and changed and forgotten all about Atlas Younger. She sat in her office reviewing the changes she had made regarding her holdings in a pharmaceutical company.

She looked up with a frown at the knock on the door. "Come in."

Hakeem entered with a bow. His dark eyes flicked toward the balcony for only a moment before returning to Elisabeta. For a moment she compared the two men. Atlas had been younger and a perfectly trained specimen. But Hakeem... he was virile, manly

—his body hardened by actual physical labor. Still, in one way, the two men were sadly alike—their intelligence.

Elisabeta waved her hand at him. "Update."

"The subjects have been moved to the facility."

"How many?"

"Thirty-six."

She looked up. "Any problems?"

"No."

She raised an eyebrow, knowing that was probably untrue. But Hakeem wasn't intentionally keeping things from her. He was simply, maddeningly, unaware.

"Have you set up the satellite link?"

"Um…"

"Go. Set it up. When you're done, send it to me."

"Yes, ma'am."

"You're excused. Send Ada in when you pass her."

He gave another deep bow before leaving. Respectful he was. Bright? Not so much. But these days she put more stock in loyalty. Gerard had shown her what happened to the bright ones.

A soft knock sounded. "Come in," she called.

Ada appeared and placed a piece of paper on the desk in front of Elisabeta before taking a seat. Ada was twenty-four and the public face for Elisabeta's philanthropic endeavors.

Elisabeta scanned the schedule. She made a note or two. Then frowned. "What's this? Two events?"

Ada nodded. "Yes. Both the Children's Coalition and your stockholder meeting are tonight. I wasn't sure which one you wanted to attend."

Ada was not a Fallen or a nephilim. She was a human and handled all of Elisabeta's public activities.

Elisabeta pushed the schedule back across the desk. "The Children's Coalition. It's much more important."

Ada smiled as she took the paper. "I knew you would say that. I'll make the arrangements. They asked that you speak as well."

"Of course. You know the cause of children is close to my heart. Tell them anything I can do to help."

"Thank you, ma'am." Ada headed to the door, then stopped and turned back when she was halfway across the room. "And ma'am? Can I just say what an honor it is to work for someone who truly understands what is important in life?"

"I have been given a great deal in my life, Ada. It seems only right to help those not so blessed."

Ada smiled again before scurrying out the door.

Elisabeta's computer beeped, and she turned to it. *Finally.* She clicked on the link, and a warehouse came into view. Four dozen redheaded toddlers sat on the ground. A large TV sat in one corner, playing a cartoon. Women wandered among the toddlers, sometimes leaning down to pick one up. Elisabeta scanned them all. "Where are you, Victoria?"

Using the arrows on her keyboard, she directed the camera to one child crying in the corner, big tears rolling down her cheeks. Elisabeta smiled. *Cry all you want. No one can help you now.*

CHAPTER 19

ASHBURNHAM, MASSACHUSETTS

Jake pulled the rented SUV up to the curb in front of the blue, two-story colonial. The front lawn was small, as was the driveway. And like most of the houses in the part of Ashburnham, it was built on a hill giving it a very steep driveway. He glanced over at Jen, who sat inspecting the house. "You good?"

"Yeah. Just—" She shook her head. "A missing kid. And right on top of their father's death two years ago. The McAdamses have already been through a lot. Doesn't seem right."

Jake opened the door. "No. It doesn't."

They made their way up the path. Two other cars were in the driveway. One was the McAdamses' minivan, and Jake thought the other might belong to a family member. The McAdams kids had seven aunts and uncles, one set of grandparents, and twenty cousins in the immediate area. According to what Jake and Jen had learned from the police on the flight over, there had always been an extended family member at the house ever since Susie McAdams had gone missing.

Jake rang the doorbell as Jen climbed up the three short steps behind him. After only a few seconds the door was opened by a tall bear of a man with red hair that sprang from his head and a matching red beard. His blue eyes narrowed. "Who are you?"

"Jake Rogan and Jen Witt from the Chandler Group. Mrs. McAdams is expecting us."

"Yeah, well, she's changed her mind. So you need to—"

"Jimmy, get away from the door and let them in. I told them to come." A small redheaded woman came into view, pushing Jimmy to the side. Her face was pale, and there were bags underneath her blue eyes. But even with that, there was a natural beauty to her. She opened the screen door. "Hi. I'm Mary Jane."

Jake stepped inside, his heart rate picking up a notch. "I'm Jake Rogan from the Chandler Group. This is my associate, Dr. Jen Witt."

Mary Jane shook both of their hands.

"This is my brother Jimmy."

Jimmy crossed his arms over his chest and glared at them.

Mary Jane sighed. "Jimmy, they might be able to help. And I'll take any help to get—" She cut off and her hand flew to her mouth. Tears sprang to her eyes.

Jimmy's anger disappeared, and he wrapped his sister in a hug. "I just don't want them upsetting you."

Mary Jane wiped her eyes. "I'll take a little upset if it helps get Susie back." She turned to Jen and Jake, taking a breath. "Sorry. I seem to burst into tears a lot lately."

"It's understandable," Jen said.

Mary Jane waved them in. "Well, let's get away from the door. Come on into the kitchen."

Mary Jane headed down the hall. Jen and Jake followed, with Jimmy bringing up the rear.

The kitchen was comfortable: white cabinets, gray countertops, and an old wooden table that dominated half the room. Old hand-drawn pictures were in frames on the walls, along with family portraits—lots of smiling redheaded kids and adults. The refrigerator was covered with school announcements, awards, and more pictures. It was the kitchen of a family—a normal family, until a few days ago.

Mary Jane sat at the table. "Please take a seat. Can I get you anything to drink? Coffee? Tea?"

"No, we're good," Jen said, sitting across from Mary Jane. Jake sat next to her.

Mary Jane turned to her brother. "Can you go see where the kids are?"

"You don't want me to stay?"

"It's okay. I'll yell if I need you."

After giving his sister a concerned look and Jake and Jen a warning one, he grabbed his jacket from beside the back door and disappeared outside.

Mary Jane turned to Jake and Jen. "Sorry about that. He means well. He's just being protective. And the Chandler Group's been in the news a little bit lately." She shrugged.

"We understand," Jen said.

"As Jen explained on the phone, we've come across some information that might be connected to your daughter's case."

Mary Jane's lips tightened and her fists clenched, but she didn't say anything. Jake could tell it was taking a lot for her to keep it together, and he prayed they weren't going to cause her unnecessary pain.

"Do you think you could run us through the details of the morning your daughter went missing?"

"She was taken," Mary Jane said. "She didn't go missing." She grabbed a tissue from a box on the table and crumpled it in her hand. "It was just a normal Saturday."

She proceeded to tell them about the abduction. Jen and Jake each asked questions, looking for more details. But Jake didn't learn anything beyond what had been in the newspaper accounts and the police file. Even as tears swamped her eyes, Mary Jane told her tale in a straightforward manner, pushing through the pain. She was strong, even with everything swirling around her and inside her. She was answering their questions, all in the hopes that maybe Jen and Jake could help her find her little girl.

Why on earth did Noriko have a vision about this? Jake couldn't see any connection. The fact that no one saw the kidnapper made it possible it was a Fallen, but Jake didn't see how that got them anywhere.

But even if it wasn't related, Jake realized he really didn't want to let this woman down.

Finally Mary Jane had answered all their questions, and now she had one of her own. "How come the Chandler Group is interested in Susie?"

Jen exchanged a glance with Jake, who nodded at her before turning back to Mary Jane. "The Chandler Group has a lot of resources at its fingertips. Some of those resources are... unusual."

"You mean the psychic stuff?"

Jen raised her eyebrows.

Mary Jane gave them a small smile even as she wiped away tears. "I think everything about your group has made it into the newspapers at some point."

With a nod, Jen conceded the point. She opened the folder that she had carried in and pulled out a piece of paper. "Well, one of our people *is* psychic. And in her last vision, she saw a child." Jen slid the image Noriko had drawn across the table.

Mary Jane gasped as she grabbed the picture, tears running down her face. "Susie."

"You're sure that's Susie?" Jake asked.

Mary Jane didn't take her gaze from the paper as she nodded. "What was the vision?"

"Our seer, she heard a child cry. Then lots of children crying. She focused on one cry and followed it. It brought her to a child sitting in a stroller." Jake nodded to the paper. "This is the child she saw. The child said to help her. To find her. To find them."

Mary Jane looked up, frowning. "Them? What does that mean?"

"We don't know. We were hoping maybe something here might help us figure that out."

"Was there anything else?"

Jake shook his head. "No, that was it. But it was enough to get us to come here. To see if we can help."

"Do you think you can?"

"The Chandler Group has done some pretty amazing things. We're hoping bringing Susie home could be one more," Jake said

Jen's head whipped toward the back door a second before it opened and two teenage boys walked in. They stopped, looking between Mary Jane and Jen and Jake. "Mom?" one of them asked.

She held out a hand, and the boys walked over. One took her hand, and the other stood on her other side, his hand on her shoulder. "These people are from the Chandler Group," Mary Jane said. "These are my sons, Shaun and Joe."

Jake nodded at them, but noticed that Jen kept her attention on the back door, where Jimmy appeared with a smaller version of Mary Jane walking in behind him. The girl's eyes were wide and her gaze was locked on Jen. She started to shake.

Jen stood up slowly, and the girl backed toward the door.

Jen put up her hands. "It's okay. It's okay."

The girl shook her head wildly, backing up quickly. "No. No. You—you took Susie."

CHAPTER 20

The McAdams kitchen was silent for a split second before all hell broke loose. Jimmy grabbed Jake by the shoulders and tried to throw him up against the wall. Mary Jane stumbled back from the table with her sons with a cry.

Shit. Jake brought his arm up between Jimmy's hands, which had a hold on Jake's collar, and slammed his forearm onto the man's arm at the elbow, breaking his hold but taking care not to hurt him. Stepping to the side, he slid his forearm up against the back of Jimmy's elbow and then down, forcing the man to bend at the waist.

"Call the police!" Jimmy yelled.

One of the sons ran for the phone, but Jen yelled, "Enough!"

Everyone went still. "Enough," Jen said, a little more quietly. "We were nowhere near here when Susie was taken. We can document that easily."

She turned to Molly. "When you said I took Susie, you meant you felt a tingle over your skin that day. Is that right? And you felt that same tingle when you neared the house today, and when you saw me, right?"

Molly nodded. Her gaze was still fixed on Jen, her terror obvious.

Oh, crap, Jake thought.

Jen looked at each person in the room. "Okay. Everyone needs to just calm down, and we are going to talk about this."

Jake watched Mary Jane. All the color had drained from the woman's face. This was not how he had wanted this visit to go.

He tapped Jimmy on the shoulder. "Okay, I'm going to let you up if you agree not to try anything,"

"Fine," Jimmy growled.

Jake looked at Jen, who nodded. Jake released Jimmy. As Jimmy straightened, he shoved Jake. "Call the cops!"

One of the boys snatched the phone from the wall. Jen blurred across the room and grabbed the phone from the boy's hand. He stumbled back, crashing into the sink behind him. "You—How—"

Jen held up her hands and looked at Molly. "Okay. This is going to be a little hard to explain. But the day of the abduction, you never saw the abductor because they moved too quickly."

Molly spoke slowly. "I thought somehow I'd just missed them."

"But you *felt* them," Jake said.

Molly nodded.

Jake looked around the room. This family had already been through so much. His chest felt heavy just thinking about the conversation to come. He let out a breath. "The world is a lot more complicated than you realize."

CHAPTER 21

Mary Jane felt like she was in a dream—a really twisted dream. They had all moved into the living room. The couple from the Chandler Group explained that there were Fallen angels walking the earth, and that they had incredible abilities. Jen and Jake believed that one of the Fallen had grabbed Susie—and that Molly had sensed them because Molly had abilities too. Now all the members of the McAdams family looked like they were in shock.

Mary Jane felt like her whole life had just shifted into an alternate universe. Molly had abilities? She was an angel?

Mary Jane had been raised Catholic. She, the kids, and pretty much the entire extended family attended church every Sunday. But she struggled with the idea of angels among them—of angels being born and living as human. Her gaze drifted to her sensitive daughter. Could *Molly* be one of them?

"So she's like a superhero?" Shaun asked.

"Sort of," Jake said. "She has strength, enhanced healing, and speed."

"How'd she get it?" Joe asked.

The two people from Chandler Group exchanged a glance, and Mary Jane tensed herself for their answer.

"She's a nephilim," Jen said. "The offspring of a Fallen and a mortal."

All eyes turned to Mary Jane. She put up her hands. "While I admit I had a bit of a rebellious period when I was a teenager, I'm certainly not in Fallen angel territory."

"But that means…" Shaun turned to a photo on the mantelpiece. A man holding up a giant fish.

"Yes," Jake said quietly. "It must have been your husband. Did you ever see anything that hinted at abilities?"

Mary Jane fell back heavily against the couch. "No, I—"

She remembered one time back when they first started dating. They had run out of gas in Billy's old Cutlass. The gas station was miles away. They had tickets for a concert, and Mary Jane knew they'd never make it in time. But Billy promised they would, and he took off running. He returned only a few minutes later with a full can of gas, saying he'd found a gas station nearby. But Mary Jane knew the closest station was miles away. She pushed it from her mind though, too wrapped up in Billy and the excitement of the concert.

And another thing: Billy never got sick or hurt. One time in the kitchen, she saw him slice his palm while making a sandwich. She insisted on treating the cut. But when she returned, there was no mark on his hand. He said he hadn't cut it at all. But she'd seen the blood.

Now she looked around at her children and brother and nodded. "Your dad, I think he might have had abilities."

"What?" Jimmy exclaimed.

"Why didn't you say something?" Shaun asked.

Mary Jane shook her head. "I didn't realize it until just now. I didn't know people like this existed. I just thought…" She shook her head. She didn't know what she had thought. She had just ignored the inconsistencies.

Joe gripped the arm of his chair. "But does that mean Grandma and Grandpa—"

"No, no," Jake said. "Fallen angels are reincarnated into each lifetime. If your dad was a Fallen angel, his siblings, his parents, they probably aren't."

"But if he was a fallen angel, does that mean Dad was bad?" Molly asked, her voice shaking.

"No." The word burst out of Mary Jane. "No. Your dad was a good man. The best man." She looked to Jake, begging him to give her children something.

"Your mom's right," Jake said. "The Fallen—they're like humans. Some are good. Some are bad. But they're not born that way. Their life, and the people around them, determine who they become. And from what we've read on your dad, he was a good man."

Shaun gave a nod, and Joe sank back into his chair. Molly, though, still looked like she was in shock. But at least two of the kids seemed to be okay.

Mary Jane looked at Jake. *Thank you.* He nodded back at her.

"What abilities will she get?" Shaun asked. He turned to Molly. "Do you have them already?"

"Um, I don't think so."

"Abilities develop slowly," Jen said. "The first one to arrive is the sense. She'll get strength, healing, and speed eventually."

"Wow," Joe said.

"But why did Molly get abilities? Why not us?" Shaun asked.

"It's possible you will have abilities some day, but there's no guarantee. Sometimes it only shows up in one offspring. Abilities show up at different times. Sometimes they emerge naturally, and other times they evolve because of some trauma." Jen looked at Mary Jane. "Maybe it was your husband's death that sparked it in Molly."

Mary Jane's mouth dropped open. *Oh my God.* "She—she was in the car."

"What?" Jake asked.

"The accident that killed Billy. Molly was in the car."

"I was thrown from the car," Molly said quietly. "I woke up on the side of the road. I didn't even have a scratch even though I went through a window."

"We all thought it was a miracle," Mary Jane said.

"And your husband? How was he killed?" Jen asked.

They were all quiet for a moment. Mary Jane knew she should speak. But Billy's death—it was just so hard to think about.

Jimmy reached over and took her hand. "He was impaled by a metal fence post. It went right through the window."

Jake and Jen exchanged a look.

They know something, Mary Jane thought. Part of her was tempted to ask, but the larger part of her wasn't, not with the kids here.

"Does this have anything to do with Susie?" Jimmy asked, and guilt roared through Mary Jane. She had forgotten about Susie for the last few minutes. *I'm sorry, baby.*

"I don't know," Jake said, "but it adds a layer that we didn't know before."

"Is it possible Susie has abilities?" Molly asked.

"At her age, it's unlikely. We've never heard of abilities manifesting so early. But I suppose anything's possible," Jen said.

"Are you saying they took her because of that?" Jimmy asked.

"No," Jake said quickly. "But it might explain why and how she was able to reach out to our seer."

"So one of these Fallen took my sister," Shaun said.

"That's what it looks like."

"Okay. Now how do we get her back?" Mary Jane asked.

Only silence greeted her question. Finally Jen shook her head. "We don't know. Not yet."

Hopelessness poured down on Mary Jane again. It was all she could do not to close her eyes and sob. *Susie.*

CHAPTER 22

BALTIMORE, MARYLAND

Danny got Yoni to give him a ride back to the estate. He texted Henry as soon as they passed through the gates. Henry promised to meet him in his office, cutting his meeting short.

"You okay, Danny? You've been awfully quiet," Yoni said as they drove along the long drive. Up ahead, the main house, with its dozens of rooms, came into view. Danny's home with Henry was a hundred yards behind the main house, in a much smaller building than this sprawling monster. It had been a lifeline to Danny when he'd come here.

An image of his mother flickered through his mind, and he tried to hold on to it, but it slipped away. She had been reduced to a fuzzy feminine silhouette with dark hair. She died when he was only seven. But he remembered how she had made him feel: loved. All kids deserved that, even if only for a little while.

And now someone was rounding up really little kids. *They must be so scared.*

"Yeah. Just some stuff on my mind."

Yoni pulled up in front of the marble stairs that led to the front door, and put the car into park. "You know if you need anything, me and Sasha are here too."

And that was the difference between Danny's life before he came to Chandler and after. Before, he'd had a biological father and brothers whose entire goal seemed to be to make him doubt his self-worth. Here, he had no one who was related to him by blood, and yet they were all his family.

"I know. Thanks, Yoni."

He let himself out of the car and ran up the steps. He said hello to a few people as he went up the three stories to Henry's office. A group of people was just leaving it. Danny ignored them as he entered, then closed the door behind him.

Henry stood up from his giant desk and walked over to Danny. Henry's eyes searched him looking for any injury, physical or otherwise. "What's going on? Are you all right?"

"It's not me. It's Victoria."

Henry went still. "What?"

Danny took a seat on the couch, and Henry did the same. Danny explained about his search results. Henry stayed silent throughout the entire recitation. Then he sat quietly thinking. And Danny appreciated that. Henry might not have shared Danny's IQ, but he thought through every situation carefully before speaking.

"I agree it has to do with Victoria, but I also agree it's a large burden to take on—rearing a bunch of children for the sake of information they might provide ten years in the future. Finding Victoria at such a young age is more burdensome than helpful."

"Yes, but by the time she reached thirteen, you would have her on your side."

"Perhaps. But I don't think Victoria is that easily swayed, especially once her memories return."

Danny agreed on that point. But he had hoped Henry might put a little more stock in that possibility. Because without that possibility, there was only one other reason Danny could think of for someone to grab Victoria at such a young age. "I was thinking that as well, which is why I don't think that's why they're looking for her."

"Then what do you think they're after?"

Danny let out a breath, hating the words he was about to speak. "Her blood."

CHAPTER 23

Her blood. Those two words coming out of Danny's mouth automatically transported Henry back to Egypt, outside the necropolis in Saqqara. To the time when he thought Jake had been killed. He'd looked at the bullet hole in Jake's forehead, and his whole world had stopped. But even then he had known he had a duty to get Laney out of there, to safety. So he had whisked her away, his heart broken at the thought that the man who was like a brother to him was gone forever.

And then, he had learned Jake was alive—because his mother had given him some of her blood. His mother was not a Fallen, or a nephilim, or a ring bearer. She was something else entirely. The first and last of her kind. And her blood could heal—as it had healed Jake.

The Fallen didn't need Victoria's blood to heal, though. They could do that on their own. But her blood could do more than just heal. It could grant someone immortality—if they used every last drop.

"But for that to work," Henry said, "they'd need to wait until she was adult. There's simply not enough blood in a child's body to have the same effect."

"I know. But they could hold her until she grew. There's no other reason for the Fallen to take her now."

An idea flashed through Henry's mind, and he recoiled at the very idea of it. Even the Fallen could not be that cruel. He shoved the thought aside. "Do we even know if they've found her? I mean, is this McAdams girl Victoria?"

Danny shook his head. "I don't know. Like I said, it's not just the McAdams girl that's missing. There are dozens of missing kids, all girls with red hair and blue eyes. I mean, Henry, there's dozens of cases. She could be any of them or none of them. I'm just beginning to gather the background data on the cases. And that's the other problem—how will they know who she is? I mean, all the children have red hair and blue eyes. How will they tell which one is her?"

"They can't," Henry said softly. "Not yet. Which means they'll have to hold on to all of them until they figure it out."

CHAPTER 24

WASHINGTON, DC

The seal of the United States was emblazoned on the blue rug in the office of Nancy Harrigan, Secretary of State. As always, she was careful to step around it as she made her way to the desk. It seemed disrespectful to tread on it.

With a sigh, Nancy placed her folder on the desk. Kicking off her shoes, she slid into her chair, leaned her head back, and closed her eyes. She'd just finished a marathon session with the Joint Chiefs on the situation in Israel. The attack on the Temple Mount had had reverberations around the world. Almost every country seemed to have a stake in it.

And they all seemed to agree upon two things. One: the Fallen could not be publicly recognized. The public's reaction was unpredictable, but no country was under the impression that learning that there were humans with extraordinary abilities would be peacefully accepted by the populace at large. And two: Delaney McPhearson must be found and made to answer for her actions.

Nancy agreed on that point—although not in the same way as the others. The incidents in Jerusalem and Australia were not the first time she had heard of McPhearson. She had been good friends with Matt Clark since her early days at State. Matt had taken her into his confidence and had explained about the Fallen years ago. Nancy herself had worked behind the scenes to help keep the funding for the SIA going and in the shadows.

After the Israel incident, she had sat down with Matt and demanded he tell her about Delaney McPhearson. Nancy needed to know if she needed to execute the woman or thank her. Matt explained about her being the ring bearer and being called into service when the world was reaching a tipping point.

Nancy hadn't known what to say. She was not overly religious. She'd been raised Protestant but rarely attended church. She believed in God, she supposed, but it was more a hedging of bets than anything else. There simply seemed to be more risk in denying God's existence than accepting it.

When Matt had first explained about the Fallen, Nancy had been able to accept that there existed people with different abilities. She had grown up reading Marvel and DC comics, so it wasn't a huge leap. And besides, she had a background in biology. She knew the potential trapped in the human genome. But she just figured these people were the next step in human evolution. Actual fallen angels? A ring bearer? That was a bit of a stretch.

By some miracle, the media's focus on Delaney McPhearson's abilities had been pushed into the background—instead, they were now primarily focusing on her past. Nancy knew that focus was pushed behind the scenes by spin doctors who were making sure the most palatable interpretation was accepted by the public.

And the most palatable explanation was that Delaney McPhearson was a danger to the public and must be brought to heel.

Then the West Virginia tape had made a splash. The woman

Delaney McPhearson had "killed" in cold blood had killed federal agents in front of the world. Anyone watching that tape would not be able to overlook the ability of the priestess to heal what should have been mortal wounds. The cat was starting to slip out of the bag.

Nancy knew it was only a matter of time before the Fallen were fully recognized for who they were—if not angels, at least humans with abilities. And once again, the world would look for someone to blame.

The United States needed to be ready for that moment.

Nancy glanced at the message on her desk. Matt had called this morning, and then again when she was in her meeting. Although no details were provided, she knew what he wanted: the location where the inmates from the SIA facility had been moved.

But in providing Matt that information, she would be breaking all sorts of rules, even some laws. And she couldn't do that. Not yet.

She drummed her fingers on the desk. Ever since Matt had told her about the Fallen, she'd known a time would come when she would have to become more directly involved. She would have to choose a side. All these years she'd kept an eye on the SIA, but always from the shadows. Now it felt as if everything was reaching a boiling point. Most of the world leaders seemed to think that the Temple Mount situation was the start of a new war.

Nancy knew they were wrong. It was the opening salvo in a new phase of an ancient war.

Blowing out a breath, she reached over and punched her intercom.

Her aide Melanie's voice answered immediately. "Yes, Secretary?"

"Get me everything you can on Elisabeta Roccorio."

"Yes, Secretary. Anything else?"

Nancy hesitated. Then sighed. "Yes. Find me everything you can on Samyaza."

Melanie paused. "Samyaza? Like in the Bible?"

"Yes. Find me everything you can from all religions on the leader of the angels who made them all fall."

CHAPTER 25

BALTIMORE, MARYLAND

The sun had started to slink below the horizon. Henry had had back-to-back meetings for the rest of the day after speaking with Danny, but he'd struggled to focus on them. He'd cancelled the last meeting of the day, his head just not there. He'd planned on getting an update from Danny, Jen, and Jake. But instead he found himself sitting at his desk and turning his chair to watch the green hills of his estate.

Danny's news had shocked him to his core. The idea that Victoria was in danger—that she was helpless, not knowing who she was or what she would become—was tearing at him. She was a child, and at this moment she was completely innocent. And now someone was trying to find her.

No, not someone. Samyaza. Henry had no doubt that she was the one behind all of this. Each lifetime she came back the same: hard and cruel. And each lifetime his mother fought her to the best of her ability. It wasn't right.

The only solace he had was knowing that she would not remember who she was, what her duty was, for her first twelve years. On the day she turned thirteen, all her memories would return, but until then, she was a child like any other child. She had a family, friends—hell, she probably even had pets and crushes. She was a normal girl.

And Henry wanted that for her. It was the least she was owed with all that she had sacrificed over her lives. And now Samyaza was trying to take that from her as well.

A tingle rolled over him.

"Henry?"

He turned as Jen walked across the office toward him.

"Hey," he said softly.

"What are you doing in the dark?"

"I don't know. I just—" He felt tears in the back of his eyes. He took a shaky breath.

Jen knelt down in front of him and placed her hand on his cheek. "Hey. What's going on? What happened?"

Henry took a breath. "Samyaza—she's looking for my mother."

Jen blinked, her surprise obvious. "Are you sure?"

Henry nodded. He had spoken with Jen and Jake earlier, but he hadn't been able to bring himself to tell them what Danny suspected. He gave her a condensed version of what Danny had learned. "It's the only thing that makes sense. I just—I hate this. I mean, we're all adults. Being part of this fight, it's our choice. But Mom, she's a child right now. She shouldn't be a part of this. She shouldn't have to fight. She should get to be an innocent for as long as she can."

Jen took his hand. "You're right. It's not fair. It's not right. But if it is happening, we need to find her. We need to help her. We need to help all of them."

He looked into her eyes, so very thankful she was in his life. "I love you."

She leaned up and kissed him gently. "And I love you."

Henry leaned his head into hers, breathing deep. She centered him. She grounded him. She fulfilled him.

Finally, he leaned back. "How are the McAdamses?"

Jen stood up and sat on the edge of his desk, shaking her head. "A mess. They're a good family. They love one another, but they've already been through so much."

"Any idea if the boys will have abilities as well?"

Jen shrugged. "Only Laney can tell."

Henry felt his sister's loss again. He hated that she was out there. He hated that he couldn't help her. Hell, he couldn't even find her. God, he felt useless. He had resources at his fingertips that most people could only dream of. He himself was beyond powerful. And yet he could not help his mother or his sister.

"Hey, stop that," Jen said.

"Stop what?"

"I know you—you're kicking yourself up one side and down the other for things that are beyond your control. We will find your mother. We will help her. And we'll help the McAdams kids and all the others, because it's what we do."

"And Laney?"

Jen grinned. "If I know your sister, she'll show up when she's taken care of whatever it is she's doing. When she wakes up, she'll find us."

Because she's still sleeping. All of them had accepted Cleo's statement that Laney was sleeping. In no small part because it was easier to picture her sleeping peacefully, than in danger.

"What do you think Cleo means by that?" Henry asked.

"I have no idea. But we have other things that we can do right now, so let's not wander off into the world of what if."

"You're right. So what's the next step?"

Jen hopped off the desk and put out her hands. Henry took them, and she pulled him up. He smiled at her strength.

"Now," Jen said, "we go have a powwow with Jake and Patrick. We need to figure out our war party."

"A powwow? Isn't that racially insensitive?"

"Nope. Because I'm going to war. How about you?" Jen gave

him a smile that reminded him just how dangerous this woman in front of him was.

And instead of being shocked or frightened, he felt emboldened. He wasn't powerless. None of them were. And together, they'd figure this out. "Right there with you."

"Great. So let's go." She smacked him on the ass.

A laugh burst from him, and he pulled her close. "I am very lucky to have you."

She leaned into his chest. "Right back at you."

CHAPTER 26

Jake walked down the hall toward Danny's office. He and Jen had just returned. Jen had gone to find Henry, but Jake had gotten a text from Danny, asking if he could stop in. Seeing as how Danny was the one who had found the McAdams link, Jake was hopeful that Danny had found something new on Susie's disappearance.

Mary Jane's family had filled his mind ever since he'd stepped out of their house. He knew a death could tear a family apart. But Mary Jane had kept her family together after her husband's death. He could see how much her children loved her. And he could also see she was their strength. They all looked to her, even her brother. He couldn't help but wonder who *she* had to lean on.

He knocked on Danny's open door. "Hey."

Danny turned from his screen. "Hey, you're back."

"Yeah. Your text said you might have found something. Can you walk me through it?"

Danny nodded, but Jake couldn't help but notice how pale he looked. *Another one struggling.* But even as he thought it, he saw Danny push his concerns aside as he brought up a screen filled with pictures of children.

Jake stepped closer. *All girls, all with red hair and blue eyes.* "What's this all about?"

"There are three hundred fifty three thousand children born every day," Danny began. He started spouting statistics and numbers so fast and furious that Jake's head was beginning to spin.

Finally, Jake put up a hand. "Okay, so if I've got this straight: approximately one percent of the children born every day have red hair and blue eyes. Half of those are female. And when you went searching, you found a link between missing kids and those born within twenty-four hours of Victoria's death. Do I have that right?"

Danny nodded, and Jake felt no small amount of pride that he'd been able to decipher Danny's explanation.

Jake turned back to the monitor. "But you said that there's, what, thirty-six kids missing?"

Danny nodded again.

"According to your numbers, there should be a lot more who match the requirements."

"There are fifteen hundred matches."

"So how'd they narrow it down? They have to be focusing on specific children for some reason."

"I agree. But what reason? All I've found in common is their birth dates."

Jake frowned as he looked at all of the little faces. "What countries are the missing kids from?"

"Uh, all over the place. The US, Great Britain, France, Australia, the Netherlands, Canada."

"All developed countries," Jake mused. He stared at the pictures. No, it couldn't be. "Where did these pictures come from?"

"They were part of the case files for the missing children reports."

"Yes, but originally: were they posted online?"

Recognition crossed Danny's face as he bent his head to his tablet. He looked back up seconds later. "All the pictures were published on social media websites. They found the kids through the internet."

"They probably checked birth records first, then ran a search of social media sites to cut those numbers down." Jake stepped toward the screen. All of the children had dark blue eyes—vibrant, almost violet—not gray blue or even pale blue.

"But even if they manage to weed out the kids by hair and eye color, that still won't tell them who Victoria is," Danny said.

"No, it won't. They must have some way to tell. They wouldn't go to all this trouble if they didn't."

"So what do they know that we don't?" Danny asked.

"A lot, it would seem." Jake turned and headed for the door.

"Where are you going?"

"To have a chat with a priest."

CHAPTER 27

ALEXANDRIA, VIRGINIA

Nancy slipped into a more comfortable pair of slacks and a cream sweater. What she really wanted was to throw on her pajamas, robe, and slippers. But even though she was in her Alexandria home, her workday was not quite done yet; she still had one more meeting to take. One she did not want on the visitor log for her office.

She glanced at her heels, and practically shuddered at the idea of putting them on. So she made one concession and threw on her slippers. There was only so much a woman could take, after all.

The doorbell rang as she was making her way down the wooden staircases. She nodded at the Secret Service agent at the bottom of the stairs, and he moved to the front door to answer it. As the door opened, she caught sight of a familiar face.

"Hello, Matt."

Matt Clark, the former director of the SIA, gave her a nod as he stepped into the foyer. "Madame Secretary. Thank you for agreeing to see me."

"I must admit you have me curious." Nancy nodded at the

agent. "Bill, why don't you get some coffee? Matt and I will be in my study."

"Yes, ma'am."

Nancy inclined her head down the hall. Matt followed her. She slid the pocket doors open to reveal a wood-paneled office with a long desk, not a paper in sight. Bookshelves held pictures rather than books, and two club chairs with a coffee table in between sat in front of the lit fireplace.

Nancy walked over to the waiter caddy by the window behind one of the club chairs. "Drink?"

"I wouldn't mind."

Me either, Nancy thought as she poured two scotches. She handed one to Matt, then took a seat in one of the chairs, waving Matt into the other. "So, Matt. What brings you to my doorstep tonight?"

Matt smiled as he took his seat. "Oh, I think you already know that."

"The SIA inmates."

"I'd like to know where they've been taken and what you plan to do with them."

"I don't plan to do anything with them. It's not a State Department matter."

Matt studied her over the rim of his glass. "But as one of the members of the oversight committee on the SIA, I'm sure you're in the loop."

Now it was Nancy's turn to study Matt as she took a sip. She had known Matt for nearly two decades, and he had always struck her as a straightforward man committed to public service and to the country. She did not like that his reputation was being tarnished by the events at the SIA.

She also wasn't thrilled about what had happened to the SIA. All their funds had been frozen, which was understandable. But allowing the ETF and Seward in particular to take charge… no good would come of that.

THE BELIAL PLAN

"As you can imagine," she said, "when the nature of the SIA facility came to light, the shit hit the proverbial fan. Everyone was tripping over themselves to condemn it."

"And after that media debacle with the priestess?" Matt asked.

Nancy grimaced. "People are falling all over themselves to distance themselves from it."

"What about you?"

Nancy looked into Matt's eyes. "I tend not to run very often. It's bad for my knees. But then again, I was not as surprised by the inhabitants' abilities as the others were. Still, the fact that there are warrants out for Delaney McPhearson complicates an already complicated picture."

Matt's jaw tightened for the briefest of seconds. He had gone to bat for Laney, pleading her case. But it had been to no avail. "She's not the woman you should be focused on."

"I *have* been looking at Elisabeta Roccorio." Nancy knew he felt it was a travesty of justice that the focus was on Delaney. And the more Nancy had dug into Elisabeta, the more she agreed.

But then again, she had a history with Elisabeta. Nancy's parents had been envoys to Italy for most of her formative years. She and Elisabeta had moved in the same circles, and Nancy had never cared for the woman. There was a cruelness there, carefully hidden beneath a public facade. Unlike the rest of the world, Nancy had not been taken in by Elisabeta's crocodile tears. That woman never cried. You needed to care deeply about something to cry, and Elisabeta was simply not capable of that.

"What about the rest of US government?" Matt asked.

"They're not touching her. She's set herself up as the victim, a symbol for other victims around the world. No. Even if some suspected, it would be political suicide to go after her with anything but ironclad proof."

"But the tape from the facility—it must have some people questioning that view."

"It does—privately. But no one is ready to do so publicly."

Matt sat back. "This is wrong, Nancy."

"You're probably right. But you also know right and wrong rarely have a place in politics."

Matt shook his head, staring into the fire. He was loyal to McPhearson. And that said a lot as far as Nancy was concerned. But without more to go on, there was little that could be done to change the forces working against her.

"Back to our original topic," she said. "The individuals who were moved from the SIA facility. I have found where they've been taken." She nodded at a manila folder on the table. "Take a look."

Matt snatched up the folder and quickly flipped through the pages. He looked up. "This is the US government's way of combatting the SIA's transparency problem?"

"No, this is the US government's way of combatting the Fallen problem and a public relations nightmare. They made a huge deal about the rights of the inmates being violated. They can't simply turn around and support your actions. So they're going to move them out of view."

Nancy held out her hand, and Matt handed her the folder. She walked to the fireplace and tossed it into the flames. "Obviously you've heard nothing from me."

"Of course."

Nancy studied him. He looked tired. "Matt, are any of those inmates good people? Any of them who don't deserve to be there?"

"Perhaps one."

Nancy shuddered. "Then if you're not a praying man, you need to start."

"Why?"

"The man they have running the facility, Moses Seward, he's not known for his restraint. And the ETF, they have very little oversight."

"The US government handed the Fallen over to a man who can do anything to them?" Matt asked.

"Yes."

"Is there anything you can do?"

"Not at the moment."

Matt stood and placed his now-empty tumbler on the table. "Thank you, Nancy."

"Whatever you're going to do next, be careful," she said. "People are all over this."

"I know. I'll keep you out of it."

"Any chance you can keep yourself out of it?"

"I'm afraid not."

"Then be careful, Matt. Be very, *very* careful."

CHAPTER 28

LOWELL, OHIO

Moses Seward sat in the control office of the black site. On the desk in front of him was a manila folder with a list of the individuals from the SIA facility who were being held in the cells below. His eyes narrowed as he looked at the last name on the list: Xia, the priestess. The bitch had fooled two of his men into thinking she was a helpless woman. They had let down their guard, and the cost of that failure had been both lethal and public. He glowered at the memory of the scolding he'd taken. His men had looked like a bunch of Keystone Cops.

The two agents who'd escorted the priestess both had concussions. As soon as they were released from the hospital, he planned on making sure they guarded nothing more critical than a Boy Scout parade.

He'd lost two men. It wasn't the loss that angered him so much as what it suggested: that he was not in control. And control was everything. He had risen through the ranks because he was always in control, always aware of the subject of his investigation and what they were capable of.

And then these abominations came along. They were beyond the scope of anything he had ever dealt with before. They were beyond the scope of anything *anyone* had dealt with before. Seward had taken down men high on drugs, who barely felt anything done to them. Those men had been tough—but these things were in a class all by themselves.

The computer monitor in front of him showed another clip of a "Fallen." A man dove off a five-story building, landed on his feet, and rolled. Even with the roll, the man broke an ankle and probably shattered his knee. He sat down with a look of pain on his face, reached down, and straightened out the broken ankle. And then, a mere two minutes later, he was hobbling away. The next camera shot—from an ATM two blocks away—showed him straightening up, the limp gone completely, before he blurred out of view.

"Fallen" was the name attached to these things, but that's not what they were. No—these things were devils. And Seward knew that every moment of his life, every type of criminal he'd ever faced, had led him to this point—when he would face the Fallen and defeat them as well.

He tapped the mouse, and the video feeds of the cells appeared on his monitor. All of the prisoners were still under sedation. If Seward had his way, they would stay under sedation forever—or until he was given the order to kill them. He expected that order to come any day now. No one would want these things out there.

One inmate, though, paced inside his cage. Seward zoomed in on that feed, his lip curling in distaste. According to the records, this one was named Cain. The fools actually thought he was *the* Cain. Seward had to admit the man's black eyes were shocking and did give him a terrifying appearance. And the effect he had on people that intended him harm—Seward couldn't explain that. He'd gone through a dozen guards and technicians before he'd accepted what was written in the report: anyone who tried to harm the man would receive sevenfold the injury they gave him.

Seward narrowed his eyes. But if that was true, the man probably was not much of a fighter. After all, who needs to fight if every opponent drops in pain the minute they touch you?

His phone rang, and he answered it. "Yes?"

"Sir, they've arrived."

Seward smiled. "Good. Get them in position."

"Yes, sir."

Seward sat back, watching the screens. The prisoner had been uncooperative, refusing to answer questions—smug in his inability to be touched. But Seward had a way around that.

He stood up and strode for the door. *Let's see what you've got, Cain.*

CHAPTER 29

Patrick turned off the television set. The tide was changing. Ever since the tape had come out showing that the priestess was alive, the media had been asking more and more questions about Laney. The right questions, finally. The governments of the world hadn't made any official statements, but Patrick had to hope that they, too, were beginning to question what her role was in all of this. They had to.

But he also knew how slowly governments responded. And more worrisome, once they had a scapegoat, they didn't always want to switch focus, even if their original scapegoat was innocent.

A picture of Cain floated through his mind. They still had no word about where he was, and Patrick was imagining the worst.

Guilt weighed him down. He should have done more to protect Cain. He should have done something to keep those men from taking him. Even as he thought it, he knew he would only have ended up right next to Cain. But wouldn't that have been better than sitting by and watching? Wasn't standing up to an injustice, no matter the penalty, the right thing to do?

He shuffled into the kitchen, not really hungry or thirsty but not sure what else to do. He reached for the kettle and started to fill it with water. *When in doubt, have a cup of tea.*

The front door opened, and Jake's voice called out. "Patrick?"

"In the kitchen." He placed the kettle on the burner and set it to high. He turned just as Jake walked into the kitchen. "Just making some tea. Care for some?"

"Sounds good."

Patrick got out some cups and saucers while Jake grabbed the milk and some Irish soda bread. A few minutes later the two men were sitting at the kitchen island with hot drinks, a plate of Irish soda bread between them.

"So, what's going on, Jake?"

"You've heard about the kids that have gone missing?"

Patrick nodded. Danny had stopped by earlier, and they'd had a long chat. By the end of the conversation, Patrick could tell Danny felt a little better—but Patrick didn't. He felt the familiar boulder sitting on his chest at the thought of those children being put in harm's way. *Every time I think we've reached the bottom of depravity, something else happens.*

"Danny and I just realized that all the children that have been taken have had pictures posted on social media sites. We think it's been a way of weeding them out."

"They're looking for Victoria's eyes," Patrick said quietly.

"Yes. All the kids have violet eyes. But they'll need to figure out a way to reduce that number even more. They'll have to figure out a way to identify Victoria, and long before she remembers who she is."

Patrick placed his hand on his chin. "You want to know if I've figured anything out from my research."

"Yes."

Ever since Victoria's death, Patrick had been looking into her life—or lives, more accurately. She had been called the Great Mother by early societies, but he also thought she might have been the inspiration for the Divine Feminine, the idea of women being the spiritual equals of men, if not leaders in the ancient world.

"Have you learned anything that might help us figure out who she was among the children taken?" Jake asked.

Patrick shook his head. "I don't—" He went quiet. *I wonder...* "Patrick?"

"There's a legend, In fact, it's so old I'm not sure that's even the right word for it. It tells of the tome of the Great Mother."

"A book?"

Patrick nodded. "Allegedly, the book contains all the information on the Great Mother's incarnations on earth."

"So it could tell us how to recognize her?"

"I suppose. But no one's seen the book in thousands of years. I'm not even convinced it actually exists."

"But you think it's possible."

Patrick studied Jake. When he first met him years ago, Jake was as straight-laced as they came. He believed only what his eyes could see. But the years and experiences since then had changed him. And Patrick couldn't blame him for that change. They had learned that Victoria was Lilith, the first woman ever created, that Cain still lived, and that Atlantis was real as was Lemuria, a civilization that predated even Atlantis. The necropolis in Saqqara was actually a prison for the Fallen. Gobekli Tepe was created by the descendants of Atlantis, as was its sister site in Montana. And these were just some of the historical events that had proven to be much more than the history books suggested.

"Yes, I think it's possible," Patrick said.

"What do the legends say about where it is?"

"That's the problem. These tales are so ancient, they've been spread across different cultures and countries. And while all agree that there is a book, none of them suggest where it might currently be, if it has even managed to survive."

"There has to be a way to find it. There must be some source, somewhere."

"There's one person who might be able to point us in the right direction."

"Who?"

"The man who has been around almost as long as Victoria—Cain."

CHAPTER 30

The cell was only four by eight feet. Cain could reach both sides with his hands easily. There was a toilet in one corner, a concrete bunk, and actual bars on one side. All things considered, he preferred the cell at the SIA facility.

Blowing out a breath, he sat on the bunk and leaned his head against the cold concrete wall. *How the mighty have fallen...*

He had been at low points over the course of his existence, but he hadn't been this low for at least—he paused, considering—a millennium or two. He had spent the last couple thousands of years in comfort, in extravagance. He was not used to this.

But it wasn't the surroundings that bothered him the most. No—he could accept a simple existence. It was the prospect of spending the rest of his days alone.

Cain had been around people ever since he had been born, but these last months had been different. He'd felt a companionship with people, a connection—something he had thought he didn't need. But that was a lie. He wanted that connection more than anything. And he'd found it—in a prison, of all places. First with Laney, then Patrick. Even his guard, Hanz, had grown on him, showing him pictures of his competition dog. And even though he had been locked up, Cain had felt, in a weird sort of way, like he belonged.

Even his concern for Laney was comforting. He honestly worried about the woman—although his worry was not as great as everyone else's. He knew that as long as Drake was with her, nothing would harm her. Hell itself would tremble under the wrath of that man. But it wasn't Cain's place to explain why. So he offered Patrick what comfort he could without explaining who exactly Drake and Laney were to each other.

Laney's face wafted through his mind. He felt a protectiveness toward her that shocked him when he first recognized it as such. At first, it was because she was Victoria's daughter. Victoria, his one constant in a sea of change. The only one who understood the blessing, and the curse, of immortality.

But as he spent more time with Laney, the reason for their bond shifted. The two of them became friends—genuine friends. That had been a balm, an unexpected gift.

And then Patrick had entered his life—another gift. Both had accepted him, something he never thought he needed, but apparently did. It was eye-opening, humbling, and fulfilling. And in a strange sort of way, they were family.

After all, Enoch was his son. He still remembered when Enoch was born. Cain had known there was something different about him, something powerful. So Cain had kept his distance from his son, afraid of him. Afraid he, Cain, would fail him.

Which I did.

And Laney was Enoch's child. That meant she was his granddaughter, a few millennia removed. But their lives were not viewed in a linear fashion anyway. Meeting her, getting to know her and Patrick... it had been a gift Cain knew he didn't deserve. But one he promised himself he *would* deserve—one day.

And now here I sit, he thought, glancing around. He had no illusions about ever getting out. The SIA had not exactly been warm and fuzzy, but they were fair. Cain didn't care overly much for

Matt Clark, but the man did run a tight ship. No violence or even threats had been made at the other facility.

But these new guards—he'd seen what they had done to some of the Fallen while they were drugged. They had taken out their anger at the priestess on everyone else. All save him. Oh, the guards had stopped by his cell to promise retribution, but Cain knew it was all bluster. They couldn't touch him. Not without experiencing unimaginable pain. But they hadn't exactly made him feel at home.

When he'd first arrived at the SIA facility, part of him had thought he should fight the guards and escape. But he was tired of running. And the loss of Victoria had cut him deep. In her last lifetime, he'd been unable to connect to her until the end. And he'd been so distraught at what was coming.

He shook his head. *Not my best moment.*

He wanted peace, even if it was in a prison cell.

He curled his lip in distaste as a spider crawled through the bars. *But this was not exactly what I had in mind.*

A rumble sounded from the wall behind him. He looked over his shoulder and saw his bunk beginning to slide into the wall. Cain jumped to his feet in alarm. *What the—*

His bunk disappeared, now just another concrete block. Behind him, metal clanked. He turned slowly as his cell door opened.

"Prisoner 173, exit your cell."

Cain crossed his arms over his chest. "Not bloody likely," he muttered.

The rumble sounded behind him again, and the entire wall began to move forward. Cain's eyes went wide, and he started backing toward the bars. *Well, they really want me out of this cell.*

With one last look at the wall moving toward him, he stepped out from the cell and into the long hallway. There were twenty cells along this hall, although his was the only one that was occupied.

Cain extended his arms to his sides. "Well, I'm out. What do you want?"

In reply, the doors on both ends of the hall slid open and men in orange jumpsuits filed in. Cain frowned. These were not the Fallen from the facility. These were humans. What the hell was going on?

The wall behind Cain thudded to a stop right against the bars, leaving him no retreat that way. He looked warily at the men circling him. "Gentlemen, I assure you this is *not* a good idea."

A few got their first look at his black eyes and stumbled back, but others took their place. One man darted forward and slammed his fist into Cain's ribs. Pain tore through Cain, but it was nothing compared to what the man experienced. He let out an ear-shattering scream as his ribs snapped.

The men stopped encroaching on Cain, and those nearest him backed away, their eyes large.

Cain held his side. "Stay back or the same happens to you."

The PA system blared to life. "Anyone who manages to land a punch will have their sentences commuted. None of you has a chance of seeing the outside world again any other way."

Some of the men exchanged glances. Then one broke free from the group with a yell. Cain turned, but the man's fist still collided with his face. The bones in the man's face shattered, but his scream was lost in the scream of the next inmate, who punched Cain in the back. The kidney shot dropped Cain to his knees.

After that the hits came fast, each one punctuated by another scream. Soon the men had to pull other inmates out of the way to reach Cain; the bodies were piling up.

Cain curled up in a ball on the floor as blows rained down on him. After a while, the screams of agony surrounding him disappeared. Everything disappeared.

CHAPTER 31

The ground was awash in blood when Cain opened his eyes again. Well, eye—one was swollen shut, and the other throbbed. He couldn't remember ever feeling this much pain. The curse meant injuries were not a large part of his life. One time a chariot had overturned, throwing him against a rock face. That had been the most pain he had ever experienced in his life.

Up until today.

A man in an orange jumpsuit lay staring at him, another man on his back. The man opened and closed his mouth like a beached fish, blood dripping from his nose. But no words came out—only wheezing breaths.

Two guards appeared and picked up the man on top of him. Cain shifted his gaze to watch them carry the man from the room. More guards were picking up other inmates. He could hear movement behind him; apparently they were gathering up the ones up on that side as well. But the thought of turning was too painful for Cain to try and look.

The man in front of him continued to gurgle; his eyes were filled with pain. Cain felt pity for him. *Stupid pawn.*

Two guards rolled the man onto his back. The man's whole body shuddered as they picked him up. He was the last one on this side. Now all Cain could see was blood splashed across the floor and the walls.

They had sacrificed these men to hurt him, knowing what would happen to them. *And they say* I'm *the evil one.*

The door opened again and two men walked in, each pushing a mop in a bucket. Without a word or even a glance at Cain, they began to mop the floor. Cain watched them for a while. Their movements, slow and deliberate, almost put him in a trance. He felt his lids close.

A door slammed behind him, and Cain's eyes flew open. The floor in front of him was clean, and the men with the buckets were gone. He shifted and sucked in a breath with a hiss. His shoulder was dislocated, his ribs broken. He'd be shocked if he didn't have internal bleeding. Footsteps approached him from behind, but he made no effort to turn. He wasn't sure he would be able to even if he tried.

Dress shoes came into view, along with the bottom of a pair of black pants.

"Tsk, tsk. You are not looking good."

Cain moved only his one good eye to get a look at the man, but even that was painful. Unbidden, a moan escaped his lips.

The man squatted down, and Cain could finally see his face. His identity held no surprise. *Seward.* When Cain had first seen him, Seward struck him as a man who needed to prove his worth. A man's man, in the worst possible sense.

"So. It appears you *can* be hurt," Seward said.

Cain said nothing, partly because he wasn't sure his jaw would work.

Seward looked around. "They cleaned the place up well. You would never know anything happened here." He returned his attention to Cain with a laugh. "Well, of course, except for you.

You thought I couldn't get to you. I think you've learned just how good I am at my job. I will *always* get to you. Don't forget that."

Seward dropped a stack of white towels on the floor, out of Cain's reach, along with a small, clear plastic bag. Cain could make out Band-Aids, gauze, and some antiseptic wipes. "I'd send some people in to help you, but I'm pretty sure they'd just get hurt. So here's some supplies. Feel free to help yourself."

Seward stood, then spit. His aim proved true; the spit landed on Cain's cheek. "You make me sick." He turned and headed for the door.

Cain could feel the spit on his cheek. He didn't even have the energy to wipe it off. He stared at the supplies, but there was no chance he could reach them. They might as well have been on the moon.

The darkness pulled at him. He closed his eyes, trying to work up some anger, but he couldn't. All he felt was pain—pain, and the absolute certainty that he was alone in this world.

Again.

CHAPTER 32

Jake paced along the windows of Henry's office. For the last twenty-four hours, they'd been trying to track down the site where the SIA inmates had been taken. Matt had called an hour ago to tell them he had news, although he hadn't gone into any detail—with the surveillance on them, it wasn't safe to say much over the phone. So they had to wait until he arrived.

Jake turned at a knock on the office door. *Finally.*

"Come in," Henry said.

Mustafa and Matt strode in. Jake waved them over to the conference table.

"Okay, what did you find out?" Jake asked.

"Nice to see you too, Jake," Matt said dryly.

"Yeah, yeah, it's a pleasure. What did you find out?"

"My source was able to find out where they're being held. It's a former black site in Ohio. It hasn't been used since the end of the Cold War."

"Okay. Good. That's something. What're the chances of getting in to see Cain?"

Mustafa and Matt exchanged a glance. "Not good," Matt said. "The inmates have been tortured."

"For information?" Henry asked.

"No—for control. But Cain, he received the worst of it."

Mustafa nodded to the tablet on the table. "With your permission."

"Please," Henry said.

Mustafa picked up the tablet. "We had some people look into the site. We got the schematics, and we also managed to get a feed from inside the facility. It—it's not easy to watch."

Jake focused on the screen, his muscles tense. *Now what?*

On screen, a hallway with maybe two dozen cells came into view. A cell door slid open, and Cain stepped out. A moment later, the doors at either end of the hall opened, and a bunch of men in orange jumpsuits stepped through. *Oh no.*

Jake watched in horror as man after man attacked Cain. Each man fell to the floor after attacking, his own injuries so much greater than what he had doled out to Cain, but they kept on coming. After the last man took his shot and dropped, Mustafa froze the frame. Cain lay on the floor with bodies piled around him.

"They sacrificed those men," Henry said.

"Yes," Matt said. "We ran facial recognition, and we know two of them are from Colorado—ADX Florence. I'm guessing the others are as well."

"Jesus," Jake said, his anger growing. ADX Florence was nicknamed the Alcatraz of the Rockies. Supermax prisons were designed for the worst of the worst. The inmates spent twenty-three hours a day alone, in cells a mere seven feet by twelve. And even when out of their cells, they were always restrained. It was a living hell, and a tightly controlled environment. Which meant—

"The US government approved this?"

"I don't think this was approved, exactly. But the ETF has a lot of pull. I think this was Seward establishing who's in charge."

"It actually gets worse," Mustafa said quietly. He fast-forwarded the recording. Jake watched as the men in orange were taken from the room. Then two men came in to clean up. And all the while, Cain lay broken on the floor. Finally Seward walked in, dropped a bag, and left.

The video continued to fast-forward, but Cain didn't move.

"It's been two hours now," Mustafa said.

"Bastards," Henry muttered.

"What do we know about Cain's healing ability?" Jake asked, his eyes not leaving the screen. He didn't have the relationship with the man that Laney or Patrick had. But no one deserved to be treated like that.

"It's hard to say. He's rarely injured. But he doesn't seem to heal any faster than a human," Matt said.

"They're going to kill him," Mustafa said. "If he doesn't receive medical treatment, he will die."

"He's not immortal?" Jake asked.

"Apparently not," Matt said. "You said when you called earlier that finding Cain was the priority. Did you know about this?"

"No," Jake said. "We had no idea they would treat the inmates like this. We were looking for Cain for a different reason." He quickly explained about the tome of the Great Mother.

By the time he was done, Matt was shaking his head. "They won't let us in," Matt said. "And without medical intervention, I don't think Cain will survive the night."

"How heavily guarded is the site?"

Matt's eyebrows rose. "Heavily. There are a dozen guards, all armed to the teeth. There's only one way in, and one way out."

"You don't think we should actually break Cain out, do you?" Henry asked.

Jake pictured the McAdams family, the devastation on their faces. He didn't want to have to tell them that he hadn't done everything he could to save their daughter. "Yes, that's exactly what I'm saying."

CHAPTER 33

Cain wasn't sure how long he had been lying on the cold floor. He dropped in and out of consciousness. Everything hurt. His mouth, his ears, his legs, even his teeth. He closed his eyes as another pain pierced him.

They were not going to help. They were going to leave him here. Maybe even let him die.

He breathed shallowly; his chest ached. He forced his eyes open and saw the medical supplies still lying where Seward had dropped them. He thought about just closing his eyes again and letting the darkness take him. Maybe he would finally die. All his long life, he'd secretly had a death wish. A wish not only for death, but for the oblivion that came with it. Maybe for him it could be a reset. A blessing.

But...

He pictured Delaney, Patrick, and Victoria. His mind stayed on Victoria. She lived life after life. She embraced life even knowing the pain that would come. The pain of losing those she loved, and the pain of her inevitable death—because most of her deaths were not peaceful. But he had never known her to give up. She had faced it all time and time again.

And she was somewhere out there right now, a child innocent of the future that lay ahead of her.

One day, she would remember it all.

Cain wanted to be there for that day. He wanted to look into her eyes and feel the bond. She was the one person who understood his pain, his loneliness. Who had experienced it as well.

He closed his eyes, trying to steel himself against the pain to come. He opened them and inched forward, a whimper escaping his lips as his broken ribs shifted with the movement. Pain pierced him, overwhelmed him. His vision darkened.

When his eyes flew open again, he knew he had passed out. The supplies were still out of reach. Tears gathered in the corners of his eyes. One slipped down his cheek, and he didn't have the ability to wipe it away.

Move, Cain. Move. The voice in his mind was not his own. He knew it wasn't hers either. His mind was playing tricks on him.

Victoria appeared behind the supplies. She knelt down, her violet eyes staring at him. "You need to move, Cain. You need to help yourself."

"I can't."

"You *can*. And I need you to help my daughter. For me, Cain. Move for me."

He looked into her eyes and wanted nothing more than to let go. But her eyes would not look away from him.

Gritting his teeth, he pulled himself forward, panting, whimpering. Slowly he made his way forward. And then, just when he thought he couldn't move another inch, his hand touched the bag. He wanted to weep.

He felt a hand run through his hair. "You did well." Victoria placed a gentle kiss on his forehead.

Cain curled the bag toward him. *Thank you.*

CHAPTER 34

BALTIMORE, MARYLAND

Henry stopped pacing along the windows in his office. "Are we really going to do this?"

Jake sighed. "Look, I get it. We're breaking all sorts of rules here."

"Not rules, Jake. Laws."

"Yes, laws. But Henry, look at what they did. They raked Laney over the coals, calling her everything including the goddamn antichrist. They raked the SIA over the coals, claiming they were unconstitutional in their process. And look what they did to Cain. I don't like Cain, but no one, not even he, deserves to be treated like that. This is the United States of America. We are better than this."

"We need to give Matt's idea a chance," Henry said. "Some more time."

Jake shook his head. Matt was pleading with his source to intervene, but none of them thought he would be successful.

"If we do this and we're found out, we'll lose everything," Henry said.

Jake nodded. "I know. But unless Matt can manage to talk some sense into his contact, what choice do we have? We have no leads on where the kids are, no way of finding them. Cain offers us a chance to find out what the Fallen are looking for."

"Is that the only reason?"

Jake shook his head. "He's going to die. Laney asked Patrick to look out for him. If Cain dies, it'll kill Patrick. And goddamn it, it's the right thing to do. We cannot leave him there."

"What about the Fallen that are locked up there?"

"They're not in immediate danger. We'll take the ETF down eventually. But until then, we need to get Cain out."

Henry's phone rang. He glanced at the screen before answering it. "Matt?" He paused, nodding his head as he listened. "Okay. I'll tell them." He disconnected the call.

"Well?"

"His contact won't be able to get anything done in time."

"So we're going."

"We're going."

CHAPTER 35

LOWELL, OHIO

Cain heard muffled noises in the background, but he couldn't work up the energy to look, or even to care. He knew he was going to die. After all this time, he was finally at the end of his long life. For years, centuries even, he had longed for this day. The day when he could finally be free.

And yet now that the moment was here, he found himself doing something he'd sworn he would never do. He found himself praying. *Please don't take me. Not yet.*

Part of him rebelled at the thought, his aching body begging for release. But then he pictured Patrick and Laney. For the first time in God knew how long, he had people who actually cared about him. He had no hope that he would land in some sort of promised land, not with the life he had led. And the idea of living just a little longer with people who cared about him... that was water to a thirsty man.

At the same time, his practical side mocked him. Even if someone out there cared about him, no one was going to come for him. Not where he was. This was where people went to die.

Anyone who set foot in this facility was risking his own life. And no one would risk their life for him.

But if the positions were reversed, if it were Laney or Patrick, *he* would risk it for *them*. He would risk it even if they asked him to help someone else. He wanted a chance to prove that. He realized, to his surprise, that he wanted a chance to be redeemed.

A door slammed. He wanted to open his eyes, but it was no use. The darkness was pushing closer. *Goodbye, Patrick. Goodbye, Laney. Thank you for being my friends.*

CHAPTER 36

Jake swept the hall, but there was no one there save for the man lying in a pool of his own blood. He hardened himself against the sight, even as it tugged at him. How could they have treated someone this way?

Five of his men entered behind him; all of them, like Jake, were covered in black from head to toe. He'd forced Henry to stay outside—with his height, he would have been too easily identified. They had taken out all of the guards in the facility. It had been surprisingly easy. But then again, the ETF still didn't truly understand what the Fallen and nephilim were capable of. And Jake had a dozen men on his team.

Jake nodded to Hanz, who stepped up next to him. "Sir?"

"Take him. But carefully."

Hanz had volunteered earlier to carry Cain out, even knowing that any injury he inflicted, though unintentional, might blow back on him sevenfold. He had been Cain's guard while he'd been in the SIA facility. According to Matt, Hanz did not socialize very often; he seemed to prefer the company of his dog to that of humans. Somehow Cain had been aware of that, and he had made a point of turning on dog shows whenever Hanz was around.

Soon the two of them would watch together, one in the cell and one outside, although they rarely spoke.

Now Hanz slung his weapon over his shoulder and knelt down next to the damaged immortal. Carefully, he rolled him over. Then he placed one hand under his neck, the other under his legs, and stood.

"Okay?" Jake asked.

Hanz nodded.

"We're coming out," Jake said into his mike.

"Roger," Henry replied. "How's he look?"

"Not good."

Two men headed out, and another two fell in step behind Jake and Hanz. Jake looked at Cain. His chest was moving agonizingly slowly, and blood soaked the front of his jumpsuit.

"Any issues?" he asked Hanz.

"No. I'm fine."

"Then let's pick up the pace. I don't think he has much time."

CHAPTER 37

WASHINGTON, DC

Moses stepped out of the office of the director of Homeland Security. He'd been ordered to the DC office to discuss the treatment of the inmates. Somehow word of their "rehabilitation" had gotten out. Moses had of course denied any knowledge of mistreatment, and promised to punish anyone treating the inmates unfairly.

Bunch of idiot paper pushers. They had no idea what was necessary to actually fight these people. They still thought the old rules applied. But as far as Moses was concerned, when it came to the Fallen, there *were* no rules.

His aide, Gavin Dryden, hustled down the hallway toward him. Dryden had done only a two-year stint with the FBI before transferring to Homeland. In Seward's opinion, the kid was as green as they came. But he was loyal and earnest—that counted for something.

"Thank God," Dryden said.

"What?"

"I've been trying to reach you."

"They made me surrender my cell phone."

"I know. I called the director's office and told his aide it was an emergency, but he wouldn't put my call through."

For the first time, Moses noticed the sweat that had broken out along Dryden's forehead and the stress lining his face. "What happened?"

"The facility's been breached."

"What? When?"

"An hour ago. I've been trying to reach you ever since."

Moses picked up his pace, forgoing the elevator for the stairs. He swung open the door. "What happened?"

"A force of twelve, no identifying marks, infiltrated at 9:07. They were—some were enhanced."

In his mind, Seward reviewed all the inmates. It had to be someone aligned with one or more of them. There was probably some kind of leader on the outside calling the shots, trying to get his minions free. "How many were freed?"

"Uh, one, sir."

Moses stopped and turned to Dryden. "One? Were they stopped before they could free the others?"

"No, sir. In fact, they used tranqs and took out the entire staff. All of our people were unconscious for about a half hour. They could have released every single inmate easily."

"So who did they take?"

"Inmate 23."

Cain. Of course. "It's the Chandler Group. They're behind this."

"I agree they're the most likely subjects."

From all reports, Jake Rogan was the point man for these kind of activities. But Henry Chandler… Moses had a feeling he'd be in on it as well.

And he realized, as they reached the first floor, that the Chandler Group had finally screwed up. No doubt they had been behind his recall to DC—but that had only brought him closer to the Chandler estate in Baltimore.

Dryden held open the door. "Orders, sir?"

"Tell the men we're heading to the Chandler estate."

CHAPTER 38

GALETON, PENNSYLVANIA

Patrick paced along the front porch, waiting for Cain. He'd been told Cain had been injured and that his condition was critical. Patrick was still trying to wrap his mind around that.

The rain poured down and the wind howled, making a mockery of the porch roof's attempt to provide cover. But Patrick didn't head inside. He didn't even think about it. Instead he moved closer to the railing. The rain slapped against his face and his raincoat as he stared at the sky and prayed the weather didn't interfere with the chopper.

This cabin had belonged to Victoria. It had been one of many properties she'd held in trust. Henry had received a box three months after Victoria died telling him and Laney about all her properties. But Victoria warned them to keep them in the utmost confidence.

And this place was special. It was the place where Victoria had told Laney she was her daughter.

A speck appeared in the distance, and Patrick held his breath as it grew larger. *Finally*. He ran to the front door and yelled inside, "They're coming."

The doctor and two nurses hurried outside and waited at the edge of the porch as the chopper landed. Patrick ran for the chopper, ducking to avoid the blades. Jordan hopped out of the cockpit and slid the side door open. "He's in bad shape, Father."

Patrick said nothing; he just reached for one of the handles of the stretcher as Jordan grabbed the other. They pulled it out far enough for the doctor to grab the handles at the other end. Patrick took a quick glance at Cain's face, then made sure to not look again, keeping his eyes on the doctor. He saw her blanch too, although she tried to hide it. That was not a good sign.

The doctor nodded. "Let's move."

Together they hustled to the cabin, quickly but carefully mounting the steps and carrying the stretcher inside. A hospital bed had been set up in the living room.

"Okay, gently everybody," the doctor said. And for the first time, Patrick noticed the saline bag on the stretcher. "You got a line in him?"

"Apparently, helping him has no effect," Jordan said. "The curse must only kick in when you intend him harm."

Patrick said a quick thanks for that. He had been terrified that they would be unable to help him without harming those who were giving him aid.

Steeling himself, he took his first good look at Cain. His knees went weak, and he gripped the side of the stretcher. Cain was unrecognizable. His cheeks were swollen. His jaw was crooked. One eye was swollen shut. Blood had been wiped from his face, but Patrick could still see traces. "My God."

The doctor was professional enough to not let the horror of Cain's injuries affect her. "Father, please back away. We need room to work."

He nodded, and stumbled away from the stretcher, his hand to his mouth. He stared at Cain as the doctors examined him.

Cain had been one of the first humans, and according to Victoria, humans had been nearly immortal in Cain's time. Diseases, violence—these were not part of their lives. Only through a horrible accident could they die. And then Victoria, as Lilith, made her decision. She condemned mankind to a mortal life, one that no matter how well you lived it, would end in your death. But Cain had been exempt. His punishment was to live forever, to pay for being the world's first murderer.

Now Patrick stared at the world's first murderer and prayed for God to have compassion and let him live. It was partly selfish; he wanted to keep Cain in his life. But it was also for Cain. The man deserved to be part of a family. After all these years, he finally had that chance with Patrick, and with Laney. And goddammit, Cain deserved that kindness. After all he had suffered, didn't he deserve a shot at happiness?

The doctor examined Cain, speaking without emotion. "Dislocated shoulder, broken ribs, fractured wrist, internal bleeding, possible ruptured spleen. We need to open him up."

Jordan put an arm around Patrick's shoulder. "Come on, Father. Let's let them work."

Patrick nodded numbly. Jordan steered him into the living room and deposited him on the couch before mumbling something about making some coffee.

Patrick rose, crossed to the window and stared out at the rain lashing against it. The trees swayed under the onslaught, and once again, he felt so very tired, so without hope. A picture of Cain's battered face stayed in the back of his mind, the face of a man who had been reviled for thousands of years. A man Patrick now thought of as a friend. And he could not get past one simple thought.

The good guys did this to him. How have we come to this?

CHAPTER 39

BALTIMORE, MARYLAND

Moses slammed on the brakes of the black Suburban, barely avoiding ramming into the back of the Suburban ahead of them, which had stopped at the closed gates of the Chandler estate. "What the hell?"

He stormed out of the driver seat and up to the Chandler security guard, who was speaking with Dryden, the driver of the other vehicle.

"Get these gates opened immediately," Moses demanded.

The guard turned slowly to Moses. He was tall, athletically slim, with large brown eyes and sharp cheekbones. His nametag read, "Fricano." "And you are?"

Moses narrowed his eyes. "The man about to shove his boot up your ass if you don't open these gates."

Fricano clicked his pen, then stood with it poised over his clipboard. "I see. And would that be your first name or your last?"

"How dare—"

Dryden jumped out of the car. "This is Moses Seward, the head of the ETF."

Fricano didn't look up from his clipboard as he wrote. "I see. And what is the nature of your business with the Chandler Group?"

Seward gestured angrily to the gates. "The nature? The *nature*? They're criminals! They just stole an inmate from my facility!"

Fricano made a note on the clipboard. "Hm. Well, I'll just put down here—legal."

Moses took a step forward, planning on showing the man exactly what he could do with his clipboard.

Fricano didn't even look up as he spoke. "Just so you know, all the entrances are fully equipped with cameras. Everything is recorded—audio, too." He finally looked up at Moses and smiled. "So, I take it you don't have an appointment."

"We don't need one. We are the United States—"

Fricano shook his head. "Sorry, but you must have missed that lesson in civics class. You cannot, as a government agent, simply storm in without probable cause."

"We have probable cause!"

Fricano grinned even more broadly. "Great! Now just go explain that to a judge, bring me a search warrant, and I will happily—well, maybe not happily, because honestly you've been a little rude—but I *will* open the gates. Now. Have a nice evening, gentlemen."

"I am invoking the PATRIOT Act," Moses snapped. "Stand aside or you will be—"

Fricano held up a finger. "Hold on one second. Hey, Dylan."

A blond guard popped his head from the security hut. "Yeah?"

"Agent…" Fricano paused and looked back at Seward. "Seward, was it?"

Moses just growled, but Dryden nodded.

"Ah, good, I got that right. Agent Seward here of the ETF is claiming the PATRIOT Act allows him access to the estate without a warrant. Thoughts?"

"Well, I have Judge Sheila Appleby of the Fifth Circuit on the line, and she assures me that that is not how the PATRIOT Act works. Agent Sewer is going to have to go get a warrant. Wait—hold on." Dylan placed his ear near the phone. "Judge Appleby says he could go to one of those secret courts. But regardless, at the end of the day, he still needs a warrant."

"That's what I thought." Fricano smiled. "Is there anything else I can do for you fellas tonight?"

Moses glared. "This isn't over."

"Of course it's not. Like I said, get me a warrant and I'll open the gates. Now, I am going to have to ask you gentlemen to move your cars? Because you're blocking the exit. And that, I believe, is a fire hazard. Dylan, is that a fire hazard?" He yelled back over his shoulder.

"Sure is," Dylan called from inside the hut.

Fricano nodded, looking sympathetic. "See? Well, have a good night." He stepped back and shooed the men away.

Moses took a step toward him, but Dryden grabbed his arm. "Cameras," he whispered.

Moses shook him off. "Fine. Get me a fricking warrant. And find out who these two assholes are."

CHAPTER 40

It took almost an hour to get the warrant, and Moses was beyond angry by the time it came through. He also got the background on the two guards at the front gate. Mark Fricano and Dylan Jenkins—both former Navy SEALs, highly decorated. They had gone to work with Chandler shortly after they left the service and had served with Jake Rogan for years. He knew they would not be easily intimidated. *Damn it.*

"We're good," Dryden said over the phone.

"Finally," Moses growled as he put the car into gear.

The gates to the Chandler estate opened slowly—incredibly slowly. It took a full five minutes for them to open wide enough for the SUVs to get past.

As soon as they were open, though, Dryden's SUV headed in. Moses was right behind him. Fricano and Jenkins stood by the hut, waving. Moses promised to find a way to make the men's lives hell.

They spent the next two hours searching the main house of the estate while another team went through the houses down on Sharecroppers Lane. And they found nothing. No sign of Cain, and also no sign of Henry Chandler or Jake Rogan. In fact, the only people they did see were the video crew that had shown up to record the search, and the fleet of lawyers who had magically appeared as soon as they had gotten out of their SUVs, two per search team. The Chandler Group chopper was sitting quietly on its helipad.

Moses called Dryden as he headed down the stairs from Henry Chandler's office. "Go to the front gate. Find out where the hell everybody is." He disconnected the call without waiting for a reply.

He stopped and whirled around to the lawyer behind him. "Where are Henry Chandler and Jake Rogan?"

The woman showed not an ounce of fear at his close proximity. "I'm afraid I do not know. As I explained, we are on retainer for whenever a government agency shows up at the estate. We are simply here to make sure you do not step beyond the bounds of the warrant."

Curling his lip, Moses headed back down the stairs. *Bottom feeders.*

As he stepped out of the main doors, his phone rang. "What?"

"Um, Henry Chandler and Jake Rogan are on the estate. They're in the bomb shelter."

"What? Why the hell didn't they tell us that to begin with?"

Dryden hesitated. "Um, sir, we never asked them."

Oh, for fuck's sake. He growled, "What the hell are they doing in a bomb shelter? Hiding?"

"Um, no. According to these guys, they go there every two weeks."

"For what? Survivalist training?"

"Um, no. Poker."

∽

Moses stormed down the path toward the bomb shelter. He'd

forgotten the stupid thing was even here. Who the hell builds a bomb shelter in this day and age?

Dryden jogged up to him. "Sir."

"Report."

"Um, the shelter was built about fifteen years ago when Dr. Dominic Salvatore joined the Chandler Group."

"What is it? A research lab?"

"Yes, but it's also where Dr. Salvatore lives. He's apparently an agoraphobe. He doesn't leave the shelter—ever."

Moses stopped short. "Are you kidding?"

Dryden shook his head. "No. From all reports, he's really close to Henry Chandler and his son, as well as Jake Rogan." A utility shed came into view up ahead. "That's it," Dryden said.

Moses stopped at the front door and looked around. There was no handle. "How the hell do you get in?"

"Um, I think it's this." Dryden pushed a button to the left of the door.

A piece of metal slid away from the left of the door at their eye line. It remained black for a second, then flicked to life, showing a bald man staring back at them. "Yo."

"Who the hell are you?" Moses demanded.

"Who the hell are you?" the man answered.

"I am Agent Moses Seward of the ETF. I have a warrant to search the premises. Now identify yourself."

"Can I see a badge?"

Seward dug in his jacket pocket for his badge, then held it up.

"Can you hold it closer to the camera?"

Moses looked around, but didn't see a camera. Dryden pointed to a small device directly above the door. "Um, I think that's it, sir."

Seward glared at him before holding the badge up.

"A little closer."

Seward reached higher.

"Great. Thanks. Let me just check this and I'll get right back to you." The screen blinked off.

"Goddamn—" Moses punched the button again. He continued punching it, but the screen stayed blank.

Fifteen minutes later, the man reappeared. "Good news! You are who you said you are."

"I *know* that. Now. Open. The. Door."

"First, I'm going to need to see a warrant."

Moses gestured to the lawyer who had followed him. "She's already seen it. She can verify that we have permission."

"Um, lawyer, could you step up to the camera?"

Moses stepped back, allowing the woman to be within the camera's range. "There. Satisfied?"

The bald man shook his head. "'Fraid not. I don't know her. She could be one of your agents playing the part of a lawyer. I'm gonna need the warrant."

Dryden stepped forward, pushing the paper close to the camera. "Here."

"Uh-huh. Give me just another few minutes."

The screen blinked off again.

"What the hell is wrong with these people?" Moses demanded.

"I'm guessing they like to make sure their constitutional rights are being protected," the lawyer said.

"Who the hell asked you?"

She raised an eyebrow, looking like a bored Sunday school teacher. "You did. The next time you don't want a question answered, you should just keep it to yourself."

Moses imagined arresting the woman and tossing her in a cell for a nice long time, but honestly, lawyers were the worst. She'd no doubt have him tied up in courts for weeks, if not longer. It wasn't worth it. But it was fun to think about.

He paced along the front of the shelter, punching the button every few minutes and demanding someone let them in. He always received the same response—an automated one. *I'm sorry. No one is available to take your call right now. Please try again later.*

After fifteen minutes, he turned to Dryden. "Call Mac. Tell him I want to find a way in there."

"Um, sir, it's a bomb shelter."

"I know what the hell it is! Find me a way in."

CHAPTER 41

Jake leaned forward, as if that would make the chopper go faster. They'd arranged for the Airbus H155, one of the fastest choppers in the world, to get them back to Baltimore. But they were still cutting it close. Fricano had called when they'd barely gotten into the air to let them know the ETF was at the estate. He'd stalled them, but they were inside the estate now.

Jordan had taken Cain to the cabin in Pennsylvania, where a medical team met them. According to Jordan, the medical team had to operate on Cain and couldn't say if the man would make it.

Behind him, Henry pocketed his phone. His voice came through the headset. "Seward finished the search of the main house. He's heading to the bunker."

"We're not going to make it," Jake said. They were fifteen minutes away. They were going to enter Dom's shelter by the same route Laney had taken when she'd slipped away, but that meant they still had to travel two miles through a tunnel to get into the bunker itself.

"We can save time by not landing," Jen said.

"You two can. But me breaking both legs will not speed up the process," Jake said.

"I can carry you," Henry said.

Jake narrowed his eyes. "How?"

"Um, in my arms?" Henry replied.

"Yeah, I don't see that happening."

"It might be our only choice," Jen said, then grinned. "Too tough to let another man cradle you like a baby?"

Jake glared at her while Henry murmured, "Not helping, Jen."

She grinned. "Not really trying to."

"Jake, it might be our only shot," Henry said.

"We might still make it."

The next few minutes were tense. Jake's phone beeped, and he looked down at it. It was a text from Dom. *They'll be here in ten minutes. You need to hurry.*

Jake stared at the field where the entrance was—and closed his eyes. *Crap.* He turned back to Jen and Henry. "We're going to have to jump."

With a grin, Jen opened her mouth.

Jake cut her off. "Not a word, Jen."

CHAPTER 42

Dryden looked dumbfounded when Moses ordered him to find a way into the bomb shelter. Moses knew how ridiculous that request was—it would take hours, if he could even do it at all. But the Chandler Group did not get to thumb its nose at the United States government.

"Um, yes, sir. I'll—"

All heads turned as the light above the door beeped and turned green.

"See? You didn't need your battering ram," the lawyer said dryly.

Moses whirled around to tell her to shut it, but she simply raised an eyebrow. "Yes?"

He growled and turned back to the door. With a puff of air, it swung open. A short bald man stood looking at them. "Oh, hey. I'm Yoni. I'll show you down."

"About time." Moses pushed past him, only to come up short at a blast door. He whirled on Yoni. "Why is this closed?"

"Shelter rules—all doors must be locked when you're through them. Give me a minute"—Yoni looked at the door and shrugged—"or five, and I'll have us through."

Moses stepped back and pursed his lips. *I hate every single person who works here.*

CHAPTER 43

Henry rolled as he hit the ground, and Jake rolled as well, right out of Henry's arms, for which he was grateful. Jake was not, in his mind, overly macho. But being cuddled against Henry's chest while Henry leapt from the chopper was a little more than his ego could take.

Henry reached down a hand and helped Jake to his feet. Jake looked into his friend's face. "It goes without saying that what just happened, dies with us."

Henry smiled. "My lips are sealed."

Jen jogged up. "Mine, too. Now let's move."

She blurred over to the entrance. Henry blurred as well, and feeling like a giant tortoise, Jake sprinted after them. By the time he reached the entrance, Jen had it open.

The tunnel was only about six feet high. It had been hollowed out of the earth to be used for the Underground Railroad. It ran from this field straight to the estate.

"You two need to go. Get to Dom's," Jake said.

Henry shook his head. "I can carry—"

Jake cut him off. "No. The tunnel's too low. You'll be running hunched over as it is. Even Jen and I will have to duck. Just get there as fast as you two can. We don't have time."

Henry's voice was laced with concern. "Jake, if you don't get there in time…"

"I know. Then Seward will know we were part of the breakout. So move. I'm right behind you."

With a nod, Jen took off. Henry gave Jake one last look.

"Go," Jake said.

Henry blurred through the tunnel, but Jake could tell he wasn't moving as fast as normal.

Jake slammed the tunnel gate behind him and began to run, his shoulders hunched to keep him from slamming his head into the low ceiling. But still he pushed on, not letting himself slow.

Please let this work.

CHAPTER 44

The trip down to the bomb shelter took twenty minutes. Each door required a separate security protocol, some of which were lengthy. Moses had moved beyond the furious stage. He knew Henry Chandler and Jake Rogan weren't down here, and as soon as he had proof, he was going to swear out the warrant for their arrests. Picturing them being cuffed was the only thing keeping him sane.

Rich guys like Chandler ticked him off. Wealthy, spoiled—life had been handed to guys like him on a silver platter. And as a result, they thought the rules didn't apply to them.

And then there was Rogan, a highly decorated Navy SEAL. All SEALs thought they were tough shit, like those two at the gate. Moses could have been a SEAL. He would have been an incredible SEAL. But he'd been drummed out of the Navy. They couldn't handle a man like him. They were *scared* of a man like him. And now, Rogan was going to go down.

"Well, here we are," Yoni said, pulling the last door open. The man had kept up a nonstop stream of conversation the entire walk down. Moses knew from his file that his full name was Yoni Benjamin, that he'd been born in Israel but had American citizenship, and that he had worked for the Israeli military before joining the Navy. And he, too, was a Navy SEAL, who'd also worked with Rogan. Apparently Rogan had hired every damn SEAL he'd ever worked with.

A man with gray and white hair and thick glasses shifted from foot to foot in the entryway.

Moses pulled his sidearm. "Who the hell are you?"

"Whoa, whoa, whoa." Yoni stepped in front of the man. "This is Dom—Dr. Dominick Salvatore. He lives here. You are in his home."

Moses narrowed his eyes, lowering his weapon. He waved Yoni to the side. With a glare, Yoni moved to stand right next to the doctor, who was shaking. *About time someone showed the correct amount of fear.*

"We are looking for Henry Chandler and Jake Rogan and a man by the name of Cain. You two will have to leave while we search."

"Wait a minute. The doc here does not leave his home. He's got a condition," Yoni said.

"I don't care." Moses nodded to two of his men. "Take them out."

The lawyer stepped forward. "You are not allowed to remove anyone from the premises. They are allowed to remain for the search. To remove them violates the contents of the warrant."

"Who the hell's going to know?" Moses asked.

Yoni nodded toward the corner behind Moses. "Everybody."

Moses turned around and saw a camera. God damn these people. They had cameras everywhere. Bunch of criminals.

"Whatever. Get out of the way." Moses strode forward.

Yoni pulled Dom out of the way, and Moses made his way down a long hall and into a giant room. He'd never been in a bomb shelter, but this one, it really did look like a home. There was a kitchen area over to the left, a living room area with a large leather sectional, a plush carpet, what looked like a greenhouse in the back of the room, and plants everywhere.

His gaze traveled across the space and stopped still at the leather couch. Or more specifically, at the two people sitting on it.

Henry Chandler stood, his height causing him to tower over the woman who stood next to him—Jenifer Witt.

Chandler inclined his head. "Agent Seward."

CHAPTER 45

Moses frowned watching Chandler and Witt. They looked uncomfortable. Something was off. He crossed the room toward them. "What are you two doing here?"

Chandler gestured toward the kitchen area. "Poker night."

On the kitchen table were the remnants of a poker game. The island was covered with takeout food boxes.

Seward looked at Jen. "And you?"

Jen nodded to Henry. "He just told you."

"*You* play poker?"

Witt crossed her arms over her chest and rolled her eyes. "Gee, sexist much?"

Moses glared at her. "Someone broke into a secure government facility and abducted one of the inmates that had been held at the SIA facility. What do you know about that?"

"Nothing," Henry said.

Jen shrugged. "I know that whoever named it a secure facility should probably lose their job."

Seward narrowed his eyes. "Why would you say that?"

Jen spoke slowly. "Because you just said someone broke in and abducted someone from there. That doesn't sound secure."

Seward stepped toward her, intending to intimidate her. But she held her ground and stared at him like she was bored. She even blew out a breath. In fact, Seward had to stop short or else he'd run into her. She raised an eyebrow at him with a smirk as if she knew he was trying to intimidate her. And it rankled Moses that she was taller than him.

"Need something, agent?" she asked.

With a growl, he stepped back. *They don't matter*, he reminded himself. He doubted either of them was in on the actual abduction. Chandler was a paper pusher, and Witt—she had no training. She was an academic.

He looked around the space, focusing on an open doorway in the back. He nudged his chin toward it. "Where does that lead?"

"Bedrooms, Dom's office, storage room, two bathrooms," Henry said.

Seward waved his men toward the door. "Check them."

Seward noticed Henry swallow. "Nervous, Mr. Chandler?"

Chandler kept his gaze. "No. My stomach's just a little queasy."

Seward scanned the space. "Where's Jake Rogan?"

Neither Chandler nor Witt answered him.

He turned back to them. "I said, where is Jake Rogan?"

"Find him yourself," Witt said, taking a seat.

"But he's not here, is he?" Seward smiled as he strode toward the back hall. Rogan wasn't here. Finally. They had slipped up. They had—

The sound of a toilet flushing interrupted his thoughts. He stepped into the hall as a door halfway down the hall opened. Jake Rogan stepped out, his hand on his stomach. His face was pale, and he was sweating hard. He grimaced. "Do not eat the shrimp," he said as he passed Seward and headed for the main area.

"Where the hell have you been?" Seward yelled.

Jake turned slowly, holding on to the wall. "What?"

"Tonight—where have you been?"

"Here, apparently eating shrimp that's going to keep me up all night. I put the fan on in the bathroom, but you still might give it a minute before you head in there."

"Is there something I'm going to find?"

"Yeah," Jake drawled, "the smell of vomit." He turned and continued down the hall.

Seward watched him go. Not possible. He knew Rogan, at least, had to be in on the break-in. He was Henry Chandler's go-to man. He could *not* be here.

But he also knew there was only one entrance in and out of the shelter. And his men had had the estate under observation for hours.

He gritted his teeth. Rogan *had* been part of this. He felt it in his bones. He just couldn't prove it.

One of his men walked up to him. "Sir, we've checked the storage room and the bedrooms. There's no sign of—"

"Oh, shut up." Seward stormed away.

CHAPTER 46

The doctor and nurses had worked on Cain for hours. They had even opened him up and operated on him to address the internal bleeding. Patrick had stayed out of their way, keeping up an almost continual prayer for the man's safety. Jordan was stationed outside, along with four other guards who had arrived to keep the cabin secured.

Now the doctor and one of the nurses were sleeping in one of the rooms down the hall. Charles, the other nurse, kept track of Cain's vitals, watching the monitors for any change. Charles was a tall, muscular, African-American vet who had been an army medic and had joined the Chandler Group after his third tour in Afghanistan.

"Is it all right if I sit with him now?" Patrick asked.

"Go ahead, Father. I'm actually going to grab some coffee, if you don't mind. Give me a yell if anything changes, okay?"

"Will do."

"Can I bring you some coffee?"

"No, I'm good."

"I'm just down the hall if you need me." Charles stepped out of the room.

Patrick pulled a chair over to Cain's bedside. Cain lay quietly, bright white sheets pulled up to his neck, his dark hair spread across the pillow. His unusual eyes were hidden behind his closed eyelids. He looked so pale.

Patrick didn't know what to say. He didn't know what to think. Cain was the world's first murderer, and he had paid a huge penalty for that act. But he hadn't been the world's *last* murderer.

Murders happened every day—every thirty-one minutes, in fact. Patrick remembered talking with Laney once about the criminal justice system. She said that even for violent crimes, most cities' clearance rates never topped sixty-four percent, which meant almost forty percent of murderers were never caught. But even that was a misunderstanding of the stats. Sometimes cases were cleared without someone being convicted. Patrick had personally heard of cases where people had done horrible things and spent little to no time locked up. Yet this man had been punished for thousands of years.

Patrick himself had taken lives—in the war, but more recently as well. It had always been in the act of defending himself or others—but did that truly make a difference? Wasn't a life a life?

He'd known what kind of men those agents had been. And he'd done nothing.

He gently gripped Cain's hand and leaned in close. "I'm sorry, Cain. I'm so sorry."

⁓

PATRICK HAD FALLEN asleep in a chair next to Cain's bed. When he opened his eyes, darkness had fallen, and his back protested. Charles was moving quietly about the room, checking the monitors and making notations on Cain's chart.

Patrick sat up quickly, then winced as pain shot through his lower back. "Am I in your way?"

Charles looked over and shook his head. "You're fine. And your friend is doing well. The doctor checked him while you were sleeping. No signs of a leak, no fever—those are good indicators. Right now he just needs sleep."

"Is the doctor still here?"

"No. The patient's out of the woods, so she and Sheila took off. She'll be back in two days to check on him, and I'll stay around the clock."

"He's out of the woods?"

"Yeah. I have no idea how, but yeah. It's going to take a while, and we'll need to keep an eye on him, but he's looking good. I'm going to get a bite to eat and then I'll sleep in here." He nodded to a cot in the corner. "You should go get some sleep yourself. I'll wake you if anything changes. But like I said, he's looking good." Charles headed out of the room.

Patrick knew he was right, but he wasn't ready to leave, not quite yet.

Cain stirred. Patrick leaned forward. "Cain?"

Cain mumbled, his words unintelligible.

Patrick leaned forward even more. "Cain, it's Patrick. You've sustained a lot of injuries, but the doctor says you'll be all right."

Cain's eyes opened slowly.

Relief flooded through Patrick. "You're going to be okay. We got to you in time."

Cain struggled to swallow. When he spoke, his voice was weak. "How?"

"Henry, Jake, Jen—they raided the facility and got you out."

Cain nodded. "Why?"

Patrick felt the man's desolation, his loneliness. And he spoke the truth, if only in part. "Because we didn't want you to die."

Cain's voice was barely above a whisper. "Thank you."

Patrick tapped his hand lightly. "Get some sleep. You need to heal."

Cain's breathing evened out, and Patrick bowed his head. Cain was going to be all right. With one last glance at his friend, he shuffled down the hall looking for a spot to lay his own head.

CHAPTER 47

BEVERLY HILLS, CALIFORNIA

Elisabeta reviewed the notes on the children. All were female, about the same size, and within a few pounds of each other. There were a dozen or so birthmarks between them. But nothing that screamed "I am the mother of all humanity."

She pushed the papers away with a grunt. *Even as a child, you're making things difficult*, she thought, picturing Victoria when she'd last seen her. But if all went as planned, she would know who she was soon enough. And then, of course, the question was what to do with the rest of them.

But that was a problem for a different day. Today's problem was identifying the correct child, and Elisabeta's patience was running thin on that count. Perhaps she should have waited before grabbing the children—but she had thought she would have had the book by now. Nothing had run as well without Gerard. That man was nothing if not efficient.

But Victoria had thrown an obstacle in that path as well. She had returned Gerard's memories to him from his first life. Elisabeta frowned, picturing the pain on Gerard's face when he realized his family was dead. Emotional attachments were weaknesses, and they should play no role in the lives of the Fallen. After all, what were they if not gods among men? And gods should not have weaknesses.

But that had not been the case for Gerard. When his memories returned, it was like he was experiencing their deaths all over again. But that was to be expected, she supposed. He just needed a little time and he would return to the fold. She had found him when he was a teenager, his powers just budding. She had crafted him from that moment. That link, that connection, was stronger than a millennia-old attachment to a dead woman and her children. He'd come around soon enough.

She had sent men to find him, but no trace of him had been found. She still had men looking, but she knew he would not be found until he wanted to be.

No doubt the fact that her current endeavor involved children had forced him to the forefront of her mind these last few weeks. Pushing Gerard from her thoughts, she focused back on the children, contemplating whether there was another way to identify the correct child. Idly, she wondered if Cain might be able to identify Victoria. But even if he was, there was no easy way to control that man. Besides, the US government had whisked him away somewhere, and she really wasn't interested in tracking him down for a maybe. And running into the US government was always tricky. She had kept her involvement from the world's eyes; she had no interest in exposing herself now.

She smiled. *At least, not until everything is ready.*

She raised an eyebrow as the sounds of a fight reached her. *That's not right.* Then a familiar tingle ran over her. She put down her pen. *It's about time.*

She leaned back from the desk, her hands folded in her lap. The door to her office burst open. A tall, powerful Fallen with blond hair and blue eyes strode in, his gaze locked on Elisabeta's face. His shirt was torn, a splotch of blood marring the designer outfit that highlighted his sleek frame.

Three of her Fallen burst in the door behind him. "Samyaza."

The man glanced over his shoulder, then turned back to Elisabeta, an eyebrow raised. "Well?"

She waved her men away. "It's all right. Leave us."

"But Samyaza—"

"Leave us."

"Yes, Samyaza." The men bowed, all glaring at the man.

Samyaza waited to speak until the door was closed. "Hello, Gerard."

CHAPTER 48

GALETON, PENNSYLVANIA

Patrick wasn't sure how long he had slept. It felt like days had passed when he finally opened his eyes, yet at the same time he knew if he closed them again he would easily fall back into unconsciousness. He pushed himself up and sat at the edge of the bed for a moment to let himself fully awaken. He glanced at his cell phone on the side table. He picked it up and noticed he'd missed a call from Sean. He put the phone down in disgust. No doubt Sean was calling again to try to get him to distance himself from Laney.

Patrick rubbed his hands on his face, trying to chase away the cobwebs in his mind. Charles had promised to wake him if Cain took a turn, and the fact that he hadn't was a good sign. But the sight of Cain's bruised and battered body was a weight on Patrick's soul. He knew he was in the middle of an existential crisis. His whole life he had been loyal to God, the church, and his country, believing they had the best interests of all mankind at heart. Oh, he knew mistakes would be made—people would fall short of goals. But how could they have fallen *so* far short?

The church wanted him to denounce Delaney. How could they think he would ever agree to that? His niece, who had done more for mankind than all those men combined. Lecturing him about responsibility, they had asked Patrick—no, *ordered* him—to turn his back on her.

And then his government, the government he had gone to war for, had beaten Cain within an inch of life just because they could.

It felt like the world had shifted radically on him. All he believed in had been turned around, leaving only this gaping hole in his chest. He wanted to believe the church would do the right thing. He wanted to believe his government would do the right thing. But at this moment, he had no faith that either of those things would happen.

Patrick rubbed his hands over his face. *Isn't life supposed to get less complicated as you get older? Not more?*

With a sigh, he pushed off the bed. After a quick stop at the bathroom, he headed down the hall to check on the patient.

Charles looked up when Patrick peeked his head in. With a quick glance at the bed, Charles stood up and waved Patrick outside.

"How is he?" Patrick asked.

"He's good, actually. He woke up a few hours ago and I offered to go get you, but he said to let you sleep. But his vitals look good. His incision is healing really well. Honestly, if you had told me when he arrived that he'd been in this shape right now, I would have called you crazy. Glad I was wrong."

Patrick felt relief flow through him. "Thank God."

"Pretty sure He had to be helping. You want to sit with him?"

"Yeah." Patrick noted the exhaustion lining the man's face. "Why don't you get some sleep in a real bed? I'll call you if we need you."

Charles stifled a yawn. "I think I'll take you up on that." He moved past Patrick and headed down the hall. Patrick took a breath, said a little prayer of thanks, and walked in.

Even the bruises on Cain's face seemed to have cleared up some, making Patrick frown. *He really is healing quickly.*

CHAPTER 49

The first sound Cain heard was the soft beep of the heart monitor. Then a sigh, and someone shifted in a seat nearby. He opened his eyes a crack and saw Patrick sitting in a chair next to the bed.

Confused for a moment, he couldn't figure out why he was here and where Patrick had come from. Then the memories returned in a wave, crashing down on him. His breathing hitched, and Patrick's head jerked up, concern and exhaustion clear in the lines on his face.

Cain calmed his breathing even as the images of the men coming at him one after the next flew through his mind. He shut his eyes as a tall African-American man, who from his clothes must be some sort of medical attendant, hustled into the room and checked the monitors before placing two fingers on Cain's wrist to check his pulse.

"Is he all right?" Patrick asked. "His heart rate spiked there for a moment."

"Well, it's normal now. It might have just been a nightmare."

"Oh, okay."

Cain heard Patrick settle back in his chair. The other man

walked around the room for a few minutes before everything settled back into silence.

Cain slit his eyes open again. Only Patrick remained in the room.

"Hey," Cain said softly.

Patrick dropped the book he'd been reading and bounded to his feet, moving next to the bed. "You're awake. How are you feeling?"

"Like I was hit by a bus. Which then backed over me and ran over me again."

"You kind of look like that." Patrick paused. "How did this happen?"

Cain closed his eyes. "In the facility. They forced me out of my cell. Then inmates, it must have been two dozen of them, surrounded me. They attacked me."

Patrick frowned. "But how? I mean, when the first one hit you, the rest must have realized what would happen to them."

"Seward—the man in charge of the facility. He spoke through the PA system. He reminded them that hurting me was the only chance any of them had at getting out. I guess I was their parole hearing."

Patrick sat back, stunned. "He offered to commute their sentences in exchange for hurting you?"

Cain nodded.

"But—but, those men—did they survive?"

Cain pictured the bloodied hallway, the bodies surrounding him. His final image was of the man who had lain in front of him, noiselessly moving his mouth. "I doubt all of them did."

Patrick stood up again and paced the room, his anger evident. "And these are the good guys. What has happened to humanity that we have come to this?" The sorrow in his eyes tugged at Cain. "I'm sorry they did this to you. It never should have happened."

Cain looked away.

Patrick walked to the bed. "You can't think you deserve this."

Cain's voice was soft. "Maybe I do. I've done some horrible things in my life, Patrick."

"But you weren't doing a horrible thing when they did this to you. They chose to attack you when you were defenseless. And they used other men as their weapons. They sacrificed those men to hurt you."

"You don't know what I have done."

Patrick pulled up a chair so he could look in Cain's eyes. "No. I don't know the extent of what you have done. But I do know the man you are now. And you did not deserve this."

Patrick's words were like a life preserver to a drowning man. But he knew Patrick was wrong—even though every cell in his being wanted to believe him. "No. What I have done, it cannot be forgiven. Not just Abel, but the others I have harmed throughout my long life. I deserve this. And so much more."

"I don't believe that."

Cain tried to shrug, but it proved too painful. "Nevertheless."

"Everyone can be forgiven. Everyone can be redeemed. Even you, Cain."

Cain wanted to believe Patrick, but a part of him, a large part, knew that Patrick's faith in him was misplaced. "I haven't done anything to deserve redemption. I *have* changed. These last months, they have changed me. But how does sitting in a cell, not hurting anyone, but also not helping anyone, how does that redeem me? Don't there need to be actions for redemption to work?"

"It starts with changing your heart. It starts with empathy and compassion for others. How did you feel when you saw those men lying there?"

Cain pictured the men falling around him, heard their cries of pain again. "I felt pity and anger that they had been treated that way."

"See? It has begun. The fire has been lit. Now we just need to fan it."

CHAPTER 50

Gerard Thompson. Elisabeta's eyes roamed over his lithe frame. When she had found him as a teenager, he had been the picture of an angel. Strong cheekbones, piercing blue eyes, hair almost white from the sun. As he'd aged, his beauty had turned more manly, giving him a look of the type that usually graced the covers of *GQ*. Gerard had been fully and completely hers, loyal to a fault.

Until Victoria had ripped him away by restoring his memories.

But Elisabeta had known it would only be a matter of time before he returned to the fold. His past life was just that—in the past. He had been shocked, hurt at first. That was to be expected. But she knew that, with time, he would see the rightness of her decisions. If not then, certainly now.

And she had to admit, it was good to see him. Hakeem was adequate in some areas—the bedroom being one—but he didn't have Gerard's mind for strategy and games. There, only Gerard had been able to match her.

Not that she would go easy on him now. After all, loyalty was demanded of all her people. And no one, not even Gerard, would get a pass.

"So, Gerard, you're looking well."

Gerard tipped his head, looking completely at ease, as if he had not just destroyed her security team. "You as well, Elisabeta."

"To what do I owe the honor of your visit?"

"Well, I ran into a few of your people. I thought they were looking for me. Imagine my surprise when I realized they were watching a child."

Elisabeta narrowed her eyes. "And what exactly happened to those people?"

Gerard smiled. "Nothing much. They should wake up in a few hours. Or maybe not. Your people need to be better trained."

"Well, I *had* an incredible trainer—but he had an unfortunate burst of conscience."

"That does happen."

"Enough, Gerard," Elisabeta said, all pretense of civility gone. "What do you want?"

"To come back."

She raised an eyebrow. "Why?"

He sighed. "Because life is short, Elisabeta. And I do not intend to waste it like the humans. Plus, I hear there is a war coming. And I plan to be on the side of the victor."

"Who said I *wanted* you back?"

"You always want me."

A thrill shot through Elisabeta at his words, but she ignored it. She traced an outline of an infinity symbol on the desk, her gaze on Gerard. "And what of Kaya, Arya, and Peter?"

Not a flicker of emotion crossed Gerard's face as he shrugged. "Lifetimes ago. I'm concerned with the here and now."

"That's not how you felt when you left."

He curled his lip. "That witch messed with my head. I needed to step back and determine what my priorities are."

"And what conclusion did you come to?"

"You are my priority. Whatever your goals are, they are mine as well."

Seconds passed, and Elisabeta continued to study him, looking for a sign that he was not telling the truth. But he gave her nothing.

She tilted her head. "Very well. I have a task that needs to be completed, and I think you may be just the man for the job. If you are successful, I will consider reinstating you."

"Whatever you need, Samyaza."

Samyaza smiled. "Good."

CHAPTER 51

GALETON, PENNSYLVANIA

Patrick paced along the porch, his cell phone at his ear. "No, I haven't asked him if he knows where the book is."

It had been twenty-four hours since Cain had arrived. He was healing amazingly well, at least physically. But the emotional wounds, those were still raw. And not just for Cain. Patrick had seen the recording of the attack. The brutality of it had left him shaken.

Jake's exasperation was clear. "Patrick, we need that information. That's the whole reason we got him out."

"That's not the only reason, and you know it. If we didn't go in, he would be dead."

Jake sighed. "I know. But we need to know where the tome is."

"I agree. But Jake, you saw him. You saw the condition he was in. He needs time to heal."

"Patrick, there are children out there in danger. There are families out there terrified of what is happening to their children. We need as much information as we can get."

"I know. I know. I'll ask."

"Good. Call me back when you learn something." Jake disconnected the call.

Patrick stared at his phone in frustration. It wasn't that he didn't agree with Jake. He did. It was just that he hated the idea of Cain thinking they only got him out because of the book.

But Jake was right—time was of the essence.

Patrick headed back inside. The cabin was quiet. Charles had left. He would return this evening to check on Cain. Patrick knew that the swiftness of Cain's recovery perplexed Charles, although he hadn't asked any questions.

Patrick paused outside Cain's bedroom, working up his courage, then stepped in. Cain was sitting up, a TV remote in his hand. He looked over at Patrick. "How is it possible that there are about three hundred channels on this thing and nothing good to watch?"

Patrick smiled. "It's one of the modern world's greatest mysteries."

Cain shut the TV off and placed the remote on the bed next to him. "So. Are you finally going to tell me why you got me out?"

Patrick searched Cain's black eyes to see if he could get a read on him, but Cain had his emotions well in check. "What I told you was true. Seeing what had happened to you spurred us into action. But the reason we were looking for you... is because we need your help."

Cain's jaw tensed. "I see."

"No, you don't. Look, yes, we went looking for you so you could help us. But we would never have left you in there, no matter what. Laney—she asked me to look after you. It's the last thing she asked me to do. And I had no intention of denying that request. I still don't. And it wasn't just because of Laney, either. You—you're my friend. Against every possible belief I had when I first visited you, you are my friend. And I would not have left you in there. And when I saw what they had done to you—it hurt to watch. It hurts to think about. And I think Seward should be punished eternally for it."

Cain gave him a crooked smile, but Patrick could now see some of the emotion cracking through his mask of indifference. "I think only one person gets an eternal punishment. And I seem to be the lucky recipient of that."

"Well, I don't think that's fair either."

Cain's mouth dropped open in surprise. Then he seemed to get ahold of himself. "Okay, so what is it that you needed my help with?"

"Victoria." Patrick quickly explained about the missing toddlers and the belief that Samyaza was searching for Victoria.

"She can't be allowed to get her," Cain said.

"Unfortunately, that's easier said than done. We don't know who Victoria is or where she is. And with the number of children Samyaza's grabbed, it's clear she doesn't either. She needs a way to identify her as much as we do. And I can only think of one way to do that—the tome of the Great Mother."

Cain was quiet for a moment, and Patrick let him digest everything he'd been told. "You think she's going to go after the book."

"Yes."

"You're probably right. But there is another way to identify her."

Patrick frowned. "How?"

"*I* can identify her."

Patrick's mouth fell open. "I didn't even think of that. Does Samyaza know that?"

"I don't think so. My dealings with her—or him, depending on the lifetime—never involved discussions of Victoria."

"Then don't tell anyone," Patrick said quickly. "It will put you in danger, and I'd rather avoid that."

Cain watched him for a few seconds before nodding. "I will agree to that for the moment. But if it comes to a choice between my safety and Victoria's, I will choose hers."

"Understood," Patrick said. "Now, the tome. What can you tell me?"

"It exists, obviously." Cain paused. "You're certain Samyaza will go for it?"

"That's what we think. Besides, we have no other leads; she's covered her tracks too well. We're hoping we can either grab the book ourselves, or better yet, put a tracker on it and let it lead us to her."

"That's *not* a great plan."

Patrick gave a small laugh. "No, it's not. And we're still trying to come up with another option. But right now it's the best we've got."

Cain was quiet for a moment. "The tome—it was highly regarded in ancient times, long before history books were ever written. Lilith—she drew people to her. And soon, people began chronicling her life. Each generation would add to the book. Her followers would search the globe for traces of her after each of her deaths, trying to find where she would appear next. They rarely found her during her life, but every once in a while they would. And they would watch her grow and transform from an innocent child into the mother of all."

"There was a group that followed her?"

"They called themselves the followers of the Great Mother. For thousands of years, their duty was to follow her, chronicle her, spread the tales of her good deeds. In the fight between good and evil, they were a weapon. What we would call today a massive PR campaign. And for a while, the message spread. It flourished."

"The Divine Feminine and the Great Mother."

Cain nodded. "Eventually that's how she became known, as her message spread beyond the initial followers. The tales of her seeped into cultures across the globe. She became Cybele in Greece and Rome, Maia in Greece, Yum Chenmo a Tibetan deity, and host of other mother goddesses."

"What happened to her followers?" Patrick asked.

"They were destroyed."

"By Samyaza?"

Cain shook his head. "No—by man. The same forces that argued a woman could not be the true way to understanding tamped down any voices that called for the Great Mother."

"And the books on the Great Mother?"

"There were six copies. Most were destroyed. The last two copies were held at the Imperial Library of Constantinople."

The Imperial Library of Constantinople was one of the last great libraries of the ancient world. It had been created by the son of Constantine in the fourth century AD, and was responsible for transferring many ancient texts from papyrus before the original parchment they were written on disintegrated. They saved many texts—at least until the Ottoman Empire destroyed the library in 1453.

Patrick's spirits dropped. "So, then. They are lost."

Cain shook his head. "No. Two were secreted away by the followers of the Great Mother."

"Where?"

"The rumors spread for years. Different places, different times. But I went in search."

"You did? Why?"

Cain was quiet for a moment. "Lilith—she is my home. She is the one being in all the world who knows me from the beginning. She is my constant. We have fought throughout time, but I loved her. I love her still. I mourn her loss every day. And I could not abide the idea of her history being lost for all time."

"All that you put us through when you knew she was going to sacrifice herself—you were frantic because you knew it meant losing her again."

Cain looked away, his chin wobbling, and he let out a breath. "It meant I was alone again. And there was no guarantee I would find her in the next lifetime. It could be centuries before I saw her again."

Patrick sat back, taking a good long look at the immortal in front of him. He had been through so much, but at his heart he, like everyone else, just wanted a place where he belonged. Victoria had been that place. "I can understand that."

Cain's head turned toward him, inspecting him. "I think you can. Laney is your home. And now you're adrift too."

Patrick felt the truth of his words. All his doubts about everything were because his foundation had been ripped out from underneath him. Laney *was* his home. It didn't matter where they were, or where they lived: they were family. And without her, without knowing if she was hurt, or alive or dead, he couldn't function the way he used to. Because nothing was like it used to be. "Yes."

"Lilith and her daughter are amazing women who inspire fierce love and loyalty in those they care about."

"And fierce hate in those they go against."

"That is true as well." Cain let out a breath. "Now, I think we've gotten off the topic. You were asking about the book. Rumor has it one copy is held in the Vatican archives."

Patrick's shoulders slumped. The Vatican archives were believed to hold everything from the petition to annul King Henry the VIII's marriage to Catherine of Aragon to the transcripts from the trial of Galileo; from the final message from the Mother of God to the three children in Fatima in 1917, to every other mystery attached to the Catholic Church. The archives covered an astounding fifty miles beneath Rome.

The archives were created in 1621 and remained closed to the public until 1881. At that point, Pope Leo XIII began to allow select Catholic scholars in. And even then, scholars were only allowed to examine the specific files they were interested in; there was, sadly, no browsing. There was also a bit of a catch-22—you must request a specific file in order to see it, but in order to do that, you had to know the file existed. And there was no table of contents.

And in any case, they were certainly not going to let Patrick, a priest currently on suspension, into their sacred holdings.

"You said there were two copies," Patrick said.

Cain nodded. "The second could have been destroyed by the elements or time. It's been hundreds of years since anyone has mentioned it."

"Where is it?"

"A group of women took it, protected it, and brought it to the New World."

Patrick sat back in shock. "The New World? It's in America?"

"Yes. I believe it may still be here, although forces did almost uncover it. But the women, they would not reveal its location. They died rather than reveal it."

"So there's a chance?"

"To the best of my knowledge, yes."

"Where?"

Cain's gaze met Patrick's. "Salem, Massachusetts."

CHAPTER 52

Jake put down the phone and stared off into space. *Salem, Massachusetts? Seriously?*

Shaking his head, he strode down the hall. He knew about the witch trials, of course. Everyone knew about the witch trials: between 1692 and 1693, over a dozen women had been unjustly accused of being a witch in Salem. Those accused were hanged, drowned, even burned, all on the hysteria built from a preacher.

But if the tome of the Great Mother was there, as Cain said, did that mean there was more to the story? Were the accused women the last of the Great Mother's followers? And who, then, wiped them out?

Jake's money was on the Council.

The Council had been around since the time of the Inquisition. They had chased down artifacts from Atlantis and Lemuria, using them to build their bank accounts and the power of those within the Council's membership. Had they gone after the tome?

The Great Mother… Jake knew very little about the religious or spiritual aspects of Laney's mother. In Egypt, she had brought him back to life through her blood. And in China, she had sacrificed herself to keep the Fallen from gaining immortality. Those were just two examples of the power hidden within the woman. What might the tome hint at?

It wasn't her power that drove him to find her—nor the fact that she was Delaney and Henry's mother. Nor even the fact that she had saved his life in Egypt. No—he wanted to help her because she was a child in danger. And these bastards had put dozens of other children in jeopardy because of her.

A picture of Mary Jane McAdams floated through his head. Mary Jane was strong. She would hold the family together. But how much more could that family take? And what if Susie wasn't returned to them? How would they survive that? How could anyone?

He called Jordan and had him get a strike team together. They discussed details for a half hour, then Jake made another few calls. They would leave in two hours.

His phone rang, and he answered it without looking at the screen. "Yeah?"

"Um, Mr. Rogan? Jake?"

Jake glanced at the screen, not recognizing the voice. "Mary Jane?"

"Yes. I know you said you'd call if there was anything, and I know it's too soon, but I just—" She sighed. "I'm sorry. I'm sure you're in the middle of something."

Jake pulled out a seat and sat down. "No. I've got time. But no, we don't have any leads that specifically lead to Susie. We did learn about something that might help us, and I'm going to run that down. Hopefully, I'll have something by tomorrow."

"That's great. I should let you—"

Jake cut her off. "You okay?"

"I'm good. You know how it is."

And Jake did. Mary Jane was shoving all her feelings aside to focus on her family, to be strong for them. But who was strong for her?

"Mary Jane, it's okay to admit you're scared."

She was silent for a moment. Finally she spoke, her voice filled with emotion. "No, it's not. Everyone here looks to me. I'm the last barrier against us all sinking into an abyss. I cannot bend. I cannot break. I stand tall so everyone around me can collapse. *That's* my job. And I will stand until Susie is back. She is my heart."

"I'm not looking to you for that. You can tell me."

"No—thank you. If I open these floodgates, I'll never be able to close them again."

The silence stretched between them. Jake knew he should get off the phone—there were still some details to handle—but instead he scrambled for something to say. "Then tell me about Susie. What's she like?"

He could hear the smile in Mary Jane's voice, along with the tears. "She lights up a room."

Mary Jane and Jake spoke for an hour, and during that time, Jake let himself forget his fear for Victoria, his fear for Laney, his fear for all the children caught up in this mess. He just listened to the love in Mary Jane's voice as she spoke about her youngest child.

A knock sounded on the door, and Jordan peeked his head in. "Jake, we need you."

Jake nodded. *Be there in a minute*, he mouthed.

"Oh," Mary Jane said. "You have to go. I've talked your ear off. I am so sorry."

"You have nothing to apologize for. You have an amazing family."

"Yeah, as much as they make me crazy some days, I wouldn't trade them for anything." She paused. "Thank you, Jake."

"Take care, Mary Jane."

"You too."

Jake disconnected the call and sat back, the phone resting against his chin. It was strange. He needed to move. They were waiting on him. But he let himself sit for another moment and enjoy the peace, the family he'd felt in that one phone call. How strange that one phone call could have such an effect.

Finally, though, he stood. The love Mary Jane felt for her family was a tangible thing, and Jake promised himself he would do everything in his power to bring her little girl back to her.

Time to get to work.

CHAPTER 53

Patrick disconnected the call after speaking with Jake, his mind whirling. He'd spent some time researching the Salem witch trials, but that had been years ago. To him, they had seemed to be a perfect example of religious hysteria run amok.

He retook his seat next to Cain's bed. "So the women accused of witchcraft, they were followers of the Great Mother?"

"Most of them. Not all. And some men were also accused of witchcraft, too."

"I don't get how they managed to land in the New World. And why."

Cain sighed. "The Great Mother's followers were loyal. They were dedicated to her. And it wasn't just her they followed, but her views as well. They were believers in the equality of all people, in the need to treat the lowest members of our society no different than the highest. Compassion and love were their ruling motivations. Those were the Great Mother's beliefs, and they held on to them even as the world turned away from those beliefs."

Though nowadays those views might not seem controversial, Patrick knew that for hundreds, if not thousands, of years they had been. It wasn't until the late seventeenth and early eighteenth century that man began to question whether biology was destiny. With the dawning of the Enlightenment, it began to be understood that through logic, rationality, and education, man could raise himself above the station in life he had been born into.

Cain continued. "The followers… at times they stood out. Not just because of their beliefs, but because as women, they were supposed to be subservient to their husbands, their fathers. They weren't. And they were hunted."

"By whom?" Patrick asked.

"At first the Fallen, but then they tried to hide their ways. That's when the Council began to track them. The Council were organized. Their searches lasted generations. At one point, they even teamed up with the Fallen, working under the guise of the Inquisition."

Patrick shook his head. "That's a dark stain on the church's history."

Cain nodded. "The last time the followers were recorded performing their ritual was in Madrid. The Council broke into their meeting place. But they weren't alone. They were working under the guidance of Samyaza."

"Were the followers killed?"

"No. They were prepared. They all escaped, save one: their leader, Marguerite. She was taken. Samyaza himself interrogated her for days. But she never revealed where the rest had escaped to, and for almost two hundred years, there was no sign of them. I had begun to think that perhaps they had been killed off. Then I heard about the witch trials in England."

Patrick was familiar with that piece of English history. Prior to the witch trials in Salem, similar trials had occurred across the pond. Demonology had taken hold of society at that point; when people committed criminal acts, it was attributed to the demon residing within them. And the punishment involved removing that demon, often painfully.

As in Salem, the witch trials in England focused on women. Women weren't equals in society at that time, so it had always seemed odd to Patrick that they had been the target.

"When I heard about the trials, I recognized the signs of a search for the Great Mother's followers," Cain said.

"Are you sure the Council was behind it?"

Cain nodded. "Matthew Hopkins, who led the charge in England, was a member of the Council, as were some of the other names associated with the witch trials. Hopkins had nineteen people hanged in one day for witchcraft. And he got paid by the towns for rooting out their witches. But really, he was looking for the followers. When I heard about the number of 'witches' he had found and killed, I knew that the followers had survived.

"Fortunately, by the time the witch trials began, most of the members had moved on to the New World, where they had become the antithesis—at least in public—of the followers. They had become Puritans."

The Puritans, Patrick knew, were a religious sect that broke away from the English Protestant church. They believed the Protestant church hadn't done enough to regulate the abuse of the church and its members. They called for a stricter interpretation of the Bible and supported a severely restricted set of behaviors for its members, particularly with regard to sex and pleasure.

Patrick frowned. "If I'm remembering correctly, the key figure in the beginning of the Salem witch trials was Reverend Samuel Parris. Was he a Council member?"

Cain shook his head. "No, not from what I could tell. I think he was a true believer, and the Council manipulated him into believing that witchcraft was the reason for his daughters' fits."

"Why do you think the fits occurred?"

"Parrish was a greedy, self-important, strict man. I have no doubt that his strictness crossed over into abuse. Then again, perhaps his daughters were simply acting out. And instead of being punished, they were rewarded. They received attention. Their father listened to them. "

"And all they had to do was point the finger at three other women."

"The three women first charged were viewed by the town of Salem as women of no consequence: Sarah Good, Sarah Osborne, and Tituba. A destitute woman, an ill woman who had not attended church in years, and a slave."

"But it didn't stop with them."

"No, it continued. And I believe that by accident, Parrish actually stumbled across one of the followers with that first set of accusations."

"Which one?"

"Sarah Good."

Patrick sat for a moment, reviewing in his mind what he knew of the woman. She had been raised by a wealthy father who had given his daughter a sizeable dowry. But when she married, her husband blew through the dowry, and after his death, she was left with debt and multiple children. She remarried to a good man, but they weren't able to make ends meet, and she was reduced to begging—and was reported to be rather unpleasant to the people who did not provide to her.

But now Patrick looked at Sarah a little differently. She had been hanged as a witch. Perhaps, once that happened, her personality had been retroactively reimagined to fit that designation, to make her death more palatable. After all, she was described as an old hag with white hair and a stooped frame, yet at the time of the trials she was pregnant, suggesting she was much younger than the "old hag" description indicated.

But why would Cain think she was a follower?

Then it came to him. "At her death, as the undertaker was about to hang her, she said the judge would die if he went through with this."

"She said he would die choking on his own blood. Years later, the judge did indeed die from internal bleeding, choking on his own blood."

"She had the sight."

"Many of the followers did."

"Then why didn't they see it coming?"

"I think they did. I think they took steps to make sure that when it came, the book was protected. The Great Mother's legacy was protected. After all, that was their sacred duty."

"At the cost of their lives?"

"Would you turn your back on what you believed if your life was threatened?"

Patrick thought about the church and how they were asking him to denounce Laney. He would never do that. He never could—not even if his life were at stake. "But they could have run."

"Where? The New World was in its infancy. Travel was difficult; the terrain was unknown. If they had run, they faced an uncertain future. If they stayed, they knew what they would face. Which meant they could prepare."

"Over two hundred were accused. Nineteen were killed—none of them witches."

Cain nodded. "Yes. But I believe that through all of that, the followers protected the book. The tome made it to the New World. They would have *made sure* it was protected."

"Sarah Good. She was the first one accused of witchcraft, and the first one hanged. Do you think they buried it with her?"

"They were brave women. Publicly, no one ever knew their connection to the Great Mother. They died to protect her legacy. You'll find the tome with one of them. But my money is on Rebecca Nurse. She was the oldest woman killed, and the most likely leader."

"How old was she?"

"Seventy-one."

Patrick started. "I had no idea they killed an old woman."

"Age was irrelevant. It was the accusation that mattered."

"The accusation," Patrick murmured, thinking of how all of Laney's actions had been twisted against her. "It seems time hasn't changed much."

Cain nodded, closing his eyes.

Patrick stood. "You get some sleep. I'll see what I can find on the witch trials and send it to Jake. Perhaps I can give them a good place to start."

Cain's voice was tired. "The Nurse farm was preserved. It will be their best bet."

"Sleep. I'll take care of it."

Patrick patted Cain's leg through the covers before heading out of the room to research a group of women unfairly maligned and killed by a public scared of their alleged abilities.

He prayed the same fate was not awaiting Laney.

CHAPTER 54

It was only a four-man team going to Salem: Henry, Jake, Jen, and Jordan. No one knew they were looking for the book, and Salem was a quiet city of less than 42,000 in Essex County, Massachusetts.

The Nurse farm sat outside the main city of Salem. It had shrunk from its original size of three hundred acres to only twenty-five acres now, but the family cemetery remained. Cain believed the tome had been buried with the alleged leader of the followers, Rebecca Nurse.

Patrick had sent over some notes on the layout, as well as a history of the Nurse family. At the time of the trials, Rebecca Nurse was well regarded in her town. In fact, her conviction was viewed as a pivotal point in the witch trials, making people question their legitimacy. Most scholars believed that her accusers, all members of the Putnam family or their friends, accused her to get part of the Nurses' large farm. It shared a border with the Putnams' and legal skirmishes had been going on between the two families for years. In fact, the Putnam family had been behind many of the accusations, starting with Sarah Osbourne.

Jake stared down at the quiet town of Salem as they flew over. In a six-month period, over one hundred men and women were accused of witchcraft here. Nineteen were hanged. The last one to die was Ann Foster, who after being convicted died in prison in December 1692.

"We're coming up on the Nurse farm," Jordan said through the headset.

Rebecca Nurse, age seventy-one and mother of eight, was convicted and executed in July of 1692. She had actually been found not guilty at trial, but her accusers had fits in the court after the verdict was read, and the verdict was changed—in part because Rebecca failed to answer a question directed to her by the judge. Of course, Rebecca was also partly deaf, which was why she failed to answer.

She was hanged on Gallows Hill, along with four other women. The bodies were buried in shallow graves at the site. But late at night, Benjamin Nurse made his way to Gallows Hill, gathered his mother's body, and brought it back to the family farm for burial.

If Patrick and Cain were right, the tome of the Great Mother was buried with her as well. The "witches" were the last of the followers of the Great Mother. Which made Jake wonder what exactly had been behind the Salem witch trials. He knew there had been witch hunts in England prior to the hunts in the New World. But had they all just been a cover? A way to hide the search for the followers? Had the women fled to the New World, hoping the distance would keep them safe?

If that had been their hope, it had been a false one.

"Nurse farm is just ahead," Jordan said. Jake glanced down. A few lights broke up the darkness, but it was late at night. No one should be around. They should be in and out in less than an hour, depending on how long it took them to dig up the grave.

The idea made him shiver. He didn't like disturbing the resting place of the poor woman. She'd been through enough. But there was no avoiding it.

The chopper began its descent into the field beyond the Nurse farmhouse.

In and out, one hour.

CHAPTER 55

The exhumation did not go as planned. Rebecca's grave was easy to find—a giant tombstone had been erected in 1885 to mark the spot. But the ground was hard due to the colder nights, and digging through it had taken some time. Finally, though, they reached the wooden coffin. When Jake pulled on the lid, it disintegrated in his hands.

Jen then carefully searched through the grave. After thirty minutes of tense silence, she looked up. "It's not here."

"What? Are you sure?" Jake shone his flashlight over the remains, as if the book was going to magically appear.

"Jake, I've searched this whole area. There's nothing. It's just Rebecca Nurse in here."

"Is it possible the book decomposed? Buried in the earth, exposed like that?" Jordan asked.

Henry offered Jen an arm and pulled her out. Jen wiped the dirt from her hands on her pants. "It depends on what it was made out of. But I have to think if it was as old as they say, it wouldn't be made of something that would be easily destroyed. And the women guarding it would have gone to great lengths to protect it. It should be here."

"So now what? We're sure it's not in the memorial?" Jordan asked, nodding to the tall stone that stood higher than any of the other memorials in the family's cemetery.

Henry shook his head. "That thing is solid. Besides, it was only erected in 1885, 193 years after Rebecca Nurse's death."

"And I already checked it to make sure there weren't any hidden compartments. There's nothing. It's exactly what it appears to be—a solid grave marker," Jen said.

Jake pulled out his phone and dialed. Patrick's voice was sleepy when he answered. "Hello?"

"The book's not in Nurse's grave," Jake said.

"What? Hold on." Jake could hear Patrick moving, then waking Cain. He heard low voices before Patrick's voice came back on the line. "Cain says the book was with the women in Salem. It should be with Nurse's grave. She was their leader."

"Okay. But even if she was the leader, it could have been buried with any of them, right?"

"Yes, that's possible," Patrick admitted.

Jake closed his eyes, frustration rolling through him. They didn't have time to dig up nineteen graves. Dawn was only a few hours away, and once the disturbance at these graves was found, he was pretty sure their chances of getting to the other graves would be next to impossible. Besides, some of the witches had been buried where they fell, and no one knew where their bodies were.

"Jake, it's possible that another one of the executed was buried near Nurse's grave. Look around. See if any of the dates were the same," Patrick said.

"Spread out," Jake ordered. "Check dates. See if any of them line up with the witch trials."

Jake started at the graves nearest him. None of the dates aligned with 1692.

"Over here," Henry called.

The other three hurried over. Henry's flashlight illuminated a grave with what looked like angel wings engraved on it. "That tombstone looks newer," Jen said.

"I know. But look at the date," Henry said.

"Patrick, we've got a George Jacobs here who died in 1692," Jake said. "The inscription on the bottom of the tomb says, 'Burn me or hang me, I will stand in the truth of Christ.'"

"Yes, yes!" Patrick exclaimed. "He was seventy and was found guilty after being accused by his granddaughter Margaret."

"His granddaughter?" Jordan exclaimed. "That's cold."

"Accusing someone else was the only way to avoid being killed yourself. Hold on a sec."

Jake could hear Patrick rustling, no doubt scrounging through a book.

"Ah, here we go. According to this, Jacobs was killed on Gallows Hill and buried on his family's farm. But the farm was sold to developers in 1992. At that point, his remains were moved to the Nurse farm and given a new tombstone in the style of the old one."

"Why was it moved here?" Jake asked.

"It doesn't say. I suppose since there were so few graves from the victims of the trials, it made sense to bury him there."

"Thanks, Patrick. I'll let you know if we find anything." Jake nodded to the grave as he disconnected the call. "Let's dig him up."

Jen and Henry broke the ground while Jordan and Jake went back to Rebecca's grave and started refilling it. They worked in silence for a few minutes before Jordan spoke.

"If his remains were moved, even if the book was buried with him, wouldn't someone have removed it?"

Jake shook his head, even though he had the same worry. "I don't know. Let's hope they just left him be."

"We've got something," Henry called.

Jake looked at Jordan, who waved him away. "I'll finish this. Go."

Jake walked over to the other grave. "What have you got?" He looked down into the hole, which was illuminated by Henry's and Jen's flashlights. "Oh, shit."

They had reburied Jacobs in a new coffin.

"My thoughts exactly." Jen straddled the grave, looking at the obviously newer coffin. She moved to one side, leaned down and lifted the lid. "That's better."

Whoever had re-buried Jacobs had apparently just placed the old coffin right into the new one. *Now let's just hope they didn't take anything out of it.*

Crouching down, Jen gently peeled back the old coffin lid. It was in slightly better shape than Nurse's had been. Jake held his breath as Jen searched.

"Might have something here," she said.

Jake and Henry leaned forward.

"It's here," Jen called out excitedly. She stood up with an object wrapped in leather in her arms. Still straddling the grave, she carefully pulled the fabric back to reveal an ivory box. Jake could see figures engraved on the box, but in the dim light he couldn't make them out.

Jen opened the box and shined her flashlight inside—on a book with an old brown cover.

Jake let out a relieved breath. *Yes.*

Jen closed the lid, and Henry reached down to help Jen out.

Just then, Jordan let out a muffled cry.

Jake turned around. "Jordan? You okay?"

Jordan didn't answer. Then Jake caught sight of him lying on the ground. "Jordan!" He took a step forward and felt a pinch in his neck. He slapped at his neck, expecting a bug, but his hand instead came away with a small dart. "What the—"

He dropped to his knees, his legs giving out, his vision narrowing. Jen and Henry collapsed behind him.

Six men slipped out of the shadows. They ignored him and Jordan as they shot more darts into Henry and Jen. Jake struggled to move, to yell, but he couldn't.

One of the men broke away from the others. He walked smoothly toward Jen and Henry. Jake narrowed his eyes as Jen's flashlight illuminated him. Gerard Thompson. What the hell was *he* doing here? The last they'd heard, he'd broken ranks with Samyaza.

Gerard pulled the box from Jen's hands. "Thank you very much." He patted Jen on the cheek as she glared at him.

One of the men called out, "You want us to finish them?"

Gerard looked around and shook his head. "No need. They're no threat. Not anymore. Let's go."

He turned and faded back into the shadows, his men following him.

And Jake could do nothing but watch him go, knowing that Gerard's words were correct. They were no threat. Not to anyone.

CHAPTER 56

Jordan was the first to be able to move. Jake managed to turn his head to see Jordan stumbling toward him, but that was all the movement he could manage.

Jordan fell to the ground next to Jake. "You okay?"

"Yeah." Jake wiggled his fingers. "Drug's wearing off. Check the other two."

As Jordan moved over to Jen and Henry, the feeling returned to Jake's hands and legs. With a great deal of effort, he managed to get himself to his knees. He thought briefly about giving chase, but he knew it would be useless. Gerard and his men had a head start, it was dark, and he could barely walk. Besides, it had been fifteen minutes, at least. They were no doubt long gone.

He got to his feet, his head spinning. Jordan had helped Jen sit up, and Henry was just pushing himself up. "You guys okay?" Jake asked.

"No. I'm pissed," Jen said.

"Join the club," Jake muttered.

"Why didn't they kill us? Why leave us alive?" Jordan asked.

"Because they didn't need to kill us," Jake said. "I'm going to check the chopper."

He walked as quickly as he could manage away from the group. Anger was crawling inside him, and he didn't want to unleash it on them. He'd been stupid. He'd thought Samyaza had no idea what they were up to—that she was ignoring them. But she wasn't. She was just waiting until they did something she was interested in.

The chopper looked unharmed. He managed a slow jog and opened the cockpit door. He stopped short. The console had been destroyed. Wires hung limply, and the stick sat on the pilot's seat.

Jake gripped the door, anger overcoming him, and slammed it shut. "Goddammit!" He paced, trying to control his anger, but he was having trouble. He was better than this. He should have brought a bigger group. He should have set up a defensive perimeter. He should have remembered whom exactly they were going up against.

"Hey."

Jake turned around and saw Jen approaching.

"The chopper's toast," Jake said.

"Yeah, we figured that when we heard your yell. Henry's arranging for another chopper, and Jordan's scoping around to see if he can find their trail."

"He won't."

"I know. But he needs to do something."

Jake just stared up at the sky. They had failed. They had failed spectacularly. But how had Samyaza known exactly where they were?

Without a word, he turned toward the chopper. He grabbed the giant flashlight from the back and ran it over the outside of the bird, examining each spot the beam touched carefully.

"Jake?" Jen asked.

Jake didn't say anything as the beam highlighted a small dark object attached beneath the bird. He ripped it off. *A tracker.*

"Is that what I think it is?" Jen said.

"Yeah. They knew exactly where we were going, because they were tracking us."

"When's the last time the chopper was swept for bugs?"

"I have them checked every morning, the same time the rest of the estate is checked."

"But that means…" Jen went silent, horror dawning in her eyes.

"Someone on the estate placed this here. We have a mole."

CHAPTER 57

BALTIMORE, MARYLAND

The dream held on to Noriko and wouldn't let her escape.

She ran through the mist. "Where are you? Where are you?" she called, but there was no answer.

She felt the presence of someone else. Her head whipped from side to side, her heart pounding as she tried to find them.

She backed up, her whole body shaking. "Where are you?"

She heard the child's cry again. She turned and slammed into a body. Her head jerked up, and her gaze met a pair of cool blue eyes.

"Noriko!"

Noriko sat up with a cry, and Lou fell back. Their room was still dark, although through the window Noriko could see the first rays of dawn breaking along the horizon. She pushed the blankets off of herself and threw her legs over the side of the bed. Bending at the waist, she took several deep breaths.

Lou sat down next to her and rubbed her back. "Hey, hey. It's okay. It was just a dream." She paused. "Wasn't it?"

Noriko shook her head. "I don't know. I was in the mist. I

couldn't see anything. I think I was looking for the kids, but I couldn't find them. And then I ran into a man."

"Did you know him?"

"I don't think so." She struggled to remember his face, but it was like a picture out of focus. All she could remember were a pair of blue eyes.

A knock sounded at their bedroom door. Lou turned to the clock. "It's not even six yet."

Noriko turned on the light on her bedside table as Lou opened the door.

Yoni stepped in. "Hey. Sorry to wake you guys."

"Actually we were already awake," Lou said. "What's up?"

"I just got a call from the preserve. Something's happened with the cats. They were hoping maybe Noriko would be able to come over."

"What's happening?" Noriko's concern about the dream receded, replaced by concern for the leopards.

"Not sure. John said the cats were all worked up. They checked the perimeter and didn't see anything that would cause it. They thought maybe you could come and figure out what's bothering them."

"Of course. Just let me get changed."

"We'll meet you downstairs in a few minutes," Lou said.

Ten minutes later, they were driving off the grounds of the school with Yoni behind the wheel. No one said anything during the twenty-minute ride. But as they grew closer, Lou frowned. She rolled down her window.

"What is that?"

The night air wafted into the car, but Noriko didn't hear anything out of the ordinary until a few minutes later. Then her eyes grew wide. "That's the cats."

The cats were screaming and howling into the night.

"Good God," Yoni muttered. "What's wrong with them?"

"I don't know." Noriko tilted her head. "They're—happy."

"Happy?" Lou asked. "That doesn't sound happy."

"But it is."

Yoni pulled to a stop at the first gate, and the guard opened it. After the gate closed behind them, the second gate opened. Noriko was out of the car before Yoni had time to stop.

"Noriko!" he yelled.

But Noriko ignored him as Cleo raced toward her. *What's happened?*

Cleo skidded to a stop in front of her. Noriko could feel the excitement coming off of her. *She's awake.*

CHAPTER 58

The chopper ride back to the estate was silent. And it was not a companionable silence; it was tense, filled with anxiety. Someone on the estate was working against them. Jake stared out the window, his fists tight.

As soon as they landed, he headed for the security office. Heads were going to roll. He spent the rest of the morning reviewing tapes, demanding answers, and generally scaring the hell out of everybody.

At lunch, Jen stepped into his office. "You okay?"

Jake thought for a moment about giving her a reasoned response. But these last few months, he and Jen had become good friends, and he knew she wouldn't let him get away with anything but pure honesty. And besides, he was too ticked off for reasonable. "Okay? How the hell am I supposed to be okay? One of our people is working for Samyaza. One of our people is working against *us*."

Jen opened her mouth, then shook her head. "I don't know, Jake." Silence fell between them.

The helplessness he'd felt last night as Gerard had waltzed in and taken the book played through his mind again. "We led Elisabeta right to it. She wouldn't have been able to separate the kids without it. We gave her what she needs!"

"I know that!" Jen yelled. "But you acting like an ass doesn't help us figure out what to do."

"Yeah, I know!" Jake huffed out a breath. "I know that. I just, I don't know what to do. Nothing's been right since Laney left." The words had escaped his lips before he could stop them.

Jen's voice was equally somber when she answered him. "No, it hasn't."

"God, I feel like we're just stumbling around in the dark." He closed his eyes, picturing Laney. He loved her. He always would. But that love had shifted from passion to loyalty. She was right: he couldn't give her what she wanted. He wanted to be someone's hero, but Laney didn't need a hero. She *was* one. Still, that didn't change his need to find her, to see her safe. They were family. All of them.

And Jake had been unable to find her, unable to bring her home. So he had turned his attention to the kids. And now he felt like he was failing at that, too.

"I'll check back later, okay?"

"Yeah, sure." Jake turned back to the stack of notes on his desk with a sigh.

A few minutes later Jordan interrupted him, his face serious. "Jake."

Jake tried not to sigh. "What is it?"

"We found the mole."

"Who?"

"His name's David Keller. He was just hired four months ago on the maintenance staff."

Jake stood. "Let's see what he has to—"

Jordan put up a hand. " He doesn't have anything to say. He's dead."

Jake sank back in his chair. "How?"

"It was made to look like a suicide. He left a note. But I think it was staged."

"Any idea why he would rat us out?"

"He's got debts—lots of them. He's been receiving five-thousand-dollar payments every two weeks for the last two months."

"Money—of course." *And then once Samyaza was done with him, she took care of him.*

"Some of our guys are going through his online life. Looks like he was big into online gambling. I'll let you know if they find anything else."

"Yeah, okay."

As Jordan disappeared back down the hall, Jake's phone rang. He felt like ignoring it. No, actually he felt like stomping the thing into the ground. He pulled it out and frowned at the name on the screen. "Lou?"

"Hold on, Jake. Noriko needs to talk to you."

"Lou, it's not really—"

But Lou was gone, and Noriko's quiet voice spoke. "Hello?"

Jake reined in his frustration. Noriko was a sweet girl and very timid. She didn't deserve to be on the receiving end of his misery. "Hey, Noriko. It's not really a good time."

"I know. They have the book."

"How do you—" He shook his head. *Right, psychic.* "Yes. So now we need to—"

"Cleo called to me. I'm at the preserve."

Jake frowned. "Cleo? What are you talking about?"

"She told me Laney's awake. She's awake, Jake. And she's coming back."

CHAPTER 59

HALFWAY BETWEEN PRUDHOE BAY AND BARROW, ALASKA

Laney sat on the couch in the cabin. Maddox and Max had left almost two hours ago, and she had spent that time looking at news coverage from the last six months. Blowing out a breath, she pushed the laptop off her lap.

Henry's company, which he had spent his adult life creating, was under siege. It seemed like every step they made was noted and documented by the media and law enforcement. Somehow, all of Henry's good works were being cast as suspicious activity. *Just like all of my activities.*

The search for her hadn't waned any, although the priestess's attack on the agents at the SIA facility had at least given some journalists pause. But the warrants for her arrest remained, both in the United States and abroad.

Laney's gaze shifted to a picture on the monitor of Henry, Jake, and Jen walking out of the Chandler School. In the corner of the shot were Danny, Lou, and Rolly. God, she missed all of them. It felt like a lifetime since she'd seen them—and in a way, she supposed it actually was.

She put the laptop on the coffee table next to the TV remote. It looked so alien. It had been four hours since she'd woken up, and the "modern" world still felt out of place.

She looked up as Drake entered the living room, his hair still damp from his shower. She tried *not* to imagine him in the shower. He was by far the most jarring part of this current life. Waking up and recognizing him had shocked her to her core. But luckily, Max and Maddox's arrival had kept them from having to talk about it—yet.

"I was thinking of making something to eat. Are you hungry?" Drake asked.

"Actually, yeah." She paused. "I don't suppose there's a pizza place nearby."

"I could make pizza happen. But I think maybe we should talk first."

Laney tucked her feet underneath her. "Okay. What do you want to talk about?"

Drake took a seat on the other side of the couch. "Oh, I don't know. How about the weather? It's been unseasonably warm."

"Global warming."

"Most likely. You humans sure *are* making a mess of this planet."

"Hey, I recycle."

"Oh, well then, no worries. The planet is saved. "

They exchanged a smile before Laney looked away.

"Well, now that that's out of the way, you seem uncomfortable around me."

Laney looked into his eyes, not sure what to say. She decided to go with blunt honesty. "I don't know how to react to you. I met you as Drake. But now I know you differently."

"Intimately," he said.

Laney felt her cheeks flush. "Yes. And I'm not sure how to deal with that. When we met in Vegas, you acted as if we had never met before."

"It was startling to see you again. I guess I felt like you feel now. I wasn't sure what to say, especially seeing as you didn't know me. All you saw was the flashy Las Vegas entertainer."

"Why didn't you tell me?"

He watched her for a long moment, refusing to let her look away. "What should I have said? That at one point we had been each other's entire world? That I had lived just for you? That you and I were each other's reason to breathe? How would that have gone over?"

Laney looked away. His words had been spoken as questions, and yet the sound of them, the meaning behind them, pulled at her. "You died protecting me."

"I did. I don't regret that. But I'm not that man anymore. And you're not that woman. And according to Max, we have more important matters to focus on." His words were good, but he couldn't seem to drop her gaze, and she couldn't seem to look away from him either.

"Right. Victoria," Laney said.

Drake finally broke eye contact and stood. "I will take care of the pizza if you take care of our next steps. But be warned: everyone from your life is under surveillance. If you stick your head out, the world will know. And most of that world would like to see that head on a platter."

Laney nodded, pulling back her thoughts from her and Drake and focusing on what Max had told her: *Life's changing, Laney. You have two paths, and you need to take both of them. But you can't. You have to choose.*

She knew exactly what he meant. She had to choose between Victoria and finding the Omni, the weapon that could make anyone a Fallen or strip any Fallen of their powers. With that weapon, she could defeat Samyaza. And if that weapon fell into Samyaza's hands, the darkness would win.

But even knowing all that, the choice was easy. Victoria came first.

She picked up her computer. *And I know someone who can help me find her.*

CHAPTER 60

BEVERLY HILLS, CALIFORNIA

Elisabeta stood on the balcony of her estate in Beverly Hills. From here she could see the eternity pool and the fountains that dotted her twenty-acre estate. No expense had been spared in reproducing her home in Venice here. But she ignored all of it, instead watching the chopper land on the east lawn.

Gerard's golden-crowned form was easy to pick out from the group that disembarked. And he had a confidence, a grace to his walk, that none of her other men could match.

He looked up and caught sight of her. She smiled. He always knew when he was being watched.

Gerard disappeared from view, and Elisabeta turned and leaned against the railing. *Soon. It will all be completed soon.*

A knock sounded at her door.

"Enter," she called, and Gerard strode in. He walked toward her, the book wrapped in fabric at his side. He held it out to her. "Samyaza."

She smiled as she took it, walked into her office, and placed it on her desk, which had already been cleared off. A thick, heavy, cotton sheet had been placed there in anticipation of this moment. "Has anyone looked at it?" she asked.

"No, Samyaza. As per your orders."

"Good." She unwrapped the heavy fabric protecting it, and when she saw the box, surprise filtered through her. It looked like the box that had once held the Omni. But no, the pictures on this box were different. They were peaceful scenes depicting humans, animals, and nature.

She scoffed. The followers had always been too optimistic for the real world.

She opened the box. A very old leather-bound book lay inside. It had no title, nothing to indicate its explosive contents.

She pulled it out and placed it gently on her desk, noting it had only a little wear at the edges. Even at a glance she could tell the pages were made from different materials—animal skin, papyrus, leather.

The book had survived. All these years, and somehow it had survived. It was a miracle. Humans might not be worth much, but every once in a while, one of them surprised her. *Nicely done, Marguerite.*

She pulled on a pair of cotton gloves and carefully opened the book. It was written in a language she hadn't seen since the time of Lemuria and Atlantis. A language long since forgotten by man. But Elisabeta didn't need to read the words to get what she wanted—for it wasn't the words she was interested in. She had eyes only for the sketches that adorned each page—sketches of the Great Mother in her various incarnations.

The Great Mother. Samyaza sneered. A woman with no power beyond memories. And right now, she was a helpless child just waiting to be identified.

Gerard moved closer. "It's beautiful."

She nodded, agreeing with him. Each page was a work of art. The script, long and flowing, was surrounded by pictures of extraordinary beauty. Flowers, buildings, mountains, animals—and of course, Victoria. On each page, her face stared back at Samyaza. Different ages, but the same face, no matter the time period.

She studied each depiction carefully, not sure what exactly she was looking for but knowing she would find it within these pages. Carefully she turned page after page, until she noticed a similarity. The page in front of her showed a picture of Victoria when she was a child, running around without clothes. Samyaza flipped back to a picture of Victoria as a twenty-year-old, wearing a long dress that draped over one shoulder. She flipped back once more, to a picture of Victoria in tunic. As she studied the drawings, her smile grew wider. "That's it."

"What's it?"

She turned to Gerard, feeling triumphant. "Look at these pictures. What do they have in common?" She turned the pages, giving him a chance to inspect each drawing. And she recognized the moment he saw it.

"The mark on her shoulder," he said. "It's a birthmark."

Samyaza smiled. "Each lifetime, she's born with the same mark. That's how we'll know who she is."

"You are brilliant."

Elisabeta's eyes roamed over the book. "Yes. I am."

"What are your orders?"

"Have all the children inspected. Find the one with the mark." She paused. "Actually, no. *I* will inspect them. I want to be the one who finds her."

"Of course, Samyaza." He paused. "And what will we do with the other children when we find Victoria?"

"They are not needed. Dispose of them."

"By dispose of them, you mean…"

Her voice was dry. "Kill them, Gerard. I assume you don't have a problem with that?"

"Of course not. I'll see to the arrangements. And I assume you wish us to leave immediately?"

She smiled. "Yes. We leave within the hour."

CHAPTER 61

BALTIMORE, MARYLAND

The gates to the Chandler estate opened in front of the SUV, and the guards waved Yoni and Noriko through.

Yoni waved his thanks before turning to Noriko. "Just two minutes more. How's she doing?"

Yoni had been giving her a running countdown of how long until they reached the main house. Noriko couldn't blame him. Cleo was pacing along the back of the Suburban, looking extremely agitated.

"She's good. She just needs to lose some energy."

"But Laney's still awake and coming back, right?"

Noriko smiled. "Yes. It hasn't changed."

Yoni grinned. Grins were something Noriko had seen on everybody's face after she told them about Cleo's statement. In fact, a new energy seemed to have infused the whole school. There had been a noticeable buzz when Yoni and Noriko dropped Lou back at the school. Lou had called the boys to let them know ahead of time, and they had all been waiting when Yoni pulled up.

Rolly pulled Noriko from the car and hugged her tight. "You are awesome!"

Noriko had laughed, but she had felt his excitement. Now Jake had asked for her and Cleo to come to the estate to tell everyone exactly what she had seen.

The main house came into view, and Cleo let out a roar. Yoni swerved. "Damn it, Cleo, not when I'm driving."

Cleo laid her head on Noriko's shoulder. *Sorry.*

"She says she's sorry. She's just excited."

"That's okay, buddy. We're all kind of excited today." Yoni pulled to a stop. "You guys hop out. I'll be up in a minute."

Noriko opened the door and stepped out. Cleo was right behind her. She gave a deep stretch on the drive as Yoni pulled away.

Noriko felt butterflies zip across her stomach. She'd never been here without Lou or Danny. It was making her a little nervous.

As if *he* was psychic, Danny appeared at the front door and jogged down the stairs toward her, Moxy at his side. "Hey. There you guys are." He rubbed Cleo's head. "Come on. I'll walk up with you."

Cleo stayed where she was. *Run.*

Noriko nodded as Cleo took off for the back of the estate. Moxy took off after her.

"Where's she going?" Danny asked.

"She needs to run. She's been hyped up since Laney woke up. She'll join us after she runs some energy off."

Noriko followed Danny into the foyer and up the circular staircase. When they reached the third floor, people streamed past them, rushing between rooms.

"What's going on?" Noriko asked.

"Henry's got people rearranging schedules and meetings as well as developing contingencies for wherever Laney pops up.

They want to be ready to move if she needs them. Come on." He led her into Henry's office.

Noriko had only been in the room once before. She liked it, especially the windows that looked over the back of the estate. There was no one by the windows now, so she walked over to them, and in the distance she saw a black shadow sprinting across the lawn. Even without the psychic bond, she'd be able to feel Cleo's excitement.

Noriko was a little more anxious than everybody else seemed to be. Laney had asked in her note that Noriko look after the cats while she was gone. Now that Laney was coming back, Noriko wasn't sure if she'd still be needed. When the idea of leaving Malama Island had first been mentioned to her, she'd been a little terrified at the prospect of facing the outside world. But now, months later, the idea of returning to Malama Island didn't hold the appeal it once did. It was still her home, but there was something about where she was right now that called to her as well.

I suppose that's an issue for another day.

She watched Cleo run laps for a few more minutes, with Moxy trailing behind her, before turning back to the room. Danny was sitting at the big conference table, his attention on the monitor in front of him. Not wanting to disturb him, she wandered around the room, reading book titles along the back wall. Eventually she made her way over to the table. The monitor two down from Danny was on, and she stared at the screen with a jolt. "Who's this?"

Danny looked up. "His name is Gerard. He's a Fallen. We thought he'd cut ties with Samyaza, but apparently we were mistaken. He led the team that intercepted our team in Salem."

Noriko frowned and tilted her head, her gaze not leaving the man's face. "That's not right," she whispered.

"What's not right?"

She pictured the eyes from her vision. They were the same. "I saw him—or at least I think it was him."

Danny came to stand next to her. "In a vision?"

"Or a dream. But I didn't get the sense that he was working against us. I thought he was a friend."

"No one's really sure what Gerard is. He helped Victoria and Max when Samyaza grabbed them, but he seems to have joined up again with the other side. Maybe your visions need to play a little catch-up."

"Maybe." But she couldn't get the blue eyes from her dream out of her mind—and she couldn't help shake the feeling that there was more to the man than they realized.

"Good. You're here," Henry said as he walked into the room, Jake with him.

"Hi, Noriko. Thanks for coming." Jake looked around with a frown. "Where's Cleo?"

"Um…" Noriko was still studying the man on the monitor, and she had to force herself to focus on the two men. "She's running. She'll be back in a little bit."

Henry gestured to the couches over by the bookshelves. "Why don't we all take a seat?"

Noriko sat down, and was glad when Danny sat next to her. Jake and Henry sat across from them.

"Okay," Jake said. "Now we need you to tell us exactly what Cleo said."

After taking a moment to collect her thoughts, Noriko recounted Cleo's words and feelings.

"Any idea where Laney is?" Henry asked.

Noriko shook her head. "No. I don't think Cleo knows either. But she's certain Laney is coming back."

"Did you have any sort of vision about Laney?"

Noriko's gaze darted to the monitor for a second before she shook her head. "I haven't seen anything about Laney."

Henry and Jake exchanged a glance. Henry turned back to Noriko. "I was hoping that perhaps you and Cleo could stay at the estate for a few days. Just in case Cleo says anything else."

"I—I guess I could."

"Lou, Rolly, and Zach are coming as well. Dom said you guys could stay with him."

Noriko smiled. She really liked the eccentric scientist. "Sure. That would be great."

"Good." Jake pulled out his phone. "And now I need you to tell Patrick everything you just told us. We haven't said anything to him yet. You okay with that?"

Noriko nodded. She knew how upset the priest had been at Laney's absence. And this was one piece of news she really didn't mind providing.

CHAPTER 62

BURLINGTON, VERMONT

Elisabeta stretched out her legs with a smile. The flight had been smooth so far; in fact, almost everything had gone as planned. The abduction of the children had spurred the Chandler Group to find the book for her. And now, within a few short hours, she would have Victoria.

And my immortality.

The children were being held at one of Elisabeta's estates. Elisabeta had picked the place up years ago through a shell company so it couldn't be traced back to her. She wanted the children physically isolated; she didn't want to take the chance of anyone spotting the children in passing. She'd had a crew clean the place up and prepare it for the children with cribs, high chairs, and all other essential child equipment.

She knew abducting the kids had been a risky move. If Laney returned, if the government—*any* government—caught wind of her involvement in Israel, everything would be in jeopardy. But a willingness to take great risks was an attribute of a great leader.

And for this particular prize, the risk was well worth it. Elisabeta had known that sooner or later, one of Victoria's brats would go looking for her—and Elisabeta could not chance them finding her first.

Because Elisabeta had plans—great plans. Victoria had stopped her once, and she was not going to let that happen again. Just this morning she had found the beginnings of another wrinkle. Time was marching on, and as powerful as she was, death was not something she could bend to her will or manipulate to her side.

"We'll be landing in ten minutes," the pilot called over the intercom.

Elisabeta looked up from her ruminations with a frown. She buckled her seat belt, her gaze shifting to where Gerard sat, his eyes closed. *Are you truly loyal to me?*

She had asked herself that same question ever since he had returned. She had to admit, his return had brought her, if not joy, satisfaction. Although she *had* expected him to return sooner.

Yet even though she wanted him back in the fold, she couldn't help but wonder about his motivations. Yes, he had said the past was in the past. And for her, that was true. But she had never truly understood why Gerard had chosen to live a simple life, a life without glory or wealth, to begin with. And seeing as how she could not understand it, she could not entirely trust that he had turned away from it—even if it *had* occurred lifetimes ago.

Hakeem was the only other occupant of the cabin. He sat sulking in the back row. He had been unhappy since Gerard had returned, no doubt because he had been pushed aside. But when it came to these two, well... there was no choice. It was like asking if someone wanted a perfectly cut diamond, or the coal that might eventually turn into one after a massive amount of pressure. Gerard was finesse and grace. Hakeem was brute strength, but also unquestioning loyalty.

The wheels touched down with a small bump, and Gerard's eyes popped open. He looked over at Elisabeta and smiled.

Elisabeta returned the smile. "I hope you're rested, because I have an important task for you."

He bowed his head. "Whatever you need, Samyaza."

"Indeed," she murmured with a quick glance at Hakeem. The large man stared stubbornly out the window.

Elisabeta looked back at Gerard, who was unbuckling his seatbelt. *And if you don't fulfill that task, well, then my blunt instrument will come in quite handy.*

CHAPTER 63

GALETON, PENNSYLVANIA

Patrick was in a daze as he ended the call with Noriko. *Laney's awake. She's coming back.*

"Patrick? Is everything all right?"

Cain stood at the edge of the kitchen, looking at Patrick with concern. Patrick was once again amazed at how quickly he was recovering. Only yesterday he had walked for the first time, and now he moved with only a little pain.

"That was Noriko. She said Laney's coming back."

Cain smiled. "Now *that* is good news. When?"

"We don't know yet. It was Cleo who told everyone." Patrick didn't understand the bond between Laney and Cleo, but he did know how strong it was. And Noriko was convinced of the accuracy of Cleo's words.

"You should go back. You should be there when she gets back. She'll want to see you."

"She'll want to see *both* of us. Let me see what I can work out. I'm not sure heading back to the Chandler estate is the best call.

The ETF has already been there, and they still have it under surveillance."

"But you could go back. I'll be fine."

Patrick shook his head. "No. We don't even know when she'll be back. When she returns, we'll find a way to see her. Until then, let's just focus on getting you all the way healed."

Patrick could see the relief on Cain's face. The immortal did not want to be left alone. "Well, how about a game of chess then? We haven't played in a long time."

Patrick smiled. "Sounds good. I saw a board in the back bedroom."

"I'll get it," Cain said. He headed down the hall.

Patrick cleared some space for the board on the kitchen table before putting on the kettle. He found himself humming as he did so. *She's coming home. She's all right.* He looked up, tears pressing against the back of his eyes. *Thank you, God.*

CHAPTER 64

BURLINGTON, VERMONT

Hakeem drove the Mercedes SUV through the winding, tree-lined roads toward the country estate. The surrounding area reminded Elisabeta of the place in Switzerland where she had stayed when she was in hiding.

The iron gates to the estate swung open as they approached. Hakeem wound through the drive at a speed slightly faster than Elisabeta would have liked. He jerked the wheel, and she slid to the side. "Hakeem!"

"Sorry, Samyaza." He reduced his speed.

Gerard said nothing, but a small smile spread across his face. Gerard was aware of Hakeem's jealousy—a blind man would be. He did nothing to egg the man on, but he'd also done nothing to reduce the animosity either.

Elisabeta sighed. Why did men so often behave like boys?

The building came into view. Two tall turrets framed a two-story home of Victorian-styled design. A deep, large porch dominated half of the front. The house's whimsical color scheme—blue siding with yellow trim and green shutters—gave it a wholesome look.

Hakeem pulled up in front and quickly got out to open the door for Elisabeta. She nodded at him, walked past Gerard, who held the front door for her, and handed her coat to Hilda, who stood waiting with a clipboard in hand.

Hilda draped the coat over her arm. "The children are all waiting in the playroom."

Elisabeta grimaced. "The playroom?"

Hilda shrugged. "That is what the nannies are calling it. It's the den with some toys."

Elisabeta waved her forward. "Right. Well. Let's begin. Hakeem, bring the book."

Hakeem hurried forward, smirking at Gerard as he passed.

Hilda led them down the hall toward a set of double doors. Even from down the hall, Elisabeta could hear the children. A shiver ran through her. Who on earth would ever voluntarily spend time with the little monsters? All they did was demand attention and food and provide nothing in return. She cast a glance at Gerard, who walked beside her, his face impassive. What had he seen in his own children that had caused him such pain at their death—and from all reports, joy at their existence? Maybe the biological bond caused some sort of chemical response that made you lose your sanity. If so, so much the better that she'd never even considered having a child.

Hilda opened the doors, and with distaste, Elisabeta stepped into the den.

It was pandemonium. A group of six children were running in circles in one corner. Another handful were sitting in a group playing some sort of clapping game. Some children sat by themselves crying. One kid was staring at the wall, laughing, while another was jumping at something only she could see; obviously those two were deranged. Elisabeta hoped neither was Victoria.

A few children sat quietly around a woman who was reading

them a story, and more had crawled into the laps of the six women that were sitting on the floor. Another four women wandered the room, three with children in their arms. These nannies did not speak any English, and had been brought in from Argentina for just this project. They were all poor, unattached, and most importantly, disposable.

Elisabeta waved Hilda forward. "Have them bring the first group."

Hilda relayed the order to three women near them. They jumped to attention and began carrying over the children one at a time, exposing the upper half of each child's right arm. Elisabeta waved them all away and gestured impatiently for the next group.

After eighteen children, Elisabeta was growing concerned. None had the mark. What if Victoria wasn't in this group? What if they needed to get more children? She had hoped that this method would bear fruit. Scouring the world for *every* redheaded female child born within a few days of Victoria's death would be next to impossible. It had taken months to get the information to winnow the number down to these thirty-six.

Elisabeta glared at the next child's unmarked arm, waving her away with a growl.

Gerard took her hand and gave it a squeeze. "Patience. We are not through all of them yet. If you would like to take a break, I will finish the task."

Elisabeta looked into his handsome face and took a breath. He was right. And here was why he was more useful than her other people. He could read her. He could read a situation.

She shook her head. "No. I want to be the one to find her." She waved the next child forward. The girl screamed, trying to claw her way from the nanny's arms. The nanny struggled to free the girl's arm.

"Enough." Elisabeta yanked on the girl's arm, ripping her shirt-sleeve. No mark. In disgust, she pushed the girl away. "Next."

The next girl sat calmly in the nanny's arms, although the nanny shook with fright. The nanny pushed up the girl's sleeve—

And there, on the girl's arm, was a birthmark shaped like a crescent moon.

Elisabeta gasped and squeezed the girl's arm tightly. The girl let out a cry.

Gerard was beside her in a moment. "Elisabeta," he said quietly.

Elisabeta let go of the girl's arm but didn't step back. Instead she peered into the girl's face. The girl looked back at her, her bottom lip trembling, a stuffed lamb clutched in her chubby little hands, tears pooling in her eyes. She leaned away from Elisabeta's stare.

Elisabeta smiled. "There you are."

The girl turned her face into the nanny's chest, and the nanny wrapped her arms protectively around her.

Elisabeta turned on her heel. "We're done here."

Hilda and Hakeem followed her out. "What are your instructions?"

"Prepare the rest of the children to be moved." Elisabeta paused. "Have the nannies go with them. We can take care of them at the same time."

"Yes, ma'am."

"Will I be taking care of them?" Hakeem asked.

"Yes. You and—" She looked around with a frown. "Where's Gerard?"

"He remained in the room, ma'am," Hilda said.

Elisabeta narrowed her eyes. "Oh, did he?" she said softly.

She knew it. He had not let go of his feelings for his family.

She marched back down the hall. The den's doors were once again shut. She flung them open.

A few of the children cried out, and one of the nannies near the door put her hand to her throat. Gerard was on the other side of the room, holding a child. *Protecting* a child.

Anger rising, Elisabeta stormed across the room. "What are you doing?"

Hakeem was at her side in flash, reaching for the child in Gerard's arms. Gerard kicked him back. "Do not touch her."

"You traitor. I knew you—"

Gerard stood straight, his eyes looking right into Elisabeta's without blinking. "I am no traitor. I thought it wise to check the rest of the children. To be sure we had the right child."

Elisabeta faltered. It was a good decision. A logical decision. "And?"

Gerard gestured to the child in his arms. "This one has the same mark."

Elisabeta reached for the child. "What? That's not possible."

Gerard turned the child so Elisabeta could see her arm. Sure enough, the crescent mark was there as well.

"There are two that bear the mark. Not one," Gerard said quietly.

Elisabeta had not considered the possibility of two. She stared at the little girl in Gerard's arms. She had the red hair and blue eyes, as they all did, but her cheekbones were more pronounced, her face longer than the other child's. And God's truth, Elisabeta could not truly see much more of a difference between the two girls. They could easily be mistaken for sisters, if not twins. And both looked liked they could grow into Victoria.

"What would you like to do?" Gerard asked.

"The rest of the children?" Elisabeta asked.

"They do not have the mark. I checked them all," Gerard said.

"Very well. We will take both."

"And what of the other ones?" Gerard asked.

"We do not need them any longer. You will be in charge of disposing of them." She watched him carefully. "Unless you have a problem with that."

He shrugged. "I see no problem."

"Good. You will fly out with them and the nannies. I don't

want it done here. I want nothing to tie it back to me. The pilot has the coordinates."

Gerard bowed. "Yes, Samyaza."

"Have that one taken to my plane along with the other one. And send one of the nannies with them. I don't want to deal with the things."

She turned on her heel and strode from the room, the fates of the other children and the nannies slipping from her mind as soon as they were out of her sight.

She pictured what awaited the two children she had found. She would search the book and find a way to determine which was Victoria.

She smiled. *And then the fun begins.*

CHAPTER 65

GALETON, PENNSYLVANIA

Patrick put the last of the dishes in the dishwasher and turned it on. He was leaning down to put the detergent back beneath the sink when he heard a creak. He stood up with a frown. "Did you hear that?"

Cain looked up. "What?"

"It sounded like someone on the porch."

But Patrick knew that shouldn't be. They were four men who were constantly patrolling the area around the cabin, but they were never supposed to come near it. Henry didn't want anyone knowing about Cain. And if the men saw any problems they were to handle it, then call the cabin and notify them. Only in an extreme emergency were they allowed to enter the cabin.

Patrick quickly walked to the side table in the kitchen, opened the drawer, and pulled out the Glock 20. There were handguns stashed throughout the cabin in case they were needed.

Cain's eyes went wide. "What are you doing?"

"You need to get in the back bedroom."

"No. If someone's there, they're here for me. I will check it out."

"You're not healed yet, and besides there's no—"

There was a soft knock on the cabin door.

"Bad guys don't normally knock, do they?" Cain asked.

"Not normally, no." Patrick moved toward the door.

Cain was right behind him.

Patrick waved Cain behind him before he grabbed the handle. "Who is it?"

"It's me."

Patrick's heart jumped at the sound of that voice.

"It can't be," Cain said.

But Patrick scrambled to open the door. He flung it wide.

A man and woman slipped inside and shut the door behind them. The man scanned the space, looking for any threat, but Patrick's eyes stayed on the woman.

"Laney?"

She smiled, her green eyes filling with tears. "Hi, Uncle Patrick."

CHAPTER 66

Laney sank into the warmth and familiarity of her uncle's hug. She would have been content to stay there for hours. Tears slipped down her cheeks, and her uncle's shoulders shook as he held her close.

Finally her uncle stepped back, wiping his eyes. "I don't know if I should yell at you for leaving or just get down on my knees and thank God you're back."

"I'd prefer we skip the yelling," Laney said, her eyes going to the man behind her uncle.

Cain nodded at her, a smile on his face. "Laney."

She stepped beyond her uncle and pulled the immortal into a hug. "I've missed you too, Cain."

Cain went still before his arms wrapped around her. A tremor ran through him, and Laney realized with a shock that this might be his first hug in years—if not centuries. She leaned back and looked at him, searching his face for any sign of pain from his injuries. "How are you feeling?"

Cain cleared his throat, his eyes suspiciously shiny. "Good. Better. Your uncle has taken good care of me."

Drake cleared his throat as well, and Laney looked back at

him. "Oh, right." She stepped back. "Uncle Patrick, Cain, this is Drake. My, uh, friend."

Drake extended his hand to Patrick. "Father."

Patrick shook it. "Thank you for saving my niece's life in Colorado. Now maybe you could explain to me why you then kidnapped her and left me scared to death for the last six months?"

Laney groaned. "Uncle Patrick."

"Don't 'Uncle Patrick' me. Do you have any idea how scared I've been? How scared we've *all* been?"

Drake nodded toward the hall. "I'm just going to take a look around and make sure our arrival hasn't raised any attention."

"Fine," Patrick said, his teeth clenched.

Cain put his hand on Patrick's shoulder. "Perhaps we could give Laney a chance to explain."

Patrick took a breath. "Okay. Right. I'll make some tea." He headed to the kitchen.

Laney watched him go, her heart sinking. "He's so mad."

"No," Cain said. "He's been terrified for you. Sometimes terrified comes out mad. He just needs a minute to get ahold of his emotions."

Laney looked up at the immortal. "You two seem to have become good friends."

"He's a good man, and yes, we're friends."

"You seem surprised," Laney said.

"I am." Cain shifted his gaze to where Drake had disappeared. "And I might be the only one who wasn't worried when I learned Drake was the one who had taken you from Colorado."

"You weren't?"

Cain shook his head, searching Laney's face. He spoke quietly. "You know who he's been to you."

Laney was, unsure what to say. Finally, she sighed. "Yes. I just don't know who he is to me now."

CHAPTER 67

Her uncle seemed to have gotten control of his anger, though Laney couldn't blame him for being mad. She knew if the positions were reversed she would have been just as worried. Ever since she'd woken up, she'd been reading about what everyone close to her had been going through: the government investigations, the media circus, the church's veiled responses, the moving of the SIA facility inmates, Cain's torture, and now the search for Victoria.

She'd been awake for less than forty-eight hours, and it had been nerve-wracking. She had wanted to sprint right back to everyone, but Drake had convinced her that they needed to come at this a little more carefully. That they could not just rush in. After all, the world was still after her.

But all of that paled in comparison to the idea that Samyaza somehow had her hands on Victoria. That she had somehow found her. The idea of that drove a knife through Laney's heart. Victoria was a child, a toddler. Targeting her at this age should be completely off-limits. But as Drake had reminded her, there was no off-limits when it came to Samyaza.

And then there was Drake. Since she had woken up, he had

been by her side. But they still had not talked about their relationship when she was Helen and he was Achilles, beyond those first few minutes. She wasn't sure if she wanted to, and at the same time, she *desperately* wanted to. But how did you ask someone who had declared he would love you in every lifetime if he still felt that way? And what would she do with that answer once she had it? Until she knew the answer to the latter question, she did not want his answer to the former.

Now she sat with her uncle and Cain, and as much as she wanted to delve into what had happened between her and Drake, there were much more important questions to address first. She turned to Drake, whose gaze seemed always to be on her. That was something she actually found comfort in. He'd been watching her ever since she'd woken up.

He nodded to her now, those incredibly familiar eyes staring into hers.

Strengthened, she took a breath and turned to her uncle and Cain. "So, there's a lot to tell. I'm not even sure where to start."

Patrick crossed his arms over his chest. "The beginning is always a good place." He turned to Drake. "Like how come you saved her life?"

Laney tensed, wanting to hear what he said.

"I think perhaps Laney should explain that."

Laney gave him a disgruntled look. "Gee, thanks."

He laughed, leaned back in his chair, and draped his arm across the back of hers. "Any time, ring bearer."

She shook her head, then saw that the two men across from her were watching this exchange avidly. She felt her cheeks burn, and she wasn't really sure why. She took a breath. "Well, it all goes back the Trojan War…"

CHAPTER 68

"And so with Max's warning in mind, I knew I needed to find Victoria," Laney finished.

She had been talking for almost an hour. She had provided a very tame recounting of her relationship with Achilles—probably for her uncle's benefit—and had told the tale as if it had occurred to someone else. But Cain could feel the emotion underneath. She had been through the wringer, and her emotions were still a little raw. She hadn't just *remembered* her life as Helen of Troy; she had *lived* it. For everyone else, months had passed—but for her, years has passed. An entire lifetime.

Cain noted how pale Patrick looked. "Perhaps Drake and I should give you two some privacy to speak alone," Cain said.

Laney took her uncle's hand. "We'll go sit outside. With the rain, it's dark enough on the porch that no one should see us."

Drake's lips tightened, but he nodded, and Cain had the distinct impression he didn't like the idea of Laney being out of his sight.

When the two had left, Cain studied Drake. He had been quiet during her speech, but his gaze had never left her. Cain knew what they had meant to one another. But the way Laney had spoken, it was as though she was describing a relationship between two strangers, not between herself and the man sitting next to her.

Drake, on the other hand…Cain had seen how he looked at her. That relationship was not in the past for him. Not by a long shot.

Cain watched Drake pace. "How did you get past the guards?" he asked. "Some of them have abilities."

"They can't sense me. It was easy enough to get past them." Drake moved toward the window. Laney and Patrick were right outside it.

"She won't appreciate it if you eavesdrop."

Drake smirked. "Perhaps I don't care what she appreciates."

Cain crossed his arms over his chest. "Perhaps you should try that line with someone who doesn't know what she truly means to you."

Drake's mask slipped for a just a moment, and Cain saw surprise there before Drake's arrogance returned. "And what do you know about it, old man?"

Cain laughed. He knew he barely looked older than Drake, but he liked being called an old man. "Quite a bit." He moved toward the living room, and after a momentary hesitation, Drake followed him.

Cain sat down on the couch. Drake took one of the club chairs.

"So," Drake said. "I don't recall us meeting."

Cain studied him. "Do you remember everything of your time as Achilles?"

Drake paused before nodding.

"I see. Well, no. We did not meet then, nor since, on any of your—I believe you call them 'sabbaticals.' But I do make a point of learning everything I can about the important players on the board. And you and Helen, well… there were no more important players at that point."

Drake kept his face impassive, but Cain noted a tensing of his shoulders. "It was a long time ago."

"Indeed it was. But the fact that you two are here together now suggests that there are certain forces in this universe that want you two together."

"I'm just helping out a friend."

"A friend? I consider her a friend as well, but I don't think we view her the same way."

"She's the ring bearer. She's about to be tested, more so than she has for thousands of years. She needs every weapon she can get. I'm one of them." He paused. "So are you."

"True. And I am at her disposal, whatever she needs."

"Good." Drake stood. "She doesn't need any ancient tales to clutter up her present."

"Maybe not. But she does need you."

The mask slipped again. "And she has me. However she needs me." He disappeared down the hall.

Drake was an interesting man. He was not the first archangel Cain had met, but he was by far the most interesting. *Of course, he's not just any old archangel*, Cain thought. *I wonder if he knows who he truly is?*

Patrick's and Laney's mumbled voices drifted through the walls, and Cain frowned. If Drake didn't know, Laney *certainly* didn't. And it would change nothing about Drake's current mission.

Cain just hoped it didn't break Laney's heart down the road.

CHAPTER 69

Alone, Noriko made her way toward Dom's shelter. Danny was finishing up some work, and Cleo was off running through the trees—for which Noriko was grateful. She needed a few minutes alone.

She didn't mind staying with Dom. She actually really liked him. But she couldn't shake the feeling that her last dream was important. Yet it had been so short, and now she wasn't even sure if the blue eyes in her mind were from the dream, or from the image of Gerard on Danny's monitor.

Her phone rang, and she picked it up. "Hello?"

"Noriko, thank goodness. I was getting worried."

Aaliyah's voice came through strong and clear, eliciting a pang of homesickness. It hit her that she was supposed to have called yesterday. "Oh, I'm so sorry. I forgot to call. How is everything?"

"Good, although we're still getting adjusted to our new reality."

After the priestess's true plan had come to light, it had been difficult for many members of Honu Keiki to move forward. Some wanted to leave the group behind entirely, while others argued for even greater isolation from the outside world and its influences. Still others suggested it was their isolation which had

THE BELIAL PLAN

led to the problem to begin with. But the one thing they'd all agreed on was who would take charge in the priestess's absence: Aaliyah. With Kai by her side, she was steering Honu Keiki through this difficult transition.

Aaliyah explained what had been happening most recently, but Noriko was only half listening.

"And then, we made a cow the final member of the high priest council."

"That's nice," Noriko said. "Wait, what did you just say?"

Aaliyah laughed. "I knew you weren't listening. So tell me, what has you so distracted?"

Noriko sighed, thinking of everything that had happened. She hadn't wanted to burden Aaliyah with it. She had so much going on in her own life. But she realized this was what family did: they shared their burdens. So she told Aaliyah everything—about the missing children, her visions, and her last dream.

Aaliyah was quiet the whole time. Only when Noriko finished did she speak. "It seems you, too, have quite a lot going on."

"I didn't want to burden you with—"

"Stop right there. You are my family. What troubles you, troubles me. I've known something was wrong, but I was waiting for you to share it. I could feel the stress in you."

Noriko realized how foolish she had been. She and Aaliyah shared a bond, one that did not always require words. She had thought with the distance, perhaps she could spare Aaliyah the angst she was experiencing. She should have known better. "I'm sorry."

"No need to apologize. But because I knew something was wrong, I've been looking into your gifts. Particularly the one of prophesy."

"Have you found anything?"

"I may have. Your visions, they come on you without any warning, without any attempt on your part to create them, yes?"

"Yes. I'm blindsided by them. I have no control over them."

"That may not be entirely true. In our history there have been people who could focus their visions, even summon them to a subject they wished to see."

Noriko was stunned. She'd never even considered the possibility. She'd never heard of anyone who had been able to do that. "Truly?"

"Yes. But it doesn't come without disadvantages."

"Like what?"

"When you tap further into your gift, you must tap into more energy. And that can be dangerous."

"How?"

"Your visions so far, you have always been able to pull yourself from them. But as your visions deepen, you may not be able to do so. You may need someone else to pull you out."

"Okay. That's not a problem."

"There's more. You may also pull someone else *into* your vision. And you may not be able to control who that is. And whoever it is… they will also be able to control what you see."

"How?"

"It's not clear."

"But the visions, or the person in them, they can't affect the viewer."

Aaliyah hesitated before she spoke. "I'm not so sure that's true."

Noriko didn't like the sound of that. "Someone else could control my vision? That's possible?"

"Potentially. The history—it's so old. And in hundreds of years, we've never needed to force ourselves to see."

The silence felt deep between them. "There's something else, isn't there?" Noriko said.

"There was one tale about a great seer. Her name was Ferniall. I'm not even sure when she lived, the tale is so old. And most likely, it was exaggerated. I shouldn't have even mentioned it."

"Aaliyah, what happened to Ferniall?"

"She forced a vision about some people coming to hurt members of Lemuria. And she fell into a deep, deep sleep."

"What happened to her?"

Aaliyah was silent for so long that Noriko thought she wasn't going to answer. And once she did, Noriko wished she hadn't.

"She never woke up."

CHAPTER 70

It had started to rain when they were inside, and now it was coming down in sheets. Patrick and Laney sat in the shadows on the old swing on the cabin's porch. It creaked as they swung back and forth. For a few minutes, they just sat together and listened to the squeaking and the rain. It was strangely comforting.

Finally, Patrick took Laney's hand. "You scared me."

Laney sighed. "I know. I'm sorry. But I knew the world's law enforcement wings were moving in, and the rest of you would be caught in the same net coming down on me."

"We never would have—"

She squeezed his hand. "You never would have let them take me. Which meant you all would have been arrested as well. I needed to go so we all could have some breathing room, some time to figure things out."

Patrick wanted to deny her words, to say that it never would have come to that. But they both knew she was right. Just as they both knew it was unfair.

He sighed. "I'm afraid not much has changed. Although I did

see one news show that was at least beginning to question the government's interpretation of events."

"Well, I guess that's a start. And I suppose that's one benefit of the feds taking over the SIA facility: everyone got to see the priestess for who she really is." Laney lowered her voice. "How's Cain doing?"

"You know what happened to him?"

Laney nodded.

Patrick frowned. "How—" He shook his head. "I guess it doesn't matter. But as to your question, it took a toll on him."

"I'm sorry I couldn't be there."

"I'm glad you weren't. When I first read your letter—when I read that you wanted me to visit Cain—I was prepared to dislike the man. But he's not what I thought he'd be."

"I had a feeling you two would like each other."

"That we do. And it was difficult to see him after what they did to him. He's a man who's lived for millennia, yet I've never met someone who seemed so alone."

"I'm glad you two have become friends. And I'm glad you got him out. If you hadn't, I would have. I was heading there when I learned of the breakout. After seeing that tape..." She shook her head, a tremor in her chin. "Those men are animals."

"You saw that too?"

She nodded again.

"You're awfully well informed for someone who's been locked away. How did you even know where we were?"

"Um, don't get mad... but Dom's been sending me messages."

Patrick's mouth fell open. "Dom?"

Laney's words came out in a rush. "He has never known where I was. I asked him before I left to find a way to let me know what was happening with all of you. He set it up so he can't even tell if I've checked the messages, and I can't reply back. The first time I was even able to check his messages was when I woke up."

. . .

"How does he do it?"

"It's a website. He makes comments there."

"We could have gotten a message to you?"

"Even if you could have, I've been asleep for months. I wouldn't have seen them."

"We have to tell Henry, Jake, and Jen you're back."

"No." Laney's voice was firm.

"No? Why not?"

"Because I'm still wanted on a global scale. They're all being followed. I can't chance them getting in the middle of something. The only reason we were able to get here was because you're so far off the grid. No one knows about Victoria's cabin."

"You're not going to tell them you're back?"

"I'll figure out a way to let them know I'm around."

He watched her carefully. "But you didn't come out of hiding just to say hello to two old men, did you?"

"Well, first off, you're not old. Cain…" She shrugged. "And actually, I did come to check up on you. But not *just* that. Dom arranged for some supplies to be sent here tomorrow."

"You're going after Victoria, aren't you?"

"I have to. She's defenseless. And what Samyaza will do to her…" Laney shuddered. "I have to."

"But if you're seen, if you're caught—"

"Samyaza is going way off the beaten path with this action, and she has as much to lose if she's caught. She won't chance anyone stumbling over her operation. "

"But if it's that important to her, she'll layer herself with security. You'll need help."

"I have Drake."

"You need more than him!"

"I know you're worried. But this is my job. I have to do this. And I'm asking you to trust me and not tell anyone you've seen me."

Patrick studied her in the dim light and realized he'd been

wrong earlier—she wasn't the same Laney who had left here six months ago. There was a calmness to her, and at the same time a determination. She had embraced her role in this world, in this fight. He knew Drake had something to do with that, because even with everything else, there was a lightness to her that hadn't been there before.

With a shock, he realized she had felt as alone as Cain. Even with all of them surrounding her, the burden of her duty was something she had shouldered alone. And somehow, Drake had lightened that burden—or perhaps shared it.

Patrick took a deep breath. He hated the idea of her going into danger again. But he was thinking as the man who had bandaged her knees and hugged away her tears as a child. She wasn't that little girl anymore. She was the ring bearer. And she wasn't alone anymore, either.

"I won't tell anyone. And neither will Cain."

Laney smiled. "Really? Because I have three other arguments ready to go."

He gave a small laugh. "I guess, like you, I'm finally accepting that you're not my little girl anymore."

She leaned her head on his shoulder. "I'll always be your little girl. But I'm not *just* your little girl."

"I know." He kissed her forehead. "But don't hate me if I wish I could protect you from all the evils of the world."

"As long you don't hate the world, or me, because you can't."

"Never."

Both of them fell into silence, listening to the night. And Patrick embraced the moment. Because he knew when it was over, he'd have to let her go.

CHAPTER 71

Noriko walked down the hall of Dom's shelter. Lou, Rolly, and Zach hadn't arrived yet, and Dom was locked away in his lab, so she had the living area to herself.

Well, almost to herself.

Cleo leaned against her. *Okay?*

Noriko thought about lying, but Cleo would know the truth anyway. "No. I can't get those missing kids out of my head."

Cleo sighed, and Noriko knew the cat felt her anguish. The kids were only two years old. And some of them were now orphans; their parents had been killed when they'd been abducted. All Noriko couldn't help them. All she'd managed to do was tell everybody that they were missing. She couldn't tell anybody where they were, or even who exactly had been grabbed.

Well, except for Susie McAdams. Noriko had looked her family up on the computer. They were a cute family—all redheads with blue eyes. And she could just tell from the pictures—the way they always had their arms around one another, the way they smiled—that they really loved one another.

And now their youngest was missing, on top of the father being killed last year. It was just too much sadness for one family.

"There you are."

Noriko looked up to see Lou coming toward them. "Oh, hey. When'd you get here?"

"Just now."

"Where's Zach and Rolly?"

Lou rolled her eyes. "Raiding the kitchen at the main house. They seem to think we'll be stranded down here for days."

Noriko cringed. "Sorry about that. You guys don't have to—"

Lou put up her hand. "Let me stop you right there. The boys are *hoping* we get stranded down here for days. They have all the seasons of *Battlestar Galactica* lined up—both versions— along with the *Lord of the Rings* trilogy. And I may have mentioned that you hadn't seen *Star Wars*, so now they're planning on making you watch all the movies."

"That can't be too many."

"There are eight."

"Eight?"

Lou rolled her eyes. "Yup. So I assure you, they're pretty happy to be 'stranded' down here. In fact, I'm pretty sure you and I will be the first two making a break for freedom."

Cleo growled.

"Sorry, three," Lou amended. "Anyway, I finished my exam early so I thought I'd see if you two wanted to get something to eat."

Noriko shook her head. "I'm not really hungry."

Lou touched Noriko's sleeve. "It's not your fault, you know."

"What?"

"The missing kids. You didn't cause that."

Noriko sighed. "No, but I'm not helping either. I'm just waiting around for a stupid vision that might or might not help."

Lou was quiet for a moment. "Have you thought about trying to *make* yourself have a vision?"

"Yeah," Noriko said slowly. All the worries in Aaliyah's voice reappeared in her mind. "I just—I've never done that before. I'm just a little…" She shrugged.

Scared, Cleo finished for her.

Noriko looked down at her. *Yeah, scared.*

"Why don't we give it a try? I'll stay with you. And if anything doesn't look right, I'll pull you out."

Noriko bit her bottom lip. She wanted to, but the idea still terrified her. What if she didn't wake up? At the same time, she really did want to help somehow. "Okay. Let's give it a shot."

They walked to one of the bedrooms so Noriko could lie down. Cleo curled up on the floor next to her.

"Do you need any special music?" Lou asked. "Or a candle or something?"

"No, just silence, I think."

"Okay." Lou sat on the bed opposite Noriko's.

Noriko closed her eyes and focused on her breathing: in and out. But after a few minutes she cracked open an eye. Lou was staring at her.

"Um, do you think you could maybe look somewhere else?"

Lou stood up. "Sorry. Maybe I'll go grab a quick bite in the kitchen. I'll come back in a bit and see if you've made any progress."

"That's good. I'll see you in a little bit."

Lou hesitated in the doorway. "You sure you're okay on your own?"

"Yeah. Go on. Cleo will get you if I need you."

"Okay. I won't be gone long."

Noriko waited until she could no longer hear Lou's footsteps, then she settled back on the bed and closed her eyes once more.

Almost immediately, a vision of the kids popped into her mind, but she knew the image didn't come from her brain. It was Cleo trying to help her.

It's okay, Cleo. I've got this.

She focused on her breathing, tuning out every other sound. And in her mind she pictured the little girl she'd seen. But the image kept shifting between the little girl and the blue eyes.

Then she felt a stirring at the back of her mind. She blocked everything else out and focused on the sensation.

It was like a wave pulling her out to sea. She was sucked into the vision.

CHAPTER 72

The mist surrounded Noriko. She pushed against it. It had substance and didn't want to let her through. But she knew she needed to get past it. She needed to see.

A hand reached out, latched on to hers, and pulled her forward.

The hand led her through the mist, but she couldn't see who it belonged to. When, the mist began to lessen, she could make out details—blond hair, a strong build, definitely male—but his face was turned away. There was something familiar about him.

Finally, the man stopped. Noriko came abreast of him, and the mist was gone. Ahead was a field, empty save for grass and a few trees.

"Where are we?" she asked.

"Where we need to be. Where you need to be." He looked down at her.

"I know you, don't I?"

The man acted as if he hadn't heard her question, and Noriko wasn't even sure if she had asked it out loud. "Find me," he said. "Save them."

"Them?" she asked. But then she heard the cries. She ran forward. "Where are you?"

The only answer she heard was more crying. And the farther she ran, the louder the cries became, until the sound was deafening, painful. She crashed to her knees, her hands over her ears.

Two hands covered hers and pulled her to her feet. With tears streaming down her face, she stared up into the man's face. His blue eyes held her captive and wouldn't let go. "Focus on me," he said. She couldn't hear him, but she read his lips.

He pulled her closer. "Focus on me," he said again.

Noriko stared into his face and let out a breath. Him, only him.

The cries began to lessen. Soon, they disappeared. She pulled her hands from her ears slowly. All was still.

But when he removed his hands from hers, the cries returned. He grabbed her hand, and the cries disappeared again. His connection was the only thing keeping the cries away.

"They're gone," she said.

"No. They're still there. You need to find them."

She looked around. They were surrounded by trees. They could be anywhere. "I don't know where we are. Can you tell me where we are?"

He shook his head. "No. But I can show you. Come."

He started to walk down the path, his hand holding Noriko's firmly.

Noriko didn't think of breaking away. The warmth of his hand in hers made her feel safe.

He stopped, looking out over a valley.

"I still don't—"Noriko began.

"Look. You need to see."

She turned away from his intense gaze and scanned the landscape, looking for something, anything. She paused, squinting at one particular spot. "Wait. Is that—"

"Noriko!" Lou shouted, shaking Noriko's shoulder.

Noriko's eyes flew open with a jolt. Both Lou and Danny were looking down at her with concern.

"Oh, thank God." Lou sat back, blowing out a breath.

"What are you guys doing? I was in the middle of a vision," Noriko said.

"Noriko, you stopped breathing. You've been unresponsive for an hour," Danny said.

"What? That's not possible. My visions never take that long."

"Well it did this time. You scared us to death," Lou said.

"I'm sorry," Noriko said, sitting up.

"Was anything different this time?" Danny asked.

Noriko remembered how the mist had tried to keep her out. "I was trying to have a vision, but I had to force my way through."

She frowned. No, that wasn't right. Someone *helped* her through. Who was it? She couldn't picture the person's face. That was strange. The rest of the vision remained crystal clear. She could even remember the warmth of the person's hand. So why couldn't she remember their face?

"Did you see the kids?" Lou asked.

Noriko shook her head. "No, but I think I know where they are. I mean, I might." She grabbed the sketchpad next to her and a pencil. She began to draw.

Lou began. "What—"

"Just let her go," Danny said quietly.

Noriko tuned them out. She pictured the valley, focusing in particular on the one spot that stood out. Her pencil flew across the page, bringing the vision to life. Finally she turned the sketchpad around for the other two to see. "I saw this. I think it's near where the kids are."

Lou peered at the picture. "Is that a face?"

On the pad, Noriko had drawn a rock wall with two eyes. She shook her head. "No, it was just eyes."

Danny held out his hand. "May I?"

Noriko handed the pad to him. Danny quickly stood.

"Where are you going?" Lou asked.

"To find out if this exists," Danny called over his shoulder.

CHAPTER 73

Danny examined the sketch Noriko had created. It looked like two eyes had been carved right into a rock wall. He shook his head, worrying that the sketch was nothing more than some representation of Noriko's subconscious. Perhaps it was her own eyes, watching the children.

"Hey," Jen called as she walked into the room.

"Hey. What are you doing here?"

"Lou called and told me about what Noriko saw. Jake's pulling together a team to be ready to go if you find anything."

"Great, no pressure," he mumbled.

Jen squeezed his shoulder. "Hey. You do what you can. We all do."

"I don't even know if this is a real place or just part of Noriko's imagination."

"Why would you say that?"

"Noriko said her visions are sometimes abstract, that she has to interpret them. Sometimes she doesn't realize they're abstract until after the event in the vision comes to pass."

"You're worried that's the case here."

"Yeah."

"Why?"

He gestured at the sketch on the desk. "Look at it."

Jen picked it up and frowned. "It looks like two eyes."

"Yeah. She said it was two eyes in the side of a wall of rock."

"Lou said this vision was different from her others. That it lasted longer."

"Yeah. She's never been out that long. And this was the first time she *tried* to have a vision. She's never done that before."

"Well, it seemed to work."

"Yeah, it did something. But I can't find anything that matches this picture."

Jen frowned again. "It looks familiar to me, actually."

"Really?"

"Yeah... but I can't place it."

Jen took the pad over to the window. She studied the picture again, then stared out the window—although Danny knew she wasn't taking in the view.

He bit his tongue to keep himself from urging her to remember. He'd seen the look on Noriko's face. She was terrified.

"I know this," Jen said quietly. "Why can't I remember this?"

"Maybe you need to walk or something. Concentrate on something else."

"You're probably right. I'll go grab my gear in case you get a hit."

"I'll keep plugging away."

Danny sat at his computer for another hour, but only grew more frustrated—and more concerned that this was just an abstraction.

His phone beeped with a message. He didn't recognize the number, and the message was only two letters: *az.*

He saw that the message had been sent to Henry and Jake as well. *That's odd.*

He stretched in his chair, then nearly fell out of it as Jen blew into the room. "I need a computer."

He stood up. Jen took his seat and quickly brought up a search engine.

"What's going on?"

"AZ," Jen said. She typed, "rock formations in Arizona." A slew of images appeared on the screen, and she began scrolling through them.

Danny rolled his hands into fists. *Come on, Jen.*

She continued to scroll, then backtracked to an image she had just passed. It was an image of a tall rock spire; it looked nothing like the sketch.

"That's it," she murmured. She brought up the national park associated with the formation.

Danny peered at the screen. "Canyon de Chelly National Monument?"

Jen scrolled through the park's website. "Yeah. It was declared a park back in 1931. It's part of the Navajo Nation, and few visitors are actually allowed."

Jen found what she was looking for. "There you are." She brought up a photo for something called "The Mummy Cave Ruin," located in the eastern portion of the park. It was a rock wall with two holes in it; they bore an uncanny resemblance to eyes.

Danny leaned forward and gasped. "It's real."

CHAPTER 74

Jake dialed quickly. "We think we have a location—Canyon de Chelly National Monument. It's in northeast Arizona. I need everything on it including who runs it. It's part of Navajo territory."

"Yes, sir. I'll have everything in a few minutes."

"Good."

Jake disconnected the call. Jen was coming over with Noriko to repeat everything she had seen in the vision, in case there was anything else that might help them. He headed downstairs to make sure the team was ready to go. It would be a thirty-man team this time. He wasn't taking another chance at being understaffed. Not like in Salem.

He reviewed the list of supplies and added a med unit, in case any of the kids were in bad shape. He considered calling Mary Jane, but quickly discarded the idea. They were working on very wild guesses right now.

He pulled out his phone and stared at the text message: *az*. He had no idea who had sent it. Apparently the phone that had sent it was in motion. Danny thought maybe on a plane.

He'd seen Noriko's sketch, and he agreed it looked like the

picture of Mummy Cave Ruin that Danny had sent him. But it still felt like everything was built on blind trust that Noriko's vision would lead them to the children.

He looked once more at the text message. *Well, whoever you are, I hope you're looking out for these kids.*

CHAPTER 75

Noriko had recounted every step of the vision three times. Now she sat quietly with Cleo while Henry, Jake, and Jen discussed their plan. No one had suggested she go along with them. No one had asked if she wanted to go.

Cleo looked up at her. *Okay?*

Yes. You?

Worried.

I'm sorry. It was a different type of vision, wasn't it?

Connected to man.

Noriko nodded slowly. *Yes.* She realized that it was that connection that was unusual. The man had pulled her into the vision. He had helped her, allowed her to see. That had never happened before.

Is he a psychic? Noriko asked.

No. Connected to you. We need to go.

Go? Where?

The image of the rock wall appeared in Noriko's mind. She gasped, then looked over at the other three, but they didn't seemed to notice.

We can't go.

Cleo stared into her eyes, not letting her look away. *Supposed to be there.*

Noriko shook her head even as she felt the pull.

Cleo nudged her.

Noriko shook her head again.

Cleo nudged her again, this time harder.

Noriko glared. *Okay, okay. Just give me a minute.*

She took a breath. She was very comfortable with Lou, Danny, and the gang at the Chandler school. But she had to admit, Jen, Henry, Jake... they intimidated her. When it came to dealing with the leopards, she was all confidence. But with humans, not so much. And Lou had told her some of what these people had done. They were like real life superheroes. She didn't want to bother them with her concerns.

Cleo nudged her again, and Noriko could feel her impatience. "Okay, okay," she muttered.

"Everything okay, Noriko?" Jen asked.

Jen, Henry, and Jake were all now looking at Noriko, and she felt her cheeks flame with color. *Great.* "Um, yes... sort of... No, actually."

Jen gave her a smile. "Something you want to add?"

"Not me so much as Cleo. She, uh, wants to go. And I think I should go with her so I can tell you what she's thinking."

Jake was shaking his head before Noriko had even finished speaking. "No. You are not trained. This is going to be dangerous. Absolutely not."

Cleo roared at Jake.

He sat back, his eyes large. "Did she just yell at me?"

"Um, yeah. See, Cleo knows that you're going after the kids. And she also knows she's the only one who can identify Victoria. She says she's done it before."

Henry frowned. "When?"

Jen answered for her. "When Victoria came to the estate. Cleo ran up to her. We all thought she was going to attack, but she didn't. She stopped and bowed to Victoria."

Cleo up sat straight and nodded.

"If Victoria's there, Cleo will be able to find her," Noriko said.

"She's right," Henry said. "Cleo may be our best chance."

"And I need to go too," Noriko said.

Jen, Henry, and Jake answered simultaneously. "No."

"Look, it's not just because of Cleo. I think—I think I'm *supposed* to be there. So I need to go."

"What do you mean you're supposed to be there? Did you have another vision?" Henry asked.

"Not exactly. I just have this feeling. I think I'm supposed to be there. Not to mention, I'm the only one who can understand Cleo."

Henry and Jake exchanged a look. Jen cut in before they could speak. "Are you sure?"

Noriko nodded.

Jen watched her for a long moment. "Okay. But you do whatever we tell you to do. Okay?"

"Okay."

"I mean it, Noriko."

"I know. I will."

Jen stared at her for a moment longer, then the three of them returned to their discussion.

Cleo gave a growl of contentment. But Noriko didn't feel content. She felt terrified.

Oh, I don't want to do this.

CHAPTER 76

The jet lurched, and Elisabeta stumbled, dropping her dress as she grabbed the side of the plane.

The pilot's voice came over the intercom. "We're in for a few bumps. There's a short batch of turbulence ahead. Everyone should strap in."

"Maybe a little more warning next time," she mumbled as she retrieved her dress from the floor and slipped into it. She had just gotten it zippered when the plane shook again. *Makeup will have to wait.*

She looked at her reflection in the full-length mirror on the back of the bedroom door. The sheath was a dark green with a lace overlay. She had matching pumps and gold accessories that would complete the look. She would look like the modest philanthropist she was. Or at least, the philanthropist she wanted people to *believe* she was.

Of course, the truth was that she did donate to causes. She had arranged for hospitals and schools to be built all over the world. So she wasn't a complete fraud. She just didn't actually believe in any of the charities she donated to. They were a means to an end.

They provided her the cover she needed to perform the activities she was *really* interested in.

And soon, all of that wouldn't matter. Soon, she could stop playing society host and embrace her real role: ruler of all.

But she wasn't quite there yet. She would give anything to avoid this idiocy in Manhattan tonight—yet another charity dinner. This one was at the St. Regis. The media would be there in full force and would cover everyone who entered. They always made a big deal about the rich and famous who attended these type of galas with the other rich and famous, as if they were a special type of species. Their giving back to society would be lauded and heralded by the media and all of the attendees' publicists.

She wondered what the public would think if they knew just how little actually went to the charities, after the expenses were paid. The ballroom, the food, the staff, decorations, invitations… the expenses went on and on. And all of it was deducted from whatever was raised at the event.

And although she would love to avoid tonight, Elisabeta would need to be seen, just in case any whiff of the children's situation drifted in her direction. She needed to be seen on this side of the country while events occurred on the other side. It was an annoyance, but it needed to be done.

Speaking of annoyances…

Elisabeta picked up her phone and dialed.

Gerard answered. "Yes?"

"Have you arrived?"

"We ran into some turbulence. The pilot needed to go around. But we will be landing in another few minutes."

Elisabeta frowned. She did not like delays. "You understand that there needs to be no evidence found."

"That will not be a problem. We have enough manpower. I will make sure not a trace is left."

Elisabeta smiled at the confidence in his voice. This was the

Gerard she knew. This was the Gerard she counted on. "When you return, we'll have a quiet dinner," she said. "Just the two of us, to celebrate."

His voice took on a husky timbre. "I look forward to it."

"As do I."

She disconnected the call. Yes, she looked forward to it greatly. It would be a nice distraction from her inability to identify Victoria.

She still had the two girls, of course; she just wasn't sure which one was Victoria. She had gone through the book again and again, but found nothing of use. She had scholars going over it now, focusing on a few passages she'd been unable to translate, and hopefully they would find the answer.

And if they didn't, she had another way to determine Victoria's identity. In the meantime, her plan would just have to adjust a little.

She would bleed them both.

CHAPTER 77

The flight across the country had been uneventful, and now Jake, Henry, Jen, and thirty Chandler operatives were barreling down Highway 191 toward the Canyon de Chelly National Monument in northeast Arizona.

It was a remote park, with few visitors, and was jointly managed by the National Park Service and the Navajo Nation. Forty Navajo families lived on the park's one hundred thirty-two square miles, farming and raising livestock

Jake had his computer open and was waiting for the satellite imagery of the park to update. Given the images he had now, it didn't look like Samyaza had arrived with children yet. *Assuming we even have the right place.* And they still didn't know exactly what they were walking into.

Truth was, they were heading across the country based on a psychic vision and a two-letter text. It was a far cry from the missions Jake had performed for the military, with pages of intel. But not long after Laney had entered his life, he'd learn not to question the path laid in front of him. As much as his younger self would balk at what he did now, he had learned that the world was much more than what he could touch and see.

But not all his lessons from the past had been lost. He had six teams of six, and he had not relied solely on his own men. He'd contacted Mustafa at the SIA, who'd arrived with a handful of agents, all trusted, and all with special skills. There were separated into five SUVs; Jen was at the wheel of Jake's. Choppers would have been quicker, but they also would have been easier for Elisabeta's people to spot.

In his mind, Jake reviewed each of the three dozen operatives that would be involved. He wasn't worried about any of them. On this trip, there was only one person he was worried about.

He glanced at Noriko, who sat right behind him with Cleo next to her. "You okay?"

Noriko nodded, but her face was pale. "Yeah. I'm okay."

"Just stay with Cleo, okay? And if anything goes wrong, you hide. We'll find you. We're going to drop you and Cleo off, well away from the fighting, then bring you in after we have the kids, so you can identify Victoria." He had tried to get Cleo and Noriko to stay back at the airport, but Noriko had insisted they needed to go along with them. "It's not too late, you know. You don't have to do this."

Cleo lifted her head and looked at Noriko. Noriko met her stare before turning back to Jake. "No, I'm in."

Jake glared at the cat. "You'd better not be pressuring her."

Cleo licked her paw.

Jake rolled his eyes. *I'm arguing with a giant cat.*

"It's okay. I'm—I'm supposed to be here."

Jake studied the young woman. Noriko had always struck him as shy, not one to push too hard. Yet she had been there to save Lou, and now here she was again. He was going to have to modify his assessment of her. But he still didn't like taking her with them.

Noriko ran her hand through Cleo's pelt absentmindedly. "It's so different here. It almost looks like a different world."

"Yeah. First time I saw the southwest, I thought the same thing."

She gave him a small smile before looking back out the window.

Jake turned back to his data, still uncomfortable with Noriko coming along.

"She'll be all right," Jen said.

"I know. I just don't like taking her in there."

"Like you said, we'll bring her in only when the kids are secure. She won't be near the fighting."

Yeah, because firefights always play out exactly as planned.

CHAPTER 78

The Arizona landscape flew past as Laney and Drake turned off 191 and onto Route 7. Laney couldn't help but think of Red Canyon, when Henry had been grabbed by Sebastian Flourent. That felt like a lifetime ago; so much had happened since then.

Laney hadn't contacted Henry, Jake, Jen or anyone from the Chandler Group yet. Dom's website had let her know where they were going. But she and Drake had already been in the air on the way there—thanks to a tip from Drake's "source," one he had been incredibly closed-mouthed about.

She watched Drake from the corner of her eye. He was focused on the road, and she was focused on his muscular forearms as he gripped the steering wheel. She had an image of him walking toward her with no shirt, only a leather skirt.

Her pulse jumped, and she turned quickly to look out the side window. Ever since she had woken up, she had been having flashes of her life as Helen—and of her relationship with Achilles. Friendship, belonging, desire—they all accompanied the visions.

But they felt like a cheat. Like she was jumping past the getting-to-know-you stage and right to the immortal-love stage.

After all, it had been years—*thousands* of years—since they'd been Helen and Achilles. He had lived all that time, and it had to have changed him. He was no longer the same man. He couldn't be.

And she wasn't Helen, either. Helen had been raised the heir to a warrior kingdom, with brothers, a sister, and two parents. Laney had been an orphan at age eight, an abuse victim until age ten, and then the only child of a priest. Her life and Helen's couldn't be any more different—which meant *she* was different. All the research said biology and environment played almost equal roles in who you became. So Laney's life experiences meant she wasn't Helen. And Drake's meant he was no longer Achilles.

So who are we to each other now? Just old loves? Because as much as she told herself her feelings were only an artifact from Helen's life, what she felt… it seemed real. And all-consuming.

Laney sighed. She needed to pull herself together. There would be time to figure this all out later. Right now they had more pressing concerns.

"You all right, ring bearer?"

Composing herself, she turned to him and nodded. He'd called her ring bearer—his attempt at reminding himself she had other priorities. *And a good reminder for me, too.*

"Are you sure the children are here? And who *is* this source of yours?" she said. Drake had shocked her when he'd told her he knew where the kids were heading.

Drake raised an eyebrow. "My source is working inside Elisabeta's operation, and for now that's all I'm going to tell you."

"Why?"

"Because I don't think you'll believe me—or him. He's one of Elisabeta's inner circle. He contacted me months ago."

"Why didn't you say something?"

"He's been quiet. He only contacted me today. It's the first time in months."

"Why you?"

Drake paused. "We knew each other in one of his past lives.

We were friends. He recently remembered that. And when he realized you were missing, he knew I was involved again."

Laney frowned. "Who is he?"

Drake just smiled. "An old friend. You can trust him, Laney. He wants those children safe."

Laney's mind whirled, trying to figure out who this "old friend" could be. But her thoughts were interrupted by a sign that appeared ahead. "There's the service entrance."

Drake turned, and the SUV bucked as they left the smooth asphalt for the dirt road that would lead them into the park.

Laney gripped the emergency bar. "Drake, I need you to promise me something."

He glanced at her and shook his head. "No."

"No? What do you mean, no? I haven't even asked you yet."

"You're going to ask me to promise to protect the children above all else, even you. And I can't do that."

"Drake, you can and you will. Because I won't be able to live if my life was chosen over a child's. You know that. So promise me."

The silence between them was heavy before Drake finally spoke. "You're going to drive me to an early grave," he grumbled.

"You're, what? Thousands of years old? I think we've passed the early grave possibilities."

"Yeah, but my life only truly began when you woke back up."

Laney went still. "Drake."

He grinned. "... is what a cheesy romantic would say. Fine. You want me to save the kids before you, you got it. You're on your own."

"Well, I didn't mean you can't help me out if I need it," she grumbled. "It *has* been a while since I fought."

"Not really. In your mind, you were just fighting in Troy. Your body remembers."

Laney looked over at him, and for a moment the air was charged. It wasn't Laney and Drake in the front seat of the SUV. It was Helen and Achilles.

Laney wasn't sure what to do. What to say. She curled her hands into fists to prevent her from giving in to an urge to touch his face. *Focus, Laney. Focus.*

Drake pulled over just as Laney felt the smallest tingle coming from ahead. "They're here."

CHAPTER 79

The Chandler Group was just two minutes outside the national park when the updated satellite images finally came in. Jake watched them unfold, his stomach clenching. "Three vans entered the park. That has to be them."

"Any sign of the kids?" Jen asked.

"No. But I'm guessing they're in the van."

"Are they heading for Mummy Cave Ruin?"

"Looks like." He glanced back at Noriko. "Looks like you were right."

She swallowed. "I guess so."

"We're dropping you well away from there. You'll be fine." He looked at Cleo. "Right, Cleo?"

Cleo placed her head on Noriko's lap. "She said she'll keep me safe," Noriko said.

Jake had picked a location far from the Mummy Cave Ruin to drop them off. He had a few other spots picked out as well, in case they weren't heading there.

"Where are they?" Jen asked.

"About a mile from the Mummy Cave Ruin." He paused. "You need to go faster."

Without a word, Jen pressed down on the accelerator, and the SUV shot forward.

Jake frowned as he looked at the image.

"What?" Jen asked, watching him from the corner of her eye.

"There's another car. It's trailing them."

"Do you think it's one of them?"

"I don't think so. It wasn't at the airport, and it's staying well back."

"So who do you think it is?"

"I don't know. But they're closer to the kids than we are."

Jen gripped the steering wheel tighter. "Then let's pray they're here to help."

CHAPTER 80

Laney and Drake trailed well behind the SUV caravan, and Laney used binoculars to keep an eye on them. Even at a distance, Laney could tell there were at least six Fallen inside and three nephilim. She frowned. That seemed like a lot of power to handle some toddlers. *Unless there's something else they have planned.*

"They're stopping," Laney said, and Drake pulled over behind some rocks.

Laney got out of the car and crept forward. "So, how exactly are we going to get the kids?"

"They can't sense either of us, but it's open ground—they'll see us well before we arrive."

Laney stilled and turned her head to the right. "Somebody else is here."

"Your friends?"

Laney nodded. "I'm guessing."

"And if we can sense them..." Drake said quietly.

There was a flurry of movement at the vans.

Laney nodded. "Then so can the Fallen."

CHAPTER 81

Gerard stopped the first van in the middle of the valley, with Hakeem's van stopping just behind him. From this spot they had a perfect view of the Mummy Cave Ruins. The ruins had been created by the Puebloan Indians and consisted of about seventy rooms three hundred feet up the red cliff face. The site had been occupied until around 1300 CE, when it was abruptly abandoned.

On either side of the ruins were deep alcoves that gave the appearance of eyes. And right now, it felt as if the eyes were watching them—which Gerard had no doubt was Elisabeta's goal. The woman did have a flair for the dramatic.

Gerard glanced at the "cargo" in the back of his van: two nannies and ten kids. A Fallen sat in the passenger seat. Gerard scanned the surrounding landscape. *Where the hell is the cavalry?*

He turned to the nanny closest behind him and spoke in Spanish. "Keep the children in the van. And keep their heads down."

"Why?" She looked at him with big eyes, and her voice trembled. All the nannies had been terrified ever since they'd left Vermont.

"These men will hurt you."

The woman nodded quickly.

Gerard stepped out of the van, and his co-pilot came around to join him. "Hey, what did you say to her?"

Gerard looked at the man and smiled. "That you're all bastards."

"What?"

Gerard ignored him and scanned the area again—but he didn't see or sense anyone else.

His co-pilot gripped his shoulder and turned him around. "Hey. I asked you a question. What did you just say?"

"I said I was going to kill you." Gerard snapped the man's neck. Pulling his knife from his sheath, he plunged it into the Fallen's heart, catching the man as he fell and lowering him quietly.

"Hey, what's going on?" another Fallen called from the second van, no doubt feeling the signal from his comrade wink out.

Well, I guess it's just me. Gerard palmed his knife and sprinted forward. He was on the next Fallen in less than a second and sliced him deep across the waist. The man let out a scream. Gerard didn't have time to finish him before he was tackled to the ground.

Hakeem leaned into his face. "She knew you'd betray her. She told me I could kill you if you did."

"Good luck with that." Gerard bucked him up with his hips and managed to get a knee in between them. He kicked Hakeem up and over. The big man crashed into the side of the van and slid down, unconscious. The nannies let out a scream from inside, and the kids began to cry.

Gerard rolled to his feet, but before he could move, another Fallen stepped forward. "Traitor," he growled.

Gerard stared at the man, weighing his moves. But there was one factor that made anything he did inherently risky: the Fallen held a girl in his arms, and had one hand wrapped around her throat.

"Look at you." The Fallen sneered. "Samyaza's great soldier. Scared to move in case I twitch and snap this little human's neck."

"Let the girl go. She's just a child."

"She's unimportant. Nothing matters except—" The man choked, and blood seeped from his mouth.

Drake stepped out from behind him, a knife in his hand, and grabbed the girl as the man fell forward.

"Took you long enough," Gerard said.

"Well, traffic was bad."

Gerard shook his head. "Did you even bring help?"

A lightning bolt tore from the sky and lit up a Fallen.

Drake grinned. "A little."

CHAPTER 82

Jen gunned the accelerator. The SUVs behind her fanned out, tearing across the dry ground. There was no cover in the park, and stealth was not an option, so they opted for speed.

Jake had his binoculars out. *What the hell?* He could see the vans, but it looked like a fight had broken out. Who the hell was fighting?

He spoke into his radio. "All team leaders—the children are the priority. Do not hesitate in protecting them. First teams, go, go!"

In a blur, the Fallen and nephilim were out of the SUVs and blurring past. Jake stared ahead, his heart pounding. It would only take the Fallen a second to snap a neck. Those children could all be dead by the time they reached them.

Another Fallen blurred toward the vans, coming from the opposite direction. He'd reach them before any of the Chandler group did.

"Who the hell is that?" Jake asked aloud.

A disturbance dragged his attention back to the vans, where another fight seemed to have broken out already. "What the hell is going on?"

Clouds rolled overhead, and a lightning blast took out one of the Fallen after another.

Jen slammed on the brakes and grinned. "Laney's here."

CHAPTER 83

Laney moved from her hiding spot. Without Drake's speed, she would never get there in time to help—but there *was* something she could do. She rained lightning bolts down on the Fallen she was able to see, making careful to keep the bolts away from the vans where the children were.

It didn't take long for the Fallen to start retreating. Laney smiled as they started to sprint from view. She sent a gale force wind to intercept them; it blew them into the air. She watched with satisfaction as they crashed to the ground.

A few blurred out of her reach, but that was okay. Drake and his friend took off after some of the blurs.

With a start, she recognized Henry standing among the vans. She had just taken a step toward them when a vision slipped into her mind: Noriko, sitting on a rock.

Cleo.

Laney whirled around. They had dropped Noriko off to keep her out of harm's way, to keep her safe. And she had been safe—until Laney had scattered some of the Fallen.

No. She began to run.

CHAPTER 84

Noriko sat on a rock with Cleo standing in front of her. Jake and Jen had practically tossed her from the car. They'd seen the vans heading in with the kids, and Jen had barely even slowed to let her and Cleo out. Even with the urgency, Cleo had had to tug her outside.

I am not cut out for a life of adventure, Noriko thought as she glanced at the pack Jen had insisted she take. It contained water, a radio, a sat phone, and a gun. She had tried to get them to keep the weapon, but they had refused to allow her anywhere near the canyon without it. And she knew she was supposed to be here. She just wasn't entirely sure why.

Cleo looked at her over her shoulder. *It's started.*

Noriko couldn't hear anything, but she didn't doubt Cleo's words. She ran a hand through the cat's pelt.

Protect you.

I know you will. Thanks, Cleo.

They sat together for what felt like forever, but Noriko knew it had only been a few minutes. Then Noriko heard a sound. She leapt to her feet and looked around. *What was that?*

Cleo growled low in her throat, the hair on the back of her neck standing straight up. Noriko's heart began to thump.

A man ran into view—and he was not someone from the Chandler Group.

Run! Cleo commanded.

Noriko stumbled back, fell. The man blurred toward them, and Cleo intercepted him with a roar. Noriko scrambled behind the rock she'd just been sitting on. *Cleo? Cleo, are you okay?*

A roar answered her, followed by a man's scream. Noriko peeked her head out. Cleo stood over the man, blood dripping from her mouth. The man had a gaping wound in his neck.

Then two more figures blurred into view. One slammed into Cleo, and they tumbled together, over and over. The other looked at Noriko and smiled.

Scrambling to her feet, Noriko ran.

CHAPTER 85

Noriko ran as fast as she could manage, but her legs were shaking so hard, and she knew she wasn't as fast as she needed to be. Even without the fear coursing through her, she would never be able to outrun a Fallen.

She scrambled up the path, her palms stinging from falling to the ground. *I never should have come. I never should have come.*

She felt the wind first—and then the man was in front of her, his hand wrapped in the front of her jacket.

"Hello. And who might you be?"

She yelped and tried to pull from his grasp. "No one. I'm no one."

Another man blurred into view next to her, and her heart broke. *Cleo. Where is Cleo? Cleo!*

But she received no answer.

No. Cleo, no.

"What are we doing with her?" the first man asked.

"Bring her. Samyaza will want to know how they found us, and this little bird will tell us. Won't you?"

Noriko could only stare back at him in terror.

Then both men spun and looked behind them. A blur

appeared, and one of the men tore off after it. But no sooner had he moved than, with a sickening thud, he suddenly fell to the ground, his neck broken.

Noriko stared, her heart pounding and her vision dimming.

The other man yelled, "You traitor! You filthy, stinking—"

A blur appeared and tackled him. Noriko screamed as she was thrown back, but a body cushioned her fall. She scrambled back quickly, and then went still. She knew those blue eyes.

He was just as shocked as he stared at her. "You."

The crack of a rifle broke up the staring match. Gerard grabbed her and rolled her so fast her head spun. He grunted as he pulled her behind a tall rock formation, hit the ground hard, and let her go.

She squirmed back from him, then noticed the blood pooling along the back of his shirt. "You've been shot."

"I'm aware." He grimaced. "I'll heal."

"But not soon enough," a man said as he stepped around the rock.

Noriko's eyes went wide as the man came into view.

Gerard sighed. "Hakeem, you really need some better lines. That was right out of a bad eighties movie."

Hakeem's mouth dropped. "That was a really good line. It totally fit."

"No, it was cheesy." Gerard looked at Noriko. "Wasn't it cheesy?"

Noriko looked between the two of them, amazed that Hakeem seemed to be waiting for her response. "Um, it—"

"Put the gun down slowly and stay where you are," a female voice called out.

A look of disbelief crossed Hakeem's face. He lowered his hand, dropped the gun to the ground, and stood still.

Noriko whirled around as a woman walked toward them, a gun in her hand.

The woman looked at Noriko and smiled. "Hey, Noriko."

CHAPTER 86

Laney's heart pounded, but she focused on keeping her voice calm and her face even. Noriko was terrified, not that Laney could blame her. The whole way here, Laney had been terrified as well—terrified that she wouldn't get to Noriko in time.

"Noriko, come stand behind me please."

"But there's a—"

The rifle blast cut through the air again.

"Laney!" Noriko screamed.

Arms wrapped around Laney, lifted her off her feet, and thrust her behind a tall rock spire across the path from Noriko. Her back pressed against the rock, she looked up into Drake's face, only inches from hers.

"Careful, ring bearer. I nearly didn't make it in time."

"But you did."

Laney heard a roar in the distance, and her heart lifted. *Cleo.* "You can let go now. Cleo took care of the shooter."

Drake nodded but didn't step back.

"Laney?" Noriko said, her voice trembling.

Laney pushed past Drake, ignoring the tremble in her own

legs. *Not the time, Laney. Not the time.* "I'm here. Are you all right?"

"Yes. Thanks to him." Noriko indicated Gerard.

The Fallen, the man who had been Elisabeta's right-hand man, tilted his head at her. "Ring bearer."

As he spoke, as a vision of a dark-skinned man with a hearty laugh and an easy smile drifted through Laney's mind. *Barnabus.*

Drake walked past her and offered his hand to Gerard. "Really, Gerard? Lying around? Don't you know we're in the middle of a battle?"

Gerard grimaced as he took Drake's hand and was pulled to his feet. "I did just save someone's life."

Drake sighed. "Yes, yes, haven't we all?"

Laney shook her head at the two of them. They were always like this. Achilles and Barnabus never seemed to—

She went still, her gaze meeting Gerard's. *I wonder if he knows.*

"Some of my memories started to return a few months ago," he said, as if reading the question on her mind. "At least, from one of my previous lifetimes." He tilted his head again and gave her a small smile. "It's good to see you again, old friend."

She felt the emotion well up in her throat and fought to keep her voice even. "You too, old friend."

Then she turned to Noriko and opened her arms. Noriko ran into them, and they held each other tight. "It's all right," Laney said. "You're safe now." She looked past her to Gerard. "Thank you for what you did. Because of you, those kids are safe."

Gerard shook his head. "Not all of them."

Laney's breath stopped. "She's found Victoria?"

"She's narrowed it down to two. She moved both of them."

"Where?"

"She didn't tell me. She's playing that close to the vest."

Laney's elation at saving the kids was dashed. Her gaze met Drake's.

"We'll find them," he said.

Yeah, but how? And what the hell had Henry and Jake been thinking letting Noriko any where near this craziness?

Laney hugged Noriko tighter. "It's okay, you're safe. But what are you doing here?"

Noriko wiped her eyes and stepped back, shooting a glance at Gerard. "I'm supposed to be here."

Laney frowned. "Supposed to?"

"Yes—it's something I needed to do."

Drake put an arm around Laney's shoulders. "No sense questioning the psychic. Just accept it."

Laney opened her mouth to reply, then shut it when she felt a familiar presence wafting through her mind. She stepped away from Drake.

He frowned. "What are you doing?"

She grinned. "Keeping you out of the line of fire."

A black shadow raced up the path toward Laney. Laney braced her legs, but Cleo knocked her down anyway. Drake let out a yell and managed to get underneath her as she fell, and Cleo stood over both of them, bathing Laney in kisses.

Laney laughed, trying to turn her head so she could at least speak. "Cleo, stop, stop. Let me up."

Cleo gave Laney one last lick and stepped back.

Laney rolled off Drake and got to her knees. Cleo buried her head in Laney's chest, and Laney wrapped her arms around her. *I missed you.*

Gone too long.

I know. I'm so sorry.

Okay?

Yes, I'm okay.

Drake stood and dusted himself off. "Um, I take it you two know each other?"

Laney smiled. "Drake, I'd like you to meet Cleo."

Cleo stalked slowly toward him, then prowled just as slowly around him.

"Uh, what's she doing?" Drake asked.

"Just making sure you're no threat."

Cleo bumped him on the way back to Laney.

"Hey," Drake yelled, stumbling.

Noriko laughed, and Laney grinned at her.

"What?" Drake demanded.

Cleo's growl cut off Laney's response. The cat was eyeing Gerard now, and the hair along her back was raised.

Noriko moved quickly in front of him. "No, Cleo. He's on our side."

Laney had a vision of Gerard jumping the fence and taking Max. Laney knew Noriko was seeing the same thing.

"I know," Noriko said. "But he's not that man—not anymore."

"He's not," Laney said softly, letting images of Barnabus fill her mind.

Cleo sat looking into Laney's eyes. Finally she nodded and went right back to nuzzling Laney.

"Um, does that mean she's not going to try to eat me?" Gerard asked.

Laney shrugged. "Not today."

"Hey, what about me?" Hakeem demanded.

Everyone turned to look at the Fallen, who was still frozen in place. Laney had completely forgotten he was there. From the look on everyone else's face, they had as well.

Drake glanced over at Laney with a wolfish smile. "I'd be happy to take care of him for you."

Laney shook her head. "No. I've got plans for him."

CHAPTER 87

By the time Jen and Jake had reached the vans, the fight was all but over. A few Fallen were down, so Jen and Jake quickly injured them further so they wouldn't spring up like some lethal Jack-in-the box.

Jen and Henry were now walking between the vans, calming the nannies. Almost all of the children were crying, and some of Jake's operatives were attempting to calm them as well.

Jake stepped away and tapped his radio mike. "Report, Mustafa."

"My men have run down four Fallen, but we're not sure what to do with them. We don't have any legal authority to arrest them."

Jake had known that would be an issue. "Keep them incapacitated until we're out of the park."

"We're leaving them?"

"Unless we want to straight up kill them in cold blood, or figure out away to convince the US government to safely incarcerate them."

Mustafa's sigh was audible over Jake's earpiece. "This is insane,

Jake. These men need to be locked up so they can't hurt anyone else."

"I agree, but until the United States government comes to the same conclusion, we can't do anything about it. We need to let them go."

"Fine. I'll let the men know. Then I'm heading back to you."

Henry walked over, and Jake nodded to the vans. "How many?"

"Thirty-four children, six nannies who don't seem to speak English, and only minor scrapes."

"It's a miracle none of them were killed." Jake looked over to the children. They were ringed by a group of Chandler operatives.

"No," Henry said. "Someone was helping us. Someone turned on Samyaza."

"Our texting friend," Jake said.

Mustafa jogged over.

"We good?" Jake asked.

"My men are sedating them. They'll follow us as soon as we're out of the park."

"Good. We'll leave you an SUV."

Mustafa gave him an abrupt nod and turned to go—but then turned back. "The lightning—that was Laney, wasn't it?"

"Yes," Henry said.

"Are we going after her?"

This time Jake answered him. "No."

Henry turned to him. "What? Why not? She's here."

"Yeah, and there's a reason she's not coming to us. As hard as it is, we need to trust that—we need to trust *her*."

"But Jake—" Mustafa began.

"No." Jake's voice was quiet but firm. "The children are our priority. That's what Laney would want. And you both know it."

Henry shook his head. "I know it, but I don't like it."

As Mustafa and Henry walked off, Jake thought, *I don't like it either.*

CHAPTER 88

Laney watched Noriko head off with Gerard toward where the Chandler Group was gathering the children. Gerard had agreed to tell them everything he knew about Samyaza's operation. If Laney and Drake were unable to get a location from Hakeem, hopefully Gerard and the Chandler resources could come up with something.

Cleo rubbed against Laney, and Laney reached down to run a hand through her pelt. She'd tried to get the cat to go with Noriko, but Cleo had refused. Apparently, now that Laney and Cleo were reunited, Cleo wasn't going to let her out of her sight.

Safe.

You're sure? Laney asked, watching Noriko disappear behind a rock.

Safe, Cleo repeated, and Laney felt a strong sense of protectiveness toward Noriko. But it wasn't from Cleo—it was from Gerard. She frowned. What was *that* about?

She looked up at Drake. "You're sure we can trust Gerard?"

"He has no allegiance to Samyaza, not after what she did to them."

"What did she do?"

"She took his joy and stomped it under her heel." Drake's voice held a deep sadness.

Still, a small twinge of doubt rolled through Laney. Could she trust Gerard? She knew he wasn't the Gerard she had fought months ago, but he wasn't fully Barnabus either.

"So what's the plan with this one?" Drake nodded toward Hakeem.

"He's going to tell us where Samyaza took the other two children."

"No, I'm not," Hakeem said.

Drake ignored him. "So we're taking him with us?"

"Unfortunately." Laney contemplated how to get the man to stay with them. She'd found that she had to be very specific with her wording to make sure that her commands had the intended effect.

Drake reached over and broke Hakeem's neck.

Laney gasped. "What did you do that for?"

Drake crouched down, pulled on Hakeem's arms, and hoisted him over his shoulders. He grinned at her. "To make him easier to transport. Unless of course you'd prefer listening to him yammer on."

"Come on. That man barely talks and you know it. But you're right: we should go before the others see us."

"You sure you don't want to see them?"

Laney looked in the direction where she knew Henry, Jake, and Jen were. She shook her head and started to walk back to the SUV. "I do—more than anything. But I can't take that chance. Someone may have reported the fight. Sound travels. And besides, even if it wasn't the Chandler Group, showing up somewhere with dozens of missing children is going to be a media circus, and I'm still wanted in half a dozen countries."

Drake wiggled his eyebrows at her. "A bad girl."

"Oh, shut up."

Drake laughed as he matched her pace, Hakeem's weight

seeming not to bother him at all. "Very well. So let's take our booty and skedaddle."

"Skedaddle? Careful, you're showing your age."

Drake narrowed his eyes. "Don't make me take you over my knee, young lady."

"Try it, old man."

"Is that a dare?"

Laney looked up at him and saw the intensity in his gaze. She swallowed, her mouth suddenly dry. "No, no dare. We should hurry up." She started to jog.

Drake stayed by her side, but Laney was careful to keep her eyes forward and not on the man next to her. And she did an admirable job of convincing herself that the uptick in her heart rate was simply an aftereffect of adrenaline.

CHAPTER 89

NEW YORK, NEW YORK

Elisabeta smiled and waved at the media as she exited the gala.

"Ms. Roccorio, Ms. Roccorio!" a reporter yelled.

Elisabeta turned to him, her perfectly practiced smile in place. "Yes?"

"Are you nervous being out in public with Delaney McPhearson still at large?"

Her again. Annoyance crept through Elisabeta but she maintained her composure and shifted her expression to one of concern. "Of course that is always in the back of my mind. But I won't let her keep me from living my life. That is what we do. We don't let the bullies win."

The reporter smiled at her as the flashbulbs went off.

Elisabeta's date took her elbow and escorted her to the car. The chauffer had the door open already. Elisabeta slid into the car, and her date went around to the other side and sat next to the driver. As soon as the chauffer was behind the wheel, he took off, and Victoria initiated the privacy shield. She pulled out her phone and dialed Hakeem again. He still wasn't answering. She called Gerard next. No answer from him either.

Something was wrong. She needed to get back.

She lowered the shield.

"Yes, ma'am?" the driver said.

"Take me to the 21 Club. The back entrance."

The ride took only ten minutes, but Elisabeta's nails had cut dark crescent moons into her palms by the time they arrived. Without waiting for the chauffer, she opened her door and strode inside.

Hilda appeared from a side room as soon as Elisabeta stepped into the foyer. "Everything ready?" Elisabeta asked.

"Yes, ma'am."

She opened a door, and Elisabeta stepped through with Hilda right behind her. In the room beyond the door waited a woman dressed exactly like Elisabeta, with her same coloring and build. Unless someone knew Elisabeta extremely well, they would be hard-pressed to tell the two women apart. Still, Elisabeta inspected the woman thoroughly before nodding. "Very good. Go."

The woman left the room. She would meet Elisabeta's escort in the hall, and they would head upstairs, where they would have dinner before attending a late performance of the ballet. Tomorrow morning, the woman and her escort would have breakfast together extremely early, and then be seen shopping throughout Manhattan for the entire day.

Hilda held up a coat. "The car's waiting outside."

Elisabeta slipped on the coat and pulled up the hood "Let's go."

They retraced their steps and entered a Mercedes SUV. Forty-five minutes later, Elisabeta was in a private plane, taxiing down the runway at LaGuardia.

"Can I get you anything?" Hilda asked.

"An update." They had tried to reach the team in Arizona on the car ride here, with no luck. "Track down Gerard and Hakeem.

Call the others with them. Use a satellite if you need to, but find out what the hell is going on. And find out where the hell the Chandler Group is right now. But first, get me the recording from the flight."

"Yes, ma'am." Hilda scurried to the back of the plane and disappeared into the office.

A flight attendant placed a glass of champagne on the table in front of Elisabeta. "May I get you anything else?" he asked, his voice husky.

Elisabeta waved him away. "Privacy."

Without a word he disappeared.

Hilda returned with a laptop. "I've queued it up for you."

On the car ride over, Elisabeta had started to watch this recording—a feed from the plane that had carried the children to Arizona. She'd had cameras placed in the cabin to make sure she would know if there were any problems. So far, she had seen nothing. The children had been crying, the nannies taking care of them. Hakeem had somehow slept for most of the flight. The rest of the team had sat along the perimeter of the plane's cabin.

But none of them were her concern. No—Gerard was her focus.

He had not been alone since Vermont. Elisabeta had made sure of that.

But he had done nothing suspicious. He slept a little. When he awoke, he jolted a little and stared straight ahead as if trying to figure something out. But besides that, he simply read a magazine and stared out the window. Nothing suspicious. And yet...

She rewound the recording to the beginning. There was something there. She knew there was. She just wasn't seeing it.

She frowned as she watched everyone settle in for the long flight. Gerard had no doubt spied the cameras. The man missed nothing. She focused on the screen, then paused it.

What was that?

She rewound the recording and replayed it. Gerard stretched

—and then he blurred for a spilt second. If she hadn't been watching carefully, she would have missed it.

She went through the recording again, frame by frame. Even so, he moved too fast for her to catch exactly what he had done. But on the last frame, she saw his phone in his hand. He hadn't had time to call anyone. Which meant—

He texted someone. She crushed the crystal glass in her hand as she glared at the screen. *What have you done?*

CHAPTER 90

CANYON DE CHELLY NATIONAL MONUMENT, ARIZONA

Noriko walked quietly next to Gerard. "Are you sure you want to do this?"

"No. But Laney asked me to, so I guess I'm going to. Besides, she's right. The Chandler Group needs to know all about Elisabeta's holdings, her plans, her strategies. I can tell them that."

Noriko was silent for a moment. "Laney, she—she seemed to recognize you. But not from now." As the words left her mouth, she realized how ridiculous they sounded.

But Gerard apparently understood what she meant. "We are old friends, she and I."

But not recently. She cast a sideways glance at him. *And you and I are old friends as well, aren't we?* The question slipped into her mind, and she knew the answer was yes. But she didn't think that bond was the same as the one between him and Laney. She wanted to ask if he felt the connection to her, but she couldn't seem to make herself.

"You should be prepared," Gerard said. "My appearance will not be greeted well."

"I know. I'm ready."

"Good. Because they're straight ahead."

Noriko could hear the voices now.

"We have all the children," Jake was saying. "We need to move out."

"I'll get Noriko," Jen said.

"No need." Noriko stepped into view. "I'm here."

All heads turned toward her—and in a flash, guns were aimed at her. Noriko realized Gerard had stepped up beside her, his hands raised.

"Noriko, get away from him," Jake ordered.

"You should step away," Gerard said quietly.

Noriko looked into his eyes and shook her head. "Trust me." She stepped in front of him. "No," she said to Jake. "He saved my life."

"Noriko—you don't know what he's done," Jen said. She stepped to the side to get a better angle on Gerard.

"I do. I know he worked for Elisabeta. But he's the one who called out to me in my vision. And he's the one who texted you."

Jen and Henry continued to move closer.

They're not listening, she thought. She didn't like the looks on any of their faces. A few other Chandler operatives had pulled their weapons as well and were moving in. *Oh, no.*

Noriko took a step back until she could feel the heat of Gerard behind her. "It's not just my word. Laney trusts him as well."

Henry went still. "What did you say?"

"Laney—she was here. She saved me. Well, after Gerard saved me. And she trusts him. She asked me to tell you to trust him too."

Henry and Jen exchanged a glance.

Jake walked closer. "Noriko, you must be mistaken. Laney would never—"

Noriko cut in. "She said he was an old friend." As soon as the words left her mouth, she knew it was the wrong tack. They wouldn't understand.

Gerard leaned into her, his breath on her ear. "You need to get away from me now."

"No," she whispered.

She raised her voice so it would carry to the others. "Cleo went with her. You know she would never leave my side if I was in danger." She looked at Jake. "She said you'd be the hardest to convince. She told me to tell you that your brother Tom visits his friend Seeley every other Sunday and takes him for a walk around the estate."

Jake's mouth fell open. "Did you see that in a vision?"

"No. Laney told me. Gerard can help us. And *she* wants you to let him."

The standoff was tense. Noriko reached behind her and took Gerard's hand, unsure who was most surprised by the action: her, Gerard, or the armed people staring at them.

Finally Jen broke the silence. "You're sure?"

Noriko tried not to let her fear show. "Yes."

Jen lowered her weapon. "Then let's see what the man has to say."

CHAPTER 91

Laney drove for an hour, following Drake's directions, before pulling over at a cabin that was little more than a shed. But it was in the middle of nowhere, which was all they needed.

Drake hauled Hakeem out of the car while Laney opened the door to the cabin. Inside were a bed, an old wooden table, one chair, and a wood stove.

"Cozy," Laney said as the others entered.

"Hunting cabin. The owner passed away fifty years ago and left it to me." Drake shrugged Hakeem off his shoulders, and the man landed on the floor with a thud.

"Drake!"

He extended his hands. "What? He'll heal."

Laney shook her head and eyed the man on the floor. "How long until he comes around?"

"As short or as long you'd like, my dear."

"Let's get him on a chair." She spied some rope on a nail over by the bed. She grabbed it and handed it to Drake. "We can tie him up with this."

Drake positioned Hakeem in the chair and raised an eyebrow.

"Are we in an old Western? Will we be tying him to the railroad tracks next?"

"We need him to stay where he is, and if he wakes up and lunges, this will give us enough time for me to command him to be still."

Drake took the rope from her. "Your lack of faith in my skills is insulting."

She rolled her eyes. "I'm sure your ego will survive."

"It is a very fragile thing." He tightened the ropes around Hakeem. "Well, that should keep him still for a good second or two."

"Oh, just shut up. So what do we do now?"

"You're asking me? I thought I was just the lackey."

She smiled sweetly at him. "Well, I'm new to kidnapping. You, however, have past experience in this area."

"That was a rescue, not a kidnapping."

"And yet somehow I still ended up unconscious—twice."

"Ah, yes." He smiled. "The memories."

She shook her head, but she couldn't seem to remove the smile from her face. "Okay, we need to know where Elisabeta took the other kids. Any idea how to get that information from him?"

"I beat him to a pulp?"

"Yeah, somehow I think that'd make him *less* likely to tell us anything." Laney studied the unconscious Fallen. "Gerard says he's not very bright. I'm wondering if he'll just tell us."

"You want to ask? Maybe if you say pretty please. No, wait: pretty please with sugar on top. That should work."

Laney held up her hand. "Well, this little ring does tend to get the Fallen to answer my questions."

"I'd still rather beat him to a pulp."

"There's more to life than fighting, you know."

Drake raised his arms. "But what is the point of this amazing physique if not to use it to make my enemies submit?"

"I'm sure you could come up with some other possibilities."

"Get your mind out of the gutter. We're working here."

Laney's mouth dropped, and she felt her cheeks flame. "I didn't mean—You know I didn't—"

"You are cute when you—"

Hakeem groaned. "Would you two get a room already?"

Laney turned to the large man, grateful for the interruption. "Hello, Hakeem. You will stay in that chair and not move until I give you permission to move."

Hakeem glared at the two of them. Then he looked down at the ropes. "Why'd you tie me up?"

Drake tilted his head toward Laney. "She thinks we're in an old Western."

"I like old Westerns," Hakeem said. "You ever seen *High Noon* with Gary Cooper?"

"I'm more of a John Wayne fan. Ever seen his movies?"

"I liked *The Quiet Man*. But I think that's because of Maureen O'Hara. I really like redheads."

Drake grinned. "Yeah, me too. Actually, I met John Wayne once."

Hakeem leaned forward, his face eager. "Really? What was he like?"

"Kind of a jerk. He cheated on all three of his wives. And he smelled like an ashtray."

"That's disappointing."

"I find most encounters with celebrities are." Drake caught Laney's gaze, and his expression immediately grew more serious. "Right, well. Back to the task at hand."

Laney shook her head. *Angels.* She said to Hakeem, "You will answer all of my questions truthfully."

Hakeem snorted. "No, I won't."

"What is your full name?"

"Hakeem Suarez."

"Where were you born?"

"Cordoba, Spain." Hakeem's mouth dropped open. "Why'd I tell you that?"

Laney held up her finger with the ring of Solomon on it. "Because you don't have a choice. Now—where is Elisabeta taking the other two children?"

Hakeem shrugged. "I don't know."

"Are you supposed to meet up with her?"

"Yes."

"Where?"

"I don't know. She didn't tell me."

"So how were you going to meet up with her?"

"I was supposed to call her after we killed the kids, the nanny, and Gerard if necessary."

Laney's pulse raced. "Okay. So you're going to call her and tell her they're all dead and Gerard is too. You're not going to mention anything about the fight. Do you understand?"

Hakeem stared at Laney sullenly. "Yes." He paused. "She's going to kill you, you know. After she makes you watch everyone you care about die."

"Do you really believe that?" Laney asked.

Hakeem didn't hesitate. "Yes."

Laney swallowed, hoping her fear didn't show. "If you give us away in any way, I will kill you first. Do you understand?"

He nodded.

"Do you believe me?"

He nodded again. "Yes," he spit out.

And Laney felt a little bit better.

CHAPTER 92

They loaded all the children and nannies into vans and SUVs and brought them back to the airfield in Gallup, New Mexico. Henry contacted the local police, who met with Yoni and the kids and a few other operatives.

They arranged to have the children taken into protective custody while their family situations were worked out. Danny forwarded all the information he had on the children to the Arizona family services, but even with that head start, it would take a while to get the children all sorted, so Yoni would stay with them while everything was taken care of. Luckily, the press hadn't gotten word of any of this—yet.

Now Henry, Jake, Jen, and Noriko sat in a private office with Gerard. Gerard had a drip attached to him; Jake had insisted on drugging him to reduce his abilities. Noriko had balked, but Gerard had told her it would be all right. And he hadn't once tried to pull the line out or escape. In fact, he'd quietly gone along with everything demanded of him. Not that his cooperation had scored him any points with the others.

Noriko had insisted on being here, even though the others had tried to talk her out of it. She couldn't help but notice the weapons at the sides of Jake, Jen, and Henry. She also didn't like the looks on their faces. They had said they'd listen, but nothing they'd done so far had suggested an open mind.

"Why should we believe anything you say?" Jake asked Gerard.

"Because I risked my life to save those children."

"Why?" Henry asked.

"My reasons are my own. But I have no allegiance to Samyaza." He nodded to Noriko. "Ask her. She knows."

All eyes turned to Noriko. "He saved me," she said.

"How did you get involved in this?" Jen asked Gerard.

"I already told you that."

"Tell us again."

Gerard sighed. "Samyaza has had people trying to find me since I broke with her. After Honu Keiki tried to kill me, I originally thought it was Samyaza, and I started paying a little more attention to where everyone was. I noted that two Fallen who worked for Elisabeta had flown into an airport near me. I thought they were coming for me. I followed them, thinking I could get the drop on them. That's when I realized they weren't interested in me at all. They were surveilling a house. I didn't know what to make of it.

"They grabbed a child from the house an hour later. I gave chase, but I only managed to catch one—the one without the child. So I asked him some questions."

"He answered them?"

"Eventually. And I learned this was not the first time Elisabeta had sent them after a child. So I offered my services to her, so I could find out why. And when I learned where they were holding the children, I planned on releasing them."

Noriko noted the absence of emotion in his words, but she could sense it boiling just under the surface. He looked up and met her gaze—and she sucked in a breath at the pain that rolled over her as she was yanked into a vision.

The huts were ablaze as Noriko walked through the village, but she couldn't feel the heat. She could see the bodies though. Some were inside, some across the doorways, some along the paths. All were dead. Men, women, and children—no one had been spared.

Voices were raised ahead of her. Someone was alive. She could glimpse a river beyond the burning huts, but no one was rushing with water to put out any of the fires. She hurried forward and stopped abruptly as she passed the last hut. Six men stood towering over a seventh man who knelt on the ground. The man held two children in his arms, a boy and a girl, both young, both covered in blood.

He looked up. Anger and grief had drawn heavy lines into his face. "Why?" he screamed at the warriors above him.

Noriko recognized the man, and gasped. It was Gerard. Her heart ached at the devastation on his face.

A man stepped toward him, flanked by two of his Fallen. Noriko knew this man was Samyaza, though he appeared as a man with long blond hair. Samyaza insulted and derided Gerard, who continued to hold his children, his agony clear on his face.

Noriko finally looked closely at the two children.

Her legs shook, and tears sprang to her eyes. The children lay still in their father's arms—dead. Yet somehow, Noriko could hear Peter's laugh and Arya's soft voice. Their deaths felt like a punch in the chest, as if her life had been pulled from her very soul.

The vision cut off, and Noriko blinked up at the concerned faces above her. She was on the floor.

"Are you all right?" Jen asked, helping her sit up.

Noriko nodded, but she felt the tears on her cheeks and the ache in her chest. She looked past Jen to meet Gerard's gaze. Tears crested in her eyes. "I'm sorry."

Gerard's mouth dropped. He gave her an abrupt nod before turning away. But she caught the anguish all the same, the devastation still fresh.

Jake looked between the two of them. "What's going on?"

Noriko's voice was soft. "Samyaza killed his family, his children. He was trying to get Gerard to turn his back on them. To slaughter humans. He refused."

Henry frowned. "He? Samyaza's a woman."

"Now. This was lifetimes ago. But Gerard remembers. It's like yesterday to him. He is not helping Samyaza. He couldn't. And the children…" The image of Gerard holding his children once more passed through her mind. "He won't let Samyaza hurt any more children. That's why he's helping us."

Silence descended. Noriko could tell Jake didn't want to believe her. But the grief coming off Gerard could be felt by anyone, psychic or not.

"Okay, so Gerard's on our team, at least for the moment," Jen said. "Where does that leave us?"

"Back where you started," Gerard said. "Victoria is not among the children you have. She was taken somewhere else. Two girls were taken. Molly Shelton and Susie—"

"McAdams," Jake said, his face pale.

Gerard nodded. "They both have a mark that suggests they could be Lilith. So Elisabeta took them both."

"Where did she take them?" Henry asked.

"I don't know the answer to that. She didn't share everything with me. She didn't fully trust me yet."

"But Laney's going after her," Henry said quietly.

"Yes. She and Drake took one of Elisabeta's men. I assume they'll get the information from him."

"What is Elisabeta planning? Are the children in immediate danger?" Henry asked.

"I don't believe the one who is Victoria is. But the other one… Elisabeta will have no need for her."

Jake cursed softly before striding out of the room.

CHAPTER 93

Jake paced along the hangar, having no clue what to do next. He vacillated between hoping Susie was Victoria so she would be safe, and hoping she wasn't so she wouldn't be taken from the McAdamses.

And if she wasn't Victoria, they would need to get to her before Elisabeta realized that.

His phone rang, and he looked at the screen. Mary Jane McAdams. Jake sent the call to voicemail, cursing himself as he did so. The return of the children had no doubt made the news. Mary Jane would be beside herself when she heard about it. He didn't want to break her heart and dash the hopes she had no doubt built up.

Taking a deep breath, he dialed Mary Jane's number. "Hey, Mary Jane. It's Jake."

"Jake, thank God. It's all over the news. Is it true? Did you find Susie?"

Jake hesitated, not sure how to say what needed to be said. He struggled to think of a way to soften the blow. But at the same time, he knew there was no way. "We did find most of the missing children."

Mary Jane gasped. "That's amazing! I—"

Jake cut her off quickly. "But Susie was not one of them. She's not here."

Silence answered him for a few beats. Then Mary Jane spoke. "Maybe you just didn't recognize her. She could be there. I'll fly out and—"

"Mary Jane, I have confirmation that Susie was taken somewhere else."

Jake could hear her heart breaking and her hope being crushed across the phone line. "Are you sure?"

"Yes. I'm sorry. But we're not done. I'm going to keep looking. We'll bring her back to you."

Mary Jane took a stuttering breath. "Thank you, Jake, but please don't make promises you can't keep." The line went dead.

Jake squeezed his phone in his fist, wanting nothing more than to hurt something, to make it feel as much pain as Mary Jane was feeling.

The sound of engines rushing toward him caused him to turn. Four government-issued SUVs raced across the tarmac toward him. They all slammed to a stop, and Moses Seward stepped out of one, slamming his door. He glared at Jake as he strode toward him.

Oh, shit. Jake shoved his phone back in his pocket. *As if this morning isn't crappy enough.*

CHAPTER 94

QUEENS, NEW YORK

Elisabeta slammed the phone down on the table. Her plane was still sitting on the runway at LaGuardia. There was a huge backup due to some sort of computer glitch at the tower. They might not be able to take off for another hour or two.

She had spoken with Hakeem a half hour ago. Apparently, the canyons walls had interfered with cell reception, keeping them out of reach. Everything had gone as expected, including Gerard turning on them. Even though she had expected that, it did sting. Still, he was no longer a worry. Hakeem and the men were on their way to Michigan, and Elisabeta would join them there.

If this plane ever takes off!

Hilda hustled into the cabin. "Ma'am, there's something you should see."

"What?"

"A broadcast. The children have been found."

Hilda turned on the TV in the cabin. A news broadcaster was on screen, his dark hair perfectly groomed, his expression a precise blend of concern and amazement. "An incredible discovery today at the Canyon de Chelly National Monument. A group of over thirty children who have been missing from around the world were found together. The Chandler Group, run by Henry Chandler, were in the park and came across the children. Chandler, of course, is the brother of Delaney McPhearson, who is wanted in connection with—"

Elisabeta snapped off the TV. "Funny Hakeem didn't mention anything when we spoke."

Hilda took out her phone and dialed. But after a few moments, she shook her head. "He's not answering."

"What about Delaney? Was she spotted?"

"No ma'am, only Henry Chandler, Jen Witt, Jake Rogan, and some Chandler operatives."

Elisabeta raised an eyebrow. "Any *unusual* weather patterns in the park at that time?"

"There were some reports of lightning." Hilda met Elisabeta's eyes, then she looked away.

Elisabeta growled. "Get out."

Hilda disappeared into the back of the plane.

Elisabeta stared out the window. Delaney McPhearson was back. *I should have moved faster.* She was undeniably on her way to the children. And McPhearson had only a short hop from Arizona, which meant she would arrive there first.

Now, how do I play this? She could alert the local authorities, but since McPhearson had Drake with her, she doubted they would be very effective. Besides, if McPhearson told them what she was up to, the locals—or worse, the feds—could interrupt her plans. And that wasn't an option, not when she was so close.

No, she would handle McPhearson herself. Apparently making the woman a public pariah hadn't been enough. It was time to take her out of the game—painfully.

She smiled. *And permanently.*

CHAPTER 95

GALLUP, NEW MEXICO

The Chandler Group had been under surveillance for months. And when the ETF had been given control of the SIA, they had taken over that surveillance. So Moses's men had alerted him immediately to their departure.

He had been livid that his men hadn't stopped them. But apparently the Chandler Group had expected that and had had their men block the road leading to the airport.

It had taken Moses over an hour to commandeer a plane and learn where the Chandler Group were heading. By the time Moses and his men touched down, they had learned of the Chandler's Group's miraculous find: thirty-four girls around the age of two, all with red hair and blue eyes.

Moses had blinked hard at the description, and he still didn't know what to make of it. But he also knew this was finally his chance to take Henry Chandler and Jake Rogan into custody. Whatever had drawn them across the country was, no doubt, illegal. And Moses was going to enjoy carting them away himself.

The whole trip here he'd reviewed the Chandler Group's

activities for the last few years, particularly with regard to Delaney McPhearson. She was the world's most wanted fugitive, and these people had helped her, although none of them had been charged.

Yet.

It was an absolute miscarriage of justice. Moses's temper boiled as he read over the incidents in Montana, Ecuador, Australia, India, Israel. These people had left a trail of destruction in their wake. The number of deaths they'd been responsible for was astronomical. As far as Moses was concerned, the Chandler Group was the world's most dangerous terrorist group. And he was charged by the United States government to take down terrorists—wherever he found them.

As he stepped from the SUV, he was filled with righteous fury. These people thought they were above the law. They thought they could do whatever they wanted. Well, they were about to find out how wrong they were.

He saw Jake Rogan open the door to the hangar.

"Stop right—"

Rogan disappeared inside.

Moses's anger spiked. Dryden hurried ahead of him and opened the door for Moses. He stepped inside.

Ten men stood talking, and gave only a quick glance at Moses and Dryden. Another dozen lounged at tables along the back, and a few even slept curled up on the floor. All of them were dressed in black tactical gear. Jake Rogan, Henry Chandler, and Jenifer Witt were not among them.

But there were two men whom Moses recognized. He strode up to Fricano and Jenkins, the front gate guards from the Chandler estate. "What are you two doing here?"

"Standing," Fricano replied.

"I mean, what are you doing in Arizona?" Moses growled.

"Paintball," Jenkins said.

"Paintball?" Moses echoed.

"Yeah. It's this game where everybody has a gun that shoots paint pellets. You break into two teams—"

Jenkins cut in. "Well, technically, you could have more than two teams."

Fricano nodded. "That's true. But we only had two teams today. Anyway, each team—"

"I know what paintball is!" Moses yelled. "But do you actually expect me to believe this entire group flew across the country to play paintball?"

"I really can't control what you believe, sir. I can only control what I do," Fricano said.

Jenkins's face was serious as he clapped Fricano on the shoulder. "Powerful words, my man, powerful words."

"Thanks."

Moses gritted his teeth. "And the children? You just, what? Stumbled upon them?"

"You know, we were pretty surprised when we found them too," Fricano said. "Right, Dylan?"

"Yup."

Moses grit his teeth. "*Where* is Jake Rogan?"

Fricano tilted his head toward the door at the back of the hangar. "In the office."

Moses turned his back on Fricano and Jenkins and nodded to three of his own men. "Make sure none of them leave." He strode toward the door and flung it open.

Jen Witt, Henry Chandler, and Jake Rogan looked up in surprise as he entered. They were sitting around a table, the remains of a takeout breakfast in front of them. A young woman was with them, and another man lay on a couch in the back of the office, a drip attached to his arm.

"Agent Seward, what a nice surprise," Henry said, closing his newspaper.

"*I'm* not so sure it's a nice surprise," Jen said, turning back to her own newspaper.

"Well, I've got you now," Moses said.

"Got us?" Jake asked. "Not sure we know what you mean."

"You are no longer agents of the federal government. You have no authority to—" He paused. "To do whatever you just did."

Jen raised an eyebrow. "Well, that was clear."

"I know you acted as an extra-legal agent when you found those kids. There will be consequences."

Henry frowned. "I'm confused, agent. Are you suggesting that the US government wanted us to leave those children where we found them?"

"Of course not." Moses nodded toward the man on the couch. "What's going on with him?"

"He got dehydrated," Jen said.

The man on the couch shrugged. "I should have drunk more water."

Great, another one. He turned to the young woman. "And you are?"

The girl looked around. "Uh, Noriko."

"And were you playing paintball?"

"Um, no. They made me sit out."

"Why?"

"The guys get a little serious," Henry said. "We didn't want her getting hurt."

"Then why are you here?"

"She's with me," the man on the couch said, his tone daring Moses to push further. Moses contemplated it. But the look in the man's eyes…

He turned back to the three who were his focus. "You are not allowed to operate in a law enforcement capacity on America soil."

"I see," Henry said. "And what exactly did we do that suggests we did what you're suggesting?"

Jen flicked her newspaper loudly and sighed. "Great. His doublespeak is contagious."

Moses narrowed his eyes. "I have my men searching your planes. I'm sure they'll find something that will confirm my suspicions."

Jake shrugged and reached for a bagel. "Okay."

Jen and Henry turned back to their papers.

Moses stood staring at them, but they acted as if he wasn't there. He turned to Dryden. "Make sure they don't leave."

Twenty minutes later, Moses men had searched all of the planes. And all they had found was guns—paintball guns, along with extra paint cartridges and paint-splattered clothes.

"Um, sir," Dryden said. "What do you want us to do?"

"Keep searching. They're up to something."

Dryden scurried away.

Moses glared at the hangar as if he could see Jake, Henry, and Jen through the walls. *I will find out what you were up to.*

CHAPTER 96

Jake paced in the office. Prior to arriving at the airfield, he had sent Jordan to dump all of the weapons at one of Henry's secure holding areas nearby, so there was no chance of Seward finding anything except the paintball equipment. But still, despite having searched the planes twice, Seward was holding them.

They'd relayed Gerard's information on Samyaza's holdings to their people back in Baltimore, but they hadn't found anything that would point to where Samyaza had taken the two girls. Samyaza's holdings were extensive. It would take weeks, if not months, to check them all. *We have nothing...*

But maybe Laney does.

It had been extremely difficult to not try to go find her when they were at the park. She had been so close. But he knew her, and she wanted them to get the children out of there. He didn't doubt that. He just hoped she was having better luck than they were.

Besides, if Laney had been with them, Seward would now have her in custody—and no one wanted that. But it would have been nice if she had given them a heads-up as to what she was doing.

Jake felt the minutes ticking away. There were still two children out there. And as long as Seward kept them here, they weren't tracking down those children.

"You need to calm down, Jake. Wearing a hole in the floor won't help us find those kids," Jen said.

"Well, sitting on our asses isn't doing a whole hell of a lot either," he said.

"No," Henry said. "But we have people working on it. And until we get a lead, even without Seward here, there would be nothing we could do."

Jake sighed. "I know. I know. I just hate it."

"Do you want to call Mary Jane again?" Henry asked.

Jake shook his head. "No. I mean, what can I offer her besides my sympathies at this point? And every time I call, I know her hopes build that I have good news. So until I have some…" He shrugged.

"Maybe you could just call her."

Jake frowned. "Why?"

Jen and Henry exchanged a look.

"What?" Jake demanded.

"Nothing. It just seems you have a type: pale redheads."

Jake reared back. "What? No. It's not like that. She's lost her child. I would never—"

Henry raised his hand. "Hey. We're not accusing you of anything."

"But if you *were* interested in her, would it be the worst thing?" Jen said.

Jake looked between them. "With Laney missing?"

Henry glanced at Jen before turning back to Jake. "Laney chose to leave. Yes, to protect us. But she's gone, and it's been months. I love her. I want her back here. But I can't make that happen. And none of us can stop living while we wait. Laney wouldn't want that. You know that better than any of us."

Jake let out a breath. "I know. It's—I don't know. Right now, my life is consumed by this search."

"Maybe that just shows you that you need to take a step back," Jen said.

"Maybe," Jake said quietly.

"Laney will find them," Noriko said. "It's what she does, isn't it?"

"It's what she does," Jake agreed.

His phone beeped. It was a text from Jordan. *Any idea when you guys will be free?*

Jake texted back. *No. Seward seems to want to keep us until he finds something.*

Well, me and the guys are napping at the northwest entrance. Give me a yell when you guys get released.

Will do.

Jake blew out a breath. This standing around doing nothing was killing him. He felt as helpless as he did those first few weeks when Laney was gone.

Jake's phone beeped again, and this time Henry's and Jen's phones did too. Jake stared at his screen. It showed a text from an unfamiliar number. *The kids are at Gradley Island in Lake Michigan.* The words were followed by coordinates.

Jake's mouth fell open. "Did you guys just get—"

They both nodded.

"It's Laney," Jen said quietly. "She's found them."

"Are you sure?" Henry asked.

Jen nodded. "There's no way she'd leave Victoria in Elisabeta's hands. Besides, Noriko said they had one of Elisabeta's men. I bet she got it out of him."

Jake realized she was right. "We need to go."

Henry shook his head. "We can't all go. We still have Seward to deal with."

"If Laney's contacting us, it's because she needs our help."

"I know," Henry said.

"I'm not staying here," Jake said.

"And you shouldn't," Jen said. "Grab Jordan, find the kids. We'll cover for you as best we can."

"But how do I get out of here without them seeing me?"

"We'll cause a distraction, and you slip out the door."

"What kind of distraction?" Jake asked.

Jen grinned, strode across the room, and flung open the door. "Where the hell is Seward?" she shouted. "I've had it with this confinement. I better be out of here in five minutes or someone's losing their job!" She continued to yell as she made her way across the hangar.

Henry laughed. "I'll go help her before she hurts someone."

Jake grinned. "Maybe you should wait a little while then."

Henry chuckled. "I think we're in enough trouble. You get going."

CHAPTER 97

After learning where the children were from Elisabeta, Laney and Drake wasted no time heading for the western coast of Michigan. Drake had arranged for a private plane to take them there from the Farmington airport in New Mexico. Elisabeta had been surprisingly forthcoming. Obviously she had not trusted Gerard completely and had expected him to turn. But Laney had realized it wasn't truly about trust with Elisabeta but arrogance. Elisabeta thought she knew what every one would do and why. And that would be her downfall.

Hakeem was now in the back of the plane, unconscious. They were keeping him with them in case Elisabeta wasn't there. But once they had the kids back, Laney wasn't sure what to do with him. Normally she would turn a Fallen she'd captured over to the SIA, but they no longer were in the Fallen imprisonment business. And she wasn't exactly on good terms with the US government.

She sighed. *One problem at a time.*

She stared at the phone in her lap. It had taken a great deal of internal struggle to get her to contact Jake, Henry, and Jen. She wanted to keep them far away from her, lest they get hurt if she was discovered. But if Elisabeta had the girls, she was going to need all the help she could get.

Jake had just sent a text back saying he and Jordan were on their way with half a dozen operatives. She had been debating whether or not to send him a text in response. She still hadn't decided. They needed to coordinate, but it felt like there was this gulf between them.

"Coming through." Drake pushed her legs aside so he could sit in the seat next to her.

She grumbled as she pulled her knees back. "There are ten other unused seats in this plane."

"Ah, but I like sitting next to you."

She rolled her eyes and ignored the butterflies dancing through her stomach. *He's Drake, not Achilles. You're Laney, not Helen.* "How's our friend?"

Drake stretched out his hands. "Once again, unconscious. You know, since you've woken up, I've been involved in more violent acts than I think I've been involved in in the last hundred years." He paused. "Actually, the most violent act before this was probably that time we spent a lovely evening at that quaint little restaurant outside Las Vegas."

"You mean the biker bar you sauntered into and managed to get the entire place to want to kill us?"

"Ah, yes. Good times." He nudged her arm. "Admit it—you had fun that night."

Laney shook her head, but once again she couldn't keep the smile from her face. "I admit no such thing." Her smile faded as she remembered that while she was here joking around, two children's lives were at risk.

"Hey," Drake said softly.

She looked up into his eyes.

"It's okay to smile. Your life is duty, but it's also a life. You are allowed to smile and laugh. It doesn't take away from your mission. It doesn't take away from the stakes. But it does make it all more bearable."

"It feels wrong. There are families out there who have been torn apart by Elisabeta."

Drake sighed. "You always take on the weight of the world. Most of the time the people you help, they get to move on from the pain and horror of it. But you *live* in that horror and pain. So yes, you do get to laugh, even though other people are crying. Otherwise you'd be crying all the time. You need to let the light in, Laney. You can't always live in the dark."

Unconsciously, Laney had started to lean toward him. And now he was only a few inches away. If she just leaned a little bit more—

She pushed back and took a breath.

Drake watched her for a moment before leaning back in his own seat. "I think I'll get a little sleep. Wake me if Hakeem tries to rip a hole in the wall of the plane." He closed his eyes and reclined his seat.

Laney watched him, studying the angles of his face. In her mind, she saw him across the firelight, his face bathed in shadow. Her heart pounding, she licked her lips and undid her seatbelt. She hurried to the restroom and splashed cold water on her face. She stared at her reflection in the mirror. Her face was pale, but her cheeks were bright red. And her eyes shone.

"It's not the time for this," she told her reflection.

Drake's words drifted through her mind. *You need to let the light in, Laney. You can't always live in the dark.*

Somehow, even with everything spinning around her, when Drake was with her she felt lighter, freer than she could ever recall since this had all begun.

She just wasn't sure if that was a good thing or a bad one.

CHAPTER 98

Jake managed to sneak out without the ETF noticing him. That was thanks mostly to Jen, but Fricano and Jenkins had helped as well. When they noticed Jake slipping out, they staged a fight to draw everyone's attention.

Jordan sat next to him as he piloted the small private plane. They had stopped by the storage supply unit where Jordan had dropped the weapons earlier, and now they were all loaded up. Six operatives were in the back getting some sleep before they landed in Michigan to face who knew what.

"I still can't believe Laney finally contacted us. You are sure it's her, aren't you?" Jordan asked.

"It's her. And she needs our help."

"But help to do what? And why didn't she contact us as soon as she woke up? I don't like this one-woman show thing she's doing."

"Well, she's not exactly on her own. She's got Cleo, and"—he paused—"Drake."

"The Vegas guy?" Jordan sounded incredulous.

Jake and the others had decided to keep Drake's identity a closely held secret until they knew what the man was up to and whose side he was on.

"He's a little more than just a Vegas guy," Jake said.

"Wait. He's a Fallen?"

"An archangel, actually."

"Seriously?"

Jake nodded.

"Wow. I never would have called that."

Me either, Jake thought.

The rest of the flight to Michigan was quiet. Jake spent the time downloading all the information he could on the area, which wasn't much. Gradley Island was a small island about a half mile off the western coast of Michigan. The mainland across from it was an undeveloped fifty acres, privately held. The island, too, had been untouched until three years ago, when someone started building, although no details were available. Satellite feeds showed nothing more than what looked like a normal house at the center of the island. But Jake knew looks could be deceiving.

"Have you tried calling her?" Jordan asked.

Jake shook his head. "If she's in the middle of something, I don't want a ringing phone giving her away. She'll reach out when she's ready."

"You sure?"

"Yes." And he realized it was true. Laney wouldn't let him go in without any info, and she wouldn't place the girls in jeopardy by keeping him in the dark.

As if on cue, his phone rang. Jake looked at the screen. It was the same number that had placed the text. He answered quickly. "Laney?"

"Hi, Jake."

CHAPTER 99

Laney gripped the phone, not prepared for the onslaught of emotions Jake's voice elicited. Homesickness washed over her, and longing. She wanted to be back in Baltimore. She wanted to be around Jake, Henry, Jen, her uncle, everyone. She had missed them so much.

"Are you okay?" Jake asked.

She took a shaky breath. "I'm good. And I'm sorry I had to disappear like that. I just couldn't—"

"You don't have to explain. I get it. You're in charge of this whole little mission. You have to make the calls, even if they're painful. And I know that one was… for all of us."

Laney felt tears press against the back of her eyes. "You've changed."

His throaty laugh came across the line clearly. "I like to think I've evolved."

"Is everyone okay?"

"Yeah. Henry and Jen are keeping the ETF busy." He paused. "There's something you need to know though, about Cain."

"I know. I, uh, saw him. And my uncle."

Jake was silent for a moment, and Laney wasn't sure what to expect. Anger, maybe annoyance, that she hadn't reached out to him. But he just chuckled. "I really need to stop underestimating you."

She smiled. "You do have a habit of doing that."

"I'm working on it. These coordinates you've sent, it's where the girls are being held?"

"That's what we think." She quickly explained about Hakeem and what he'd revealed.

"Okay. So what's the plan?"

Laney took a breath. "Drake, Cleo, and I will go in and get the girls out. You, Jordan, and the rest of your team will wait on the shore. We'll get the girls to you. Your sole responsibility is getting the girls to safety."

"We're not helping you?"

"You are. The girls come before anything. If anything goes wrong, we need you there to get the girls out."

He was silent for a moment. "Okay. We'll wait for you."

"Thank you." She paused. "The girls' families—do you know anything?"

"One of them, Isabel Somerfield, her father was killed trying to protect her."

Laney's heart clenched. *Oh, God.* "What about her mother?"

"She died from breast cancer a year after Isabel was born."

"So she's alone?"

"There's some extended family, but no one close."

Laney wasn't sure if that meant she should hope Isabel was Victoria—simply because it would disrupt fewer lives. "And the other girl?"

Jake paused. "Her name's Susie. She's from outside Boston. She's got a mom, two brothers, a sister, and a very involved extended family."

Jake's words were straightforward, but she heard a little something behind them. "You know them?"

"Jen and I met them not that long ago. Susie's disappearance is what clued us in to the missing kids."

"And the family? They're a good family?"

Jake's voice softened. "Mary Jane's an incredible mom. And she's got great kids. The father, he died last year in a car accident. Jen and I think he was a Fallen. The other daughter, she's fifteen, she's just starting to come into her abilities."

Laney wasn't sure what to say. She hadn't considered one of the children coming from a Fallen. But she also couldn't miss the pride in Jake's voice when he spoke of the girl's family. "You like them."

"They're a good family. They've been through a lot. They deserve some happiness. And I really hope Susie isn't Victoria. Have you figured out a way to identify her?"

Laney looked down at Cleo, who was stretched out next to her. "Yeah. I've got that covered."

"Good."

"We're about twenty minutes away. I'll text you when we land."

"We'll be right behind you."

"I have no doubts." Laney paused, knowing she'd conveyed everything she needed to convey, but not feeling quite ready to hang up yet.

"It'll be okay, Laney. You've got this."

She gave a small laugh. "Not so sure about that."

"We have reports that Elisabeta's in Manhattan."

"Yeah, I heard that too. But it doesn't make any sense. I can't see her being that far away. Not when she's so close to her goal."

"You think she'll show up?"

Laney nodded. "I'm counting on it."

CHAPTER 100

Laney, Drake, and Cleo had touched down only an hour ago at the West Michigan Regional Airport. Laney had almost forgotten she was wanted by the world until Drake handed her a hat and sunglasses as she prepared to get off the plane.

Luckily no one had raised the alarm, which was amazing, especially when Drake had to haul Hakeem out of the plane and into the car. But the only time anyone noticed them was when Cleo was slinking her way down the plane stairs and into the SUV. Two kids saw her, but by the time they got their parents' attention, Cleo had disappeared from view.

After that, they made the trip to Lake Michigan in little time. Now they stood on the bank across from the island, hidden by the tree line. A dozen guards had been stationed throughout the acreage across from the island, but they were all human, and Laney and Drake knocked them out easily and tied them up.

"Well, that is definitely more of what I expected," Laney said as she lowered her binoculars. The island looked impenetrable. Guards roamed the shoreline, and a giant fortress of concrete and sharp corners rose from the center of the island.

"Samyaza does like to set a scene, doesn't she?"

"Has she always been so dramatic?"

"Oh, yes. Remember that lovely time period when people placed the heads of their enemies on pikes? Guess who started that little practice?"

Laney shuddered. And this was the woman who currently held two small, defenseless children—and who had already tried to kill dozens more. "We need to get over there. Any ideas how we can do that without being seen?"

Drake looked up at the sky. "It'll be dark soon. We'll take a boat."

Laney shook her head. "They'll hear the motor."

"Who needs a motor when we have your power and mine?" Drake looked around. "Should we be worried about your cat?"

Cleo had disappeared into the surrounding wood, but Laney wasn't worried about her. She could still feel her, and she knew Cleo was keeping track of her as well. "No. She's just stretching her legs. She doesn't like being cooped up in planes. I can call her back when we need her."

Hakeem groaned behind them. Drake reached back and snapped his neck.

Laney cringed. "How many times have you done that now?"

Drake shrugged. "Not sure. Lost count. Are we bringing him?"

Laney stared at Samyaza's man. He'd been coming to every thirty minutes. If they left him, he could awaken and warn Samyaza. If they brought him, he'd be dead weight.

"Until we know Samyaza is inside and the kids, yes. So I guess we're bringing him along."

Drake sighed. "Wonderful."

CHAPTER 101

Laney pulled out her phone and typed a quick message to Jake. *Land on the southeast beach. We'll bring the kids to you.*

"We good?" Drake asked.

Laney nodded.

When Cleo had come back, she had spotted a canoe not too far away, and she and Drake had retrieved it. Luckily, Hakeem had stayed unconscious the whole time. Laney really wished she had some amobarbital, like the SIA used; it would make this easier. Drake had suggested just killing him, but even though she knew who he was, Laney still couldn't condone cold-blooded murder. So they were taking the man.

Drake loaded Hakeem into the canoe and pushed it into the water. Laney waded toward it and jumped over the side. Cleo slipped into the water behind her and started swimming toward the opposite shore.

Drake slipped in behind Laney and nodded toward Cleo. "Will she be okay?"

"Oh, yeah. She likes to swim." Already it was difficult to make Cleo out in the dark.

Drake put an oar in the water, but Laney shook her head. "I've got this." She looked toward the sky and called on the forces. It felt good to feel the familiar tingle, the power spreading out from the ring and through her blood. She focused on the canoe, and Drake stumbled, catching the side to keep from tipping over as the canoe shot forward, pushed by the wind.

Drake leaned forward and whispered in her ear. "Head to the left. It's darker. We can slip in easier."

She focused on where he pointed and tried to ignore the heat of him right behind her. She squinted, looking for Cleo, and finally spotted her. *More to the left*, she told the cat.

Laney steered the canoe to the shadows. She kept her focus on the wind pushing them forward even as she felt a tingle roll over her skin.

Drake leaned up next to her and spoke in a low voice. "There's a Fallen along the beach. Thirty feet in. I'll take care of it."

Stay in the water, Laney thought to Cleo.

She brought the canoe aground in the shallow water. As soon as it stopped, Drake was out and disappeared into the shadows. Even though she knew the Fallen couldn't sense the archangel, Laney was still tense.

A grunt of pain sounded from up ahead, then Drake rematerialized from the dark. "We're good."

She noted the blood on the knife in his hand, but didn't comment. *Come, Cleo.*

She nodded to Hakeem. "What do we do with him?"

"We'll have to stash him somewhere until we find the kids."

"He's been out for only about thirty minutes each time. We'll have to move fast."

Drake hauled Hakeem out of the canoe with one arm and slung him over his shoulder. "We'll stash him behind some rocks."

Laney jogged behind Drake. Hakeem groaned when he was tossed on the ground.

"Right on time," Drake said, then snapped Hakeem's neck.

Laney gathered some seaweed and driftwood and draped it over him. She shrugged. *Good enough.*

"Not yet." Drake plunged the knife into Hakeem's heart and twisted.

Laney grabbed his arm. "What are you doing?"

"He's a risk, Laney. You know that."

She knew he was right, but it just didn't sit well,

"It's done now, and it's on me, not you."

Laney met his gaze before turning to look toward the center of the island. "Let's go."

CHAPTER 102

Laney and Drake made their way toward the house, staying away from the path. The island was crawling with guards. Laney had hoped they'd be able to sneak in, but they'd seen a dozen different men already. Sneaking in wasn't an option. She hated not having more time to get the lay of the land. But with both children in danger, time was of the essence.

But they also couldn't simply fight their way through everyone. Stealth was the best shot at getting the girls out safely. This area only seemed to have those three though, so it was possible if they took them out, no one would notice for a little while.

Or their shift's about over, and we'll be uncovered shortly.

But most importantly the three guards were human, which meant once they went down, they'd stay down for a while.

"One for each of us?" Drake whispered.

"Sounds right," Laney said.

Cleo remained at Laney's side, but Laney could feel her eagerness.

"Ladies first." Drake waved them on.

Laney crept forward, Cleo at her side. Laney waited until she had reached a tree only six feet from one of the men. She looked down at Cleo. *Ready?*

Yes.

Laney focused on a tree across from the men. A wind slammed into it, breaking off one of its long branches.

The men whirled toward the sound. "What was that?"

Laney and Cleo burst from their hiding spot. Cleo pounced on one of the men, cutting off his yell. A blur raced past her, and Laney knew Drake was going for the man farthest away. Laney spun, slamming a back kick into the back of the third man's lower back. He grunted in pain, his back arching. She yanked him by the shoulders, pulling him back, and then her hands were around his neck, twisting in opposite directions. He dropped like a stone.

Cleo stood over her kill. Drake had taken down his man as well.

Drake looked at Laney, his head tilted to the side.

"What?" she asked.

He shrugged. "Nothing. It's just nice to see you in action. I've missed it."

Laney wasn't sure whether he meant the last time they were in Vegas, or farther back in time. And she wasn't sure she wanted to know.

Drake pulled his man up. The man groaned in pain.

"He's still alive?"

"I thought you might want to ask him a question or two."

"I won't answer any—"

Drake pulled the man's pinkie back and broke it. Then he crushed his hand over the man's mouth so his cries were muffled.

Laney stepped closer to the man. "There are two little girls. I want to know where they are."

The man shook his head.

Drake grabbed the man's index finger. The man shook his head and screamed, the sound muffled by Drake's hand. "Answer the lady's question," Drake said.

This time, the man nodded. Slowly, Drake removed his hand from the man's mouth.

"Where are the children?" Laney asked.

"I'm not sure."

Drake yanked the man's hand up.

"But, but, there's a lot of activity in the basement. I'm not allowed down there. Only the boss's special guard."

"How many guards are there on the island?"

"About two dozen."

"How many in the basement?"

"I—I don't think any. We're all stationed outside."

It made sense. Elisabeta wouldn't want any of her guards to know what was going on. They might try to take the immortality for themselves.

Drake punched the man in the back of the head. He pitched forward.

"Drake!"

"What? We got what we wanted, and I didn't kill him. Win-win. Now, shall we, ladies?" He gestured up the path.

Cleo moved ahead. *I like him.*

Laney shook her head. *I am not telling him that. His ego is already too big.*

Cleo huffed out a laugh.

Drake leaned down to Laney's ear. "I think she likes me." He paused. "I think you do too."

Laney had no response for that, so she just picked up her pace.

As they approached the mansion, Laney sensed six more Fallen within a few dozen yards. But none of the Fallen could sense the intruders, and they were able to sneak around them without any trouble. Soon they were just beyond the halo created by the lights of the house. It was a two-story concrete building. Laney found nothing warm about it.

"There's no one ahead of us," she whispered.

"I'm going to go do a quick scouting and see if I can find an entrance to the basement from the outside," Drake said.

Laney grabbed his arm. "You're not going to try to go in without me, right?"

"Who, me?"

"I mean it. We're coming with you."

He sighed. "Fine. But let me scout alone. I'll be back in a minute." He blurred out of sight before she could respond.

Cleo sat next to Laney, her warmth helping fight away the chill. *Children here.*

You can sense them?

Cleo nodded.

Is—is Victoria here?

Yes.

Laney jolted. She had known this was true, but part of her was still having trouble wrapping her head around it. Her mother, the mother of all, was a child. And she was inside that building.

A slight wind ruffled Laney's hair, and then Drake was beside her. "There's a side door around the back. I think the stairs to the basement are near it."

"Did you sense anyone?"

"No Fallen. But I heard movement inside. Human staff." Apparently Samyaza's paranoia survived across lifetimes.

Laney stared at the building, feeling how surreal this whole moment was. "Okay. Well, time to rescue my mother, the toddler."

CHAPTER 103

Drake led Laney and Cleo around the side of the building. The trees were closer to the house here, and there was less open space to cross.

"Where is everybody?" Laney asked. She could feel the Fallen out on the grounds, but none were near the house. There were no human guards either.

"Samyaza has always been both paranoid and arrogant. She doesn't want any Fallen near her precious project, and she's only worried about people getting on the island."

"Well, her paranoia and arrogance are our gain."

"Follow me."

Drake blurred toward the door. He had it open in a second, and Cleo and Laney slipped inside. Voices could be heard down the hall, but they quickly disappeared down the basement stairs.

Cleo sniffed the air, and Laney could sense her confusion.

What's wrong? Laney asked.

Children—upstairs and down.

Did they split them up?

Both upstairs and down.

Laney frowned. Cleo was registering the children in two places at once. *We'll try downstairs first.*

She tapped Drake's arm and nodded toward the door across from them. Drake silently crossed opened the door. Laney and Cleo followed.

They had entered a short hallway with three doors—one on either side and one straight ahead. Laney waited for a beat, but heard no sounds.

Cleo?

No one.

Laney moved to the first door. It opened it onto a large room with two hospital beds and a bunch of medical equipment. On a board near the door were printouts. Laney scanned them quickly. They discussed the vital signs and basic health of "Subject 1" and "Subject 2," both two-year-old girls.

"Laney," Drake said quietly. He stood by a refrigerated container.

No.

She hurried to his side and looked inside. Her stomach rolled. There were rows of vials filled with blood. One side of the refrigerator was dedicated to the blood of Subject 1 and the other to Subject 2.

"They don't know which is Victoria," Laney said. "So they're draining both of them."

"They're taking as much as they can each day while keeping the girls alive."

Laney's mouth hung open in horror. She knew Samyaza was evil, but this—this was a whole new level of depravity. "We need to destroy these. She can't have even a drop."

"How?" Drake spread his arms wide. "There's not even a drain in here."

Laney looked around and realized he was right. And of course, Samyaza would have made sure getting rid of the blood would be difficult. "There must be a way."

"We could take the blood with us," Drake said.

"With us? Why would we do that?"

Drake's eyes were intense. "So *you* could take it. So you could be immortal."

Laney backed up. "Immortal? I don't want to be immortal."

"I am."

Laney saw the longing in Drake's eyes. But the idea of it, not just ingesting blood, but of living forever… No. She didn't want that.

"Drake, even if I could, this is the blood of two terrified children. No one should use this. This is evil."

Drake shrugged. "It was just a thought."

Laney shoved the idea from her mind. She had never considered immortality, not since she'd had that conversation with Victoria at her home in Maine. After that, immortality had lost its appeal, real or imagined.

She looked at Cleo. "It was the blood. It made you think they were down here, didn't it? Can you lead us to the other place?"

Yes.

Laney turned to the lab equipment. There had to be something they could use. "Hold on." She headed to the door, then stopped with her hand on the handle. She glanced at Cleo. *Is there anyone outside?*

No.

Laney opened the door and looked both ways before crossing to the door across the hall. It was a supply closet, just like she'd hoped. She scanned the shelves and grabbed two bottles of bleach and a bucket. *This should do nicely.*

Back across the hall, Drake helped her pour all the blood into the bucket. Then Laney poured in the bleach. "Well, that should do it. There's a drain in the closet across the hall."

"I've got it." Drake picked up the bucket and left the room.

Laney peered into the hall. No one had come down the stairs, which seemed odd. But she was thankful.

Drake emerged from the closet.

"Good?"

"Someone's chance at immortality is officially down the drain." Laney groaned. "That was really bad."

"What?" he replied indignantly. "That was a good one."

Shaking her head, Laney turned to Cleo. *Find Victoria.*

Cleo padded down the hall to a second staircase. Laney knew there were no Fallen nearby, but the lack of people was surprising. *Well, small blessing, I guess,* she thought as they headed up the stairs.

Cleo waited as Drake opened the door. And then she let out a roar. Drake blurred in front of the two of them as the gun blast sounded.

CHAPTER 104

The blast was deafening, and Drake fell forward as the bullet punched through his chest and came out the other side.

"Drake!"

Cleo charged the gunman and clamped her powerful jaws around his forearm. He dropped the gun with a scream. Laney ran forward as three more men appeared behind the first gunman. "Release!" she yelled at Cleo.

Cleo let the man go, and Laney grabbed him by the lapels and propelled him back toward the other three, using him as a shield. She plowed him right into the man in the middle, slammed a sidekick into the man on her left, then sent another sidekick into the man on the right. She twisted the shoulders of her shield into the man on her left and shoved. The men dropped in a heap.

The man on her right started to bring his gun hand up. Laney clamped a hand on his wrist and kicked him in the groin, then elbowed him in the face. She twisted his gun hand and slammed her forearm into his elbow, breaking it. He screamed, and the gun dropped to the floor.

She back-kicked the man coming up behind her, followed by a round kick to the knee.

From the corner of her eye, she saw the last man get to his feet. She wrapped her hand around the second man's neck and twirled him in front of her just as the third man pulled the trigger. Three bullets slammed into her new shield. Cleo roared and leaped on the gunman, slamming him into the floor. Her jaws ripped into the man's ribs.

Laney tossed her man to the side, reached up, and broke the man's neck. She looked down at the man Cleo stood on. He was either out cold or dead. "Good job, girl."

"You two are quite a team," Drake said from behind her.

Laney rushed over. "Are you all right?"

"Almost completely healed. Although, I will admit that hurt."

"We need to move. They know we're here. Cleo?"

She turned to the stairs and slunk up them. Her heart pounding, Laney hurried behind her, Drake bringing up the rear.

Cleo paused on the steps. *Danger.*

The word floated across Laney's mind a split second before Cleo charged up the stairs and leapt out of view. A woman's scream cut off abruptly. Laney tore up the stairs and rounded a corner at the top. Cleo stood there, looked up at Laney, her eyes shining. A woman in fatigues lay on the ground at Cleo's feet, a gun in her hand.

"Guess that was the 'nanny,'" Laney said.

"Don't think she was only a nanny," Drake murmured.

Cleo stepped away from the woman, nudged open the nearest door, and disappeared inside.

"I'll stay out here," Drake said.

Laney paused only a second before stepping into the dark room.

CHAPTER 105

It took Laney's eyes a few moments to adjust to the darkness —or at least that's what she told herself as she stood, unmoving, just inside the door. She knew the gunshots had probably been heard and she should be moving quickly, but she needed a moment to prepare herself.

There were two cribs against the far wall. Cleo sat in front of one of them. *Mother of all.* Then Cleo walked past Laney and out of the room. *Outside.*

Laney barely registered her thoughts, she was so focused on the cribs. *Mother of all—Victoria's here.* A cavalcade of memories of her mother rolled through her mind, ending with her last memory. "Every time, I think I can't love you more. And then I do."

Laney blinked back tears, swallowing down all the emotions threatening to overwhelm her. *Later—deal with it later. Get her to safety now.*

On trembling legs, she moved forward.

A small girl with red hair lay in the crib, sleeping. She had a small bandage on her right arm. Laney gently ran a hand over her hair. "Hi, Mom," she whispered.

The girl didn't stir.

She looked in the other crib and saw a girl who could be the twin of Victoria. "Hey there." Laney reached down and touched the girl's cheek. She didn't stir either. Frowning, Laney reached down and picked the girl up. Her head fell back limply, and Laney quickly supported it, realizing what was wrong. *They drugged them. Those bastards.*

"Drake."

He slipped into the room. "The house is quiet. How are they?"

"They've been drugged. Can you grab, uh, Victoria?"

Drake's eyebrows rose, but he reached into the other crib and picked up the girl.

Light flickered across the room. Laney whirled, cradling the child to her chest, as a TV in the corner came to life.

Elisabeta looked coldly at them from the screen. "Hello, ring bearer."

CHAPTER 106

On screen, Elisabeta raised a hand, and a red dot appeared on each of the girls. "Not sure if your power works through electronics, but I wouldn't try it. If you command me to do anything, I will put a bullet through these girls."

"You wouldn't hurt them." Laney clasped the girl tightly to her chest. *Cleo, find the shooters.*

Elisabeta smiled sweetly. "Hurt them, yes. Kill them, no. They'll survive a bullet or two. And besides, I don't need their brains functioning. Only their hearts—to pump that beautiful blood through their bodies."

"How heartless can you be? You stole all those children, dragged them from their families—"

Elisabeta laughed. "Families? Who cares about a few mortal families? Do you know what I stand to gain?"

"All at the cost of children's lives," Laney said.

"Please, I'm going to attain immortality. Nothing will stop me. Certainly not you."

"You made sure of that, didn't you? Trumping up those

charges? Forcing me to go into hiding, leaving you to do whatever you wanted?"

"You made it too easy, my dear. Always rushing into danger, helping whatever feckless fools had endangered their own lives."

"And you twisted it all, made me look like the villain."

"What can I say? Humans are sheep, easily led. They were looking for a villain. I just pointed them to you."

"And away from yourself."

"Well, *I* certainly couldn't become a pariah. That wouldn't quite fit in with my plans, would it? I have to admit, I am a little disappointed. You got here a little faster than I had planned. I was hoping I'd be able to greet you personally."

"That is a shame. I was hoping we could 'chat' as well."

The lights on the girls winked out.

Dead.

Elisabeta frowned, then sighed. "I see your stupid cat has been busy."

"So we'll be leaving now," Drake said.

Elisabeta laughed. "I don't think so. Look out the window."

Laney stepped toward it. The tingles ran over her.

Drake shot out his hand, holding her back. "No." He handed Laney the other child before moving to the window himself and peering out.

"How gallant," Elisabeta purred.

"Drake?" Laney asked.

His jaw set, he turned to her. "At least twelve. I sense another ten around the back."

"And that doesn't include the humans, or, as I like to call them, cannon fodder," Elisabeta said.

Laney felt her fear escalate. Drake walked over and took one of the girls.

Elisabeta sighed. "Such a dilemma. You could save yourselves, fight your way out. But you'll never be able to do that while holding those children. Best you just leave them behind and be on your way.

"And Delaney, before you get any grand heroic ideas about saving those two precious children, you should know my people have been ordered to kill you. I'm done playing. But don't worry—no weapons. I want to make sure your death lasts." Elisabeta paused. "Unless of course, you get through my men. Then the humans have been ordered to open fire."

Laney pulled her gun, aimed it at the TV, and pulled the trigger. The bullet went right through the spot where Elisabeta's face had been. *If only that had been real...*

She turned to Drake, who raised an eyebrow. "That was a little dramatic."

"Well, sometimes drama is called for. Let's go." Laney adjusted the girl in her arms and headed for the door. *Cleo, can you get back in?*

Coming.

"Where's Cleo?"

"Still outside. She's going to try to get back—"

A yell went up from the side of the house, followed by a scream and the sound of a window breaking. Drake pushed Laney against the wall, his body tense.

Laney felt her heart rate spike. *Cleo?*

Inside.

She put a hand on Drake's chest. "It's okay. It's Cleo."

Anyone else inside?

No.

"No one else is inside. I wonder what they're waiting for," Laney mumbled.

"I think they're waiting for us."

Laney took a breath. "Well, let's not disappoint them."

CHAPTER 107

As Drake and Laney made their way down the stairs, the tingles ran over Laney's skin. Drake had been right. There were dozens of them.

Drake looked over at her, one of the girls in his arms. "They're coming."

"A lot of them. Let's go."

Laney examined both girls. Neither moved, but their breathing seemed all right. Still, she knew Elisabeta was right: they'd never be able to fight their way out while holding the girls. *Especially not if I'm their focus.*

Cleo prowled ahead of them, the hair on her back standing straight up. *Outside.*

Laney moved silently to the door, the girl still held tightly to her chest. She peered through the transom glass. At least two dozen people stood along the drive, all of them Fallen. And she could feel still more of them somewhere out of sight.

She swallowed and looked up at Drake. "We're surrounded."

A man stepped forward from among the Fallen—Hakeem. "Come on out, ring bearer," he yelled.

Drake cursed. "Apparently I didn't plunge that knife in hard enough."

"Yup." Laney shifted the girl in her arms and ran a hand through her hair. The girl looked up at her sleepily, and for a moment Laney s breath caught as Victoria's eyes looked into hers.

Laney felt tears push against the back of her eyes as she laid a trembling kiss on the girl's forehead. "You don't deserve any of this."

Victoria had done so much, for all of them. For all of humanity. And now Samyaza was trying to rip her years of peace from her as well.

Laney looked at the girl held in Drake's arms. She was just a poor innocent who had nothing to do with any of this. And yet here she was in mortal danger.

"What do you want to do?" Drake asked, his eyes intense.

And in that moment, Laney knew he would do whatever she asked. He would sacrifice himself, without hesitation, to save her. And the lifetimes slipped away. "Jake will be arriving at the shore. You need to get them to safety."

"You mean *we* do."

Laney shook her head. "No. *You* get them to safety. I'll keep these guys busy."

And for a moment, it wasn't Laney and Drake, but Helen and Achilles. And she was sending Achilles away with Clytemnestra and Morcant.

Then Achilles died.

Laney swallowed down the fear and the anguish. *Not this time.* He would not die this time. She would not allow it.

"Get them to safety. You're faster. You can get them there. I can't. Cleo and I will distract them. When you hear us move, you go out the back."

Drake shook his head. His voice was a fierce whisper. "I am *not* leaving you."

Laney looked once more at the two girls before looking back

at him. "They come first. And you are their best chance of getting out of this alive. Cleo and I can keep them busy while you run. It's the only chance they have."

Drake's jaw clenched, and he stared at a spot above Laney's head. She was afraid he wouldn't do it. That he would insist on staying with her. "You don't know what you're asking me to do," he said.

"Yes I do," she said softly, feeling Achilles's death all over again. She would give anything to prevent that.

Drake grabbed her and pulled her close. "Do not die. Do you hear me? You are not allowed to die."

She stared into his face and couldn't think of a single thing to say. So instead, she wrapped her arms around his neck and pulled him to her. His lips pressed down on hers, and her whole body felt alive. She clung to him, her life, Helen's life, crashing over her. *Achilles.*

With regret, she pushed him away and leaned her forehead into his, feeling breathless. "Go. You need to go."

He stared into her eyes, looking like he wanted to say more. But he took the girl from her arms.

Laney nodded back down the hall. "Go out the back. They can't sense you. As soon as you hear the commotion up front, you run. Jake will be on the beach."

Drake gave her an abrupt nod but stayed where he was.

"Go. Keep them safe," she said quietly.

Drake gave her one last look and disappeared down the hall.

Taking a deep breath, Laney looked down at Cleo. "You ready, girl?"

Cleo let out a roar in response. The hair on the back of her neck was standing straight up.

Shoving all of her fear aside and pulling up all of her anger, Laney opened the door and stepped outside, with Cleo by her side.

Hakeem snarled from thirty feet away. "Where's your boy toy?"

Laney shrugged. "You know men, so fickle. Now get—"

Music blared from speakers, drowning her out. Metallica's "Hit the Lights" played through the night. Hakeem grinned, and Laney's heart sank. She wouldn't be able to command them. But that wasn't her only trick.

She touched Cleo's back. *I love you, Cleo.*

Lightning crashed, piercing Fallen after Fallen. Then Laney yanked the gun from the back of her belt and fired at the closest Fallen.

Hakeem let out a yell and charged—along with every other Fallen she could see.

CHAPTER 108

The lightning could be seen clearly from the opposite shore. Jake and Jordan looked at each other for only a moment before picking up the Zodiac and running for the water. They dropped the boat in, did a quick weapon check, and they were on their way, along with two other men. The rest of the men would stay on the shore, weapons trained on the far island. They'd provide cover fire if necessary.

"Looks like Laney's in the thick of it," Jordan said.

Jake just nodded. He could picture Laney in the middle of a fight, protecting the two children. She would lay down her life for them. He knew that without a doubt. He just prayed it didn't come to that.

He also feared they wouldn't arrive in time. That Laney wouldn't succeed. And that he would have to face Mary Jane and tell her that her child was dead. Jake had done some difficult things in his life. He'd broken the news of the death of a loved one to family before. But never about a child. And never to a family who'd already been through so much.

He pictured Mary Jane crumpling to the ground, her children joining her. And then he realized he'd have to have the same conversation with Patrick if things went badly. *Please don't let it come to that.*

Jake scanned the coast as Jordan steered them toward the open beach. Muzzle flashes appeared on the shore. Jake put his weapon to his shoulder and returned fire as Jordan set them on a zigzag course. Then Jake's men opened fire from the opposite shore, and soon the gunfire on the beach ahead of them stopped. Whoever had been there was now gone or dead.

And everyone else is probably focusing on Laney.

Jordan beached them, and Jake was quickly over the side. "Clear."

"Where is everybody?"

Cleo's roar provided the answer. Jake nodded toward the wall. "That way." He took a step, but a shape blurred toward him. "Shit."

"Do not shoot!" Drake stopped twenty feet away, two small children held in his arms.

Jake put a hand on the muzzle of Jordan's weapon. "Hold. Drake?"

Drake nodded and walked toward them—but a half dozen shapes blurred behind him.

"Get down!" Jake yelled.

Drake dove for the ground as Jake opened fire. Jordan tossed a grenade, lighting up the path. And Jake could see more people coming.

"Incoming!" Jake yelled.

His men spread out, offering suppression fire.

Drake rolled to his feet and pushed the two children toward Jake. "Laney wants you to get them out of here."

"She's in trouble?"

Drake nodded, and Jake could see the fear in his eyes.

"I'll go with you," Jake said.

Drake shook his head. "No. She was clear. Getting these two to safety is your priority. She wants them out of harm's way. We'll find you when this is over."

Jake looked down at the two girls. Tears streamed down their faces, although they made no sound. They were probably in shock. He knew he needed to get them away.

He looked back at Drake. "Take care of her."

"With my very life," Drake replied before sprinting back up the beach, zigzagging between the Fallen and dropping them as he passed. Jake's men continued to engage them, firing chest shots.

While Jake got the girls onto the Zodiac, Jordan backed up with him, never taking his finger off the trigger. Their men leapt into the craft as Jake started to pull it away from shore.

"We're not helping her?" Jordan asked.

Jake let out a trembling breath. "No. We're following Laney's orders. These two are our priority. Let's go."

Jake heard a roar and knew Cleo was in the thick of things. He also noticed that the lightning blasts had slowed. He hated leaving, but it was Laney's order. He just hoped that what she wanted didn't get her killed.

CHAPTER 109

Laney was a blur of motion, not thinking, just moving—block, move, strike, duck, hit. Her lightning bolts struck randomly; she was unable to focus on specific targets, so she just made sure it didn't come near her or Cleo. But it was thinning the herd.

Her bullets depleted, she twirled from Fallen to Fallen, her knife slashing and stabbing, necks being broken. She didn't know how many she had taken down. Sometimes she even got close enough to command them to defend her against their comrades.

She had never been more scared in her life. She could hear Cleo somewhere to her right, but she couldn't stop to look. *Please let her be all right.*

Her energy was beginning to wane. And then she misjudged a punch, fading when she should have moved, and took a hit right in the stomach. Her breath left her, and she fell to the ground. Cleo let out a roar but couldn't reach her.

Laney's hands went to her throat. Her voice was gone. She couldn't command the Fallen to do anything.

A man came at her, and she rolled out of the way, kicked him in the face, wrapped her legs around his neck, and yanked him to the ground. She rolled to her knees. Movement caused her to move to her left just in time to avoid a kick to the face. She punched the man in the groin, rose to her feet, grabbed his leg, and pushed it above his head. He crashed down onto his back, and she kicked him in the face, knocking him out.

Feeling like death warmed over, she looked around, surprised that no one was charging her.

That was when she saw the circle of Fallen and nephilim surrounding her. They'd been toying with her.

Hakeem stood directly in front of her, smiling.

Laney forced herself to speak. She needed to stall, to give herself some time to recover. In this fight, seconds counted.

She opened her mouth, but her voice didn't carry above the music.

Hakeem replied. She couldn't hear his words either, but it didn't take a genius to figure them out. "Goodbye, ring bearer."

CHAPTER 110

Drake knew he had never run so fast in his life. The fate of the two girls, along with the men he'd entrusted them to, had been pushed from his mind, shoved away by his all-consuming need to get to Laney. When Fallen blocked his path, he showed them no compassion.

At the same time, he had a horrible sense of déjà vu, knowing he had raced to save her like this before—only to lose his own life.

And he didn't care. He would gladly trade his life ten times over for hers.

But as he crested the hill, he stared in horror at the scene below him. Laney was surrounded by over a dozen Fallen, with Hakeem in front of her.

And in that second, Drake knew two things for certain. One, Hakeem was going to kill her. And two, even with all his abilities, he would never be able to get to her in time.

CHAPTER 111

Laney reacted as fast as she could, but it wasn't fast enough. She dodged a hook to the head only to take a hit to the shoulder. She stumbled back, and someone grabbed her shoulders. Without thinking, she stepped to the side and tossed him over her hip. She stomped his face, then slammed a sidekick into the Fallen charging her.

A Fallen grabbed her left shoulder, and she reached back and snapped his pinky while kicking another in the chest. She ducked the man coming from the side, having to release the man behind her, who kicked her in the back and sent her flying forward. She knew he had broken some of her ribs. She staggered to her feet.

And then the bullet punched through her chest.

Laney's eyes went wide, her breath disappeared, and her knees turned to liquid. But there was no pain. *Shouldn't there be pain?*

Hakeem jumped back "Damn it! Who shot her? No weapons! That was the rule!"

Laney collapsed to her knees, then fell backwards. And that's when the pain arrived. It screamed through her as blood bubbled up her throat. *I'm going to die.* Time slowed down and sounds became muffled. She was vaguely aware of Cleo bellowing—in pain or anger she didn't know. And through their bond, she could feel Cleo frantically trying to reach her.

No, Cleo. Save yourself.

Hakeem knelt down and grabbed her by the hair. She barely felt it. He leered at her. "Who's the bitch now?" he asked.

He punched her in the face, and her whole world went black.

CHAPTER 112

Drake had never been so scared in his life as he was when he saw Laney drop. He emptied the magazine of the gun he'd grabbed from one of the downed humans and shot every single Fallen he saw in the head as he made his way to Laney.

When the magazine was empty, he tossed the gun to the side. The gun he'd used to shoot Laney.

It was the only way. It was the only way, he repeated to himself as the image of Laney dropping replayed in his mind. He bulldozed past half a dozen Fallen before they'd even realized he was there. And when they did, they turned their attention away from Laney —who lay on the ground, her blood slowly draining from her.

All thought, all emotion left Drake. He simply fought—efficiently and brutally. From the corner of his eye, he saw Cleo reach Laney with an ear-shattering roar. One Fallen tried to reach Laney, but Cleo turned as if psychic and leapt across Laney's body, slammed into the Fallen, and sank her teeth into his throat. The message was clear: any Fallen that approached would receive the same treatment.

Good girl, Drake thought, turning his attention back to his own fight. It took only three minutes, but each second felt like an hour. And Drake was supremely aware of Laney's blood pooling around her. *Hold on, Laney. Please hold on.*

Finally the last Fallen was down. Half had taken off running at the sight of Drake, Hakeem the coward among them. Drake yanked back the arm of the last man, practically ripping it from his socket, then shoved him away, sending him sailing.

He sprinted for Laney.

With a roar, Cleo barred Drake's way, her teeth bared.

Drake stumbled to a stop and put up his hands. "Easy, girl, easy. I just want to help her."

Growling low in her throat, Cleo moved toward him.

"Cleo, I don't want to hurt you. Please get out of the way so I can help her."

Cleo stopped and stared into his eyes. Drake didn't move, but his anxiety grew. He didn't want to hurt the cat, but if she didn't move, it would soon be too late.

Finally, Cleo stepped aside.

Drake sprinted forward and dropped to his knees next to Laney. He cradled her head in his lap and put his hand over the wound in her chest, which still oozed blood.

The wound he had caused.

"Come on, come on," Drake begged. "Come on, Laney. Come back to me."

Cleo inched forward and lay her head right next to Laney's. Her eyes were on Drake.

Drake ignored her, pouring all his focus into Laney's wound. He had spent his time since she'd woken up keeping his distance, telling himself she needed time. But now, it was crystal clear that neither of them had the luxury of time.

"I have waited lifetimes for you. Don't you dare die on me. You will live. Do you hear me? Do not make me wait another thousand lifetimes to be with you. You are supposed to live. You are supposed to be with me. So damn it, come back to me."

He hadn't used this skill in eons. He wasn't even sure it would work. He felt the warmth spread through his hand, but he wasn't sure if that was just her blood or something more.

"Laney, open your eyes. Please open them."

When he'd seen the Fallen surrounding her, he'd known they would kill her. His only desperate hope had been to injure her so badly they'd leave her alone. Because he knew if he injured her, he could heal her as well—a small gift from the maker.

His hand began to glow. The healing was agonizingly slow, but it was happening: the blood flow slowed. Then the wound itself began to glow.

At last, the warmth in Drake's hand began to recede, and the glow dimmed and disappeared altogether. He pulled his hand away and looked down at the wound. Or at least, at the spot where the wound used to be. All he saw now was untouched skin.

"Laney?"

She groaned, and her eyes opened. "Drake?"

Cleo let out a whimper and licked Laney's cheek over and over again. Laney reached up a hand and scratched Cleo behind the ears. "I'm okay, girl."

Cleo rested her head on Laney's shoulder with a purr.

Drake sucked in air, feeling like he hadn't taken a breath since Laney had been shot. Since he had shot her.

"What happened?"

"It doesn't matter. You're all right." He gently took her into his arms; Cleo gave him a disgruntled look. "We need to get out of here before these guys wake up."

Laney looked around, shock splashed across her face. "What happened to them?"

"Me and Cleo, and a little bit of you. Come on." He pulled her into his chest and knew she could feel his heart hammering away. And in that moment he made a decision: he was never letting her go.

CHAPTER 113

Jake, Jordan, and their team had hustled the girls back to the airfield. His men had set up a perimeter around the plane, which was idling outside the hangar. As soon as the medical team looking over the girls gave the all clear, they would take off.

Jake had seen the needle punctures in their arms, which made him see red. And both girls were exhausted. Jake just hoped there weren't any serious medical issues with either of them. He hadn't called Mary Jane yet, because until he could tell her that her daughter was fine, he didn't want to get her hopes up.

Jordan jogged out from the hangar. "Not done yet. But the doc says so far, they look good. He thinks they may have been sedated, and he's pretty sure blood was taken."

Jake curled his hand into a fist. *Bastards.* "Are the girls awake?"

"They woke up during the exam. They seem pretty calm."

"Are they in shock?"

"Probably. But Doc says overall, they look good."

"Well that's something."

"So, what's the plan? Are we really going to wait here while Laney's in trouble?"

"If we leave, the girls are unprotected. And we know Samyaza will come for them as soon as she can. The minute the girls are cleared to be moved, we need to go."

"So we're leaving her," Jordan said.

Jake whirled on him. "Do you think this is what I want? It's *Laney* back there. You know what she means to me. Romance, no romance, she's my family. But she's right: we need to start fighting smart, not by emotion. Her leaving? That was the right move, as much as we all hated it. It bought us time. And right now, the right move is to get those girls to safety as soon as the doc okays them to go."

"I don't like it."

"Well, I *hate* it, so I've got you beat. But this is war, and we're soldiers. And we've been given an order. Are you planning on disobeying it?"

Jordan looked at him for a long moment before shaking his head. "No. But I don't have to like it." He returned to the hangar.

Jake continued surveying the area around them. *No, and I don't have to like it either.*

CHAPTER 114

The doctor had given the girls the all clear. He'd run some rudimentary blood work, and everything had come back clear except for traces of a mild sedative in their blood. He would have to run more extensive tests back at his lab, but for now the girls were free to travel.

The nurses who would accompany them on the plane ride were getting the girls settled in. Jake planned on calling Mary Jane on the flight, once they were safely in the air.

Jordan stepped up next to him. "Any word?"

Jake shook his head. He had meant what he'd said to Jordan: the girls were their priority. But the idea of leaving Laney behind when she could be in trouble... He was having trouble physically placing himself on that plane.

"We're doing the right thing, right?" he asked quietly.

"Victoria needs to be protected. There's no doubt about that."

Jake stared out into the darkness. *Come on, Laney.* "Jordan—"

Jordan clapped him on the shoulder. "Go. I've got the girls. Henry is sending people to meet us as soon as we land."

Relief flooded through Jake. "Okay. I'll—"

A shadow separated from the darkness and streaked toward them. Both men had their weapon in their hands in an instant.

Jake paused, his finger over the trigger. "Cleo?"

The black panther stopped in front of them. Dried blood was around her mouth and along her coat. Then with a second blur, Drake appeared beside her, Laney in his arms.

Jake's whole world came to a stop as he rushed to Laney's side. "Laney!"

Jordan was already running for the plane and calling for the medical team.

Laney's jacket was covered in dried blood, and in the center of the blood was what looked like a bullet hole. Jake felt his knees weaken, and his gaze rose to meet Drake's.

"She's all right, Rogan. No permanent injuries."

"How can you say that? She's been shot."

"That's already healed."

Jordan returned with a doctor, a nurse, and a gurney. Drake gently lowered Laney to the gurney, pushed her hair from her forehead, and stepped back. The gurney was whisked into the hangar. Cleo followed.

Jake had glimpsed Laney's untouched flesh through the hole in her jacket. "She'll be okay?"

Drake gave a stiff nod, his gaze never leaving the doorway where the team had disappeared with Laney. "Yes." He turned to Jake. "Laney gave me instructions for you involving the girls."

"She did?"

Drake nodded, a small smile on his face. "I've found she seems to have a plan for everything."

Jake smiled in return. "That she does."

CHAPTER 115

Elisabeta's driver pulled to a stop next to the dock. Hakeem had contacted her just a few minutes ago, and she had stopped him in the middle of his recounting of events. She had a feeling she'd want to see his face when he explained how he had failed so spectacularly.

The speedboat was idling, waiting to take her over to the island. Not waiting for the driver, she flung open her door and strode toward the boat.

Hakeem stepped off and initiated a deep bow. "Samyaza."

"What happened?" she asked through gritted teeth.

"The ring bearer arrived just after you called. We surrounded the house after she entered. We had her."

"*Had?*"

"The archangel with her—he shot her."

Elisabeta reared back. "*Shot* her? You expect me to believe the *archangel* shot her? There weren't supposed to be any weapons. It was supposed to be a long, painful death."

"It would have been. But the archangel must have gotten a weapon from one of the boundary guards."

"Why would he kill her? The wound would have left her

unable to defend herself. He only made it easier to kill her."

Hakeem wouldn't meet her eyes.

"Hakeem, you did *kill* her, didn't you?"

"Uh, well, she was down. It was a mortal wound. It should have killed her."

"*Should* have? She's still alive?"

"Um, the archangel... he, um, healed her."

"He what?"

"I watched. He healed her."

"You *watched*?"

Hakeem straightened. "Yes. I knew you would want a full report."

"I see. And the girls?"

"Uh, they took them as well."

Elisabeta rolled her hands into fists. "How?"

"Laney and her cat distracted us. The men charged the front, and the archangel must have slipped out the back with the girls."

"I see. So both of the girls are gone, and McPhearson is still alive. Is that correct?"

"Um, yes."

"So tell me, why are you still alive?"

He frowned. "Samyaza?"

"You said you watched McPhearson heal. Why didn't you kill her and the archangel?"

"I—I thought you would want to know—"

Elisabeta lashed out. "That McPhearson was dead! *That* is what I wanted to hear. I am not hearing that. I am hearing failure at every turn. Gerard is alive. McPhearson is alive. The girls are gone. Tell me, what have you done for me lately, Hakeem?"

Hakeem dropped to his knee, his hand to his heart. "Samyaza, I am your most loyal servant. I would do anything for you. Even die for you."

She stepped closer and ran a hand through his hair. "Yes, I know."

She crushed his throat with her hand. His eyes bulged. "Maybe you can at least die correctly." She pulled the knife from the sheath at his waist and plunged it into his heart over and over again.

She stepped back as he fell forward. "Well, look at that. You *did* die for me. Good boy."

Hilda walked up behind her and handed her a towel. "Ma'am."

Elisabeta wiped her face. "Report."

"There have been no further sightings of McPhearson. And her legal status remains unchanged."

"The children?"

"We have reports that Jake Rogan is headed to Boston with a child. I believe they're returning her to her family."

"And the other?"

"There's been no sign of her."

"Or McPhearson."

"Yes, ma'am."

Well, I guess I know which one is Victoria. Elisabeta looked out over the water. "What about the blood on site?"

"It was contaminated. It's unusable."

Elisabeta counted to ten to keep herself from Hilda's throat. Hilda was an incredibly capable assistant and not easily replaced. And none of this was her fault.

Her gaze went to Hakeem. *If only I could kill him again.*

"All right. McPhearson still remains a fugitive. That hasn't changed. What about our other project?"

"They've reached the tomb. They said they should have something to report in a few hours."

Elisabeta nodded. *Good.* One avenue to immortality had been closed. But it wasn't the only one. And Delaney McPhearson was way behind in that particular race.

"Good. And make sure my doubles are seen. Tip off the paparazzi." She waved to Hakeem's corpse. "And have someone take care of this."

CHAPTER 116

ASHBURNHAM, MASSACHUSETTS

The blue house looked quiet as Jake rolled to a stop at the curb. Dawn had barely broken across the sky. He'd tried to reach Mary Jane last night, but she hadn't answered the phone. No doubt the toll of everything was catching up with her.

In the rearview mirror, he saw a pair of bright blue eyes. "You're going to make a lot of people happy this morning."

Susie took a drink from her sippy cup in response.

Jake smiled. She had become agitated halfway through the flight home, and no one had been able to calm her until Jake had taken her in his arms. He walked up and down the plane, telling her how happy her family was going to be to see her, and she began to settle, finally letting her eyes close. But when he went to set her back down, she woke up, grabbed his jacket, and wouldn't let go. So Jake settled into a chair with her curled up in his lap. She fell asleep again, and so did he. When he awoke, it was to her little hand on his cheek and her blue eyes staring into his.

Now he climbed from the driver's seat, opened the rear door, and started unbuckling Susie from the car. Getting the car seat strapped into the SUV had been a humbling process. Eventually the pilot had taken pity on him and done it for him, explaining that he had three kids and that it just took practice.

With Susie securely snuggled in his arms, Jake walked up the path to the house. Susie laid her head on his shoulder, and Jake rubbed her back. *Almost there, sweetheart.*

He opened the screen door and knocked softly, not wanting to startle the whole house awake. It was a few minutes before he heard someone moving toward the door. It swung open, and Sean stood there, wiping his eyes.

"Mr. Rogan? What are—"

His jaw dropped, and he just stood staring at Susie for a moment. Then he yelled, "Mom! Mom! Come quick!" He took off running up the stairs.

Jake looked down at Susie. "Well, I guess we'll let ourselves in." He stepped into the foyer.

Sean appeared at the top of the stairs, pulling Mary Jane by the arm.

"Sean," she said, "what are you—" Her gaze fell on Susie, and she sprinted down the stairs, tears streaming down her cheeks. "Susie!"

Mary Jane pulled Susie from Jake's arms and dropped to the floor, hugging her daughter to her chest and sobbing. Sean dropped down next to her, his shoulders heaving. Molly and Joe appeared at the top of the stairs as well, looking fearful.

"Mom?" Joe called out.

Jake realized they couldn't see their sister from their vantage point and probably feared the worst. "It's okay," he said. "Your sister's home."

Molly and Joe looked at each other before running down the stairs. They skidded to a halt in front of their mom, then piled onto the crying fest on the floor.

Jake felt tears press against the back of his own eyes. Quietly, so not to disturb them, he let himself back outside and headed down the path.

"Jake!"

He turned to find Mary Jane running down the path toward him, Susie still held protectively in her arms. "Where are you going?"

"I didn't want to intrude."

She grabbed his hand. "You're not intruding. You brought my daughter back. You—" She swallowed, tears sparkling in her eyes. "Stay—for breakfast. It's the least we can do."

Susie reached for him, and Jake took her little hand in his with a smile. "Yeah, I think I could do that."

CHAPTER 117

GALETON, PENNSYLVANIA

Laney felt a presence next to her on the bed. She opened her eyes and saw Cleo sleeping quietly next to her. She ran a hand through her coat. *Hey, Cleo.*

Cleo slowly turned her head to look into Laney's eyes. *Better? Better.*

Laney looked around the room. A familiar figure was sitting in the chair next to her bed. Drake's head was down, his eyes closed. He looked almost the same as he had when she'd woken up in the cabin in Alaska.

"Hey," she said quietly.

He sat up. "Hey." He leaned forward, studying her face. "How are you feeling?"

"Sore. Pretty much everywhere. Apparently you shouldn't jump right into fighting dozens of Fallen if you haven't worked out in six months."

Drake smiled. "I will have to keep that in mind."

Cleo snuggled closer to Laney. *Tired.*

Go to sleep. I'm not going anywhere.

Good, Cleo thought back at her as she drifted back to sleep.

Drake nodded toward the cat. "She hasn't left your side. I think she missed you."

"The feeling's mutual." Laney paused. "Drake, who shot me?"

Drake went still. "Uh, we can talk about it when you're feeling better."

He rose from his seat, but Laney grabbed his hand. "Don't go."

He looked down at her, his eyes filled with pain.

Laney patted the bed next to her. "Sit."

He still hesitated.

"Please," she said.

With a nod, he sat on the bed next to her, his whole body tense.

Laney had awoken on and off through the night, but while she slept her subconscious seemed to have worked something out. "I was shot in the chest," she said.

Drake wouldn't meet her gaze.

"And you healed me."

He nodded, still refusing to meet his eyes.

She took his hand. "You shot me, didn't you?"

"Laney, there was no other way. I couldn't reach you in time."

Laney closed her eyes, reliving that moment. The Fallen had surrounded her and then charged. Her voice was gone, her strength was failing. She had known in that moment that she would not survive the fight.

And then she'd been shot.

"You know, when we left Alaska to see my uncle, I spent some time researching Achilles."

His head jerked up.

"There was one interesting story. Apparently Achilles found himself fighting Telephus, the son of Heracles. Achilles wounded Telephus. But then the oracle explained that Achilles could heal the ones he wounded. So, in exchange for Telephus showing the Greeks the way to Troy, Achilles healed him." Laney paused. "You knew if you shot me they would stop; they would think I was done. And then you'd be able to heal me."

"I didn't know. I hoped. I haven't used that ability in forever. I could have killed you."

"But you didn't. You saved me."

Laney stared into Drake's eyes, and he stared into hers—and it was as if the entire world disappeared.

Then she heard her uncle and Cain down the hall. She looked around. "Are we in Pennsylvania?"

Drake nodded. "Yes. I figured you'd want to see your uncle and Cain when you woke."

Laney was touched. "Thank you."

"That's what I do. I'm an all-service archangel."

The door opened, and her uncle poked his head in. "I knew you'd be up. She's up!" he yelled down the hall.

"Be in in a minute," Cain yelled back.

"He's bringing in some breakfast for us all," Patrick said. "I know you probably won't be able to eat much, but I thought if it was okay, we could eat in here."

"I'll just get out of your way," Drake said.

"No," Patrick said quickly. "I'd like you to stay. We made enough for you too."

Surprise flickered across Drake's face. "Well, then I'd be happy to. I'll go see if I can help." He disappeared through the door as Patrick stepped in.

Patrick took the spot Drake had vacated on the bed. He put a hand to Laney's forehead.

"I'm fine, Uncle."

"Well, you look like you went ten rounds with Mike Tyson."

"All things being equal, I think I would have preferred Tyson."

Laney heard the unmistakable sound of a child's laugh, and her gaze flew to Patrick.

He put up his hands. "We need to discuss a few things."

"Before we do, can you bring me my jacket?"

"It's covered in blood and—"

"I know, but I need it."

Patrick gave her a long look before going to retrieve it.

Laney waited anxiously for him to return. *Please let it have worked.*

Patrick returned with the jacket and handed it to her. She looked carefully at the camera lens on the lapel. It looked undamaged. She let out a breath. " I think it's okay."

Patrick looked surprised. "You were recording?"

"Dom was. I need to speak with him. Can I use your—"

Patrick handed her his phone. Laney dialed Dom.

"Patrick?" Dom answered.

"No, it's Laney. Did you get—"

She could practically hear Dom's smile on the other end of the line. "I got it. I got it all."

CHAPTER 118

BALTIMORE, MARYLAND

Henry disconnected the call and walked back to the bedroom. When the phone had rung he'd left the room so he didn't wake Jen.

They had only gotten back to Baltimore three hours ago. The ETF had held them for hours, refusing to let them go, and Henry had thought Seward was going to have a stroke when he realized Jake was missing. It had ultimately taken the intervention of the US Attorney General to get them released, and Henry still wasn't sure how he had even gotten involved. According to Brett, the ETF had been recalled, essentially removed from any dealings involving the Chandler Group. Brett didn't know why it had happened, but he thought it was a very good sign.

"Everything okay?" Jen sat up on the bed, her hair a mess and her eyes clear. She had been dead asleep when the phone had rung.

"Yeah. Jake's going to stay at the McAdamses for a little bit. He said he wanted to make sure the security for Susie was taken care of."

Jen grinned. "And that, folks, is a big fat lie."

Henry sat next to her and leaned back against the headboard, pulling Jen with him. "Yup. But let's let him lie for a little bit longer."

"Any word on Laney?"

"She disappeared with Drake, Victoria, and Cleo. And she was hurt pretty bad."

"I hate this. I hate that she's out there and can't come to us."

"We'll figure out a way."

Henry's phone beeped, and he looked down at and read the text. Then he grabbed the remote and tuned to a news station.

"What's going on?" Jen asked.

"I don't know. Dom said we need to watch."

The news was broadcasting a video of a brutal fight, apparently taken from the point of view of one of the combatants. But it was the words at the bottom of the screen that made Jen gasp and Henry feel lightheaded: *Delaney McPhearson Fights Off Multiple Attackers in an Attempt to Save Two Abducted Girls.*

"Henry," Jen said softly, touching his arm, and he realized just how tightly he was holding her.

He released her quickly. "Sorry, sorry." He turned up the volume.

"We've received word that while Delaney McPhearson was shot during the altercation, she is in fact alive and remains hidden. Although, I would argue she may not have to for much longer. The existence of this tape calls into question the case brought against her. I think it is safe to say that the US government will be spending quite a bit of time deciphering the actions on this tape and investigating Elisabeta Roccorio."

Henry muted the set as the program went to commercial.

The two of them sat there in stunned silence before Jen reached over and switched the TV off. "She did it," she said quietly.

Henry, still wrapped up in the horror of what Laney had been through, turned to her. "What?"

Jen gestured to the TV. "Laney. She figured out a way to come back to us. The world will have to investigate Elisabeta. Laney's going to come home."

It took a moment for Jen's words to register. When they did, Henry smiled and pulled her close. "Thank God."

His phone rang, and he wanted to ignore it, but it was Patrick. Wiping his eyes, he answered, still smiling. "Patrick, did you—"

"Hi, big brother."

He grasped the phone. "Laney."

CHAPTER 119

GALETON, PENNSYLVANIA

Laney stood on the porch, watching the little girl walk slowly up to Cleo, who lay on the ground. The girl's blue eyes sparkled as she carefully leaned down to touch the giant cat. Cleo purred and rolled over. The girl jumped back and ran for Cain, who scooped her up into his arms with a laugh.

"She won't hurt you, little one."

Cleo walked up to the two of them. Holding the girl, Cain leaned down, and the girl reached her hand toward Cleo's face.

Cain smiled. "Good girl."

And Laney smiled as well. Cain looked content.

"He has a way with her," Patrick said, stepping up next to her.

"He does."

"What do you know about her parents?"

"She was born to Fiona and Iain Somerfield. And from all reports, they adored her. Fiona died a year ago—cancer. But Iain, he picked up the pieces and made a life for them."

"What will you do about him?"

Laney shook her head, a lump forming in her throat. "He died trying to protect her."

Her uncle made the sign of the cross. "She was loved. For her first years then, she was loved."

Laney saw the joy on Cain's face as Victoria toddled after a butterfly. "She still is."

"What about extended family?"

"Both her parents were only children."

"So does she have any other family?"

Cain laughed again, and Laney said, "She always has a family."

"So we're keeping her?"

"Not sure we can just keep her, but we certainly can't let her go. Henry's working on the legal angles."

"You spoke with him?"

Laney smiled. God, it had been good to hear his voice. He had been shocked when he'd seen the recording. It *had* been a risk wearing the wire. And an even greater risk sending the recordings to the news station. They weren't exactly reliable, but they seemed to be beginning to grasp the situation. It hadn't been an easy choice to put everything out there, but at this point, it had been the only move. Laney's absence from the world had emboldened Elisabeta, and that could not be allowed to continue.

Henry had wanted to come to Pennsylvania immediately—in part just to see Laney. But she knew he also wanted to see Victoria. Unfortunately, until the governments rescinded some of their warrants, he needed to stay away.

"Did I hear a helicopter a little while ago?" Patrick asked.

Laney nodded. "Henry sent more men. Drake's checking them out."

Patrick raised an eyebrow. "And should I ask you about Drake?"

"No," she said quickly. "I don't know what to say anyway."

Patrick was quiet for a moment. "When Henry told me who had taken you, I was not relieved by what I read about the man online. I mentioned it to Cain, and he said I had nothing to worry about. He said if Drake was with you, he would let nothing harm you. And the way Drake watches you… I think Cain was probably right. He would lay down his life for you."

Laney gave him an abrupt nod. Dom had sent her the full recording from her camera; what had been sent to the news channels was an edited version. She had seen and heard Drake's anguish. And she knew Patrick was right. Since she'd woken up, she had been struggling to figure out what she felt for him—and what he felt for her. But there was so much going on, she'd been pushing the thoughts off.

Her uncle was right though: life was short, and she knew how she felt. And now she knew how he felt as well.

"Do you want to know what I think?"

Laney cringed. "I'm not sure."

Patrick chuckled. "Well, I'm going to tell you anyway. You have all this responsibility on your shoulders. And I know you can handle it. But I like the idea of someone who's rather difficult to kill sharing that burden—and even sometimes protecting you from it. And… he makes you smile."

"Yes."

"So, Delaney McPhearson, you need to embrace the good in your life. Don't deny yourself happiness for duty, especially if there's someone out there who has no problem sharing you with that duty."

He squeezed her hand before walking down the steps to join Cain and Victoria.

Laney watched them, but her mind was on Patrick's words. Was it possible? Could she have both? A love and a duty?

Drake appeared at the end of the porch.

"Everything okay?" Laney asked.

He joined her at the railing. "The men seem all right. I mean, they're not Spartan-trained, but what can you do?"

Laney chuckled. "Well, so few are these days."

"Did you speak with your brother?"

Laney smiled. "Yeah."

"Will you be going to see him?"

"Not yet. But Henry has the legal department working overtime trying to get the charges dropped. And they're hopeful now, especially after people started coming forward."

The nannies had been interviewed, and a few of the families had identified some of the Fallen in Elisabeta's employ. The net around her was tightening. It wouldn't be long until she was recognized for what she was.

"It won't stop her," Drake said.

"No, it won't. But hopefully, it will at least mean that law enforcement won't get in our way when we fight her."

"We're going to fight her?"

"It's always been heading to this. I just never realized it. When I'm called, it means war. So we fight."

"You said 'we.'"

"And I meant it. I can't win this without help. Everybody's help. Especially yours."

"Having an archangel on your side—"

"Not as an archangel. I need *you* on my side."

He tilted her chin up and looked into her eyes. "And you have me—however you need me."

CHAPTER 120

WASHINGTON, DC

When the video of Elisabeta and the children hit the airwaves, the effect was explosive. Every news outlet covered it—constantly. It seemed as though every person who had ever known Elisabeta in any way was interviewed. And the nannies had been able to direct authorities to the house in Colorado.

But the question remained: If Elisabeta was the bad guy, who was Delaney McPhearson?

Nancy Harrigan turned off the TV in her office and just stared at the blank screen, knowing her opinion was going to be called for. She had been preparing for this moment.

Her door opened, and she looked up, expecting to see her aide. But it wasn't Melanie.

She rose quickly to her feet. "Madam President."

Margaret Rigley waved her back down. "Sit, sit. I have a feeling we're going to be run ragged today, so take advantage when you can."

Nancy smiled and sat down. "How can I help you, Madam President?"

The president took a seat next to her and raised an eyebrow. "I think you've known me long enough to know exactly why I'm here."

Nancy studied the president. She respected her. She was a political animal, but also a good person. A combination not often found in politicians. "You want to know about Delaney McPhearson and Elisabeta Roccorio."

"It's a goddamn mess. McPhearson was supposed to be the bad guy. What the hell happened? And what the hell is a Fallen?"

"Madam President, I think we, along with the rest of the world, made a mistake when it came to Delaney McPhearson. She's not the one we should going after."

"It's Roccorio."

"Yes."

"I assume you have a file for me?"

Nancy pulled a thick manila folder off the table and handed it to her.

The president raised an eyebrow, and Nancy smiled in return. "I had a feeling you might be stopping by. I was about to order some breakfast."

The president opened the file. "I'll have whatever you're having. And make sure they send lots of really strong coffee. I think we're going to need it."

Nancy grabbed her phone to make the call. *I have no doubt.*

CHAPTER 121

CHICAGO, ILLINOIS

The penthouse overlooked the lake. Huge cathedral ceilings rose thirty feet in the air, and one whole wall was glass. When Elisabeta had bought it, it had been three apartments. But she'd combined them all, creating a single twelve-thousand-foot apartment encompassing three floors.

She pulled the belt of her silk robe tight as she took a seat at the dining table by the windows. The sky was overcast, and rain was expected. Already a strong wind was blowing, and every once in a while the windows would whistle as the wind rattled them.

The weather perfectly matched Elisabeta's mood.

She pushed the newspaper away in disgust. The headlines were about the Chandler Group's rescue of the children.

The front door opened. Elisabeta's head whipped around as Hilda hurried across the room.

"What are you doing? Get out. I told you I don't want any—"

"I've been calling you all morning." Hilda picked up the TV remote and turned to a twenty-four-hour news station. "There's something you need to see."

"For those just joining us, there's been a remarkable development in the Delaney McPhearson mystery. Early this morning, a recording was received by this station that seems to show Delaney McPhearson coming to the aid of two small children. However, most startling is the revelation that world-renowned philanthropist Elisabeta Roccorio may be the mastermind behind the children's kidnapping, along with a series of other crimes. Personally, I am still stunned by the potential ramifications of these recordings. The tapes are still being authenticated, but I'll let you be the judge."

Elisabeta's face appeared on the screen, inside a TV. Elisabeta watched as the conversation between Laney and herself in the nursery was played for the world to hear.

"That bitch! She was recording me."

Hilda muted the TV. "That's not all. Apparently McPhearson was wearing a recording device nonstop, beginning in Arizona. She's provided all of the recording to multiple stations, and the news channels have been playing them nonstop since seven a.m. We're being besieged with requests for interviews and comments. I've been trying to reach you."

"I turned off my phone." Elisabeta stared out the window. "What exactly is the spin on this?"

Hilda took a breath. "They're not sure, but they seem to be beginning to understand that there are some humans with increased abilities."

That wasn't too bad. It was going to come out at some point.

"But they also strongly suggest that you are using those people to fulfill your own goals."

Elisabeta shook her head. "We'll simply make it clear that I was protecting myself from Delaney, and that she's casting—"

"I don't think it will be that simple. On this tape, you are heard threatening the lives of the two children she's trying to save. You also admitted that you had trumped up the charges against her. I'm not sure how to spin that in your favor."

Hilda's phone buzzed, and she looked down at it. When she looked back up, her face was pale. "The FBI is downstairs. They want to speak with you."

Elisabeta looked back at the TV. It was still muted but the closed captioning was working. Drake's face filled the screen, but it was Delaney's words that were scrolling across the bottom: *They come first. And you are their best chance of getting out of this alive. Cleo and I can keep them busy while you run. It's the only chance they have.*

Elisabeta struggled not to gag. God, the woman was so dramatic. Always offering to sacrifice herself for the greater good. It was sickening.

"Elisabeta?"

Elisabeta turned from the screen. "My chopper's still on the roof?"

"Yes. And I contacted the pilot. He should be warming it up."

A loud knocking sounded at the door. "Elisabeta Roccorio, this is the FBI. Open the door."

"What do you want me to do?" Hilda asked.

"Stay here. Deal with them. You know nothing."

"Yes, ma'am. And what about you?"

Elisabeta smiled. "They think they've found their villain? They haven't seen anything yet."

Delaney McPhearson's journey continues in The Belial Witches. *Now available on Amazon*

To be notified of new releases, and for exclusive content, join R.D. Brady's mailing list. You can sign up here or at her website, rdbradybooks.com

FACT OR FICTION?

I know, I know. *The Belial Plan* did not have the same number of unusual archaeology and history that I usually sprinkle throughout a Belial novel. I promise *The Belial War* will more than make up for that. But for now, on to the facts (or the fiction)!

The Witch Trials in England. I was surprised to learn that the witch trials had actually been going on in Europe for almost three hundred years prior to them beginning in the United States. When I was in graduate school, we discussed demonology - the belief that someone commits a criminal act because they are possessed by an evil spirit. During the witch trials both in the U.S. and abroad, that was the most accepted reasoning for why someone engaged in criminal behavior. When researching the English trials, there was one case where over forty people were killed in one day.

The Salem Witch Trials. Of course, the Salem Witch Trials occurred. As mentioned in *The Belial Plan*, Rebecca Nurse was one of the women who was hung as a witch and the details of her life are accurate: she was in her seventies, partially deaf, and was originally found not guilty before some girls had 'fits' in the courtroom. Following the girls' outbursts, the judge asked her a question and she didn't answer it. As a result, she was found guilty. Her family's farm is now a tourism site and the grave of George Jacobs, another witch trial victim, was also moved there when developers took over his family's farm in the 1990s.

PATRIOT Act Abuses. The information on the PATRIOT Act abuses is sadly true. I remember my criminologist friends and I were concerned with the increased latitude provided to law enforcement included because history has shown that while a law's original intent may be focused, its application often becomes much broader after a few years. My first exposure to the abuses actually came to me through a student. Back when I was teaching college, one of my students told me how a no-knock warrant had been executed on his apartment. This was about five years after the PATRIOT act had been made into law.

So I did a little research and found that people were trying to tie the war on Drugs to the War on Terror. It's not completely separate-drug manufacturing does support some aspects of terrorism. But that is a far cry from college students with a dime bag of marijuana. And so yes, the PATRIOT Act is now used more for non-terrorism related crimes than terrorism related crimes.

Mummy Cave Ruin. The Mummy Cave Ruin is a real place in the Canyon de Chelly National Monument. When I first saw a picture of the sight, I though it looked like two eyes in a rock face. And I thought Elisabeta would like the drama of that idea. All the details of the Canyon de Chelly Monument are accurate to the best of my ability. If you'd like to learn more about the site, you can do so here.

Red Hair and Blue Eyes. I had learned years ago about the uncommon nature of red hair and blue eyes. It is indeed the least common combination in the world with only one percent of the world's population displaying it. When I learned this I was pretty surprised for good reason: both my father and sister have red hair and blue eyes. And I also have a niece with red hair and blue eyes as well as two cousins, wait no three. I forgot about the Scottish cousins. So to me, it has always been a rather common trait. :)

Achilles's Healing Ability. There is an interesting little tidbit in history about Achilles. According to one story, the Oracle declared that anyone that Achilles harms he can also heal.

Gradley Island. Gradley Island does not exist. It is pure fiction.

The Followers of the Great Mother. The Followers of the Great Mother and the tome attributed to her are my creations. However the Great Mother is in fact a force that played a role in early human cultures. In fact, some do indeed argue that at one early point the world was more matriarchal than patriarchal as a result. The idea that the Great Mother morphed into differing goddesses across cultures across the world is also well established.

Jake. So, when I started the Belial series, I liked the idea of Laney and Jake together. But then as Laney developed I realized they were no longer a good romantic fit. Jake is a good man but he wants to be the hero. And standing back and letting Laney fight the fight, it's too hard for him. So I knew their romance had to be important but short-lived.

He gave her his support in the most difficult time of her life and she will always love him for that. But they were both changed through this process. Now, my editor suggested I kill Jake. I mulled it over for an hour, but could not bring myself to do it. Jake deserved better than that. Enter, Mary Jane. A strong woman, a mother, and someone Jake can take care of who will appreciate him for it. So Jake lives and he's got this normal family that thinks he's a great man. So we'll see where that takes him!

ON DECK

So, there *is* a lot coming up. I am in the middle of writing a new Trilogy, *The Unwelcome Trilogy* which will be out in the Summer of 2017. I hope you'll consider giving it a chance. Before that, I will be publishing the second book in the *A.L.I.V.E.* series, *D.E.A.D.* If you haven't had a chance to try the series yet, consider signing up for my mailing list. All those who sign up will receive a free copy of *B.E.G.I.N.*, a short story prequel to the *A.L.I.V.E.* series.

I am also, of course, working on the Belial series. When I was researching *The Belial Plan*, I was looking for a location in the states where it would make sense for the tome of the Great Mother to be hidden. I went back and forth on different sites, but I also knew there needed to be a strong female storyline in that historical site. Then I stumbled across the Salem Witch Trials.

The more I read, the more fascinated I became by the trials themselves. The idea that this group of women could be killed with no evidence but merely the word of 'afflicted girls' was terrifying. The more I read though, the more the lives became clear in my mind. I knew I'd found my location, but I felt like I was forcing the scenes I'd seen in my head into the book. So I decided I would simply write a short story to provide more of a backstory.

ON DECK

Now I am not so sure that is going to work. As I'm writing, it's turning out to be a little longer. I don't think it will be a full-length novel, but it will probably be longer than a short story. Keep an eye out for its release and of course, for those on my mailing list, I will send you an email when it is available.

Once that is out the door, the next in line for the series is *The Belial War*. Yes, it's time.

ABOUT THE AUTHOR

R.D. Brady is an American writer who grew up on Long Island, NY but has made her home in both the South and Midwest before settling in upstate New York. On her way to becoming a full-time writer, R.D. received a Ph.D. in Criminology and taught for ten years at a small liberal arts college.

R.D. left the glamorous life of grading papers behind in 2013 with the publication of her first novel, the supernatural action adventure, *The Belial Stone*. Over ten novels later and hundreds of thousands of books sold, and she hasn't looked back. Her novels tap into her criminological background, her years spent studying martial arts, and the unexplained aspects of our history. Join her on her next adventure!

To learn about her upcoming publications, sign up for her newsletter here or her website (rdbradybooks.com).

BOOKS BY R.D. BRADY

Hominid

The Belial Series (in order)
The Belial Stone
The Belial Library
The Belial Ring
Recruit: A Belial Series Novella
The Belial Children
The Belial Origins
The Belial Search
The Belial Guard
The Belial Warrior
The Belial Plan
The Belial Witches
The Belial War
The Belial Fall
The Belial Sacrifice

The A.L.I.V.E. Series
B.E.G.I.N.

BOOKS BY R.D. BRADY

    A.L.I.V.E.
    D.E.A.D.
    R.I.S.E.
    S.A.V.E.

The Steve Kane Series
    Runs Deep
    Runs Deeper

The Unwelcome Series
    Protect
    Seek
    Proxy

The Nola James Series
    Surrender the Fear
    Escape the Fear

Published as Riley D. Brady
    The Key of Apollo
    The Curse of Hecate

Be sure to sign up for R.D.'s mailing list to be the first to hear when she has a new release!

Copyright © 2017 by R.D. Brady

The Belial Plan

Published by Scottish Seoul Publishing, LLC, Syracuse, NY

All Rights Reserved. No part of this book may be reproduced or transmitted in any form or by any means, electronic or mechanical, including photocopying, recording, or by any information storage and retrieval system without the written permission of the author, except where permitted by law.

Printed in the United States of America.

❀ Created with Vellum

Printed in Great Britain
by Amazon